Music mentioned:

"Diamonds on the Souls of Her Shoes"
Performed by Paul Simon and Ladysmith Black Mambazo
Lyrics and music by Paul Simon and Joseph Shabalala
Warner Records Inc

"Somewhere Over the Rainbow/What a Wonderful World"
Performed by Israel "IZ" Kamakawiwo'ole
Lyrics and music by Harold Arlen, Yip Harburg, Bob Thiele, and George David Weiss
Big Boy Records

"Time to Say Goodbye"
Performed by Sarah Brightman and Andrea Bocelli
Lyrics by Lucio Quarantotto, Music by Francesco Sartori
East West Records

For Marc

# Chapter 1

The muscles in Gian's shoulders constricted. I felt them as if they were my own. The Touch was back. Was the curse? This couldn't be happening. I wanted off the hillside and back in our villa.

He remained inside me but stopped thrusting. I could feel the tension in his gaze. "What do you mean you can feel what I'm feeling?" he said.

"The Touch is back. It's fucking back."

"There's no way. It can't be." He concealed his arm behind him.

"You're showing three fingers. Four. Pinky."

"Fuck."

I closed my eyes, trying to get a grip on the situation. My heart was pounding out of my chest. Or was that Gian's? He pulled out of me and sat upright, bringing me with him. I wrapped my arms around his shoulders for comfort. The Mediterranean Sea was off in the distance. Our town, Novara di Sicilia, sat nestled in the valley below. None of it was helping. If the curse was back, we would be in so much danger. Our families were exposed.

Nera, the Priestess of Death, materialized in front of us wearing a hooded robe as if she had stepped from the Bible. Her curled black hair and motherly face added to the illusion.

I lifted the corner of the blanket to my chest. "What the hell is happening, Nera? Why is the Touch back?"

"Calm down. It's nothing bad. You both need to come with me." She tossed a stack of clothes by my feet. "Put these on. Hurry."

Nothing bad? I was so confused. As soon as I let go of Gian, the Touch was gone. I grabbed his arm, bringing it back.

"I can't feel you when we're apart."

He looked over at Nera. "What is going on?"

"Linsey, Gian, we have to go. We're under a tremendous time crunch. Your questions will be answered. Right now, you need to get dressed."

I crawled over to the side of the blanket and plucked my bra and panties off the ground.

"Only the clothes I brought," she said.

I positioned Gian between us. He was bent over, stepping into the pants. The T-shirt she gave me seemed new, but the pants were thick natural cotton from another era. The fabric was rustic yet soft against my legs. I felt more comfortable once the shirt was on.

When I reached for my tennis shoes, Nera raised her hand in protest. "The eyelets are metal," she said in Italian but saw that Gian didn't understand. "The metal holes. Nothing unnatural can be on your body."

"What are you talking about?" Gian said.

"This is important. Is there anything on you that isn't a part of you?" She noticed my ring and took my hand. "Is that what I think it is?"

The natural high from moments earlier came rushing back. "He proposed minutes ago." I presented my ring proudly. Mom's diamond glistened in the sun. I caught Gian's eye and he smiled wide. The kind of goofy smile only love can bring.

"I'm so happy for you," Nera said.

"I love this woman so much," he said.

His words touched my soul. I sank in on myself, staring at his gorgeous face. A week in the Mediterranean had darkened his Sicilian skin to perfection. Mine was just getting burnt.

"You're both adorable," Nera said. "Time is short. What else is on you?"

I couldn't think straight. "My birth control, but it's plastic."

"Show me."

I lifted the sleeve and slid a finger across the raised skin on my arm.

A small folding knife appeared in her hand. She sliced through my flesh without warning.

"Ow! Jesus."

Nera ignored me as she dug the implant free. "Don't forget it's gone," she said, tossing it aside.

A wave of her hand created a tingling sensation that replaced the pain. Within seconds, the wound vanished, leaving only blood. She handed me a napkin to clean up.

"What is this?" She was pointing to a black mark on the back side of my arm.

My posture slumped in shame. "Pencil lead from a mean girl in junior school." I felt stupid saying it.

"Bullies," she said, slicing the lead free.

"Damn it, Nera. Give me a warning." The pain was less this time, but it still upset me.

"Linsey, we don't have time." She was performing the healing ritual. "What else?"

Gian removed his earring and handed it to Nera. "Don't lose this. It's her mom's." The old Gian wouldn't have been so thoughtful.

"It's safe with me. What else?" Nera said.

"Um. My teeth," I said. "I have a bunch of fillings and a crown."

She held my jaw, spreading my mouth wide. A well-worn stick appeared in her palm.

"Bite on this. We have to remove those, or your head will explode on entry."

"What? You said it was nothing bad. Heads exploding is bad. Where are you taking us?"

"You've been summoned to the Underworld. No more questions."

No more questions? I had a thousand questions. Nera placed the stick in the side of my mouth. I think it was more to shut me up.

"What the hell, Nera?" Gian said.

3

"Stop with the questions. This isn't easy."

Her focus was on my mouth. She didn't use any tools — only magic. I don't know what was worse, the cracking sound of my fillings breaking loose or the pain of the air in the holes. The longer she waved a hand in front of my mouth, the less I felt. I ran my tongue across my teeth. They were whole and perfect. Even the tooth with the crown had grown back.

"I have a metal implant," Gian said. He took the stick from me and bit down on it.

I translated for Nera the best I could.

Her hand shook as she tried to remove the post, but all that came was the crown. "I'll get the rest of the fillings out."

One small piece flew from a front tooth.

"Is that all?"

He removed the biting stick. "There's only the one filling. I lost the other tooth skateboarding."

"Whatever you're doing, keep it up," Nera said.

He gave me a winning smile. The time he spent brushing his teeth every day was ridiculous. But after today, I'd have to let go of that frustration.

She worked on repairing his missing filling. The enamel flowed inward, filling the gap until it was perfect.

Nera closed her eyes briefly. "Bianca is searching for a safe dentist to get your post out. I think there's one still in your village."

From a satchel, she retrieved a glowing orb the size of a BB. Greens and blues pulsed and swirled as if it were alive.

"This is going to hurt." She pressed the orb into the flesh between Gian's thumb and forefinger. A thin stream of smoke emerged as the orb sank inside. I cringed. He barely flinched. His squinted eyes spoke volumes, but he didn't complain.

"Your turn," she said, forcing an orb into my hand.

4

The pain surged through me like a thousand papercuts. I glared at Nera, rubbing the area around the wound.

A note fell from the sky in an arc-like drift. Nera caught it.

"Here's Dr. Vianti's address. They're waiting for you. His office is a block north of the piazza from your celebration. I'll get you to the scooter. Be more careful on the side streets."

The bee who stopped us from crashing *was* her. Gian shied his eyes away from me. His guilt was adorable.

Nera retrieved the scooter keys and slipped them into his pocket.

I grabbed her wrist. "Won't that explode on entry?"

Gian covered his bulge reflexively.

"Not on the surface."

I wanted answers but knew I'd be chastised.

She took his hand. "Traveling to the Underworld is complicated. Before I show you how to disappear, you must know how to materialize."

I've experienced crazy things, but this was hard to rationalize. Gian and I looked at each other, stunned.

"All you do to reappear is think totale. The potenza will take care of the rest." She tapped his hand where the orb had entered. "It's set to Italian, so use a heavy accent."

The word potenza means power. I wondered what she was getting us into.

"Say it. Totale. Burn it in. Figure out a rhyme to remember it."

I couldn't think of a rhyme that worked in Italian. Instead, I repeated the word, hoping it would stick.

"Now we learn to turn invisible. You first," she told me. "To vanish, you say invisibile in your head and tap the back of your upper teeth twice. What are the words?"

"Invisibile and potenza?" Gian said.

"Totale. Totale," she said, smacking him on the head.

I followed her steps and the world became bright white with only energy showing. None of me was present except the glow of my potenza. The shrubs emitted subtle colors that were barely noticeable. Gian was outlined in a red aura. Nera's was a greenish blue. I went to speak, but no words emerged. The silence was deafening.

Gian's energy imploded. All that remained was the blue of his potenza. Nera followed. Her orb twisted in an arc as if she was opening a door. A rip widened to a vertical oval shape, revealing what I thought was the street and Uncle Emilio's moped. They passed through and the opening sealed. I couldn't comprehend what I had seen. Did they just go through a portal?

I thought *totale* and found myself alone on the hill. A kaleidoscope of colors glistened like I was wearing novelty glasses. It took a moment for my eyes to adjust to normal. I laughed nervously and gathered our belongings.

The blue of an orb appeared and Nera materialized. She grabbed the picnic basket and a stack of clothes.

"Get behind me and hold your hand with the potenza like this." She held her arm straight back with her palm facing upward.

Once I had the pose, she took my other hand. Holding onto her and our stuff wasn't easy, but I managed.

"Don't let go of the pose or we'll be lost in the channel. This will feel weird. Reappear only after I do."

I was scared but thrilled all at once.

She turned us both invisible and opened a portal. Even though I could see the energy of a room on the other side, it was as if I were falling a thousand feet, only forward. Streams of multicolored light raced by. We emerged in what I thought was our villa. Nera's aura was back as she materialized. I thought *totale* and fell to the ground in my kitchen. My ears popped as if I had flown.

She slipped my mother's ring from my finger and pulled mom's earring from her pocket, setting them both on the bar.

"We have to travel a great distance to get to the gate. This will be strange," she said, taking my hand. "And then, there's the gate itself. Try and relax."

How was I supposed to relax when I had no idea what was happening? "Wait, hold on." I broke her hold. "What is the Underworld?"

"Linsey. You can't knock me off like that. We could have both died. Your questions will be answered when we get there."

Nera retook my hand and we vanished. She opened a portal to our destination, which was somewhere in nature. As I stepped through, colors flowed inward, creating a radiant tube. Nera's energy was stretching and I panicked. I kept my arm behind us as we were sucked into the void.

We ended our journey atop a small hill with sloped edges surrounding us below. Was this a crater? The energy from a hiker was crossing the other side. I think it was a hiker.

Nera's orb gestured away from us and I placed my hand in position. I was pulled into the center of the crater. My body felt torn ruthlessly, with half of me remaining on the surface. An immense weight pressed against my soul as if I were slipping through solid rock. There weren't as many colors on our way to the Underworld, just streaks of gold racing by.

We arrived in a small square space. The wall behind me was radiant, almost glowing. I fell backward up to my shoulders. Nera helped guide me out. I was completely disoriented. In front of me was the word TOTALE in blue light. I read it and materialized. The walls were smooth and white except for the back one. It was a slab of a gorgeous blue gemstone with rich tones like a massive opal. But how could one be so large? Despite the sterile look of the room, it had an unpleasant odor of sulfur.

I felt drugged. Electricity pulsed through my ears in waves. I cringed each time it passed.

Nera handed me a red clip from a shelf in the wall. "Put this on your ear."

I clipped it to my lobe as she had. Once in place, the high reduced, but I was strangely disconnected, like an echo of myself.

"You scared me," she said. "I thought you were going to materialize inside the rock."

"I don't feel right, Nera."

"Your life force is on the surface. This is important. You can only separate from yourself for so long. If the connection starts fading, we need to leave immediately. I'll be right back. I have to retrieve Gian. You're safe here, don't worry," she said and vanished.

"What the fuck?" Oh my God, she left me.

Her clip dropped to the floor. I set it back on the shelf. The ceiling began lowering at a steady pace. It was now a glowing translucent white. I panicked as it approached my head.

"Please hold still," a deep yet pleasant voice said. "The field will remove impurities from your body. Without this cleansing, we could perish."

*We,* I thought as the light enveloped my body. It passed through and became the floor. The smell was gone. Everything was clean and fresh. My thoughts were flying a mile a minute. I needed a pen and paper.

The wall before me vanished, revealing a naturally formed stone tunnel. Glowing blue veins wove throughout the smooth walls, but it wasn't the light source. That came from the ground. I could hear strange singing from beyond the tunnel.

A short, naked creature at my feet startled me. He had enormous dark eyes and devil horns twisting from his head. I shrieked, and he reached up for my arm.

"Calm down, Linsey. I'm not evil."

Not evil? Everything about him was evil. His nose was barely a bump with two connecting holes like an infinity sign. He had goat's ears and a wide mouth turned up in a crackled, devilish grin.

"My name is Teriko. I'm your muse. It's a pleasure to meet you." His voice was deep, larger than himself.

"My muse is a demon?" I tried breaking free from his grasp. He hovered until he was at eye level.

"I'm not a demon. We're aliens. Trapped deep inside your planet."

I couldn't catch my breath. It was all too much.

"Do you need me to slap you?"

The question was so out of left field. "What? No. Why would you want to slap me?"

"Gian did that in the lake to bring you to your senses. Don't worry. We are nonviolent. Our role as muses is not by choice. The way we monitored your species turned into an unbreakable bond."

I was looking at an alien. An actual alien. It was such a trip. Teriko's body was thin and gangly. His skin was iridescent, reflecting the gray and blue of the stone. That's why I couldn't see him at first. A cute devil's tail flipped behind him. Although naked, he carried himself with the utmost confidence. I glanced at his genitalia and blushed.

"Humans have such shame. Our bodies are our greatest gift."

I gestured to the room. "Is this thing going to screw up my immune system?"

He laughed. "Not at all. It will make it sharper. You're now immune to the flu and the common cold. Excuse me, dear, please step from the chamber. Your boyfriend's arriving."

I joined him in the tunnel, eager to have Nera and Gian with me. The wall of the cleansing room filled in but was translucent from our side. Two blue orbs floated in the air. Nera appeared, and the word TOTALE glowed backward on the wall. Gian materialized. A drop of blood rolled from his mouth. He smiled wide, exposing his missing tooth.

"You didn't say it would be this good." He was hanging onto Nera, trying to catch his balance.

"Hi, Gian," I said.

"Hey, baby." He looked around, trying to see me.

His high affected me and I lost my footing.

"You need to put this on," Nera said. "It will set you straight."

"Why would I do that? This is amazing."

"You'll go insane. Those are the inspirations from all the muses. Our human brains can't handle it."

"Fine." He clipped the apparatus to his ear. Once attached, I could breathe easier and stood taller.

The ceiling flowed downward, cleansing them, and the wall separating us vanished. The blood on Gian's chin was gone.

A female muse came running up. "Wow, it is you," she said to Gian. Her voice was deep and raspy. She was cute in a devilish way.

"Holy shit, you *are* aliens," Gian said. "I didn't believe Nera."

How come he got answers?

Nera responded to my thought out loud. "It would have taken forever to get you here."

Gian looked at her confused, then back at the muses. He spread his arms out wide with his palms up. "I come in peace."

"Of course you do," the female muse said. "I'm Sariant. I write your music. I'm sorry it isn't that good."

"I write my music."

"We write it," she said, taking his wrist.

"I fight with you," Teriko said to me. He gave a kick and a punch.

"My talent is fighting?" I was disappointed.

"You can't choose your gifts, and we can't choose our humans. Why do you think Elton John could play piano without taking a lesson? That was his muse, skilled through years of practice, syncing with Elton's talents. Your music is fighting. Please get back in the ring. I miss it."

"I will, I promise."

"Where's your muse," Gian said to Nera.

"I don't have one. I'm the bridge. The way here. I wouldn't be able to travel if I had one."

Gian was staring at me. "What's up with your hair? It's a natural blonde, like when you were sixteen."

Had the cleansing chamber replaced my highlights?

"Is my nose better?" he asked.

"Better? What do you mean? It's perfect."

"I think it's too big."

"You're nuts." I had no idea what his problem was. His nose complimented his dominant chin. If anything, he was too handsome.

The muses were handsy. Neither wanted to let go of us.

Teriko must have sensed my discomfort. "Please understand. Our connection on the surface is through your minds. Everyone will want to touch you."

"I don't mind," Gian said. He was having an easier time with the experience than I was, so much so that he disrobed to be naked with the muses.

"How about it?" he said to me.

"That is not happening, but I'll carry your clothes."

"When in Rome," Gian said.

Both muses reached out and felt Gian's member. Not in a sexual way. Pure curiosity.

"I apologize," Sariant said. "You're our first male visitor. It's big compared to ours."

"That's quite all right," Gian said, amused at the attention.

"You picked a good specimen," I said.

"Let's get moving," Teriko said. "You've been summoned by Penderdash."

We lifted a few feet and raced along in a standing position. Nothing was under us, even though it felt solid. I

11

didn't dare move my legs. Sariant and Teriko floated at our pace. Nera stood directly behind us.

The tunnel opened to a meadow in a massive cavern. I didn't understand how the air could be so fresh underground. Muses were sitting cross-legged in random spots, lost in meditation. Others were flying in a laid-back position as if they were sliding feet first into home plate.

"We call this place Azule," Teriko said. "Or in our language—" No possible combination of letters could transliterate the word or phrase he said, if you could even call it speech. It was more like singing.

"That was lovely," I said.

"It wasn't a lyric. That's our native tongue."

The singing in the distance wasn't music. It was the muses talking, which made it all the more beautiful.

"How come you guys don't fly around like Superman?" Gian asked.

"Too many broken horns." Teriko gestured to a muse flying by. "That way still feels cool."

"It's badass," Gian said.

"You mentioned being trapped here," I said." Can we help you out?" Nera nudged me lightly.

Sariant sighed. "There's no escaping your planet. We were only supposed to observe. And that's all we did for hundreds of years, but a muse fell restless and allowed himself to be seen on the surface. The Alliance took his presence as a threat. They destroyed our ship and everyone in it."

"What the fuck?" Gian and I said. I looked at him, smiling at our vulgar synchronicity.

"The muse on the surface, is that where the story of the devil comes from?" I asked.

"No, well, not at first," Teriko said. "The pasture reflected upon his skin in a calming green. He was the inspiration for Pan, the Greek god of nature. Pagans also worship this loving god. Satan was invented hundreds of years later to force Pagans into Christianity. With the tale, they could accuse reluctant followers of worshiping a horned god, the devil incarnate. Religion can be wicked at times."

I remembered Grandpa fighting for religion at dinner. I didn't want to let him down. "There's good in Christianity," I said. "Look at Jimmy Carter."

"He is a virtuous man indeed," Sariant said. "Penderdash almost became his muse."

"He's a rarity. Not all our hosts are good," Teriko said. "It's hard to shake that off. Or worse, if you're attached to someone utterly stupid with a boring gift. If we're lucky, we sync with a fun human, like David Lee Roth. Although I hear he's exhausting."

An alien joined our journey. He carried a small rectangular device with a digital display.

"My name's Tiki Gander. Would you like me to fix your tooth?" he asked Gian. "I felt your pain."

"There's nothing to fix. It's gone."

"Gone," Tiki said, laughing. "I can replicate it from the one on the other side. It *will* hurt. The growth starts from the root."

"I don't like dentists. Fine. Do it quickly."

The aliens could revolutionize dentistry with this technology. I wondered why they didn't.

Tiki rose slightly above Gian. After triple-checking that he was replicating the right tooth, he pressed the trigger and a grinding sound emitted, followed by a ding.

"Squeeze my hand," Teriko said. "You can't hurt me."

"Don't breathe," Tiki said. "That will make the pain worse."

He moved to the missing tooth. The device activated and Gian crumpled inward. He screamed out in absolute agony but quickly shut up. His moan was like a dying animal. It was hard to watch. He soon relaxed, and within minutes, there was a tooth.

"Oh my God, that was so painful." He slid his tongue across the new tooth.

"I'm sorry," Tiki said.

"Why? You saved me thousands."

"Your monetary system is strange. We don't have that in our culture."

"What do you have?" I asked.

"Trust. Would it be all right if I rode with you?"

"I insist," Gian said.

In the distance, an alien draped in a purple robe approached, flying in a standing position. She was the only muse I'd seen clothed.

"What a treat," Teriko said. "You'll want to meet Sty Ling."

I smirked at the name.

"Sty Ling was Amadeus's muse," he said, putting me in my place. "Since losing Prince, she is lost. Be kind."

I looked at Gian. Did Prince die?

Sty Ling was almost too beautiful to look at. Unlike the other two, her skin was smooth and youthful, her horns mere nubbins. Without the aging in the lips, her smile was inviting.

"Gian," she said and hugged him. "You feel of life." Her tone was youthful and high-pitched.

She pulled me in. "Linsey. I love you." Her large eyes expressed more emotion than I could handle. She was a walking god. I almost fell to my knees.

"I love you too," I said.

"May I join you?"

"Of course."

The cavern we crossed opened to a grander one with a lake adorned with glowing boats. Vegetation was abundant and foreign. The trees resembled massive plants with thick, healthy green trunks. A flying rain machine passed overhead but didn't get any water on us. There were farms with odd animals. Some slithered, others hopped. A giant of a beast stepped over us. Bugs were flying by. Gian

14

swatted at one, but Sty Ling snatched his wrist before he made contact.

"Those are Dracks. Don't discard the small. Everything has a purpose."

She began singing in her native tongue. I thought she was talking but recognized the melody in Prince's "7."

I've never experienced a performance so mesmerizing. Sty Ling's singing was heavenly. Her arms rolled with her body like waves in an ocean. Gian and I were brought to tears.

"I miss my purple man," she said and floated away.

"You'll have to excuse Sty Ling," Sariant said. "She's lost in the fog of grief. Usually, she's the most charismatic muse in the room. Time will give her the strength."

Silence overtook the group. I couldn't believe Prince was dead. Poor Sty Ling. How do you get over someone you were a part of?

Teriko looked over at me. "You know the dream you shared with your brother about your other me driving you around when you black out? That was spot on. It's us taking the helm."

"We love a good alcoholic," Sariant said.

"God bless the drunks," Teriko said.

"They make terrible hosts but are so much fun to steer. It's the closest we get to being human."

"We can also share your animal's minds and nudge them along," Teriko said.

Sariant smacked him lightly. "Don't tell them that."

Three new muses joined our group. One was the inspiration for the Nestle Crunch bar. I liked him. They were all leaning in, hanging onto us.

Our journey took us through a wide tunnel. The floor and walls were lined with houses carved into the stone. The connecting edges created rounded Gothic columns. There was purpose in the bizarre. Intermixed paths wound throughout, even where a path shouldn't be, like the one where a muse was walking along the ceiling.

15

The homes glowed with warm light, offering an inviting beauty.

We emerged into a massive cavern. Twin mountains towered in front of us. Their bases nearly touched, creating a passage between them. As we advanced, more muses attached to us until we were almost smothered. Once we reached the left mountain, they dispersed.

"It was a pleasure meeting you," Sariant said.

Teriko's eyes were glistening. "I will talk about this day for years."

We said our goodbyes, and they headed down the path together.

Nera startled me. I forgot she was behind us. "Don't stare at Penderdash's small horns like you did Sty Ling's. His body has regenerated. It's not polite. And no talking religion. He was Jesus' muse. He doesn't discuss it."

I was floored, scared, and unworthy.

"He also mused for Muhammad. Humanity ruined him. He will never attach to the surface again. All we do is disappoint."

"Does this mean God exists?" I asked.

"Yes." Nera tapped my head as if to say in here. Gian laughed. I didn't care for the non-answer.

A portion of the rock wall opened to reveal a passageway.

"Do not talk religion," Nera reminded.

The wall solidified as soon as we passed through the opening. We followed Nera, crawling along a winding tunnel. The dwelling we entered was futuristic, combining smooth white walls and the mountain's stone. We had to hunch over to avoid the ceiling.

Gian pointed to a mirror in the hall by the kitchen. "Check out your hair."

I was delighted with the color. He was right. It was my youthful blonde. Everything else looked the same.

"You're my princess," he said.

16

I was a teen again, wrapped in the warmth of his compliment.

Nera strode past us. "Let's keep moving."

The living room opened to a balcony facing a lake far below. In the distance was a modern city clustered with skyscrapers. To the right was the other mountain with dwellings at various lecovels. It didn't seem like we'd climbed that far, but we were hundreds of feet up.

We could have hovered to the balcony. Instead, they made us arrive on our hands and knees. It had a humbling effect that I didn't believe was coincidental.

A lone figure was on the floor with his eyes closed. The three of us joined Penderdash, sitting cross-legged like him.

The balcony had no protective railing. Who needs one when you can fly? It was unnerving being up so high.

Penderdash was leaning back at an impossible angle as if sitting in a chair. He was adorable. But saying that could be an insult.

In the adjacent mountain, muses stepped onto their balconies. They acted nonchalant like they weren't there to gawk, but I could feel them staring.

Nera removed her robe and placed it on Gian's pile. I reluctantly disrobed. Once naked, I was finally comfortable. It was the opposite of what I expected.

Penderdash snortled loudly, waking himself up. He rubbed the sleep from his eyes, looked over and jumped.

"Hello. Gian, Linsey. Hi, Nera. Hugs, hugs, all around."

Penderdash's embrace was comforting, which was good because he insisted on cuddling between Gian and me.

"Is Penderdash your first or last name?" I asked. It was such a stupid opening. Who was I to even start the conversation?

He took a moment to answer. "Yes."

"It's an honor to meet you," Gian said.

"Absolutely," I said.

"Who are you, you asked yourself? Nothing less than our salvation."

Now, I was speechless.

Nera handed our clothes to him. He held the pile with care.

"Thank you for the fabric."

A muse rose over the balcony and carried the gift away.

Penderdash leaned in close to me. "Honey, you have a little prejudice."

I was mortified.

"Don't worry. Everyone does. Would you like me to remove it?"

"Will it change me?"

"Only for the better."

He placed a finger on each of my temples and tapped once.

"I don't feel any different."

"Prejudice hides in your subconscious. Fill the void with love."

"Do me," Gian said.

Penderdash gazed at him with a smile. "There isn't any."

"It left with your healing," Nera said.

I pictured Gian lifeless in the field. It would have destroyed me if the High Priestess hadn't brought him back.

"The reason I called for you is dire. Lifting the curse caused a rift in your world. We tried reinstating it, but your grandfather signed the treaty in blood."

Finally, we were getting answers. Christ! Oh shit, I took the lord's name in vain. Penderdash looked over with a devilish smirk. He had read my thoughts.

"Are you sure it's not back?" I said. "I felt the Mirror's Touch."

"I can't lose my empathy," Gian said. "It would kill me."

"You won't. The Touch is there for you to complete your mission. You must be able to find each other no matter where you are. In time, you will also feel its powers."

Gian sat up with a smile, but it turned to concern. "Will we turn homicidal every three days?"

"No one has the curse anymore. You're safe. Your empathy is safe."

I relaxed with a sigh of relief.

"That doesn't mean your task will be easy. Five humans in five corners must die." He held up a hand to our objections. "They were supposed to die. It is their time. The world will be in great peril unless they do. Only the ones who broke the curse can execute this task."

"I don't want to kill anyone," Gian said.

"Too many people have died because of me," I said.

"You're telling *me* that? Me? Jesus and Muhammad's muse."

I relented. "You win."

Nera spoke. "When the time comes, all you have to do is lay your hands on opposite sides of their head, and the potenza will do the rest. You will only be a conduit."

That made me feel a little better. "What did these people do?" I asked.

"They haven't done anything. It's what happens if they live that's the problem. One is pregnant with a child who is pretty much Satan," Penderdash said.

"Yeah, that's a lot," Gian said. "Wait, I thought Satan was made up. Is he Satan or pretty much Satan?"

"Pretty much?"

"Make her miscarry."

"We can't interfere, and neither can you."

I leaned back as if in an invisible chair. It was weirdly comfortable. "What happens with the second person if they live?" I asked.

"She purposely runs over a Klan leader and starts a race war. The worst is an angry bloke who kills the man who cures pancreatic cancer."

"Won't we be interfering by killing them?" I asked.

"Not at all. And don't feel guilty. Good always balances out the bad, even in the extreme. Take Ted Bundy. He was a prolific murderer, yet he helped people on a suicide hotline. The gangster Al Capone came up with the idea for soup kitchens. Hitler hated cigarettes so much his scientists discovered the link to cancer."

I didn't like where he was taking this. "Are you relating these horrible people to what you're asking us to do?"

"No. Oh my gosh. I was just saying good always balances out bad. Do this task and you'll emerge clean. I assure you."

"When do we begin?" Gian said.

"You already have. Nera will teach you how to visit the five. Each person must know they are going to die."

"Won't that knowledge rock the foundation of society?" I asked.

Nera interjected. "They won't be able to talk about it with anyone but you. The witches will see to it."

"That will be a huge mind fuck. Oops, sorry."

"It's just a word," Penderdash said. "And yes, it will be a huge mind fuck. But they must die at peace with themselves. It's imperative. Otherwise, we can't kill them."

That didn't make sense. "Why do they have to be at peace with themselves if they were supposed to die anyway?"

"It fixes what was supposed to happen. Eases them through the system so you and Gian aren't noticed."

The system? Where do we go when we die? I wanted so badly to ask him. Penderdash shook a stubby finger, No, at me.

"What if they run?" Gian asked.

"Two will," Nera said, "but you'll always know where they are. Each has a tracker embedded in their brain. It is that which you will short out in the end. They won't feel a thing. Their death will be instantaneous."

20

"I like that," Gian said.

"There is something else," Penderdash said. "When we tried to reinstate the curse, a funny thing happened. If a Hunter or the Cursed try to kill each other, the one attempting the act will die."

I stood up abruptly, slamming my head into the stone ceiling. "That's not a funny thing. I need to warn our families."

"Bianca has already warned the hunters and those who were cursed," Nera said.

"All of them?" I asked. "How?"

"She spoke to their subconscious. They'll warn themselves. You didn't get the message because you were here."

I sat back down, uncertain that would work. My family was awful stubborn. I let it go for now. There were bigger questions. "If we agree to this, how do we know you won't ask us to do more and more?"

Penderdash looked me in the eyes. "You have my word. Nothing else will be asked of you."

My body felt odd, empty. I reached behind Gian and rested my arm on his back for comfort. We merged as the world shook around us. He stared into my eyes.

"I can feel you," he said. "I can feel the Touch."

His heart beat wildly. I was him as he grew erect.

"Gian!" I scolded, but he couldn't help it. The harder he became, the more my pussy pulsed in response. It was as if our senses caressed each other.

Penderdash removed himself from the awkward situation and gazed at the view. "You have to go. Your time has run out."

That was the odd sensation—my life force on the surface dimming. I failed at the one thing to remember.

"It was an honor," I said.

"I won't forget you," Gian said.

Penderdash shrugged his shoulders, staring at Gian's erection. "You may."

21

Gian concealed himself the best he could.

"Do you have any advice to help in our task?" I asked.

"Be true to yourself."

The clips dropped from our ears, and I stumbled backward, high as fuck.

Penderdash clapped. "Get off!" A bunch of Dracks jumped from the back of our hair like a cloud of dust. One passed close to my eye. They looked like fairies. It smiled and waved at me.

"All of you," Penderdash said.

The rest flew off and amassed a few feet away. Their complaints were barely audible.

Nera gathered Gian and me in a chain and raced us to the surface. We shot out so fast that our group landed high on the bank. I collapsed in what I believe was snow. The lake the island sits in looked familiar. From a standing position, I was sure we were at Crater Lake. But why did the island have a smaller crater, and why was I casting a shadow? Oh my God, it was my dying life source. She reached toward me with open arms. I dropped to the ground and absorbed into myself. With a blinding flash, I was whole again but still invisible. I leaned back, elated.

Nera opened a portal and whisked us back to Italy. The light in our villa was blinding. I grabbed my head as a migraine dropped me to my knees. Nera placed her fingers on my temples. The pain receded and I collapsed on the floor. Gian was soon next to me, working to catch his breath. Nera removed her headache last.

The three of us were naked. I'm pretty sure I was the only one faking comfort.

"What a trip," Gian said.

"I interrupted your celebration," Nera said. "There should be another bottle of Moscato in the fridge. I'll meet back here in two hours to begin your training. But first, you need to answer the door." With that, she vanished.

# Chapter 2

We dressed and headed downstairs to see who Nera said was there. As we reached the door, the intercom rang from upstairs. Our shoulders collided and the Touch engaged. An odd giggle followed Gian's shudder.

"The Touch is so freaking weird."

"Let's make this quick," I said, opening the door halfway.

Our visitor had a scar above his right eye, traversing to his cheek. He was frightening, yet I wasn't afraid; just confused that it was nighttime. I didn't think we were in the Underworld that long.

"Hello," I said.

"My humble apologies," the man said. "Don Trentino needs to talk to you." He handed a phone over.

"Sure," I said.

Gian gave me a look. Along with my prejudices, some of my common sense was gone. I needed to be careful.

I put the phone on speaker.

"Mr. Trentino, to what do we owe this honor?"

"Linsey!" Gian barked.

"Gian is correct to be skeptical." He was using an app that translated his words into English. "I promised you would not hear from me again. I'm sorry for the call. This is important. Please go inside to your villa so we are alone."

"Scusi," Gian told the man at the door. He led me back to our kitchen.

"We're inside," Gian said.

The Don said thank you in English, which translated to grazie. "One of my men has died at the hands of a Hunter. What is going on? Has the curse returned?"

I panicked, thinking of my family. "There's a bit of a glitch," I said. "If a Hunter or the formerly cursed tries to kill the other, the aggressor will die. The witches should have used your subconscious to convince you of this."

"The witches tried. Tell them to stay out of my head." His stubbornness was frustrating but not unexpected. It was the same reaction my family would have. I wasn't worried about Gian's. They were more rational.

"Is there anyone you wouldn't mind getting rid of?" Gian asked. "Someone who was cursed that you no longer trust?"

"Antonio," the Don said bluntly. "The man at the door."

"Have him shoot the Hunter who wronged you. See with your own eyes. Antonio will be the one who dies. He will rid you of himself."

There was a massive hole in his plan. "That won't work," I said. "He received the same warning."

"He will do it," the Don said forcefully. "He's the reason my cousin is dead. Keep the phone until you hear back from me. The lock is all zeros. Buonasera."

"Ciao." I turned to Gian. "What day is it?"

He checked the phone. "It's still Friday. Barely. How were we gone ten hours?"

"I have no idea."

He pulled up the news. Prince's death was the cover story. He had died a day earlier. "Oh man, that sucks." He held my arm and flinched. I had felt him before he touched me.

"It's getting stronger," I said.

"Why don't you call your family? I know the warning's on your mind."

"Thank you. I'll be quick." I kissed him passionately. He couldn't contain himself and thrust his hand between my legs. I felt his heartbeat increase from the excitement.

"It's pulsing," he said, rubbing my clit. "Go. Go. Make the call."

Max answered Dad's phone. "Hey, sis, what's up? You ready to come home?"

"There's been a change of plans. We're on a mission for the witches." I tried to explain but couldn't speak. They were constricting my throat. It was like getting the wind knocked out of me, except my voice was the breath I reached for.

"Are you there? What are you talking about?"

"Yeah, I'm here. That's all I can tell you. Trust me."

"How come you still get to do cool things?"

"It's not cool at all, brother. Please heed the warning. Do not try to kill a Dread. You'll die instead."

"We know."

"Good. I've already seen it happen. Thank Grandpa for us. His signing the treaty in blood saved the truce."

I could feel Gian approaching from behind. He grabbed my breasts.

"I have to go. Love you."

"Love you too. I'll talk to Dad and Grandpa."

"And Mary."

"She's Joan, not Mary. And she knows."

I pictured Joan of Arc to remember the name.

Gian handed me a flute of Moscato. I took a slow drink and brought his lips to mine. The warmed liquid flowed into his mouth. He started giggling, and I could feel his lips curl into a smile.

"The Touch is too fucking weird." He cupped my pussy and his cock throbbed in response. This made my inner walls clench in response, which he answered with an even more intense wave of pleasure that made his cock quiver. We couldn't stop the reverb. He ended up coming in his pants. The crazy part is I could feel what was happening in his head. I'd never been able to do that before. His orgasm was concentrated in quick, powerful bursts. Women have fireworks. Men get efficiency.

"That was crazy," he said.

Nera had interrupted our lovemaking on the hillside. What I was consumed with now was pure, unadulterated lust. Making love could wait. I dropped to my knees and released his glistening cock. His wonderful musk was gone. Teriko had cleansed us too well.

The head was untouchably sensitive. I focused on his balls, then moved up his shaft, licking the cum off him. The tart and salty combination was a welcome delight. I love his flavor.

He dropped us gingerly to the floor, shifting into a 69, pulling me with him.

With the Touch it's impossible to focus on Gian when I'm getting eaten out. "There's no way."

"Come on."

He drove his face home. I barely had the tip of him in my mouth when darkness closed in. Instead of fear, I smiled as I drifted off. Told him so.

Gian was unconscious as I came to. I looked at the clock on the wall. We were only out for a few minutes. He opened his eyes, dazed.

"We'll have to ease into this," I said. "You kind of pop a fuse in your head."

"It's nuts," he said. "I love the Touch. Make room for the master."

His confidence and eagerness had me going. He lowered himself until he was inches from my pussy. His warm breath flowed across my clit. He backed away, probably from feeling it through me. Instead of diving right in, he manipulated my energy, touching and rubbing the surrounding skin. He used the nerve endings, working outward, pulling me along. My clit pulsed, begging for attention.

He grinned widely. "Joy knew."

She does have a vagina, I wanted to say but could barely mutter a garble of words. He hadn't even brushed it and already had me melting.

26

Two fingers slid upward across my clit toward my stomach. He laughed in response and massaged my lips, playing with their reaction. He could have made me come from that alone.

Then came the tongue. Holy fucking shit. He guided every movement precisely. His laughter was gone. He *was* the master, and I was being conquered.

All reasoning and thought washed away in a swell of ecstasy. Energy raced through my clit, but he knew where it was heading and captured the power from the other side, tossing it up and catching it again. He was squeezing my belly. No, that was my orgasm brimming. I was shocked at how fast it had blossomed.

"Am I hurting you? What is that?" he asked.

The orgasm began to recede. "Don't stop," I demanded.

"Oh," he said, realizing what it meant. "Why does it do that?"

"Just keep going."

He dove back in, coaxing me along. It didn't take long for the finish line to appear again. I was on my back, my hips shaking, and my spine arched. The ceiling became bright white, like the cleansing room. I pushed the thought from my head as I screamed in a chorus with him. Gian's body lost control as he melted into me.

He began crying. "I think I saw God."

"That was your reflection in my eyes."

I was serious with my compliment, but his laughter was infectious. Feeling someone laugh is hilarious. It's deep and boisterous. I loved it. After about fifteen minutes, not so much. We begged the other to stop but it made things worse. Moving to separate rooms didn't help.

He found me on a balcony lounger. "I can end this." He lifted my legs. My sides hurt from laughing. I giggled as I positioned my legs on his shoulders. The thought of fucking dampened the humor. Nothing brought us closer. With the Touch, this was going to be epic.

His eyes locked on mine. I felt his perspective of slipping into me as he experienced the initial stretch, filling me to capacity. This was always my favorite when I had the Touch before. I wondered how it felt for him. I got my answer in the form of a deep moan.

It took a moment for him to get the timing. I knew from experience that this was from the oddity of feeling both sides. A smirk formed on his face. He was me as I was making myself tighter with my inner muscles.

A closed-lip kiss sent sparks between us. He would meet my tongue as if we were in a synchronized dance. It was the best kiss I've ever had. I believe it was the same for him because he stopped fucking. We rolled around, making out feverishly. I gripped the back of his head and pressed his lips closer to mine. We kissed for a solid half hour.

"That was nice," he said.

I grew lost in his aqua-green eyes. "I love you so much."

"I love you too, baby."

Happiness overwhelmed me. I'm sure I had the stupidest look on my face, with a smile so wide it almost hurt.

Gian gave me a quick peck and slipped back inside. A tear rolled down his cheek and he quivered. He orchestrated his rhythm, pulling me along. It was as if he was controlling me. A spot he found deep inside made the hairs on my body stand on end. I closed my eyes and drifted with him into a sea of ecstasy. Sweat dripped off him. His luscious scent was back. I soaked him up.

Another orgasm was soon blossoming. He smiled greedily and hit the spot more aggressively. I was fading.

"No fucking way," he said, thrusting his cock deep. The jarring pain shocked me awake. My orgasm ignited his. We came together in triumph, with his cresting as mine reached a fevered pitch. It was too much and we were out.

Nera tapping on my arm woke me up. Gian was flaccid but still partly inside me. It was warm and comforting from his perspective. I reveled in the feeling of him sliding out of me.

"Hi," I said, embarrassed.

Gian was startled to see her. I felt his flight reflexes.

She draped a blanket around us and handed me my mom's ring.

A smile warmed my cheeks. "I'm engaged." I slipped the ring on, never wanting it to be off again.

"You'll be with child too if you're not careful." She tapped a finger where my birth control had been.

Gian shrugged like he wouldn't mind. I tried to hide my reaction, but I'm sure he felt me sinking inward in glee.

"Why don't you get dressed," she said.

I headed to the bedroom to change. My reflection freaked me out. I was so blonde. The color wasn't bad, just unexpected. I can't believe I dyed this black at sixteen.

Gian joined me. We searched for clothes without metal rivets or zippers. My sweatpants and a T-shirt would do. He had a pair of gym shorts that were perfect. We headed back to ask about our sandals.

"Metal isn't an issue on the surface," Nera said. "What you have on is fine for what we're doing. You can go barefoot."

Gian leaned close and whispered, "Honey, let it out."

I ran from the room, mortified. He could feel me holding in my gas. There's no way to gracefully fart. Gian giggled as he felt it release. Guys are such children.

They had moved to the front room. I walked up to Gian. "I know you hate rules, but no bodily function talk."

He was crushed. "Even if it's funny?"

"Please."

"I'll try."

Nera ignored our conversation. "We're going to learn how to teleport."

I looked at Gian excited and mouthed, holy fuck!

"Well, not teleport. That's impossible. What we do is open portals in two places and pinch time together. For safety, it will only open if you're invisible. Practice disappearing and returning. Invisibile and totale," she said, reminding us of the words.

I thought *invisibile* and tapped my teeth with my tongue. The room became a world of energy. I could see the wires in the walls glowing. There was nothing from my ring, only a slight flicker from the diamond. I brought myself back as Gian was emerging. My eyes adjusted faster to the colors.

"Good. Good. Turn invisible and open a portal to the altar on Lake Pergusa. If you get lost, think of being at home. I'll go first so you can find me."

She vanished and I followed. Her orb turned as a slit opened in the air. On the other side was the energy of the altar. She stepped through and was gone.

I thought of the altar and placed my hand in the air. Nothing happened. There was no handle or doorknob. Gian's orb was floating through his portal. Nera returned and materialized. I joined her.

"What am I doing wrong? I thought of the altar, but the portal didn't open."

"Sorry, don't think of the altar. Picture yourself on it." She vanished and crossed over.

I thought of standing on the stone slab and a slit opened up. A turn of my wrists widened the portal enough to step through. The journey wasn't long, but it was still wild. I appeared upside down and landed on my shoulder.

I materialized to Nera saying, "Graceful."

I looked down at the stone, embarrassed but proud of making it there.

"You'll get used to traveling. You both did well."

"Can you believe we just did that?" Gian said.

I was numb, maybe in shock. All I could get out was, "So cool."

"What did you see after you arrived?" Nera asked.

"A soft blue light concentrated in a wide area," Gian said. "What was that?"

"Our security camera. Go invisible. Emerge when you're out of range."

Once I saw the light, it was easy to avoid. I materialized off in the corner.

"What did you do wrong?"

I was disappointed. I thought we did well.

"The gardener saw us," Gian said.

"That is correct. And now he must die."

I backed away from her. "What? Oh my God, no!"

She laughed. "It's all right. That's a scarecrow. But if someone sees you, we must eliminate them."

I couldn't contain my mischievous grin.

"Don't you dare materialize around your school bullies," she said.

I failed at acting innocent. The thought of the clique girls perishing brought a smirk to my face. That can't be healthy.

"It's easy to see which way a person faces," Nera said. "The energy around the head changes. I'll face the house, so you know which way I'm looking. Walk around me."

I vanished and circled her. It was clear when she was looking in my direction. Streams of energy followed her gaze. Beyond that was the glow of her thoughts. The view from the back of her head was blank. I materialized.

"These are dangerous powers," she said. "Who knows if our planet is still monitored? Do you want to get the human race wiped out by being spotted materializing? From what the muses say, the Collective is not forgiving."

I looked into the stars. "We'll be careful."

"Not just careful, certain."

"We will. I have a question. What color is my aura? I can't see my own."

"A vibrant blue," Gian said. "It's beautiful. What color is mine?"

31

"A very sexy red."

A bag of clothes appeared on the altar. Nera tucked it under her arm. "Let's head back to your place. Think about being home."

My portal took me on a journey far away. I realized my mistake on arrival. I wanted to materialize and hug Grandpa, but returned to Italy.

"There you are. Where did you go?" Nera asked.

"My home in the States," I said, embarrassed.

"Don't be so hard on yourself. You were able to correct and return. You're doing great, Linsey."

I ate the compliment up. We didn't get a lot of those growing up.

"Here, put these on." She handed me a summer top with a cute pair of shorts and sandals.

I stepped out of my pants and into the shorts. "Wow, normal pockets." I thrust my hands deeply.

"Bianca's Tasca line is taking off like wildfire."

"Love the name." Tasca means pockets.

Gian was given a cute T-shirt with a blue tropical flower pattern. Nera had him wear the sandals they made him.

"The first of five is on the Hawaiian island of Kauai."

"Nice," Gian said.

"This isn't a vacation."

"I can still enjoy myself."

"You're here to kill these people. Enjoy that."

"Jesus, Nera," I said.

"This is serious. Subject number one is Don Fernau. Think about joining him. Being with him. It may take blocks to materialize safely, so don't get impatient." She vanished and I followed.

The energy in Hawaii was bright and inviting. We were in a room full of people. One of them had a glowing orb in his head. This was Don. Gian and I followed Nera, but she had us go ahead. We led her to a safe place to materialize. She let us know we were right by doing that.

Before I materialized, I saw a blue streak in my peripheral, but it was gone when I turned my head.

Kauai's air was warm and muggy. It was a little much at first. Palm trees swayed high above us. I was in Hawaii. What a trip.

We returned to Don's restaurant and found a table near his. The place was open-air with dark wood decor and a wonderful Polynesian ambiance.

Nera didn't need to point Don out. I knew who he was. The man was older, maybe in his sixties. He looked Hawaiian, but I could have jumped to conclusions because of where we were. Don had a round head and a slightly wide nose. His features were comforting, like a grandfather. There was sadness in his eyes.

"Sorry boys, I forgot my wallet," he said as the check arrived.

One of the men in his group pounded his fist on the table. "You cheap bastard." The group of men laughed. "When we get to the office, you're paying me back."

Don didn't look embarrassed, just annoyed. His ruse was over.

My piña colada arrived in a cored-out pineapple. It was the best I've ever tasted. At twenty dollars a pop, it should be.

"Why him," I whispered.

"Does he bore someone to death?" Gian asked.

"Humor will get you through this. Use it."

I scrunched my eyebrows, confused. "You're giving mixed signals here."

"Sorry for my outburst before. There isn't much time. I let the pressure get to me. Gian's right. Go light. It'll help you prevail."

"I know when he has to die," he said. "Twenty-nine days, three hours, and forty-two minutes and… twenty-two seconds."

I was about to ask how, but thinking about Don's time, I had the countdown in my head. "But why?"

"Does it matter?"

"Yes."

"If he doesn't die like he's supposed to, he cuts in line, causing an argument that slows a man enough to set the timing of a horrible car wreck. Sixteen people perish. One of them has to live."

"Fucking line cutters," Gian said.

I chuckled.

"Drink up. We need to head to an oil rig in the South Pacific."

It was amazing that we could pop around the world like that. The aliens really needed to share their technology.

Gian set a debit card down but Nera objected. "This is business." She replaced the card with three twenties. "Besides, how would you explain that being used in Hawaii?" The card was tossed back to him. "Always carry cash."

We headed back to where we had materialized.

Gian took my hand. "I wanted to feel you."

"I can feel you without touching."

"You'll get there," Nera said to Gian. "This next jump, we'll have to stay hidden. You can't just show up on an oil rig in the middle of the ocean. That's where Troy Rothburg works."

Hearing his name, I could picture him. He was a fit, handsome, blond man in his early thirties. Arriving on his rig was strange. Everything was artificial. Plus, we were so high off the water. It was disconcerting. Troy was across from us, pulling a long pipe or cable from a casing. He would be dead in twenty days.

We followed Nera to a storage closet and materialized. I grabbed onto a wall to steady myself. The oil rig wasn't swaying. I was just off.

"Subject number three is a woman from New Orleans hiding in the US Virgin Islands."

"Wait, what does Troy do to deserve to die?" Gian asked.

Yeah, what the hell, Nera?

"I'll tell you after we meet Rowanda Zimbell." She vanished.

Gian and I looked at each other, frustrated, and shot to her location. Rowanda was the hostess of an outdoor restaurant at a beachfront hotel. She had beautiful dark skin and a short, tight haircut. Her demeanor was warm and inviting as she showed us to a seat in a circular outdoor bar with a thatched roof. A welcome breeze cooled us down. The humidity was more reasonable here.

"Best seat in the house," she said.

I was expecting a Cajun accent, but she sounded Caribbean. It was an act. She couldn't hide for long. Rowanda would be dead in twenty-six days.

Our table overlooked the beach. I had never seen sand so white.

Both Gian and I ordered drinks.

"Might want to slow down," Nera said. "The travel can make you sick."

"The role is making me sick," he said. "Nothing wrong with a bit of self-medication."

I took her advice and nursed my whiskey when it arrived.

"Troy causes an explosion that kills everyone on his rig, including a traveling dignitary who needs to live. Rowanda steals a maintenance van and runs over a white supremacist she recognizes from Louisiana."

"Her destiny doesn't sound so bad," Gian said.

"Well, first of all, it's not her destiny. We're here to ensure that doesn't happen because it starts a race war that nearly destroys the US and drastically changes the world. It's worse, getting worse. Negativity snowballs. Speaking of that, you need to watch your actions. If you abuse your power too much, it can have repercussions."

"Does that mean we can abuse it a little?" he asked.

She gestured with a tiny gap between two fingers.

"A little."

I caught myself staring at Gian's nose. It was perfect. If someone as stunningly handsome as him could have insecurities about their looks, where was the hope for the rest of us?

"Before we head out, can we walk the beach?" he said. "It'll help with the stress."

I was pretty sure he was asking for me. His body felt relaxed.

"Sure. There's time. We had to get here quickly because Rowanda's shift is nearly over."

Our waitress brought us to-go cups, and we had a pleasant stroll on the sugary sand. The roar of a jet engine couldn't detract from the tranquility. An airport must be nearby.

"We have two more. I'll save the worst for last. Subject number four is Janet Narmel, a rape victim carrying Hitler 2.0. Maybe worse. I've seen what this child becomes. He's a monster."

"Hey, I was a monster," Gian said.

"You could control it," she responded.

At the end of the beach, Nera led us into a thicket of trees. "Follow me back to your villa."

Gian downed his drink. I kept mine in my hand, wondering if it would travel. After he vanished, I picked his cup up. The muses wouldn't appreciate us littering. The Underworld is so clean. Back in Sicily, I tasted the whiskey. It wasn't affected by the journey.

"Oh, thank you," Gian said, taking his cup. "I wasn't sure what to do with it."

Nera had us dress in warm clothes. They just appeared on her. We jumped to Anchorage and materialized behind a Walmart. The crisp mountain air was almost as refreshing as the underworld. Then came the odor of garbage. The wind had shifted.

We found Janet in the baby section, looking at infant clothes. Her face lit up when she heard her phone ring but sank when she saw who it was.

Janet was a country girl with long, dirty blonde hair. Her dominant chin and pointed nose were slightly masculine, giving her a party girl look. She had a kindness about her.

My sense of smell was heightened. I wondered if it was from the cleansing chamber. An unpleasant stench was in the air—a vile mixture of body odor and despair. It took a while to figure out it was the store. That gave me the giggles. Nera looked over with a smirk like she had read my mind.

"Her college friends abandoned her when she became pregnant," Nera said.

What kind of friends are those? I thought college would be different.

Janet hung up and sat on the floor dejected. The tears started flowing. I wanted to hold her.

"She's a sweetheart. Don't get attached."

Eleven days, I thought.

"OK, Last one. Robert Langfield." Nera led us from the store back to our jumping point. "He lives in the English village of Dunster."

I could picture him. "Crazy Robert."

She nodded. "He hasn't been the same since his roofing accident. Fell on me noggin," she said in an English accent. "You won't be bored with him."

We stepped through to England and materialized. Dunster was a charming village, hundreds of years old. The street was lined with connecting buildings, most made of stone. Artful signs hung from the shops, luring in patrons. I felt at home.

A pub door opened. Crazy Robert was being escorted from the premises by two hefty men. He lost his footing and fell to the ground.

Robert was a scrappy man in his fifties with a short buzzcut that screamed, I'm an asshole.

"What are you looking at," he yelled at Gian from the ground.

Gian held his palms out to show him we weren't a threat. Robert jumped up and rushed him. My training kicked in. I dove at Robert, knocking him off his feet. On the way down, I struck him twice in the head.

He shook it off. "I like her. Give me a kiss, love."

God, no. "Pass."

Gian laughed at my response.

Nera pulled me away. "Buy him a drink. Explain why you're here. We need to start now." She handed me a couple of hundred-pound notes. "There's more in your safe."

"He kills the man who discovers the cure for pancreatic cancer?" I asked.

"Yes."

"We need to talk," I said to Robert.

"Right on. Hey, not the wet wipe."

It was such a good insult that we both laughed.

"Yes, him too." I slipped Gian the money.

"I don't do dudes."

The thought of having sex with him was repulsive. If he kept pushing, my drinks were coming up.

"We're not having sex."

"I'm buying," Gian said.

He led us to a pub across the street. We made it two steps inside when the bartender yelled. "Get out of here, Robert."

"But I have friends."

"Fuck right off." The bartender waved him away.

It was too bad. The pub was adorable.

"I've been kicked out of them all," he said almost with pride.

I believed that.

There was a corner store at the end of the block. We bought a fifth of whiskey.

"Let's go to your place," Gian said.

"All right, but you're just going to watch."

He was persistent. I'll give him that.

38

Robert headed down a side road, then another. The stone wall we were following flowed into a cottage of the same material. The place was his. I fell in love with it from the living room alone. Old beams lined the ceiling. A massive fireplace was the focal point. Sketches were everywhere, offering a glimpse of his mindset. He had an erratic style of drawing. Quick lines with odd directions, yet it worked. His nature paintings drew me in—especially one of a lovely garden.

"I painted that before me accident. I can't do life anymore."

"Perfect," I said.

"I think he meant he can't paint life anymore," Gian said.

Robert pointed at him in agreement. He headed to the bathroom, and I ducked into a corner of the kitchen to vanish. I found a hidden camera in the front room and another in the hall.

When he returned, I handed him the bottle.

"Pour us a round."

"What are we drinking to?" he said.

"A new outlook on life."

"Good luck there."

"What we have to say is pretty astounding," I said.

"Whatever." He handed over full glasses. "To a new outlook on life," he joked.

"To Robert," Gian said.

"To Robert."

He picked a good bottle. The whisky was smooth.

Robert had calmed down by his second glass, but something inside snapped. He got up in my face. "Let's arm wrestle. I'm Dunster's champion."

I wasn't arm wrestling this bastard. "Gian will." Somehow, I knew he would win.

His glance wasn't as assuring. He passed on the offer, but Robert persisted relentlessly.

"If it will shut you up, fine," Gian said.

They moved to a corner of the dining room table and locked hands. Robert became distracted and started in on a story. Gian slammed his arm down and bounced to his feet triumphantly.

I cracked up. "I knew you'd win."

"I wasn't ready," Robert said. "Best two out of three."

"No, we did it. I won."

Robert became enraged. "Two out of three!"

"Whatever," Gian said.

I was sure Gian would win this round, also. They assumed the position, staring each other down. Robert was distracted again and his arm slammed to the table. It was even funnier the second time.

"What the hell!" Robert said. "Go again."

"Nope, I'm retired."

"You can't retire."

"The hell I can't."

No amount of complaining would change Gian's mind. He was Dunster's new arm wrestling champion.

"We should get down to business," he said. "Do you want to tell him, or should I?"

"Let the lass tell me. Are you coppers? What did I do now?"

"We're not cops." I walked over to the first camera, unplugged it, and removed the one in the hall.

"How did you know those were there?" Robert yelled.

He dove for me, and I vanished as he dropped through to the floor. I reappeared and helped him up.

"Have a seat, Robert," Gian said.

"I need my medicine. I'm seeing things."

"You're not seeing things." I refilled his glass. "Drink this."

Robert calmed down after taking a long pull of whisky.

"We're not the police," I said.

"We're angels of death."

God, we were angels of death. "In thirty-one days, you're going to die. We're here to see that you make peace with yourself."

"Why do I have to die?" he whined. I wasn't expecting that.

"It just is."

"You'll never find me." He snagged his keys and raced out the door.

"Let him go," I said.

"Gladly. I'm beat."

"Can we get a bite to eat before we head home?" I asked.

"Sure. I love English cuisine."

It took a minute to realize he was mocking me. I searched on my phone for meat pies. There was a pub in town that served Cornish pasties. He was about to eat his words.

In the street, we passed a man whose poise was military perfect. I rolled my shoulders back. Gian did the same, feeling me. The Touch was going to do wonders for our posture.

"Did you notice that you felt the Touch without holding onto me?"

"I did. It's weird, though. Not as strong as when we're touching."

"You'll get there. Mine's almost returned. So, what did you think of Robert?"

"He seems like the type that doesn't return his shopping cart."

# Chapter 3

Gian didn't show up to my home in Seattle. I stepped through to our place in Sicily.

"There you are," he said.

"I thought of my house when you said let's go home. That was a little presumptuous."

"Not at all. You're homesick. We can visit them."

I wrapped my arm around his waist, pulling him close.

From the kitchen counter came the vibrating sound of a text. He glanced at it, then handed the Don's phone over.

"It's in Italian."

I read the message to him, following along with my finger so he could read what I translated. "Buongiorno. You were right. Antonio held a gun up to the temple of the Hunter and fired. The bullet went through Antonio's head, nearly hitting me. I apologize for contacting you when I promised I wouldn't. The phone is yours. Addio."

"Sweet," Gian said and grabbed the iPhone. "Wait, thank him for us. I'll be right back." He vanished, heading north.

I was taken aback by his callous attitude toward getting one of his kind killed, even if he was a mobster.

He returned with a bottle of Sir Donald's favorite scotch.

"Do I want to know?" I said.

"What a rush. Don't worry. I'll replace it. There were enough that he won't notice."

I couldn't believe he went to Scotland without me.

He slid an arm around my waist. "I didn't like being away from you. I can feel your heart beating faster. Can you feel mine?"

"Every time."

"Let's go visit your family."

"Right now?"

"You've gone there twice. This bottle is for them."

I guess I could forgive him.

We were about to turn invisible. Gian rubbed his cock against my ass. I wasn't in the mood but humored him. He worked my pants down and slid himself inside me. The dual feeling of insertion sparked my lust. I guess we're traveling together.

"It feels so weird from your side as I press inside," Gian said. "The two feelings at once are amazing."

"Let's hope we get to keep it this time."

I took his hand and disappeared, pulling him into the portal. Our hands remained locked, but the rest split apart, sending us tumbling. I freaked out at the thought of him losing the pose and trapping us in the void, but he held us steady. It was weird being the lead. The falling sensation was more of a dragging. Upon arrival, I could see the energy of my family's porch. Security cameras were everywhere. There wasn't a corner we could safely appear. We ended up blocks away at the base of the park.

Gian's member was still out when we materialized, but the travel had made him flaccid. He brought me deeper into the woods and fucked me against the sturdy trunk of a maple before we made our way to my family's house.

Joan saw me through the living room window as we walked to our front yard. She had her red hair pulled tightly into a ponytail. Her scream of excitement was so loud I heard it through the glass.

She was coming out the back door as I was running to it. We both did an excited dance before hugging. Gian strolled around the corner.

"There's your handsome man," she said, hugging him.

"What are you still doing here?" Gian asked.

44

"She's with me," Max said from the door. His blond hair was getting long and floppy. He hadn't cut it in months.

"A Hunter and a Huntress," Gian said. "Good lord, imagine your offspring."

"I don't think they'd like you," Max said dryly.

I was relieved when Gian laughed and gave my brother a chuck on the shoulder.

"Where's your luggage?" Joan asked.

Gian was quick. "It's at my place."

"What is all the ruckus?" Grandpa said, walking onto their deck. His short beard was back. "Son, get out here."

Dad poked his head out the sliding door. "Hey, guys." He had received the driving cap I sent him. It was so him.

"Mr. Cameron. Mr. Cameron," Gian said, reaching up to shake their hands.

"Call me Bram," Dad said.

"You have a cool name," Gian said.

Dad smirked.

Grandpa didn't correct Gian's Mr. Cameron.

"What are you doing in town?" Dad asked. "I thought you were staying in Sicily for a while?"

"We only have a few hours before we head back," I said.

"A few hours?" he said.

Shit. Why had I said that? "We're on a mission for the witches. That's all I can say."

Dad nodded.

"For this special occasion." Gian handed the bottle over.

Grandpa noticed the 'Aged twenty-five years' label. His eyes widened. "Come on over."

Once they were out of earshot, I asked Max, "What's wrong with Dad? He's acting weird."

Max laughed. "You're not used to the smile. Now that he doesn't have to keep us safe, he's kind of fun."

"Dad, fun?" That I had a hard time believing.

We followed Max and Joan to the basement door. They were holding hands. I found that adorable.

Upstairs, Dad had tumblers out and was pouring our drinks.

His toast was short and to the point. "To family."

The room grew silent as the liquor washed over our palates.

"That is good scotch," Dad said.

"It's from Sir Donald's private collection," Gian said. "You're drinking his favorite."

Grandpa took a healthy drink. "What an honor. Please thank him for us."

Yes, thank you, Sir Donald, for letting us steal your liquor.

"Can I talk to you for a moment," Gian said, leading me to the deck. Our magnolia tree was blooming. It was stunning. I'm glad we got to see it. For the rest of the year, it's just a tree.

"How about you move in with me and offer your brother your room?"

"Really?"

"I want to live with you. We're getting married."

"That we are." I held him tightly. "You smell good. What is that?"

"My new deodorant. Supposed to be more of a cologne."

It gave him a wonderful scent that didn't overpower his own. I soaked him up. "Don't change it."

I took his hand and led him back inside. Dad didn't seem comfortable with this simple act of affection, but his face softened when he saw the ring. "So?"

"Of course, I said yes."

"Welcome to the family, Son," Grandpa said, holding his glass up.

"Speaking of family." I looked at Max and Joan. "We want you to have my room. Make the other one a guest room for us."

"Guilty about losing at hide and seek?" Max said. No one but him and I knew what he was talking about.

"Thank you," Joan said.

"A girl needs an ensuite."

Dad wouldn't look at me. When he finally did, I saw tears welling in his eyes. "Linsey, you can't just throw something like that at us. I don't want to lose my girl."

"You're not losing me. I'm just growing up."

"Don't think of it as losing a daughter," Gian said. "You're gaining a monster."

The room grew awkwardly silent. Grandpa let out a bellowing laugh that got the room rolling.

"Son, you're not a monster. You're a good boy."

I thought the Reckoning would bring Gian to tears, but he kept it together.

"Tell us about your trip," Dad said. "From what Max was saying, it sounds amazing."

"It was so awesome," I said. "But first, I need you guys to know the witch's warning is real. You can't kill any Dread. It's you who will die."

"We know," Grandpa said.

"Good," Gian said. "A Don in Sicily has already lost two men to their foolishness."

"You know a Don," Max said.

"He's our friend," I said.

Gian snapped at me. "He's not our friend."

Nera had us head out straight from Seattle. We didn't have time to see Gian's family. She brought our beach clothes to his condo, and we were off to Kauai.

We arrived on a dirt road as Don drove by in a clunker of a Jeep. The air wasn't as muggy on this part of the island, but there was the comforting warmth. Gian pointed to a spot around the curve. We made it far enough ahead of Don to materialize. He saw us on the side of the road but looked away.

"Should we show up in his car?" I asked.

"He could wreck. Let's wait until he stops."

"I know where he's going." I took Gian's hand and stepped through a portal to a small park. There were only two cars. We materialized behind the bathrooms.

"I saw something in the sand. Follow my light." I vanished.

As I rounded the corner, I saw a glowing ring. I placed my blue orb above it, and Gian dug through the sand.

I returned after materializing. "What is it?"

"A wedding ring with a huge-ass diamond. How did you see it?"

"It glowed."

"Why doesn't your ring?"

I held it to the sunlight. "Maybe because it's silver." The ring in his hand was gold.

Don's Jeep barely made it up the hill to the parking lot. It knocked for a while after the engine was off. He did a double-take seeing us, and walked by.

We followed him along a sandy path through long grass and emerged on top of a massive dune high above a vast beach.

I put my hand on his shoulder.

"You can see me?" he said.

I was confused. "Are you a ghost?"

"No, just old," he said, dropping his gaze.

"Hi, Don, I'm Gian, and this is my angel, Linsey."

"We're actually both angels," I said.

"Aloha," he said sarcastically, brushing us off.

48

He continued down the dune at a swifter pace. Far off to our right, the beach butted up to a cliff that stretched into the ocean. To the left was endless beige sand. It was a muted color, like how apartments are painted, but here it was bliss. A gentle breeze flowed from the ocean as waves broke upon the shore. The weather was comfortable. Perfect.

Don laid out a blanket and we joined him.

"What do you want? And how do you know my name?" The sun was on his face, forcing him to smile.

I didn't know how to tell him. With Robert, it was easy. He was an asshole.

"This will be a lot to take in," Gian said. "I'm just saying it."

"No, don't," I said.

"It's the best way. You're going to die soon. But it won't be painful."

Don laughed. I nodded in agreement. He jumped up, backing away. "That was you on the road. How did you beat me here?"

"That's not important. Your time is drawing near. We're here to guide you home."

"Why are you telling me?"

"To give you time to make peace with yourself," Gian said.

"I've saved my whole life to retire." His eyes drooped in sorrow. "It's a year away. Have I wasted everything? How much time do I have?"

I felt as low as dirt. What a fucked up thing they're putting us through.

"Twenty-eight days," Gian said.

And twenty-two hours, eighteen minutes, and six seconds, I thought.

"Why?"

Gian went to speak. "I can't tell you. I seriously can't get the words out. Try it," he said to me.

I couldn't say it either. The witches were blocking us.

"This is all we can tell you."

"Well, fuck this." He gasped. "I'm sorry. I usually don't swear."

"It's all right, Don. I would swear, too." I put my arm around him.

Gian comforted me, and I caught a whiff of his new scent again. I wanted to bury my face in his pits. That would make for a great impression.

My phone rang. It was my brother. I let it go to voicemail. He called right back from the app we use for privacy.

"Maxwell never calls twice. I have to take this." I tapped Accept on my phone.

"Gian's Uncle has a gun to Dad's head. Put him on."

The extreme of going from a sad paradise to constricting panic overwhelmed my senses.

"Lindsey?"

"Fuck. Sorry. Are you at home?"

"What? Yes. Put Gian on," he stressed.

"We'll be right there."

I heard him say, "What?" as I hung up.

"Don, we have to go. We'll be back."

"Follow me to Dad's basement," I said to Gian.

"Can I stop my death?" Don asked.

I looked at him earnestly. "No. All you can do is prepare."

I ran to the protective grass in the dunes and stepped through to my house. When we arrived, I could see everyone's energy upstairs.

"You have to stop Uncle Tony."

Gian raced up the stairs with me on his heels. In the front room, his uncle had a gun pressed against Dad's forehead.

"Don't do it," Gian yelled.

Everyone looked over.

"You'll kill him. You'll kill my father-in-law. You were never cursed. Stop it."

Dad had a startled look of realization. Within seconds, he had Tony's arm knocked to the side and the gun safely in his hands. The hammer had clipped Tony's head. Blood flowed to the beat of his heart. Knowing Dad, he did it on purpose to teach him a lesson.

Tony crumpled to the floor in defeat. Gian sat next to him and lifted him into a sitting position in his arms. His uncle let out a wail and rocked back and forth.

Dad sat on the other side and cradled him with Gian. "You'll be all right."

"No, I won't." Tony's words came out in a whimper.

"Yes, you will," Dad said.

I headed to the bathroom for bandages. But really, I was hiding my tears from Dad. I returned when I had my emotions under control and dressed the wound.

"Why was he never cursed?" Grandpa asked.

"It didn't affect gay people," Gian said.

Grandpa caught my eye. "You couldn't feel him at the storage unit. I'm so sorry for not trusting you."

I couldn't let him know I knew. I had put our family in danger by allowing Uncle Tony to go. I nodded.

"How did you get here so fast?" Maxwell asked.

We didn't know how to respond.

"What's going on?" Dad asked. "It looks like you're headed to the beach."

Grandpa brushed sand from my leg. "Or were just there."

I heard Nera say in my head, *We're setting things right.* Before I could say it, Gian did.

"What does that mean?" Uncle Tony said.

Gian tried to speak but couldn't. "Please, no questions. All I can say is we need you alive. I need you alive."

Dad continued to hold onto Tony with Gian. It was the longest act of love I'd seen him perform.

"I have to go," Uncle Tony said, trying to stand.

"We're going to talk first." Dad led him to the TV room. "Could you pour us a drink?" he asked Grandpa.

Dad's kindness touched me. He *had* changed.

"We need to get back to Don," I told Gian.

"I know."

We hugged my family and headed downstairs to vanish. Don's back was to us as we approached. He sat still, staring at the sea.

I followed his gaze to the blood on Gian's shirt.

"What the hell?" He scrambled away from us.

"It's not what you think," I said. "We saved a life."

"Save me," he pleaded.

"We can't. All we can do is save your soul." I was proud of how well that sounded.

"But why me? Why do I have to die?"

"If you don't, a man who has to live won't," Gian said.

"How do I cause this?"

Gian tried to speak. "God, that's frustrating. It's not important how. There's only one way to stop it."

Don leaned over and up came his lunch. His arm went to his lower back. I could see pain on his face even though he didn't verbally express it. Gian helped him back into a sitting position.

A rainbow sat at the same angle as the end of the cliff. Clouds cut off the top like it was floating past the rocks. I pointed it out to distract Don. He took my hand and we stared in wonder.

I had an even better distraction. "We found a ring. Do you think you can find the owner?"

Gian stared at me in astonishment. I mocked his look back. I couldn't believe he thought we would keep something as sacred as a wedding ring. He reluctantly handed it over.

Don seemed pleased with the task. "I'll find its home." He turned the ring around in his hand. "This should be easy. Their names are inscribed in the band."

"Will you be all right?" I said. "You're one of five. We have to talk to the others."

"How do I know this is real?"

*Let him see you vanish,* Nera's voice said in my head.

"Walk with us."

In the safety of the dunes, I turned to face Don and vanished, then stepped through a portal to the oil rig. Gian followed close behind.

Troy was in a kitchen, bussing his plate. We followed him to a small room with no people or cameras. He sat on the floor with his legs stretched out in front of him. We materialized as Troy was pulling his cock from his open jeans.

We all screamed for different reasons.

"What the fuck," Troy said to Gian. He put things away. "Oh, hello," he told me, toying with his fly.

"Uh, no," I said.

Troy was a cute blond roughed up by life. His hair was short and spikey. I think it was styled from sweat and oil, not product. The sides were shaved so tightly it almost looked like he had a mohawk.

A knock at the door sent us invisible. A man peered his head in. There was frantic movement from Troy, but we couldn't hear what he was saying. As soon as the man closed the door, we materialized.

Troy scrambled back against the wall and stared at us. He closed his eyes, but we were still there when they opened. His hand moved toward me as if he expected it to pass through.

"We're not ghosts. We're angels of death," I said.

"You're not taking me." He pushed past us.

"You have twenty days," I yelled to him.

"Don't mess with me," he said. "I am not in the mood."

He was a feisty one. I liked him.

"You have to die, or everyone on this rig will," Gian said. He looked at me. "Why was I able to say that?"

"Then I'll just leave."

"It will still happen."

Nera was feeding him the lines.

"Dying is the only way to stop it. But first, you have to find peace with yourself."

"Peace with myself. What kind of hippy mumbo jumbo is that?"

"All right, let's do it now," Gian said.

Troy screamed and dashed from the room, leaving the door open. We moved to the side and vanished. Gian's reverse psychology hadn't worked. I didn't know what we were supposed to do.

Troy led us to a bunkhouse with no cameras inside. There sure were a lot on the way.

He barely flinched when we appeared. "Is that a phone?" Troy asked, pointing at Gian's pocket.

He nodded and pulled it out.

"I need to act like someone called with an emergency."

Troy dialed his cell and left the line open for a few minutes. He then texted a message that his mom was in Family General. And to hurry.

I looked over at Gian, wondering if we should be doing this.

"There's a supply helicopter coming soon. Kick me in the balls. It's the only way I can cry," Troy said to me.

"I think you have to stay here." Nera wasn't telling me this. It just felt right.

"Screw that. I'm going to have some fun before I die. Now kick me in the nuts."

"Get a lemon," I said.

"There's no time. Fucking do it."

Gian held his fingers out, ready to flick.

Troy pulled up the front of his pants from the top, giving himself a hideous moose knuckle.

I turned away. A quick double snap brought a muffled, high-pitched scream. Tears were streaming down Troy's face. He scrambled from the room hunched over.

"Want to ride in a helicopter?" I asked.

"Let's make sure Uncle Tony is okay first."

"Of course. I'm sorry."

"Don't be. This whole thing is crazy."

"We only have two more people to talk to," I said.

"You think it'll stop there?"

The weight of reality was overwhelming. "We have to guide them, don't we?"

He cocked his head. "Yep."

"This is not going to be fun."

"We'll get through it."

He held onto me, and with a quick peck, vanished. I followed him to my house. His trail was a leash dragging me along. Joan was doing laundry in the basement. We materialized in my kitchen. Maxwell's cat backed away from us. She sat on her haunches and stared. Was a muse controlling her? I waved hello, but it didn't faze her.

"Hey, Max, you home?"

He screamed from his room and came bounding down the stairs. "Hi, guys."

"Can I borrow a shirt?" Gian asked, showing him the blood. "Short sleeve."

"If you tell me what's going on."

"OK." He gestured to his mouth with both hands. No words came out. "I literally can't tell you."

"Whatever," Max said, heading upstairs.

"We're not fucking with you," I yelled.

Max returned with his favorite summer shirt. The gesture was touching.

Gian handed over his bloody one. "You'll want to soak that in cold water."

"I know how to get blood out," Max said in a snotty tone.

Joan walked in the front door. I gave her a friendly wave.

Gian looked into Max's eyes. "How's my uncle?"

"Drunk. But better. Dad was surprisingly helpful. Tony never recovered from his boyfriend's death. He needs a friend."

"Yeah, he does. I don't want to bother them. Can you give him a note?"

"Fer sher."

He hadn't said that expression in a while. "I'm so happy that's back."

"Tell them your new catchphrase," Joan said. "The one from dinner the other night."

Max shook his head, embarrassed.

"Come on. It's the best."

A massive smirk formed on his face. "You're so jizz."

We all laughed at the stupid phrase and had trouble stopping.

"You have any more pot?" Gian asked. I hadn't noticed that Max was stoned.

"Oh my God, I got Dad high a week ago. It was so funny."

"What? No way," I said. "You're so jizz."

We were laughing again.

"Well, he got himself high," Max said. "He Found some chocolates in our freezer. Luckily, I saw him eating them or he would have had a third piece."

"How was he?"

"Pretty freaking high. Grandpa and I ate some so he wouldn't be alone."

"Grandpa," I laughed. "What did you do?"

"Played video golf and ate a lot of pizza. Dad sat next to us, barely moving. He would close his eyes and talk about this magical world he was in with all these colors. It was hilarious. He crawled to the bathroom, thinking he shit his pants. Grandpa and I were rolling. We lost it when he found out he hadn't."

I pictured Dad crawling around. I couldn't stop laughing at the story. I missed my silly brother.

"Are there any chocolates left?" Gian asked.

"We can't talk to these people high. It's not respectful."

"For later," he said.

I gave him a look.

"For stress relief."

"I have something better," Max said and returned with an opened bag of gummies. "They're CBG. Euphoric, same as what we smoked. Start with a quarter piece. They're only ten milligrams but weirdly strong."

---

The supply helicopter for the rig was massive, Coast Guard size. We didn't have time to materialize. It had shown up early. There must be gold on circuit boards. They glowed brightly. It wasn't only the cockpit. Golden circuits were all over the chopper.

Troy waited for the outgoing supplies to be loaded before boarding. His aura was like fire, with an orange base and bits of yellow at the tips. He was the only passenger and talked his way up with the pilots. We sat behind him.

It was impossible to stay centered in our seats upon takeoff. We kept having to climb out of the middle of the padding. This was a huge mistake.

*Don't materialize,* Nera yelled in our heads. *The portal is always in front of you.*

*You could have warned us not to go in here.* I swear I heard her laugh.

The helicopter shot forward like a rocket. I was in the air, falling, silently screaming. The energy of the ocean rapidly approached. I clawed at the air, trying to climb up. There was no resistance, not even the sense of wind passing. I spread my arms wide, hoping to slow down, but kept falling.

Gian fell through his portal. I was relieved that it worked. Mine opened, and I followed him to the Virgin Islands, rolling on arrival. There were too many people around to materialize. We walked to the back of a maintenance shed. As soon as I was solid, I let out a long scream.

"It came from back here," a voice said.

We vanished.

Gian was still laughing at my scream when we approached Rowanda. It was a nice icebreaker.

"Welcome back, my friends," she said.

"It's good to be back, Rowanda," I said.

She froze in her tracks. "How do you know my name?"

I pointed at her name tag, but it said Tina.

"That's not important. We need to talk."

"I ain't talkin' to no one." A little New Orleans had slipped out.

"Fine, we'll meet you at your place."

"Yeah, sure. Let's do that."

She wasn't going home.

"I need a drink," I told Gian.

"Right this way." Rowanda led us to a beachside table. Gian tripped on his feet twice on the way. Did he eat a gummy? What the hell?

Our bartender was an older white guy with a deep tan. "What can I get you, folks?"

"Scotch," I said. "Fill it to the rim."

"We had a bit of a fright," Gian said.

The man laughed. "I think I heard you scream."

Gian pointed at me with a smirk. "What's the alcohol of the Virgin Islands?"

"This is the Caribbean. The land of pirates. It's rum," the man said in a throaty tone.

"And Coke," Gian said.

"Would you like to make it a double to keep up with the missus?"

"Why not."

The bartender took his time with our drinks.

"The Touch is getting stronger," Gian said. "I'm having a hard time walking next to you."

I smiled, realizing how wrong I had been. "The trick is to walk in sync. Then you can tune me out."

"Thanks. I'll try that."

"Rowanda's running," I said.

"She's heading to another island. I know where."

"I do, too. She's heading to a bar called the Soggy Dollar. It's bizarre how we know this."

"I'm digging it," he whispered. "It doesn't seem real. Like we're in a movie."

"I hope it ends well."

"That depends on us. We can see gold."

"We're not stealing," I said forcefully.

"There's no need. We can walk along rivers picking it up. Or buy an old mine. Maybe hunt for buried treasure. Like he said, this is the land of pirates."

Greed overtook common sense, and I grinned mightily. However, deep down, I knew we shouldn't be taking advantage of our situation.

"You could always help me win a poker championship. We would only need one."

"I'm not helping you cheat. We can't take the muses' goodwill for granted."

He looked disappointed. "I'm just throwing out ideas. Do you want to work after this? I sure don't. I want to travel."

He had a point. "Normal life will be boring," I agreed.

"So will flying."

I know he was talking about on an airplane, but hearing this, I pictured the muses flying in that cool, laid-back position.

"How come we haven't talked about the aliens?"

"Where do we begin? It's blowing my mind."

"How was I even able to say that out loud?" I said.

"Who on earth would believe us."

I couldn't tell if he was being clever with his earth comment. "Witches were huge. This is astronomical. We met aliens. Aliens!"

"It's all kinds of crazy," he said.

"What we're doing is crazy. I feel like I'll wake up soon from a dream."

"As long as you're still by my side."

His eyes were on my chest when I shifted in my seat. A slight movement of my breasts was all it took to feel his arousal. "We have about forty minutes. Want to fool around?" The Touch was making him insatiable.

I rubbed myself for his pleasure. His cock pulsed in return.

"Phone, STAT," he demanded.

I picked it off the table and tossed it over. He raised his hand and caught it without looking. It was a lucky catch right in the center of his palm. He nonchalantly unlocked the phone as if he meant to do that and pulled up Maps. "She's heading to this island. I'll find somewhere isolated."

"Switch it to the satellite view." I brushed my hand across my nipple, letting my finger traverse the areola.

"Think of the phone sex."

"I don't know. We have to be close for the Touch to work fully," I said.

"I can feel you far away."

"It's different, more you as a whole."

"Like we're connected by a nerve syncing us as one."

I totally got him. "Yeah," I agreed. "Find a place quickly."

He called the waiter over. "Can I get bottled water and the bill?"

"Let's fuck on a beach," I said, low and throaty. I was getting worked up.

Gian switched to satellite view and scrolled around the island. "None of the beaches look deserted."

"Go back a bit. How about up top by this old lava flow?" I zoomed in. "Right here on this flat rock."

We left from behind the shed and materialized in the shade of a giant boulder. There was no making it to the flat rock. We undressed each other in a rush to nakedness, ending up in only our sandals. His eyes roamed across my body. I felt vulnerable in the bright sunshine but forced myself to stand tall so he wouldn't sense it.

The wind tossed his hair around like a model in a photo shoot. His tan completed the effect.

I wasn't surprised that he was drawn to my breasts. It's what brought us to this moment. I reveled in the delight he felt exploring them. I couldn't get in his mind, but was him as he fondled and caressed me. Nothing takes self-doubt about your breasts away like a man loving them.

He lowered his hands to my waist and spun me to face the boulder. The move was smooth and exhilarating. I shifted my stance to steady myself. I was having trouble clearing my mind of the guilt from our task. *Let it go*, I told myself. It wasn't working. He cupped my pussy from behind. A finger glided across the slickness.

"I'm gonna wreck this pussy," he growled.

The aggressiveness of his statement brought me fully to the moment. "Oh God, yes."

He steadied his cock as I lifted my hips back onto it. His girth felt perfect inside me. Gian didn't disappoint. His thrusts were powerful and fierce. I had to hang onto the rock wall to steady myself. The pounding was relentless, but he could feel how deep to take it. The pain was brought to the brink but never further. The dueling pleasure was all-encompassing. We were one body. One mind.

61

I gasped for breath in loud, broken moans. The sea air mingled with his musky, primal scent.

Being intertwined with the Touch was overwhelming. It felt like my eyes were going to pop out of my head. "You're the best. The fucking best."

He was a beast, ravishing me, ravishing us. It was all I could do to hang on. The world grew black. It was too much for the Touch. He thrust his cock deeply, but it didn't bring me back. His determination was strong as he knocked his head into the rock wall. The pain shot across my forehead. Light appeared as if we were coming out of a tunnel. We both screamed out, having beaten it. He kept his relentless pace. Pounding and pounding. My back arched and I lifted my head back, eyes closed.

"I can feel it building in you." He placed a hand where the tightness of my orgasm was brimming and brought both palms out as if directing the energy. The pulsing waves spread deep into the pit of my stomach and exploded, sending me into a million pieces, searching for their way home. The world shifted as we rode it out. He held me up as my legs had become useless.

I'd barely had time to recover when he turned me to face him, positioning one of my legs hooked around him, and resumed fucking me. Slower this time. He moved in for a kiss, never missing a beat on his thrusts. I enjoyed the sweetness of rum on his breath. The kiss didn't last long. My smile was too broad. I grew weightless as our rushing hearts sent a flood of energy through our bodies.

"It's too much." I wasn't sure if I was going to throw up. It came out of nowhere.

"Do you want me to stop?"

"No," I said between breaths, but I turned my head, in case.

"Stop thinking about it. Focus on us."

"I love you so much."

"I love you more than I ever imagined I could."

That sent me into silent, happy tears.

He pulled out and began stroking his cock. I dropped to my knees. I wanted to taste his goodness, but he aimed for my chest as he came. I looked up at him, disappointed.

"You weren't feeling well."

It was such a dirty way of thinking of me. I rested my back against the boulder. "I'm just exhausted. Can we sleep after we talk to Rowanda?"

"If Nera will let us. We should have started with Janet. She has the least amount of time left." He used a hand and the wall to clean himself off me.

"I'm not looking forward to that talk. She's a mother-to-be. It's fucked up."

Gian held me close. "It's all fucked up. But, yeah, I'm not looking forward to that either."

My head was throbbing with his. He massaged my temples gingerly until both our headaches were gone. A kiss on my forehead made it all better.

He gazed at me with a content smile. "We should beat Rowanda to the bar if we want to make an impression."

"If we have to."

The Soggy Dollar is an open-air bar nestled in sparkling white sand, surrounded by palm trees. Sailboats and catamarans were tied to buoys in the harbor.

Our bartender was a weathered older black man. I liked his straw hat. It went well with the ambiance, especially with the reggae playing in the background. The casual beat slowed my vibe even further.

"What do you recommend with rum?" Gian asked.

The man laughed heartily. "Oh, wait, you're serious. A Pain Killer, of course."

"What's that?" I asked.

"Did you just get here?"

"Today," Gian said.

"You'll love these. It's the drink of the BVI. Our bar invented them."

"Two," I said. "Make 'em doubles."

"No need to say that."

"You sure you want one?" Gian asked.

"Yeah, I'm feeling better."

"Three," Gian told the bartender. "We're expecting a friend."

The mix he added to the rum was a tan shade of orange. I was confused when he shaved nutmeg in like an egg nog, but I wasn't confused as to why it was the drink of the BVI. It was delicious.

"What's the BVI?" I whispered to Gian.

The bartender gave me a confused look. "The British Virgin Islands."

I had another question but had sufficiently made a fool of myself.

"Do you take US dollars?" Gian asked.

"That's all we take." He gestured to a row of money clipped on a line. "You'll be in the groove in no time."

I followed Gian to the beach. He found three plastic chairs to bring to the water's edge. We sat with our toes splashing in the ocean. I wanted to vacation in this paradise.

Rowanda was rounding the corner of the bay. She had a hand on the engine's throttle. The white sports bra accented her skin perfectly, showing off her muscles. She tied up to the dinghy line and swam in. I was distracted by the blue water. The white sand made it glow brilliantly.

She was walking through the shallow surf when she saw us. Her eyes grew wide, and she shook her head. Gian held up her drink to call her over. She reluctantly sat down. Water dripped off her. It hit me why they called it the Soggy Dollar, and the reason the bartender had bills hanging on a line. I am so slow.

"You have no jurisdiction here," she said. "This is British territory."

"Calm down," Gian said. "We're not cops, and we're not here to arrest you."

"Good," she said, relieved.

"It's not good either." I looked to Gian for help.

64

"We're here to prepare you for your death."

"Whatever religion you're selling, I'm not buying."

He cut her off. "You're going to die in twenty-six days."

"Did Margaret hire you? Jesus, The money is in a cemetery in New Orleans. Take it."

"Rowanda, it's not that. You're going to die."

"How?"

"It's more why," I said. "You run over a Grand Wizard of the KKK, leading to a massive race war." How was I able to say that? Gian flipped his head toward me, shocked.

She took a long swig of her Pain Killer. "That sounds about right."

We both laughed. I liked her.

"Can't I not kill him?"

"We can't stop destiny. You're supposed to die before this happens. We're here to help you make peace with yourself before crossing over."

"Honey, I'm sick of running. Let's go right now. Take me."

"It can't happen early," he said. I was thinking the same thing. I had no idea why.

"Well, then, can you bring me my money? If I'm going to die, I don't want to waste time working."

"It's not really your money, is it?" I said.

"You ever have a narcissist boss?" she asked.

I hadn't, I'd never had a real job, but Gian nodded his head. "At the theater."

"Then you'll know why I embezzled. Fuck her is why."

"How about I give you money, and we help you turn in what you stole?" he said. "How much would it take to get you through the month?"

"Eighty-one-hundy," she said.

He laughed.

"That's only $300 a day. Vacation is expensive."

She had a point. Our time in Europe was spendy, even if it wasn't our money.

Gian looked confused at his bulging pocket. He reached in and pulled out a large money roll. Both Rowanda and I were wide-eyed. "It's all here," he assured her.

She took the money in a smooth tuck of her arm and slipped it into her pocket.

"Can you make more?"

"Do you want to keep that?"

I liked stern Gian.

"Yes," she said, protecting her pocket.

"Then don't get greedy."

"Are those Tasca?" I asked, pointing to her shorts. The money had fit so easily in them.

"Hell if I know. Found 'em at a thrift shop. They have the best pockets."

I checked the tag. They were Bianca's. Had Nera seen this moment and steered her to buy these? It would explain the money arriving so fast. I found it odd that with money and clothing, I needed an explanation, but jumping from one location to another, I accepted.

Gian reached over and scratched an itch on my lower back. It must have been bugging him, too.

"My money is located —"

Gian cut her off. "We know where it is."

"Don't worry, we'll get Margaret," I said, humoring her. I was amazed that I had remembered her boss's name.

"Am I supposed to like you?" she asked.

"It wouldn't hurt," he said.

She had finished her drink. "Another round?"

"Next time," he said. "We've been up for at least a day. We need sleep."

"Nera wants us to talk to Janet first."

"Damn it," he said.

"She has ten days."

"Fine."

"What that bitch do?" Rowanda said.

That made me laugh, but the truth didn't, although I stretched it a little. "She's carrying the devil's child." How was I allowed to say that?

We headed to Gian's condo in Seattle to change into warmer clothes for Alaska. I thought I would need to jump to my place, but some of my clothes were in his closet. Nera thought of everything.

The sun wasn't out in Anchorage like it was before. Cold air burned my throat with each breath. I rushed to Janet's location to get out of the elements. We found her slumped forward in a central pew of an old church. The altar's backdrop was brick rising to the ceiling like a wide chimney. Jesus hung from a cross, looking more like fireplace art than savior. I was glad there wasn't a hell. I would surely go there for that thought.

We reached Janet's aisle. Her eyeliner was a mess from crying.

I forced a warm smile. "Do you mind if we join you?"

"Not at all." She took a tissue out of her purse to wipe the tears away.

Gian walked around the row, entering from the other side.

"I'm Janet," she said to him.

"Gian, and this is my fiancée Linsey."

Hearing him call me that was the best. I almost raised my hand to my heart but stopped myself. It was selfish of me to think of myself at a time like this.

"Fiancée? That's too bad." She sat up. "I didn't mean it like that," she told me. "He's very handsome. So are you. I'll quit talking."

He put an arm around her. "It's OK, Janet."

I had no idea how to approach the subject. I was waiting for Gian.

He turned and looked into her eyes. "We know about Eddie."

She recoiled and nearly ended up in my lap. I put my hand on her thigh. "Calm down. Everything's all right."

She glanced back and forth between us. "I haven't told anyone. Is he bragging about raping me? That evil f—" The swear wouldn't come out in church.

"No, we haven't talked to him," I said. "We're here..." I couldn't finish. How do you tell a mother-to-be that she's going to die?

"Janet, we were sent here to..." Gian looked over at me. "I can't say it."

"You're going to die," I said. "You have to die. It's your baby. He's evil." I was shocked I could say that. "He will destroy the world if he lives."

"What are you saying?" Janet searched for a way out. She tried to climb over the front pew, but Gian pulled her back.

"Just get rid of it," he said.

"I'm Catholic. I can't abort."

That's why we could tell her—wicked witches. But why could I tell Rowanda? Maybe because she didn't give a shit. But neither did Troy and I couldn't tell him.

"You have ten days until we take you," Gian said.

"What? Oh my God." She covered her mouth and looked up at Jesus. Without warning, she projectile vomited onto the floor.

The smell was atrocious, sending my cocktail shooting out of me. This caused Janet to throw up more, which reverbed back to me. Gian backed away with a hand to his mouth, trying to hide that he was laughing.

"I have to get out of here," he said.

Janet followed him, stepping carefully from her seat. I couldn't get up quick enough. Our area looked like an exorcism gone wrong.

Gian met us in the hall. "Sorry for leaving. I have a strong stomach, but come on."

"The benches sure lived up to their name." They both stared at me, not getting my joke. "Pews."

68

As dumb as it was, Gian got a bad case of the giggles. It was wonderful making him laugh. He always gazed at me lovingly when he did. It was my favorite look.

We headed to the bathroom to clean up. Gian joined us in the washroom.

"I hate to do this," he said, "but we have another affair to deal with. We'll be back. Are you going to be OK?"

Janet's face grew stern. "Am I going to be OK? Am I going to be OK?" she said louder.

I didn't know what other affair Gian was talking about. "I'm so sorry, but we've been summoned," I said. "We'll be back soon."

Gian hugged her and then disappeared. I felt him heading to Sicily.

Janet backed up against the wall. "What are you?"

"Your salvation," I said and vanished.

I opened a portal to Sicily but closed it. We forgot to tell Janet something important. I reappeared and found her up against the counter, bawling. She jumped when she saw me and shied her eyes. I wrapped my arms around her and we cried. I didn't know if I was strong enough for this.

"You have to find peace with yourself. That's why we came to talk with you."

"What? What does that mean?"

"Only you can make peace with yourself." Nera fed me a line. "You'll be stuck in limbo if you don't."

I kissed her forehead and vanished. Gian was in the shower when I reached Sicily. I went to the sink to brush my teeth. Well, more my breath.

He wiped the steam off the shower door to see me. "What took you so long?"

I spit out my mouthwash. "We forgot to tell her about making peace with herself."

"It's only the main reason we were there."

I joined him in the shower.

"She was crying when I came back. I hate this."

"So do I." He held me close. "That's why I bailed. I thought I'd be stronger."

His comment brought a deep silence. The warm water beating upon us was delightful. I fell asleep in his arms. The slight drop jarred me awake.

We washed and headed to the bedroom. I was too tired to put on underwear and climbed into bed naked, hoping Gian didn't take it as an invitation. "Can you get the curtains?"

He gave me a kiss goodnight. "You're going to love what I found." With the point of a remote, blackout blinds rolled into place.

"Nice." My eyelids grew heavy and I dozed off.

I had a full night's sleep. In the morning, Gian pulled me close and I rolled over to see his beautiful face. He was on his side with his head propped up in his hand. A tuft of hair was shooting out at an odd angle.

"Morning, sunshine. You up for massaging each other?"

"Oh, hell yes."

"I'm brushing my teeth first."

As soon as he was out of the room, I quickly dressed in sweats and jumped to the States to use his bathroom. I couldn't have him feel that. Gian was sitting on the bed in boxer-briefs when I returned. He rose and hugged me warmly. Having his arms around me soothed my frayed nerves.

"After the day we had, I needed this."

He held me a little snugger.

"You first," he said. "We'll go back and forth."

I was excited for a massage with the Touch. I stripped down to my panties and crawled onto the bed, lying on my chest.

"Relax your body. I can feel your tension."

I shook out my arms and legs, letting my body sink into the mattress. He kneeled behind me, resting his weight on his legs, not mine. I found that sweet.

His hands hovered above my body. This was how a Reiki massage should be. He ran both hands along my spine and then used varying pressure to explore my back. Feeling myself through him was distracting.

"Your right shoulder and both sides of your lower back have knots. The one on your shoulder is tight." He ran his hand over it lightly.

"Do you know massage?"

"No, not at all. The Touch guided me. I would have found them anyway. They're warm."

"Weird. I thought I felt you feeling heat."

He started on my shoulder using both hands, working in a circular motion, but kneading forward was way better. I melted with each pass of his hand. Feeling my reaction and sensitivity, he could apply the perfect amount of pressure.

"I can feel your muscle loosening. It's so strange."

"It's so good," I said.

He worked on the knot for a few minutes. With each pass of his fingers, the muscle relaxed further until it was loose.

"Did you feel the energy?" he asked.

"I think so. Did you?"

"Totally. I could feel it pushing away like I was creating ripples across your skin." He ran his hand over the area.

"It's not warm anymore," I said.

"I wonder if I could find your knots with a temperature gun?" That was such a guy thing to say.

He massaged the other side, then moved to my lower back. I lifted my hips as he lowered my panties a few inches. His touch was gentle and loving.

"You're storing something down here. I'll get it out."

That was a weird thing to say. It sent my thoughts scrambling and the stress we were under tried to sneak in. I pushed the thoughts away with an image of the Soggy Dollar's beach.

He worked on the left knot first. It was the biggest. I winced when he pressed too hard. He lightened his touch.

"Don't let up," I said.

"Just relax. I've got you."

This time, I did feel the energy escaping, especially the final wave. Who knows what was stored there, but releasing it produced tears. He held onto me until I was cried out. The other knot had the same weird effect.

"That was so odd," I said.

"It was sweet." He kissed me lightly on my lower back.

"I'll do your neck. Then we'll switch."

He used his thumbs in a kneading rolling fashion up into my hair. It was heavenly and left me lightheaded.

Gian's knots were both in his shoulders. He was right. The combination of physical touching and feeling from his side led me to them.

"Is this what you were doing?" I pressed my palm into the knot and worked upward.

"It's perfect."

I could feel the muscles relaxing with each pass, like a clenched hand slowly opening. Waves of energy flowed ahead as if I was pushing it away. I felt the massage more giving it than receiving. Would we be fighting to give massages? When the knot relaxed completely, he let out a sigh.

"That was weird," he said. "If we run into a masseuse, let's ask if emotions get trapped in muscle."

It was a strange suggestion but it left me wondering if it does. I soon had both of his knots released. Massaging his hips felt wonderful, but his neck was the best. I could almost hear the energy escaping as I pushed it around. He rolled his head in ecstasy.

He had me lie on my back and started with my temples. The stress I was carrying there melted away and I sank into the mattress. His hands moved to the back of my neck.

"OK, this is a better way to get to that area. Feels so good."

I didn't open my eyes. "It's wonderful."

He held my head, working upward along my neck. I moaned in sync. He repeated the move over and over. Each time was heaven. His hands retreated as he gingerly set my head down. Next was the upper part of my cheeks. I felt it in my sinuses.

"Yeah, get that," I said. "Bouncing between climates and altitudes is killing me."

The tightening under my eyes loosened up. A smile pushed into the area.

I expected him to play with my tits, but he was an angel, focusing on the muscles above them. We went back and forth with our massage. Moving to the arms, then legs. It never grew sexual. I appreciated that, knowing it wasn't from a lack of want. He had been growing semi-erect through the whole experience. It was sweet that he never let himself grow hard.

Out of everything, the bottom of our feet was the best. The Touch allowed us to find the exact spots that lit up our senses. Along with massages, there would be more foot rubs in the future.

Once I finished with his feet, I lay next to him, fully relaxed. My body was tingling. It felt alive. He took my hand in his and glanced over with a warm smile. "I'll make us coffee."

# Chapter 4

We had a slow start to the day. It was nice after the hectic one yesterday.

"Linsey, can you come out here a minute," Gian called from the balcony.

He was at the side table with a child's globe. I wondered why he had jumped to town. Push pins marked the locations of our five subjects. Mint dental floss was strung from pin to pin.

"Look at the pattern. It's an upside-down pentagram."

The bottom and left sides were proportional, but the Virgin Islands pin was too close. And the one in England was quite far.

I pointed to England. "This one is a bit of a stretch."

He didn't laugh at my pun.

"I see a pentagram, even if it's a messed up one."

Nera stepped out onto the patio. She grabbed the globe and ripped the pins out by the strings. "What is this bullshit? The pentagram is a sign of peace adopted for evil. The muses are pure and wholesome beings. Respect their culture."

"Sorry, sorry," he said.

"It's all right. Be thoughtful. You did well yesterday. That couldn't have been easy."

"It was horrible," I said.

"The travel is fun," she said.

I couldn't disagree there.

"How come you gave Rowanda money?" Gian asked. "She's a thief. Why would you reward her?"

Nera held a finger to each of his temples. His head jerked back, and he opened his eyes, alarmed.

"What the fuck? Get that out of my head." He was breathing heavily.

"I can't undo the visions. They'll go away."

"Don't do that again. Margaret is so horrible. My boss was a saint compared to her."

"Sometimes it's best not to know," she said.

I reached over to hold Gian's hand. He pulled it back, recoiling against himself.

"You need to rescue Troy," Nera said. "He's in a bit of trouble."

I laughed at her understatement. She shared a vision of him locked in a Honduran jail.

"If you don't get him, he'll be executed in three days. First, drop in on Robert. The stubborn fool doesn't believe you."

"He's at his house," Gian said. "I thought he'd be on the other side of the country by now."

"He came right back as soon as you were gone. Be quick." She vanished.

"I told you it was a pentagram," he said.

I shushed him.

---

We appeared in a safe corner of Robert's living room. He was working on a sketch — his pencil shot into the air with a scream.

"No. No. No. You're not real."

"We're quite real," I said.

Gian ripped a camera from the bookshelf and stepped on it. I pulled the one down from the hall.

"Quit putting these up," I said.

He was up in my face. "Piss off." His breath was a vile mixture of the previous night's debauchery.

Robert went for my throat. I had to sock him in the stomach to get him off me. This should have incapacitated him. Instead, he was enraged. It took both of us to restrain him.

"Calm down," I said. He twisted around in our arms. I cinched on his neck, cutting off his oxygen, and he relaxed his grip.

"We're not your enemy," Gian said. "You gonna be cool?"

He stared daggers, then dropped his head. "I'm fine."

"You need to get back on your medication," I said.

"I'm on my medication!"

Nera made the bottle glow for me. I walked over and held it up.

He snatched it away. "Fine."

"We can end this now if you want," Gian said.

"Do I look like someone who cares?" Robert said.

Gian approached him. "Let's do it."

"No. No. I'm cool."

"If you try to hurt Linsey again, I will end you early." Gian puffed up his chest and vanished. I winked at Robert and followed Gian back to Sicily.

A stack of weathered clothes was waiting for us. We changed and headed to a police station in Honduras.

I materialized in the surveillance room. Four officers and three prisoners were in the building, but they were all knocked out. I paused the six cameras. Gian appeared on the seat next to me.

"Aren't you afraid of materializing inside objects?" I asked.

"I am now."

I tossed a set of gloves over.

The precinct was dingy with the look of a converted mini-mart. The two cells were fenced boxes inside the room. Nera directed me to the key.

The door of Troy's cell creaked as we opened it. Both Gian's and my back tightened out of fear. No one stirred.

My heart was beating so fast from the tension I thought it would wake people.

I shook Troy's shoulder. He was confused to see me and went to say something, but I put my finger to his lips. I waved him forward. Gian locked the door behind us. Everything was happening so fast I barely had time to think. We were in reaction mode.

*You need to wipe his record,* Nera said in my head.

A book on the desk was glowing. The light was coming from a single page. I ripped it out. Gian was doing the same to a pad from a guard's pocket. The safe's door sprung open, and I grabbed a stack of money. Troy tried to snag it from me.

"That's my money."

I pulled out three bills and gave them to him. "That's your money."

He smirked at me.

With Nera's help, I found Troy's belongings and threw the envelope to him.

Gian and Troy left through the back door. It was thrilling how quickly we got him out of there. I stayed to reset the security cameras. We met a few blocks away.

Troy held the money up to me. "How did you know just these were mine."

"They were the only clean ones. No more stealing."

"I was just having fun. Haven't you wondered what robbing a bank is like?"

"They would have killed you in three days," Gian said. "How fun is that?"

"What do you want me to do? You tell me I'm dying in weeks. I'm going to live."

"You can't live by dying," I said.

"Where's the risk?" he said.

"You'll screw everything up if you die early," Gian said.

Nera warned of a man approaching. "Wait, hold back." We pressed up against a shadow in the alley. The man walked past the entrance. "OK," I said and proceeded the opposite way.

*Linsey,* Nera said. *Steal the brown car over in the shadows. Gian will think you're the coolest. The keys are in the ignition. Don't worry. The owner will get it back.*

A smirk appeared on my face, but I pulled it back.

"Let's take that car," I said.

Gian laughed like I was joking.

"Get in the fucking car," I said more firmly.

I had it started before they were inside.

"What, you get to steal?" Troy said.

"You made me do this. Power off your phones so they can't track us."

It was an hour to the base of the jungle. Half the route was dirt roads. From there, we left on foot.

"It's this way," I pointed.

*Get everyone to stop.* "Hold up." *There's a mine off to your left.*

I vanished. The explosive material gave off a dull, almost undetectable energy. We would have to pay close attention.

"There's a mine right over there," I told Gian. "Go invisible so you can see what they look like."

"You guys are fun," Troy said.

*Can you blow it up or at least mark it?* I asked Nera.

*When you're safely at home. I need to stay ahead to guide you around dangers.*

*Thank you. I can't be responsible for more deaths.*

I felt safer with Nera close.

One of us was always invisible to ensure we didn't blow ourselves up. Or get shot. Nera steered us around three sets of patrols. It was a couple hours until we crossed the border into Guatemala—another hour to the coast.

"Thanks for busting me out."

"You're welcome," I said.

"I've got to know," Gian said. "What was robbing a bank like?"

"It was the biggest rush of my life. I loved it."

"Don't encourage him," I said.

"You just broke me out of jail," Troy said. "A jailbreak. What was that like?"

I held my tongue, but not for long. "It was thrilling, all right. Are you happy?"

"I *am*," Gian said.

We found a Zodiac chained to a dock. "Not that one," I said. It was the sole source of the man's income. There was a communal boat a few docks away. The lock fell apart in Gian's hands. The power the witches were sharing was going to my head.

Troy rowed until we were far enough to start the engine without being noticed. His blond hair glowed in the moonlight, giving him an angelic look.

It was another three hours to Belize. The wind was against us, and there were naval vessels to avoid.

Off in the distance was the coastline. Gian cut the engine and we glided to a stop. The air was thick with the pungent smell of algae. A large patch surrounded us. I had pictured Belize with pristine waters.

"No more robbing banks," Gian said.

"Not just banks. No more stealing," I pressed.

"Fine," Troy said.

"Do you need any money?" Gian asked.

"No, I'm good."

"You robbed it for the experience, didn't you?" I asked.

Troy smiled wide.

"You'll want to row the rest of the way," Gian said. "That's the southern tip of Belize. There's a trail twenty yards in from the shore. Follow it to the town of Punta Gorda. Don't head West. That's Guatemala. If anything, go north to Mexico."

"Thank you for saving me. I do appreciate it."

I nodded and vanished, waiting for Gian to show me the way. He didn't leave until Troy was safely on shore and down the path. Gian's trail led to Sicily.

He was gathering our winter clothes when I arrived. I was hoping for rest.

"Not Robert."

"No, we're popping in on Janet. She's making a terrible mistake."

I zipped up the parka and headed to Anchorage.

"Hurry," Gian said, running to the church.

The cold air burned my nose. I'd never been so eager to be in a church. Warmth encased me as we passed through the large wooden front doors. Janet's voice rose in anger from a back room. We ran there and burst through the door.

She saw us and tried to speak, but the witches stopped her.

"It's not what you think," a pastor said. A young boy about nine was tying his sweatpants bottoms. He looked mortified.

Nera explained the situation to me. "You have it all wrong," I said to Janet. "The boy fell in mud." I walked over and retrieved his dirty pants to show her. "Your pastor is a kind man. He would never hurt a child."

The pastor was nodding insistently.

"Are you sure?" Janet said. "Why did he have a pair of boy's sweatpants?"

"They're from the donation bin." I pointed it out in the corner.

She cried and fell to her knees at the man's feet.

"It's OK, Janet. You had the Lord's intentions but were clouded by your conclusion."

"I could have ruined your life."

"Now, now." He looked from Gian to me. "How did you know?"

"One must not question miracles," I said, hoping I sounded biblical.

"Thank you, my angels."

Nailed it.

"Let's get you a coffee," I said to Janet. She was shaking as we exited the church. The cold air was painful again. Jumping from one extreme to another couldn't be healthy. At least we weren't going to catch a cold.

Janet brought us to a cafe overlooking a harbor. I'd heard how beautiful Alaska is, but being there overwhelmed me. The mountain range alone was enough to take my breath away.

Our table had a fantastic view. Pleasure boats lined the docks with sailboat masts offering a calming visual.

A cold breeze slipped through a crack in the window frame. I had us move over one table.

"I'm so glad you cleared that up," Janet said. "Am I bad for wishing it was true? Wishing church was a lie? Wishing I could abort?"

"I don't see how that wouldn't be normal," I said. "You're in a shitty situation."

Gian was on his phone, distracted. I looked over and saw the price of gold: $1,280 an ounce. Now I knew why we were really in Alaska. He glanced up and nodded with a smile. I tipped my head to Janet.

He set his phone face down. "So, how are you doing?"

She laughed and started crying. He crossed to her side of the table and put an arm around her. That's all she needed — human comfort.

A waiter approached our table. He had a hipster twenties mustache that curled inward.

Janet wiped her tears away. "The clam chowder here is killer."

"Is the Deep Powder Porter any good?" Gian asked.

"It's my favorite," the waiter said.

"I wish I could have one," Janet said.

"We have iced tea," the waiter suggested.

Gian ordered chowder and a beer.

"Double that," I said.

The pints arrived after Janet's drink. Beer hit the spot, but I hid my enjoyment, not wanting to make her feel any worse. It wasn't just the taste; the bubbles felt good in my throat, easing me from the climate.

I took her hand. "Are you OK?" I cringed. Gian had basically asked her the same thing.

"Not really. I'm going to die in a matter of days and can't talk to anyone about it. When I try, nothing comes out. My family thinks I'm losing my mind. Maybe I am."

"You're not crazy. You *can't* talk about this. It's not allowed."

"By who?"

"We can't talk about that," Gian said dryly. It hit us funny and we laughed nervously.

"I'm not ready to die."

"No one ever is," I said. "You're a good person. You'll be fine." I motioned to the room, to the world. "None of this matters." That last line wasn't my own. It was fed to me. I wondered if it was true.

An alert rang from Janet's phone. "Oh crap, I'm late for an appointment." She searched through her purse for her wallet.

"We've got this," Gian said.

"Have my soup," she said and left.

He waited until she was gone to speak again. "That was easy."

"It was fucked up."

"But short." He smiled, seeing our chowder arriving.

"You need to be more supportive of Janet," I said.

"It's hard. We're killing a baby. I can't handle it."

"What, do you think it's easy for me?"

The conversation hung heavy in the air. We ate our meal mostly in silence.

At a fishing store, we found hip waders, a strong shoulder bag, and thick rubber gloves. They didn't have a shovel. We had to go to a hardware store for that.

"So where are we going?" I asked.

"Panning for gold. Well, looking for gold. Want to be the spotter?" he said, not asking if I even wanted to do this.

"Sure."

"I've been reading up on hot spots. Follow me."

He opened a portal deep into the wilderness. We were under the cover of trees, but the snow was still up to my waist. The chill of Anchorage was nothing compared to the fridged mountains.

"We need one-piece snowsuits," he said. "Back to Anchorage."

We returned to the forest properly attired. I remained invisible for warmth and led the way to a broad yet shallow stream. There was a sparkling array of gold, but it was all tiny, like pixie dust. I materialized. My chest constricted, limiting my breath.

"I'm not seeing anything major."

"I have another spot," he said.

"Give me a minute. It's weird being invisible that long."

The second stream housed a massive nugget in the middle, but the water was too deep. I walked along the shore and spotted a piece the size of a quarter. Gian dug his shovel in and dumped the mud in a pile. I pointed out the gold using the orb. He washed the nugget off in the stream and held it to the light. His neon green happiness shone brighter than the gold.

There was a smaller nugget a few steps away. After he had it in his hands, I materialized.

"How are we doing?" I asked.

"Brilliantly," he said. "We easily have three ounces, maybe four. That's over $5,000. Easy money, baby."

"Nice." I headed off to continue the search.

Around the bend was a massive glow across the river. We stepped through a portal to the other side. I led him to a baseball-sized nugget just under the surface. He was jumping up and down, shouting like a fool.

"You're going to get us killed," I said.

"And you're going to make us rich."

"It's only a couple pounds."

"Only," he laughed. "That's forty thousand dollars. Come on, let's keep moving."

That's a lot of money. It could add up fast. I liked prospecting. Except for the cold, my chest was stinging. "Can we trade off? I need a break."

"Sure," follow me. He vanished, and I trailed his glowing orb.

Gian wasn't as lucky at first. But it was still fun finding the small pieces. We traded back and forth until the daylight faded. Our pack was weighted down by the time we finished.

I sat on a fallen trunk to rest my aching muscles. "So, what's the plan?"

"What do you mean?"

"How are we going to sell this? We can't walk into Anchorage and unload a bag of gold when we're supposed to be five thousand miles away. Unless Sicily is known for prospecting, we're screwed."

"Well, fuck." He sat on a rock and stared out at the river. "We can hide it and grab the loot after all this is over."

"Works for me."

I didn't feel like celebrating back in Sicily, but he talked me into getting a bottle of Prosecco from the local market. Nera appeared at the pop of the cork.

"Did we do something wrong?" I asked.

She moved her hands before her like she was weighing our actions. "Who knows? The muses can be fussy. Don't get greedy. What they give, they can take away."

"For what they're putting us through, they can let things slide," Gian said.

85

"Keep doing good deeds, like getting that ring to the young couple. Their honeymoon is back on track."

"Don found them?" I asked. "That's so sweet. I wish I'd been there."

"I think Don was happier than they were. You hit on something. He's out right now giving money away."

I found that hard to believe. "You're talking about Don Fernau?" I asked.

She laughed. "I know, right."

# Chapter 5

I looked at the clock on my phone. Had I slept ten hours straight? I sat back against the headboard and stretched wide. Gian walked to the kitchen from the balcony. I felt him reach for the coffee beans. I jumped to his condo to use the bathroom. When I returned, my coffee was on the nightstand.

We cuddled in bed for a few hours until it was time to leave for New Orleans. The Saint Louis Cemetery is the oldest in the city. Walking between the above-ground tombs is like traversing a city of the dead. The two groups of people I was watching headed away from us, but a man across from the mausoleum we needed to break into wouldn't leave. He just stood there. Even though I was invisible, his features were noticeable. He was more than an aura. It was bizarre. I gave up and left to materialize. The man was gone when I met back with Gian.

"Finally. That guy wouldn't leave. It was creeping me out."

"What guy? No one has been here."

"The guy that was standing right over there," I said, pointing down the row.

He walked toward the area and vanished. We were out in the open. What was he thinking?

Gian's body trembled when he appeared.

"He's still there. That's a ghost."

A chill ran down my spine. Gian's shoulder blades moved inward as if he felt it. "Let's do this and get the hell out of here."

"Shouldn't there be more ghosts in a cemetery?"

"You would think so."

At the base of the crypt was a cornerstone. Gian rocked it back and forth until it was free. After taking a picture of the cash inside, he returned the stone.

I opened the email we'd drafted. It was from a new account set up in Rowanda's name. We reread the message, hoping it carried her tone.

"Send it," he said.

We ran to a sheltered area and stepped through a portal to Margaret's office. Rowanda had given us the layout of the floor. A woman stood by the cubicles with her arms crossed. Her aura was a putrid brownish green. The energy surrounding her was dark, making the gold in the computer's circuit boards shine brilliantly. She stormed into Margaret's office and slammed the door. It was her. The workers' auras grew colorful as the peace returned.

Margaret moved her mouse and froze. Was she reading our letter? We followed her out of the building and down the street to her car. The traffic was slow enough that we could hold on. Still, we kept slipping into the seat. At one point, I was in the trunk. We could have jumped ahead, but trying to hang on was fun.

She followed our map to the crypt and pried the stone out without looking around. The ghost had moved closer and stood glaring with dead eyes. Was it his grave we were desecrating?

Money emits zero energy, making it look as if Margret's aura was pretending to hold something.

I was surprised to see her go to the police. Had we underestimated Rowanda's boss? No, she didn't disappoint. This was a bank. Two employees led her to the vault. I held my hand to the safety deposit box where she stashed the money. Gian unplugged the two cameras and we materialized to get the box number.

A guard was approaching. I opened a portal, and we jumped to a rooftop above the cemetery where we had set up a camera. Gian rewound the video and hit pause. I was expecting someone ugly. That was just her insides.

Margaret was an adorable brunette with a deceptively cute face. This made me hate her more.

My phone chimed. I'd set an alert for the email account we made for Rowanda. It was Margaret replying to our message.

"Bitch said the money wasn't there." I showed Gian the picture she'd sent back of the empty hole. "She told Rowanda to turn herself in."

"Don't respond. Let's head to my place to edit the video."

I rested on his balcony while Gian put together a package for the CEO of her company. The trees in the park behind his place were a lush green. Spring in Seattle is gorgeous.

It took an hour before he was satisfied with his work. We jumped to the CEO's office and slipped the package onto his desk when he left the room.

Hawaii was a perfect place to rid ourselves of Margaret's negativity. Don was in a lounge chair in the yard of a fancy beach house. I didn't realize he had that kind of money. He was bent over in pain. Bruises and a few scrapes marred the side of his face.

"What happened to you?" I asked.

Don flinched but relaxed when he saw it was me.

"Long story."

Gian pulled up a chair. "We have time."

Don stared out at the sea as he spoke. "I found the young couple who lost that ring. They're on their honeymoon. The gratitude was infectious. I cashed out my retirement and set out to do good. But first, I rented this place." He pointed back at the house.

"Nice digs," Gian said.

"Yeah, but I think vanity turned on me. I spent this morning clearing people's payday loans. It was wonderful. The relief in their eyes brought tears to mine."

"Don, that's the sweetest thing I've ever heard," I said.

"Until I was jumped. It wasn't enough to take the rest of the day's cash. They beat me. Broke a couple ribs, I'm sure. It hurts so bad. What they broke the most was my spirit. I'm afraid to give anymore."

I was horrified by his story.

*I'll heal him through you,* a woman said in my head. I flinched backward but played it off as wanting to stand. It was Bianca, the High Priestess.

"Show me where it hurts? I'll heal you."

Gian tilted his head in confusion.

Don motioned to his left side. I kneeled beside him, and Bianca entered my body. It was invasive and wrong. I wanted her out but persevered. She positioned my hands over his ribs. I was her as we recited a spell in an ancient language I didn't know. There was a blue flash and I was out.

"Linsey. Wake up."

Someone was lightly tapping my cheek. Gian and Don were above me, faces lined with worry.

"There's my girl," Gian said and kissed me. He helped me to my feet.

"Thank you," Don said. "I can't even feel my ribs anymore." He wiggled his body to show me.

I couldn't see any scrapes or bruises on his face. Even the bags under his eyes were gone.

"My back doesn't hurt. It's been years since I've felt this good." He started doing jumping jacks.

"How did you do that?" Gian said.

"It was Bianca. She was inside me. I didn't like it."

"I did," Don said happily. "I had a herniated disk. It's fixed. I know it is. I can't feel anything. Wait until my chiropractor hears about this." He looked over at me. "I probably shouldn't tell him, huh."

"Not unless you want it to reappear."

"No. Don't bring it back. I won't say anything."

"I have a feeling you wouldn't even be able to make the appointment."

"Now you can continue your charity," Gian said.

His face tightened in a grimace. There was the old Don.

"You can do it," I said. "Focus on the good."

"I'll think about it." He shook his head as if to shake away the thoughts. "Let me show you to your room. It will be here as long as I am. Stay whenever you'd like. I enjoy the company."

"You don't have to do that," I said.

Gian gave me a side-eye. "Thanks, Don. Much obliged."

Our room was in the back of the house with only a garden view. I say only. The house he rented was magnificent. I loved the dark wood and openness of the place. My favorite part was the covered lanai next to the pool. That alone probably cost more than our last house. The home was on the end of a cove with the lawn butting up to the ocean. There were no houses in sight. I walked to the edge. A small strip of sand crossed below. Off to the right was a rocky shore perfect for exploring.

"What beach is this?" Gian asked.

"Anini," Don said. "It used to be Wanini, but a local took a shotgun to the W."

Gian chuckled. "Nice."

"Snorkeling here is out of this world. There's gear if you want to join me." He pointed to a bin in the corner. "I haven't been able to in years."

"We'll have to take a rain check," Gian said. "There's another Don I want to talk to. See if he can take care of your charity concerns."

That didn't sit well with me. "He's not a man you want to owe favors," I said.

"It's not a favor. It's a good deed." With that, he disappeared. I felt him heading to our place in Sicily.

"What the fuck." I looked around to ensure no one saw.

91

"Are you talking about the mafia?" Don asked. "I don't want to owe them anything."

"You won't. It will be on us."

I waited until I was in the house to disappear.

Gian was about to dial when I arrived. "Put it down."

"What?"

"We need to think this through," I said.

"I have. Don needs to continue to give. I need this."

"We can figure this out without owing the Don a favor."

"It's not a favor. I'm buying his service." He nodded toward the baseball-sized gold nugget we brought back as a souvenir.

That didn't help to calm me down, but I relented. "Call him." I couldn't believe I said that.

He switched to the speaker, and it rang.

"Perchè diavolo mi chiami a quest'ora?" the Don said angrily. In English, this is why the hell are you calling me at this hour? I checked the time. We had woken him.

Gian heard the Italian. His back tightened in panic.

"Good morning, Don Trentino," I said in Italian. "It's Gian and Linsey. I apologize for waking you. We didn't realize the hour. We're on a mission for the witches and ran into an issue that only someone of your stature could help. A good and honest man has been wronged. I humbly ask for you to listen."

"Proceed."

Even a neutral word came out threatening. I explained about Don's charity and how he was robbed and beaten.

"Why is this man important?"

I went to tell him but couldn't. "I'm not allowed to say. His good deeds are vital to continue. Nothing less than the world depends on it. I can pay you in gold."

"Where is the man located?"

"Kauai, Hawaii."

"I'll call you back." He hung up.

I sent a picture of the nugget next to a one-euro coin for size.

The phone rang an hour later. "Buongiorno, Don Trentino."

"Buongiorno, Signora. Have your friend do his charity tomorrow. There will be protection. Text me the details."

"Grazie. Where can I send the payment?"

"Keep your gold. What you and Gian did for our people is a debt we can never repay. It is you we owe."

"You are in our hearts. Thank you. I will let our friend know he can continue."

I hung up and smiled at Gian. "We're still good with the Don."

"What about the Hawaiian Don?"

"He'll have protection."

"Nice. Let's go tell him."

We materialized in our room in the beach house. I checked beforehand for cameras. I felt bad for not trusting him.

"Don," I yelled into the hall.

"I'm on the patio," he responded.

He was sitting at the outdoor bar, well into his drinks. His hair was matted and wet. "Mai Tai?" he said, raising his cup.

"I would love a Mai Tai," Gian said. "I've never had one. Linsey?"

"I think I'll hold off. We've traveled a lot today."

"Maybe later," Don said. "It's homemade."

"Is it cool if I have an edible?" Gian asked him.

"Sure, if you have some. Pot's not legal in Hawaii."

Gian returned from our room with a gummy in a plastic wrapper.

"Do you want some?" he asked me.

"We'll be stuck here for a few hours if we do." I waited for Nera to advise against it, but she was silent. I took that as approval.

"Spend the night if you like. My house is yours."

I loved Don's generosity but was concerned about enjoying ourselves while on such a fucked up mission.

Gian sliced the gummy and took half, then quartered the rest. I wondered if the beach's calming vibe made me take a piece or all the stress.

"I didn't think you were going to," Gian said.

I let the comment go, realizing he didn't mean it negatively like I had taken it.

"Can I have the rest?" Don asked. "It's been years. Like in college."

That I did not expect.

"Sure. If you want more, it's in the left nightstand."

"Is there a town nearby? I need a swimsuit," I asked.

"Princeville is ten minutes away. You can take my Jeep if you want. It's a pretty drive."

"Should we jump?" I asked.

"This won't hit us for at least forty minutes," Gian said. "Even if it does, I can drive on it."

I rushed Gian through shopping. I didn't want him driving stoned. Don wisely recommended long-sleeved swimming shirts so we wouldn't burn. I found a cute bottom to go with mine, plus a swimsuit for later.

We were driving along the shore back to the beach when the subtle effects of the edible kicked in. "I think I'm getting high. My face is starting to smile."

Gian laughed at how I said that. "I shouldn't have done half. Your brother was right. These are strong."

"Want me to drive?"

"Nah. We're almost there. Max says this one comes on hard but mellows out. That it's a euphoric high."

"What I smoked with him was called Where's my Bike. If it's anything like that, it will be."

He loved the name.

Don was happy to see us safely home. He had a broad, silly grin. The roundness of his face worked with the happy.

"I almost forgot," I said. "You're safe to give away money tomorrow."

Don shrank in on himself. "I don't know if I can."

I placed a hand on his shoulder. "It's OK. You'll have security. We'll go too, just in case."

"Let me think about it. I enjoyed helping."

Clouds had rolled in. We took cover under the roof of the lanai. The rainstorm lasted only a few minutes, and the sun returned. It was surreal from being high. The green foliage glistened brightly. I was falling in love with Hawaii. The humidity, not so much.

"Let's go snorkeling," Gian said.

"I've never been," I said.

Don motioned to the pool. "You can practice."

We headed off to change and almost had sex in our bedroom. Being high and seeing Gian naked was too much. His bathing suit didn't help. The outline of his cock was prevalent. I wanted him so badly. We rolled around, making out. Somehow, we managed to refrain.

Gian gave me a peck on the lips. "Tonight."

It took a few tries in the pool before I had the hang of snorkeling. Once I did, it was second nature. Seeing how silly we looked in the masks was harder to manage. Our laughter made us have to keep surfacing to drain the water.

Don was sitting at the pool's edge with his feet dangling in. He was getting a kick out of watching me learn.

"There were a bunch of turtles when I was out."

I hopped out of the pool to join him. "Where? Show me."

He stood up and pointed off to our left. "About fifty yards out from the neighbor's place."

I didn't like the sound of that. There was no barrier. This was open water. But, the opportunity to see turtles got me in the water.

95

There was a coral reef throughout the bay. All we found were schools of brightly colored fish. That in itself was enough for me. They were beautiful, almost fake-looking. Movement in my peripheral caught my attention. Swimming next to me was a massive turtle. It was dirty, natural, and so freaking cool. I grabbed Gian's arm and pointed to it. His eyes grew large.

We swam with the turtle for at least a half hour. But being high, it was probably only a few minutes. I surfaced and didn't recognize the surroundings. I couldn't see the house anywhere. Someone was on the beach waving us in. It was Don.

Swimming against the current was difficult. We were exhausted by the time we made it to the shore.

"I'm so sorry. I should have checked the conditions. That was totally on me."

"It's fine," I said.

"Yeah, it's fine," he said sarcastically. "I almost killed you guys."

"Almost is not doing," I said. Did that make sense?

"Was that a turtle you were chasing?"

"It was the coolest turtle," Gian said.

"Let's head back. I'll cook stir fry before the sunset."

"A Hawaiian sunset," I said dreamily.

Gian found two halves of a coconut in the sand. He knocked them together, making clomping noises like the knights in Monty Python's Holy Grail. I knew the movie through Grandpa. I raised my hands as if holding reins and galloped along. Don cracked up and mounted a horse to join me. At the house, he brought his steed noisily to a halt.

Back in his kitchen, I had Don make a piña colada. The ocean had calmed my stomach.

"Can I ask what you guys really are? I don't see angels."

"No questions, Don," Gian said.

"But I have so many."

96

He measured three cups of white rice and poured water from the tap.

"Always wash white rice. I've seen pictures of the warehouse floors where it's stored. That's all I'm going to say. Trust me." He shifted the rice around with his hand, then poured out most of the water, filling it again with fresh, repeating the process until the water was relatively clear.

He retrieved a can of SPAM from the cupboard and set it by the chopping block. From the bottom of the fridge, he pulled out beef. He chuckled to himself as he put the SPAM away. I'm not sure why he thought that would bother me. A Hawaiian stir fry sounded delicious.

Don worked without a cookbook, eyeing the amount of the sauces to add to the beef. He set the bowl aside to focus on the vegetables.

"What else would you put in?" he asked as he wrapped up.

Gian peered around him into the wok. "Cashews. Just cashews."

"Perfect." Don searched his cupboard. "I knew I bought some." He held a jar out triumphantly and shook a bunch into the wok. "I think we're about ready. Gian, if you could carry the rice."

I brought our drinks and a water pitcher out to the lanai to join them. The boys waited for me before digging in. My mom would have been proud of their manners.

Snorkeling was exhausting. I dished up a hearty plate and dug in. The flavors danced across my tongue. "Where did you learn to cook? This is the best stir fry I've had."

"You're high," Don said.

"Yeah, but it would be just as good sober."

"My wife taught me."

"Wife?" I asked.

"Cancer," was all he had to say. "I guess I'll be seeing Emilie soon." Instead of getting sad, he had a comforting smile. It was Gian and I who were crying.

"It's OK," he said.

"We're supposed to be comforting you," I said. "Not the other way around."

"You are. I'm enjoying the company." He filled our water glasses. "Don't worry. I'm not afraid."

An alarm went off on his phone. "Oh, crap. The sun's almost down. We have to walk to the end of the peninsula to see it. Leave the meals. I'll reheat them."

From a cabinet, he retrieved covers that fit snugly around the plates. We left after he secured the lids on the rice and serving dish. I didn't want to know what bugs were out there.

Don brought us back to where he had rescued us. Even from there, the sun was nearly obstructed by the land. I sat on a rock, wishing I'd brought my drink.

"Watch as it vanishes beyond the sea. At the last second, you sometimes see a green flash. If you do, you'll never go wrong in your love."

I so wanted to see the flash, but a low cloud swept in, blocking the horizon.

"It's elusive," Don said. "You'll have to come back."

My first Hawaiian sunset was a dud with dark clouds void of color. We headed back to the house.

After we finished our meals, Gian excused himself to wash the dishes. I offered to help, but he had me relax and enjoy myself. Don and I stayed at our dinner table.

"Can you believe how lucky I am to have found such a good man?" I was talking about love with a widower, but the words were out.

"You were meant for each other. I don't believe in luck."

"Don't tell Gian that. He's a poker player."

Don laughed. He leaned in and whispered. "Watch yourself around poker players. They can tell when you're bluffing."

I panicked, thinking of how I lied to protect Gian from my family's actions.

"What?" he said.

"Nothing. You had me questioning something. What about you? Wouldn't you like to spend your last days with someone?"

"I am." He looked at me warmly. "Besides, I have Emilie. While I was handing out money, I felt her clear as day. She's here to guide me home. We'll see each other soon enough."

I hoped that was true. We gazed in silence at the last lingering bit of light. The wind had picked up. Waves were crashing against the shallow reef.

"Can I bother you for a dance?" he said. "I haven't in years. My back."

"I've got this," Gian said from behind. He pulled out his phone but grew frustrated. "I can't get it to sync to the Bluetooth."

He found a jack by the barbeque. After a few tries, he had the speakers above us working. Paul Simon's "Diamonds on the Soles of Her Shoes" played.

Don jumped up. "Emilie and I used to dance to this."

The way he marched around the floor made us laugh. That only encouraged him. We danced to four more songs before he needed a rest. I wanted to keep going, but the sadness in Don's eyes drew me to him. We joined him at the bar.

"Sorry, I was thinking about Emilie." Don's head dropped and he rubbed his hands. "I should have let her live."

"There was nothing you could have done," I said.

"No, I mean live life to the fullest. Live. I was so cheap. So focused on our retirement. She wanted to travel. I denied her travel. Look at me now. Everything was wasted."

"I think you're living pretty hard," Gian said. "You're doing good deeds and staying in this amazing house."

"Time is fleeting," he said.

"No thinking about it." I felt like dirt.

"I don't mean to mope. Put another song on."

The three of us danced together. I tried to be good but Gian would brush against me, sending my lust through the roof. He throbbed his cock, hitting me below like a thunderclap. The response was a quivering pulse that made me lose the beat.

We waited a few hours before we couldn't hold off any longer. I think Don was being polite when he excused himself for bed.

"Don't stay up too late. It's a bit of a drive to town."

"We can meet you there," I said.

"You'll want to see the views. We have to leave at eight-thirty to have time for breakfast."

Gian took my hand. "We'll be ready. It's been a pleasure, Don."

"It has," he said.

He hugged me. "Thank you for fixing my back."

"You're welcome." I wasn't sure if Nera was listening, but I asked her to please thank Bianca for me.

Gian was on me as our door was closing. He pulled away from our kiss. "Minty." I had brushed my teeth earlier. "I'll be right back." He headed to the bathroom.

I followed him in. He was putting a dab of toothpaste on his brush.

The massive walk-in shower was calling. The humidity had me all sticky. "Let's take a quick shower."

"Why take a quick one?" he said, sending foam dripping from his mouth. He wiped it away with a guttural laugh like he was severely challenged. I took his hand and led him to the shower. Thankfully, he didn't turn the water on too hot like usual.

"Let me do your back," he said.

Who would turn that down? His knees buckled as he soaped me up. "That feels so weird," he said. I concentrated on my back to tune out what he was feeling.

100

Next was my front. I should have returned the favor and cleaned his back, but was distracted by his chest. I soaped up his abs and traced the contours of his muscles. He slipped too close to my armpit, and it tickled. Instead of torturing us with more like he did when we were teens, he pulled back. I lifted my eyes to his and smiled in appreciation.

He rubbed my hip, working out a knot. The dual sensations lifted us to another plane. By the time he reached my chest, I was in heaven. My hand glided past his stomach, and I wrapped my soapy grip around his cock. Electricity raced to his chest. I caught it with a lick of his nipple. He slid a hand below.

Gian soaped and massaged my mound, then tugged at my clit, sending currents in all directions. I stroked upward and focused on the head of his cock. His shoulders curled inward and he let out a gasp. I found a rhythm and didn't let up until he came on my belly. It was a gift feeling his orgasms, like I was getting bonus ones.

He used two fingers to direct the cum onto my clit, using it as lubricant needed for the water. With his fingers, he coaxed my release. I was holding myself up with locked knees, sending energy down to my thighs. It rebounded as if it had hit a springboard.

"I can feel it approaching," he said. "I'm in your head."

My eyes were closed. I couldn't respond. He reached from behind, and I gasped as his finger pressed against my asshole and then slipped inside. My eyes shot open, and I saw stars shoot toward the ceiling. He rode the waves of my orgasm in time, bending and flexing with me. We crumbled to the floor breathing heavily. I fell into him and he cradled me, trailing butterfly kisses along my neck.

"I love you so much," he said.

It took all my energy to lean back and nestle my cheek against his. Gian sat with me until I was ready to get up. I turned on the second shower across from us and rinsed off. It was weird feeling water hit us from all directions.

"Let's go fuck," I said throatily.

He stepped out of the shower to dry off. "We can do it on that beach we first went to." With a blanket in hand, he disappeared.

I followed his jump trail to the top of the dunes. We materialized into a strong wind. Stinging sand pelted our legs.

"Nope." He headed back to Don's.

When I materialized, he was in the shower, rinsing his feet. The droplets of water glowed wildly until my eyes adjusted. I stuck one foot in at a time.

"We could go out front," he said.

"I don't need a beach. Wherever you are is my paradise."

He took my hand, leading me to the bedroom, and threw me on the bed. I bounced with a laugh.

I raised onto my hands and knees and lifted my hips. His heart raced with excitement.

"We'll need some lube."

"Oh my God, no," I said. "In the puss."

"Fine."

"We'll try that sometime," I said, unsure if I meant it. He's bigger than I think could fit.

He kissed my neck and started dry humping me between the top of my cheeks. The soft friction was arousing. I rolled my hips to his rhythm, enjoying what he was feeling. His creativity in bed always surprised me.

He stopped. "Sorry, that felt good." He moved his cock lower.

"That's a silly thing to be sorry about. Go back. I liked it."

He continued humping me, moving slowly and sensually. His back was arched, with his head even to mine.

My spine tightened. "Troy's in danger. We have to go."

"Damn it!" he said, frustrated. I was right there with him.

Gian put on his shorts and sandals. I found sweatpants and a light jacket in the closet. My tennis shoes weren't where I expected them. I grabbed my flip-flops and a shirt for Gian. We were off.

I couldn't comprehend where we were. It was up high. There were only three of us in the area. I materialized and panicked. We were at the top of an Olympic ski jump. I fell protectively backward into the bar Troy was on, nearly toppling over. The sign behind us said Park City. A biting wind sent a shiver to my core.

"Don't do it," Gian said. "You need to live."

"I need to live to die?" Troy asked.

Gian grabbed his shirt from me. "You need to live to find peace with yourself."

"That's what I'm doing, living." He pushed himself from the starting block and slid down the tracks in the jump.

"His helmet," I said, seeing it on the ground.

Troy shot from the end and somehow managed to stay upright. He was flying with shouts of joy echoing through the frigid mountain air. We stepped through a portal to meet him. I could barely watch, but he managed to land without crashing.

His eyes were wide and alive. "I made it. Did you see that?"

"You're nuts," Gian said.

Off to the side, the beam of a flashlight was approaching. "See ya," he said, heading down the hill and disappearing over the side.

Gian vanished and I followed him back to our room. We cuddled under the covers for warmth—our hearts pounded in harmony.

"Why didn't I sense when Don was in danger?" I asked.

"Troy wasn't in danger. Well, not technically."

103

"I think maybe the witches are fucking with us." If Nera was listening, I hoped she hadn't taken that wrong.

Gian was distracted by the word fucking. He reached under my robe to caress my breast but pulled back. "My hand is freezing."

We were on our sides facing each other. I wrapped a leg around him and mounted his cock. The adventure had fueled his fire. He thrust with wild abandon as I held onto his shoulder for support. My nerves were shot from the height of the ski jump. Tingling pulses raced through my body.

A scream of ecstasy was brewing, but I didn't want Don to hear. Without a verbal release, my body would surely explode under the pressure. I grabbed Gian by the neck and brought his mouth to mine. He bit my lip, ending with a slight tug. It was as if he was pulling the orgasm out of me. I thrust my head back and took a deep breath. He pressed his hand over my mouth. I let out a muffled scream as my orgasm took control. When I opened my eyes, he was staring with affection.

We rolled around making out. I was in love to my core. We must have kissed for at least an hour.

"This is like a dream," he said.

I risked guessing what he was thinking. "Because you're so in love." It came out sounding so stupid.

"Yeah," he said, holding me closely.

I guided him into me again. He moaned as I rode him. I picked up the pace and rocked him into tomorrow.

---

We woke up in time to leave with Don, although it wasn't easy. Sleep was calling me back to bed. Don said he had the best night of sleep in years.

I had wondered why he always had the hard top on the Jeep, but I understood after it rained three times on the way out of town.

Don pointed to a mountain that was the rainiest place in the US—the lush greens melded with the dazzling blues of the North Pacific. I'm glad we drove. The views were breathtaking.

He grew nervous as we entered the town of Kapa'a. I laughed at the name. Words in Hawaii have so many vowels.

Don had us stop at a bank to pick up the day's donations. He was back in the car, with me guiding us with the map on my phone. "Up here on the right. The Snack Shack."

"That has to be them," Gian said.

Five comically large Hawaiian men were standing near two dark SUVs. Don pulled in front of them, and Gian and I stepped out.

A massive shirtless man with ceremonial Hawaiian tattoos stepped forward. "Gian? Linsey?"

"Yes, Sir," Gian said.

"I'm Big Lou."

"This is Don." I pointed to him, stepping from the Jeep.

"Don Trentino?" he asked.

We both laughed. "No, the Don that was jumped."

The big man nodded. "We'll have your back at the payday loan."

"How can I repay you," Don said.

"By giving again. How much did they steal?"

"Fifty-two hundred."

"We'll try to get it back. What did these guys look like?"

Don's eyes fixed on the ground. "Skinny white meth heads. Both dirty blonds with medium-length hair like they hadn't been to the barber in a while."

"Give us a half hour before you head over."

They piled into their cars and were off.

We sat outside a café until it was time. The payday loan shop was in a run-down strip mall four blocks over. Don parked his Jeep and sat motionless. "I'm not scared of dying, but this terrifies me."

His choice of words hit deeply. I forced myself back into the moment. He needed reassurance and strength. "Think of the positivity," I said. "How good it felt to give money away. Tap into that."

He held his fists clenched by his temples with a pained expression.

"OK." He exited the car and headed toward the payday loan shop.

Two men approached from behind a dumpster. Don let out a shriek.

They were thin white guys, more meth than menace. Dark circles under their eyes spoke of many a sleepless night. This had to be the men. Why they were dumb enough to return was a mystery to me.

"Well, well, well. Look who's back for more."

Don retreated into a run. The two guys didn't see the gang of Hawaiians until they were on top of them.

Big Lou held each by their arms. "Are these the ones who robbed you?"

Don nodded.

The man lifted both guys and slammed them to the pavement. "Why did you idiots come back? What is wrong with you?"

One of the losers went to speak, but Big Lou shut him up with a solid punch to the face. He struck him so hard that the man's head bounced off the pavement. His right pupil grew wider than the other. That couldn't be good.

"Kick 'em," he said to Don.

"I can't do violence," Don said. "It's not in me."

"Well, shit. Things just got worse for you two 'cause that's all I am."

"No, don't," pleaded the guy who wasn't punched.

"We'll find the money. Somehow," the other said meagerly. He was a shell of a man.

"You don't have his money?"

"We spent it on drugs and a hotel."

"You spent $5,200 on drugs?"

"And hookers."

Big Lou got a smirk on his face. "Looks like you're about to get fucked again. Run along, Don. This don't concern you no more. If anyone messes with you, tell 'em they'll be dealing with Big Lou."

The men's eyes grew large upon hearing the name, making their faces look skeletal. I'd seen the effects of meth in pictures. Seeing it in real life was disturbing. *Meth is fun,* I said to myself.

Big Lou towered over them. "You're gonna die today."

Did we just get them killed? I felt sick at how bad we were fucking up.

Don grabbed Lou's arm. "Please, no."

"Don't tell Big Lou what to do," a gang member said.

Don looked Lou square in the eyes. "I'm begging you. Don't sully an act of charity."

Lou cocked his head to the side. "You're for real, aren't you?"

"I'm trying my best," Don said.

Lou snapped his finger at his men.

One of his henchmen handed an envelope to Don. "That's $5,200."

Lou's eyes lowered to the scum on the pavement. "That's your life. You have twenty-four hours to pay me back. Every day, the price doubles." He held up his hand before they could speak. "You don't get to talk. Let's go."

"Thank you," Don said.

The two tweakers were thrown into the back of an SUV, and they were off. The second carload stuck around to ease Don's giving.

He walked to the hood of his car and threw up, then stumbled back and slumped into the driver's seat.

"I hope he keeps his word."

"Don't tell Big Lou what to do," Gian said. It was so silly I had the giggles.

"Whatever happens, they did that to themselves. Gian and I did that. Not you."

"I need a second. Will you come in with me?"

"There'll be way too many cameras," Gian said. "We'll be out here. Plus, Big Lou's men are here." He gestured to them. "There's no need to worry."

"Hang tight." I bought a pack of gum for Don. Breathing vomit on people isn't very giving.

He was safely inside the pay day shop when two police cruisers drove through the parking lot, barely missing the action. I was relieved. Big Lou would not have appreciated us getting him in trouble.

Watching the people come out of the payday loan stunned with enormous smiles was fun. Gian had to step in a couple of times to make sure the call they were making wasn't to tell people what Don was doing. That was the first rule he had. The second was to agree never to get a payday loan again. For that, he gave them an extra $500.

Within three hours, Don returned to the car out of cash. He had a satisfying smile on his face. "That may have been the best day of my life. Thank you for making me go back."

"It was our pleasure."

"I feel so alive. What a day. I want to keep going. Find another way to help. Care to join me?"

"I'd like to, Don," I said, "but we have someone else to visit."

"No problem. I'm going to thank Big Lou's men, and we'll be off."

He had a smile on his face when he returned. "They'll be here whenever I need backup."

Gian looked at me. I think he was expecting praise for calling Don Trentino, which I wasn't doing. It had been risky.

Don dropped us off on a secluded section of the highway, and we jumped to his place.

The lanai had an air of solitude as we enjoyed a sandwich.

"I wouldn't mind moving here," Gian said.

I looked around. "Would it be the same without these digs?"

"I'd be fine with a condo off the beach."

"We could buy a vacation rental. Build up equity."

"That could work." He kissed me. "Care for a walk on the beach?"

"That sounds nice." I needed the calm after the morning we had.

I followed him down the steps to the shore. He weaved his fingers in mine, and we headed left toward the park. The soft sand between my toes was heavenly.

A fallen tree lay across the beach. Gian climbed upon the trunk, sitting with his feet dangling in the water. He glanced over and shied his eyes.

"What is it, baby? The mission getting to you?"

"It's not that. Can I be open with you?"

"We're going to be married. Open is what we have to be."

"Here's the thing. When I was cursed, I had to pretend to be a good person so I wouldn't lose you. But now that I have empathy, I'll say something and think, who are you? Why are you being so nice? Is my niceness still fake?"

I couldn't help but laugh. "That's just your negative voice. I have one, too. I think it's there to make sure life isn't easy."

"But the voice when I was cursed was on my side."

"Yeah, it's your negative voice. I can see it striving inside a Dread. Push back on the negativity. Tell it to go fuck itself. Life is good now."

"Thanks. I thought I was going crazy."

"We're all a little crazy. It's what makes us unique."

"You're not going to get bored because I'm too nice, are you?"

"Not at all. I don't need you to be an asshole. But if you're being one, you know I'll tell you."

He chuckled. "I love that you don't take any shit."

I put a hand on his leg to stress the point I was about to make. "I like the new you. And you're not too nice. You're sweet. But don't hold back. Be yourself."

"That's the problem. I don't know who I am anymore. Unless I'm looking in the mirror, I feel like I'm walking around in someone else's body. I felt that way even before this fucked up task. It's like I'm a kid again."

"You're lucky you're a guy then. You don't have to grow up."

He laughed.

"This could just be you still working through the Age of Reconning. I'll wait as long as it takes for you to find yourself. Trust that I'm happy. You make me happy."

He pulled me in for a hug and cried.

"I guess there's a little of the Reconning left," he said.

My phone chimed from Rowanda's email. I ignored it.

"You can look," he said.

I brought up her account and smiled. "They've arrested Margaret."

"Rowanda is going to love that."

"Not as much as this. The CEO is looking into dropping the charges in return for her testimony."

"Let's go tell her," he said.

"You sure you're good? We can talk some more."

"I'm fine. Thanks for listening."

I looked him in the eyes. "Any time."

# Chapter 6

Rowanda lived in a viewless apartment in the middle of the island. We knocked on the door instead of materializing inside. She didn't seem like the type who would take kindly to being startled.

"If it isn't the bane of my existence."

"Not today," I said. "We have good news."

"I'm not going to die?"

Well, shit. I wasn't using that line anymore.

"Not that good, but you'll like this," Gian said.

I showed her the initial email we sent Margaret and then the video of her at the cemetery.

"Look at that bitch." She read the response where Margaret said the money wasn't there. Rowanda was livid.

"Hold that thought. We sent a package to your CEO. Check out his response."

I expected her to scream and holler, but she cried softly. "What's the matter?" I asked.

"I may be able to go home. Momma's been so worried. I don't want to die without seeing her again. Thank you for telling me. I was about to pay for a month's rental in the BVI."

"We need to get to Alaska," Gian said. "Janet's in the hospital."

I saw a vision of her pushed down a flight of stairs. "Why didn't Nera warn us?"

"Go," Rowanda said. "I'm good here."

We raced to his condo to change. He had us grab our snow gear. It wasn't an appropriate time for prospecting, but he insisted.

Janet's tracker led us to a hospital room. She was in bed with golden circuits surrounding her. The energy from her fetus was glowing brightly, giving her a magnificent shine. I didn't like that its aura was the same color as Gian's. We materialized and Janet's eyes tracked to mine. There were deep bruises on her arms and a huge one on the side of her face. Her vulnerable state made her look younger. She looked away.

"Eddie did this. At least now he's in jail. He wanted to kill the baby because I won't have an abortion."

"Can you heal her?" Gian said.

I couldn't sense Bianca around. I shook my head.

"It's not bad," Janet said. "Mostly bruises. Eddie, true to form, couldn't even do this right. They have me overnight for observations."

There was a knock on the door. We vanished. I hope it wasn't suspicious that our gear was out in the open.

We reappeared when the orderly left.

"Is there anything we can do for you?" I asked.

"Maybe let someone know you're here?" Gian said.

"I'm good. I just need sleep."

"We'll hang around until you're out," I said.

Gian took her hand and she smiled. Whatever the nurse gave her was working. Her eyes grew heavy, and she was soon asleep. She had a cute, catlike snore.

The last remnants of daylight were waning. We stopped in a closed hardware store for headlamps. I stubbornly insisted we leave money and a note for the manager. I didn't think the muses would appreciate stealing.

Gian had done his research. The new location produced a nugget in the first couple of minutes. It was cold going. We had to trade off frequently.

A deep glow off to the side led me away from the bank of the river. Gian waited for me. I materialized back at his side.

"There's a big one over there." I pointed. "It's huge."

"Holy shit! Lead the way."

He trudged through the deep snow, following me. I was invisible to stay out of the cold. He eventually joined me for ease of movement.

At the site, Gian reappeared with a huge grin on his face. "It's massive. Looks deep. This is it, baby."

Digging through the snow to reach the nugget was easy until we struck solid ice.

"I'll be right back," he said.

Gian returned with a pick axe. "I'm only borrowing it."

I hadn't said anything. We were becoming close enough that he knew when I'd be upset.

We took turns digging. Once we made it past the bedrock, it was another three feet before we were close.

"Careful not to damage it," he said. "The big ones are worth more naturally." I handed the shovel back to him.

He dug below the gold, then broke it free with his hands. Gian held the colossal nugget up to his light. It sparkled in the darkness. The shape was oblong, like a giant peanut. "It's glorious. At least ten pounds."

"How much do you think it's worth?"

"At auction. Who knows? A million at least."

It was like winning the lottery. I couldn't wipe the smile from my face.

"We'll be able to do whatever we want," he said.

"What I want is to stop for the day. I'm freezing."

"Absolutely." He placed the nugget in his shoulder bag and was off.

I hadn't been to the hiding place. We appeared at the base of a cliff up to our necks in snow. The steep wall was intimidating.

"You know I'm not good with heights."

"It's not up there," he said. "That's what's so good about this spot. It's hidden in an opening behind the shrubs."

He disappeared, and I followed. His pack glowed brilliantly from the gold. There was a small space between the fallen rocks and the wall for us to stand. Gian placed our bounty into a nook hidden in the cliff. He stood, brushing his hands off. To the side, he left our tools.

"We need to return the pick."

"Sure. I'll meet you back in Sicily."

I materialized in our shower to rinse the sweat and dirt off my clothes. Gian was soon at my side.

We left our clothes hanging and headed to bed, exhausted. He hit the button for the blackout shades. I was sure that dreams of money would keep me awake, but I was asleep before the blinds closed.

The feeling of Gian masturbating shook me awake. He was in the front room on the couch. I had barely swiped a finger across my clit when he appeared in the bedroom doorway.

"Get back out there." I meant it sexy, but it may have come across as harsh.

"Fine." He headed to the couch.

I sank my fingers deep and heard him moan while feeling his back arch with mine. He stroked his cock in long, even movements. I loved the feel of him masturbating. I slid a finger across my clit, and a tremble flowed through his body. I had to switch to my left hand so it differed from the one he was using. My eyes were closed, and I was both of us as I stroked my invisible cock but felt his in my grip.

He was getting close but relented until the feeling subsided. It was as if he reset the orgasm. Soon, he was stroking again. He paused a few more times, waiting for me. I increased my speed and pressure. He couldn't hold off for much longer.

"I'm close," I yelled.

"I know."

My body let go and the orgasm broke free. He stroked his cock aggressively and joined in. It was all too much. I passed out.

I didn't wake up for a few hours. Gian was asleep on the couch. I washed his belly using a warm face towel, waking him up. He pulled me over him and snuggled in my arms.

A knock came from the hall. "Are you decent?" Nera asked.

"Just come in," Gian said. "We've been naked together."

She stepped inside. "I need you to be more careful. You were recorded materializing on the ski jump."

"Oh, shit," I said.

"I took care of it."

"You didn't have to kill anyone, did you?"

"Unfortunately. The guard saw you vanish."

My stomach tightened and I almost threw up. "Fuck."

"Did he have a family?" Gian asked.

"He did, and they're fine. He's fine."

"What the hell?" I grasped my chest, trying to catch my breath.

"He didn't see you. But your arrival was caught on video. I erased it when he was gone."

"How did we not see that there was a camera?" I asked.

"I had the same question. You were far enough away that the snow washed out the blue. It wasn't so fun thinking he died, was it? Be more careful."

I glared at Gian.

"What?"

"Don't do it again," she said and vanished.

"What?" he said to me.

"You've grown careless when vanishing."

"I'm sorry. But this one's on both of us."

He placed his hands softly on my back, and my disposition softened. After a long massage session, Gian made omelets for breakfast. Our internal clock was screwed up. It was dark out. We had given up on time zones and clocks, only looking to see if the person we were visiting was up.

115

"Why haven't you made these before?" I asked, savoring my last bite. The seasoning was perfection.

He smiled proudly.

"I'm going to visit Janet today. She looked like she needed a friend."

"We're not her friend," he said.

"I know, but I can be there for her, to listen."

"You're very sweet. I need to practice my card game anyway. There's a two-day tournament here in Sicily next week. I could use your help."

I slammed my fist on the counter. "I'm not helping you cheat! Quit asking."

I retrieved a deck of cards from his nightstand and spread a few upright on the table. "Turn invisible. Tell me what you see."

He vanished and reappeared. "I couldn't read them. They're blank."

"Yeah, quit asking."

He smiled. "You looked to see if we could cheat."

"No. I checked to prove you wrong. We need to be as pure as can be." I went to our bedroom to change into warm clothes.

Before Gian could join me, I headed to Janet's hospital. I materialized down the hall from her room to stay when the nurses came in.

Janet was dressed and sitting up in bed. She smiled when she saw me. "Hi. I thought you were the nurse coming to release me. They're taking forever."

"It's just me. Here as a friend."

She went to speak but started crying.

How were we going to go through with this? She was so young. So sweet. I sat on the bed and placed my hand on hers. She leaned onto my shoulder and cried herself out.

"All my friends deserted me. Were they even friends? It wasn't my fault what happened. Why am I being punished so badly?"

116

I should have prepared better. I had no idea how to respond. "This has nothing to do with you. You're in the shittiest of shitty positions. All I can tell you is your sacrifice will be rewarded." I can't believe I said that. Who knows what happens when we pass?

"I don't want to die. Is it wrong to wish my baby hadn't made it in my fall?"

"No, Janet."

"My rapist could have been my savior. How messed up is that?"

We sat in silence. Wishing a baby dead to save yourself is horrendous, but so was this baby. I hated him.

She looked up at me. "Have you met Jesus, like for real?"

I sat up. "No, but I've spoken to his closest advisor."

"Seriously?"

I nodded.

"He's real." She smiled dreamily.

"Very much so."

Nera warned me that Janet's sister was approaching. I think she just wanted me out of there.

"Your sister is on the way up. I'm heading out."

"Thanks for coming. Will I see you again before you take me?"

"Of course. You're not alone in this."

I passed Janet's sister in the hall. It was obvious they were related. She had the same boyish chin.

---

Before heading home, I had a stop to make. Kristen, the queen of the clique girls from my old high school, had moved to Hartford. I was surprised that Nera allowed me to find her. She lived in a run-down apartment in a seedy part of town. I needed to talk. I needed an apology for her bullying. I needed closure.

It took three times to find her building. Jumping to new places isn't easy. I remained invisible as I ascended the stairs. My nerves were out of control. Inside her apartment, she had her arm up protectively. The aura of a man was charging. He struck her across the face. Energy resonated outward in a wave. I raced outside to knock on the door.

Nera appeared next to me and held my arm.

"Don't interfere."

"I have to." I knocked with my free hand. Nera vanished.

The door flung open. "What do you want?" an angry man yelled.

I lost my composure and sucker-punched him in the nose. The bones crunched under my fist. It was broken for sure. The satisfaction was enormous.

"What are you doing?" Kristen shrieked and went to him. She looked older than our age. Still pretty but haggard.

"I need you to come with me," I said.

"Fuck you. This is my husband."

"Your husband do that?" I pointed to her bruising eyes.

"That's none of your business. Wait, are you Janice? Get out of here, loser."

I should have been angry, but I was just sad. I offered a hand. "Come with me. I can get you to safety."

"You broke my nose," the man whined.

I got up in his face. "Your eye socket is next if you don't shut up."

"Go, please," Kristen said and shut the door.

"You don't deserve this." I leaned back on the wall, dejected.

"Told you not to go in there," Nera said.

I followed her down the steps. "Did you know?"

"I'll show you." She brought her hands up to my forehead.

I backed away. "Keep that bitch out of my head. Just tell me."

"Her father sexually abused her throughout her childhood. That's why she lashed out at you in school. It had nothing to do with you."

"Why would you want to show me that?" I sat on the railing, defeated. "How could I have not noticed?"

"Nobody did. She hid it well."

Nera took me to a safe area to leave.

"Go back to your boyfriend. Be grateful for who he is."

I held Nera's hands in front of me. "Thank you for being here."

I vanished and opened a portal home. There was pounding coming from the bathroom but I barely felt Gian.

"Hi honey, are you there?"

He opened the door further and I felt his entire force.

"Perfect timing." He pointed at the room. Decorative stainless steel sheets were attached to the walls and ceiling. He was giving me privacy to block the Touch. Privacy in the bathroom.

"Nera delivered the panels today, one at a time. If I had done it, you would have felt me. She had a couple of men from town help install everything." He stepped from the room. "The door is solid steel. See if it works."

As soon as I closed the door, the Touch vanished. I couldn't feel him at all. I started crying. It was all too much. The day. Nera's help. His sweetness.

He opened the door, and the Touch returned with a mild shockwave. "Come here, sunshine."

I crumpled in his arms and had a good cry. I was better afterward.

"I'm sorry I let myself get mad," I said. "You want to win. There's nothing wrong with that."

"No need for sorries. You were right." He brushed the hair from my face.

"You don't need my help anyway. I believe in you."

"I'll hold the thought close. What I'm worried about is my poker face. With empathy, can I still bluff?"

"Go play and find out."

"You don't mind?"

It hurt that he would ask. "This is your passion. Go."

He pulled up Maps on his laptop. There were little gambling halls all around Sicily.

"I can't tell if they have poker. It looks like only slots."

"Search on poker," I said.

A new list came up. Near the bottom, I saw his name.

"Look, Gian's Poker Coffee. It's a sign."

"I think that's a coffee house."

He scrolled back up and selected another. "This one looks good. They're still open. I'll be right back."

I felt him heading to the States. He returned with dark sunglasses and a black cap.

"This is going to be fun," I said.

He gave me a worried look.

"For you, I meant. Of course, I can't watch. What if I played?"

"You know Texas hold 'em?" he asked excitedly.

"I can learn."

"No offense, baby, but that won't fly with the rest of the table."

I laughed. "Go. I could use some downtime."

"Thanks." He went to our wall safe and counted out a thousand euros. "You sure this is cool?"

It actually wasn't. That was the witch's money. "Of course." I straightened his collar and kissed him. "Have fun."

"You're the best," he said and vanished.

I jumped to my room in Seattle for my dance shoes and swords. I thought I was in the wrong place, but recognized Max's clothes. His new bedroom was clean and had a feminine touch. I bet he hated it. They did a great job setting up my new guest room. My sports bras were even in the same place.

With my dance equipment in hand, I headed back to Sicily. I placed the swords in a cross in the living room and hit play on my Highland mix. It had been a while since I danced. I began slowly but soon flew around the four sections made by the cross. I needed to dance more. The rush was exhilarating. I fell onto the couch, lightheaded and out of breath.

Gian had cleaned the tub for me. I couldn't think of a better way to unwind than a bath, but enjoying my soak proved difficult knowing about Kristen's abuse. I was glad I didn't let Nera put her crap in my head. That didn't stop my thoughts from drifting to the guys who'd attacked me when I was a teen. I could almost smell the stench of that creep's breath. My heart started pounding, and I tapped my fingers together while repeating my therapist's mantra, "I am in control." It wasn't working. I tried her trick of listing things to distract my mind. Naming pop groups eventually calmed me down.

I pulled the chain on the plug with my toes and stepped out. I wanted to call Dr. Killourie. What I needed was to hit someone. The time back home was four in the afternoon. I texted Joan.

You up for a little sparring?

It's about time. Come on over.

Be right there

Someone was in the yard when I showed up. I jumped to the woods by our house and walked back. Was fighting so soon after traveling a bad idea? Nera wasn't stopping me. As my driveway grew close, I thought of my muse.

121

"Teriko, you ready for this?" I knew he was excited. He had to be.

I went to my room to change. Grandpa was on his porch when I stepped out the back door. It was nice to see him.

"Hi, Bepa."

"Hey, Linsey. What are you doing here?" He strolled over to the railing.

"Popping in for a little sparring."

He smiled. "It's good to see you fighting again. You're a natural."

"Thanks. Hey, I have a question. Is Uncle Tony the one who stabbed you?"

"No. No. That man was younger. He was no one from our celebration. I was looking."

"That's good to know."

"Even if it were Tony, I wouldn't hold it against him after what your dad and I did."

"I can't imagine you would. Is he going to be OK?"

"He is. Your dad took him to a grief support group. Turns out Bram needed it more. This will be good for both of them."

"Yeah, Dad could use that." I thought about Mom. Tears built behind my eyes. I pushed them away as I learned to do as a kid. I looked toward the garage. "Joan's waiting."

"Love you. You've got this."

My heart was pounding as I walked into the garage. I hadn't fought in months. Max was in the cage with Joan, practicing an overhand. At least I knew what to look out for.

"That's not how you do it," Max said.

"It is too," Joan said. "Can't you just agree with me?"

"I could, but then we'd both be wrong."

Her obnoxious fake laugh was the perfect response to that tired saying.

"Are you rooting against me, brother?" I asked.

Joan screamed and skipped over to me with a dance in her step. She did an excited shuffle, rolling her fists.

"I haven't fought in a long time," I said. "Go easy on me."

Joan laughed. "Come on. I've been waiting so long to fight you again."

I was always able to beat her. That calmed me down a bit. But I still insisted on headgear. I walked to a corner of the cage to gather my nerves and focus.

"You ready?" Max said.

I stepped to the middle and tapped her glove with mine. Max rang the bell.

With her shorter reach, it was harder for her to get inside. She had to eat a few punches to get there. Joan came in strong with two jabs to my head. They were so fast. Her arm flexed as she went for an overhead. I dodged and came in hard to her temple.

She dove at me and weaved at the last second, grabbing me around the waist from behind in a body lock. Then she kicked my leg out, and I was down. She had me defenseless for a ground strike, but I broke free. We were going back and forth with serious jabs, connecting solidly. I was in the zone.

I heard Gian scream my name. I looked over. Joan took the opportunity to land my signature move. I barely saw the blow coming and was out.

"Linsey, wake up."

"What the hell, Joan?" Max said. "That wasn't cool."

My head was pounding. I opened my eyes. Gian was on the ground by the doorway. His sunglasses were knocked off behind him. I ran over to help.

"Gian, honey, wake up. Wake up, baby." I shook him on the shoulder.

He groaned and opened his eyes. "What the fuck?" His hand went to his forehead and he winced.

"You're OK," I said.

"Are you? I felt you getting hit and rushed over."

"What the fuck?" Max said. "Does he have the Touch?"

"Shut up. Just shut up," I said. "No questions. You'll get us killed."

"Is our family in trouble?" Max asked.

"No, just Gian and me. Please, stop talking. The curse is still broken. Everything is cool."

I helped Gian to his feet and walked him to the door.

"I'm sorry, Linsey," Joan said.

"Don't be. That was fun. We'll have to do this again. No following us."

I took Gian into the house and upstairs beyond the security cameras.

"Remember how to hold your wrist out."

He nodded.

We headed back to Sicily. He was weak when we arrived. I wanted to get him into bed, but he insisted on returning to the poker table.

"I'll take you there. Let me change real quick."

I stepped into a pair of pants and threw a sweatshirt over my sports bra.

Once invisible, I pulled him along, taking us to where Gian materialized by the gambling hall. He fell forward, holding his head.

"Come on, let's go home," I said.

"No, I'll be fine once we're apart. You're tough. How do you take that?"

"Lots of training. It's easier with adrenaline flowing."

"There was plenty. I thought you were in danger. Sorry for barging in. I wasn't thinking clearly."

I held his beautiful face in my hands and kissed him. "Never apologize for coming to my rescue. Do you need me to walk you in?"

"I'm all right."

"Call me if you can't make it back."

"I will."

I yelled for him as he was entering the building. "Wait. How's your game?"

He looked back at me. "I'm kicking ass. It feels good. Although the people I'm playing aren't the greatest."

"And your poker face?"

He flushed the emotions from his face and stared blankly. His poker face was solid.

I jumped to the family lair and erased the video of Gian materializing in the garage. I heard the deadbolts inside the door sliding open. Max jumped when he saw me.

"What are you doing?" I said.

"Nothing."

I glared at him. "Don't fuck with me. You were going to look at the tapes. Get the hell out of here."

"Sorry," he said, soft and pouty. It was strange hearing this timid response.

"Why do you guys still have so many cameras running, anyway."

"We're bored. OK."

"Get a job."

"You get a job," he said.

"I'm on one."

I left through the back door and headed to the park to jump to Sicily. It was three more hours before Gian returned. I would have been worried if I wasn't able to feel him.

"I'm…" He pointed to the bedroom. I helped him onto the mattress. He was asleep before I could get his second shoe off. In his pants pocket was a roll of cash. He was up €2,300. That seemed like a decent evening.

He slept for twelve hours straight. The rest did him well. We were at our kitchen bar having our morning coffee.

"I had a dream about my neighbor Clara," Gian said. "She's this lady I used to help in the Bronx."

"Helped how?"

"Nothing like that. She's a sweet older woman. The dream was crazy real. I should see if she needs anything. Maybe do some yard work for her."

125

"You mind if I go with you?" I wanted to meet a woman worthy of a Dread's support, one who could bring empathy from the lacking.

"Of course you can come."

We dressed down and headed to New York. Gian materialized in what I assumed was Clara's kitchen. I joined him. The dust on the counter wasn't promising.

"I hope she's still around. It was seven years ago."

Nera appeared next to us. She held her hands out and walked around the place. "I can sense her." She stopped at a chair in the front room. "She's alive." With that, she vanished.

"That was weird," Gian said.

Nera returned and handed me a business card for a convalescent home.

"Room 107."

That's all she said and was gone.

I pulled up the address on my phone. It was twenty miles away. We found a place to arrive using the satellite view, but overshot our landing even with that.

The security at the front desk was lax. We used fake names to get inside. Elderly people in wheelchairs lined the halls. Their eyes lit up, thinking we were coming for them. It was heart-wrenching.

Clara's door was closed. Gian hesitated, then knocked.

"Come in," a weak voice responded.

Her room was drab. At least she had one to herself.

With all his talk about the old neighborhood, I was expecting an Italian woman, but she was white. I dug her long gray hair. The look was youthful, like an aging rock star.

Clara cocked her head with a squint of her eyes. Then came a smile. "Stefano? Is that you?"

He walked over and took her hand. "Hi, Clara. It's Gian now. We're no longer running."

"Gian? What? What happened to you? There was a fire and your family was gone."

"We had to skip town. I couldn't say goodbye. I'm sorry."

"That's OK. You're here now. Introduce me to your friend."

"She's not only my friend. This is my fiancée, Linsey."

I smiled wide upon hearing the term.

Clara brought his hand to her lips and kissed him. "I am so happy for you."

"It's a pleasure to meet you," I said.

"I apologize for my appearance. Would you be a dear and put my hair up? My nurse didn't come back after my shower."

The damn staff had left without finishing. That's such bullshit.

"It would be my pleasure," I said.

"There should be a brush and a tie in the bathroom."

"What happened to you?" Gian asked. "Why are you in here?"

"My heart. It's not what it used to be."

I lingered in the bathroom, giving them time alone.

When I returned, Gian helped her sit up for me. I moved behind the bed and brushed her hair out.

"I can do a messy bun that's super cute," I said.

She looked up at me. "Oh, I'd like that. Keep it high so it doesn't press on my head when I lay back."

"Is there anything we can do?" Gian asked.

"You being here is gift enough. It's nice having visitors."

"There must be something. Can we clean up your place? We stopped by earlier to help."

"I was wondering what was up with your clothes. You were always a fashionable boy. It would be better if you could find someone to sell my house. Sorry, that's too much to ask."

"It's not too much at all," he said.

"You are so sweet. I don't have the strength to go home, and I can't afford assisted living without selling the place. I hate it here. They're mean."

"We'll help you fix her up to sell," he said.

I wasn't as enthused. We didn't have time for that kind of commitment.

Clara whimpered and almost cried. "You're my angel. You always have been. Bring me my purse. I'll get you the key."

I was finished with her bun. It was adorable. I took a picture so she could see.

"Oh, I love it. Thank you."

"You looked just as cute with it down."

The real estate agent we chose, William Dollar, met us at the house. We found him off a billboard across from the convalescent home. He had his name listed as Dollar, Bill. That fit as money is what Clara needed.

William was a short, bald man in his mid-thirties. His ridiculously thick mustache didn't complement his baby face.

"Thank you for making the time," he said.

"I was going to say the same to you," Gian said. "Here's your copy of the key."

"We don't need to go in. The land is zoned for business. She'll make more selling the parcel. There's not an emotional attachment to the house, is there?"

I couldn't believe he asked. Of course, there would be.

"I didn't mean it like that," he said, reading my face. "If I can't sell the house for removal, it will be torn down. Prepare her for that."

"We can talk to her now if you have time," Gian said.

I was relieved that we wouldn't have to fix up the place. There was enough on our plate.

Gian sent me home. He returned to Sicily a few hours later.

"That went well," he said.

"She's all right selling it for land?"

"As all right as she could be. At least it will get her in a better place."

"Doesn't she have family who can help?"

"She has a son, but he's in prison."

"Lovely."

"He was framed, Linsey."

I'm such an ass. "Sorry. Didn't mean anything by that."

"No worries."

"Nera stopped by," I said. "She loved that we're helping Clara but said we need to check in on Robert."

"Oh, God."

"I know. We can't ignore him. He needs to find peace with himself."

"What does that mean with crazy?" he asked.

"I don't know. Get dressed. We'll see what we can do."

"Can I at least get a coffee first?"

"Let's have one in his village."

We found the cutest cafe in Dunster. I chose a window seat so we could watch the townsfolk walk by in the darkness. I felt Robert's approach. He did a double take when we waved.

Robert let out a muffled scream and ran off. We both laughed.

"Let's see if we can find a bar that will allow him in," Gian said.

We started with the furthest pub from his house. Six pubs later, and still no luck. We finally found one by his place that, after a lot of convincing and a bribe of a hundred-pound note, would allow us to bring him in.

"Did you ever replace the bottle you took from Sir Donald?" I asked Gian.

"Oh shit, I completely forgot. I'll get it this week."

"I want to go with you."

"It's a date."

The thought of being back on my family's land brought me peace.

We opened a portal to Robert's location and stepped through. He was hiding in the woods behind his house, watching. We materialized behind him.

Gian crouched to his level. "What are you looking for?"

Robert screamed and ran for the house. We beat him inside. Gian tackled him around the waist, and I held his arms back. He thrashed around, almost breaking loose.

"Calm down, Robert," I said.

"We're not here to hurt you."

"You're not real," he said.

"Clearly, we are," I said. "Let's go get a pint."

"I can't. No one will let me in anymore."

"We talked to the man in the Three Lions. He said we can bring you."

"Really?"

"Really."

"The big redhead? Looks like a Viking?"

"Yep."

Robert's disposition changed. "I'll need a shower first."

"Take your time," I said. "We'll be shopping."

"Nothing will be open at this hour."

"Window shopping then. We'll find you."

Gian led me out the front door. What I liked best about Dunster were the cobblestone sidewalks. They would be hell to walk on in heels, though.

I was sad for the villagers having to put up with Robert, but if you look closely enough, any town has troublemakers.

There were a couple of cute dresses in a shop down the road. I took a picture of them and the store's sign. A driving cap in the next window caught Gian's eye. We turned around almost in unison, knowing Robert was approaching. I would have walked past him if I hadn't sensed his tracker. He wore a fabulous gray knit sweater and a wool cap.

"Stick with me," he said. "I'll keep you out of fights."

"You'll get us into them, Robert," I said. "This is your last chance for social drinking. If you're good, maybe they'll let you back in later."

"Don't count on it. Charlie's a wanker."

Gian laughed. "That's not helping."

Robert glanced over at him. "Look at me walking out in the open with a wop."

What the fuck? Damn it, Robert.

Gian threw his arms up. "That's it, we're done."

"What?" Robert said.

"Come on," I pleaded with Gian. I didn't want to fail our mission.

"Watch your mouth," he said, sticking a finger in Robert's face.

We had Robert wait outside until we made sure he was still good to come in. The pub was old and charming, with a massive wooden bar lining the far wall. You could smell the age in the place.

Charlie's raucous sailor's laugh was welcoming but cut short when he saw us. He pointed to a side table, away from the other patrons. "Keep him under control."

"We will," Gian said.

I went out to get Robert. "Would you like to walk in with me on your arm?"

"Would I ever," he said, adjusting himself.

"Well, you blew that," I said. "Just get in there."

All conversation stopped when we walked in.

"We're off to the left," I whispered. "Be a saint."

Some of the patrons were looking at Charlie for help. He turned away.

131

"Did he see me?" Robert asked when he sat down.

"He did," I said.

"When he comes over, how about you apologize for your past behavior."

"Why would I do that?"

"Because you should be sorry," Gian said.

Robert pounded the table with a fist. "But I'm not."

Charlie cleared his throat and nodded to the door. I held my hand up.

"Seriously, apologize," I whispered. "Even if you don't mean it."

"Whatever."

"I'm sorry for my past behavior," I repeated.

"I got it," he barked.

"Lose the tone or we're leaving."

Gian nodded in agreement.

Charlie walked over to our table. "Robert."

"Charlie. I want to apologize for me past behavior. I've been going through troubles. It's rough. The truth is I miss coming here."

Charlie was trapped. "I said for the evening. We'll see how this goes."

Robert's face grew stern. Luckily, Charlie had turned to me.

"We appreciate the hospitality," I said.

"We'll take three pints," Gian said. "Robert's choice."

"Guinness."

I smiled.

"Coming right up," Charlie said, which I think was a joke on the time it takes for a proper pour.

"So, what do you do for a living, Robert?" I asked.

"What does it matter?" he said.

"I'm just making small talk."

"I was a roofer until I fell and smacked me noggin."

I shouldn't have laughed. "I'm laughing with you."

"It's nice to hear it. I don't get many visitors. Maybe dying is for the best."

"I wish it could be different. I really do. So what do you do now?"

"I'm still in the business. They have me feet on the ground. I'm a master thatcher. I didn't lose the skills. It keeps me busy. Tamps the demons."

Charlie presented our beers. The pour was magnificent.

"Thank you," Robert said.

I smiled.

"I know how to thank people," he said roughly.

"Robert, not every statement is an argument. We're your friends."

"You're not my friends. You're here to kill me."

I raised my glass. "Not today."

"Don't tell me when. I don't want to know."

"It's a deal," Gian said.

"Will it hurt?"

"You won't feel a thing. You'll switch off like a light."

"That's good." He took a sip and looked toward the other side of the room. "My schoolmate, Jake, was in here when we arrived. He's gone now. Won't even talk to me."

"Have you tried therapy?" Gian asked.

"With my friend?" he asked. "We're not poofsters."

"No, for yourself."

"God, no."

"Would you try it for me?" I asked.

"Please," Gian said.

"Maybe."

"I'll pay. You won't even need to go anywhere. You can do it over the computer."

"If I say yes, will you stop yer pestering?"

Gian tipped his glass, yes.

"So, what brought you to Dunster?" I asked to change the subject.

"Me family lived here. I'm in the cottage I grew up in."

"Where are they?"

"Dead. They came to visit me and were hit by a Yank driving in the wrong direction. Happy birthday to me."

"Oh, Robert, that's horrible." I put an arm around him.

He recoiled a bit but kept it there. "It was a long time ago."

"Doesn't make the pain any less," I said, thinking of Mom.

"No, no, it doesn't. I miss me brother. He was a fine bloke. Better than me."

# Chapter 7

I woke the next day to Gian shaking me. My period had begun. I was cramping badly. The whole left side of my abdomen was buckling in pain. I wish he would have let me sleep.

"Linsey, there's something wrong. We need to get to the hospital."

"Oh my God, what's up, baby?"

"It's not me. Can't you feel that pain? It's killing me."

"Welcome to menstruation."

"That's normal?"

"The cramps aren't always this bad, but yeah."

"Jesus Christ. Can I get you anything?"

"Ibuprofen? There's some in the medicine cabinet."

Gian practically dove to get it. He closed the door in the bathroom so he couldn't feel me. His metal sheeting worked wonders. The Touch was blocked entirely from my side.

He returned with a glass and gingerly handed the pills to me. "Here you go, sunshine."

"I appreciate the love, but no need to baby me. I'll be fine."

"I'll try, but shit—the pain. Women are tough. I didn't know. Mad props."

"We put up with a lot," I said.

"Would you like a quiet day to yourself?"

"Sure. That sounds nice."

"You've got it. I'm helping Clara figure out what to keep for her new apartment. There's one opening up in two days."

"They're letting her move in before she gets her place sold?"

"Yeah, she's using her savings."

"You're a sweet man for helping."

"You would do the same."

My quiet day turned into two. Clara was moving in a day early. I offered to help, but Gian's friends from the old neighborhood pitched in. Nera brought him home drunk the last night. I didn't mind. I wish I had old friends to drink with.

---

Gian still wasn't feeling well the following evening. We headed to Hawaii for a bit of relaxation. Stepping from our room, we were blinded by the sun shining into Don's beach house.

He was out of mixers. I was in the mood for a vodka soda. Don was in a Safeway an hour away. Gian could sense his location on his phone's map. I hadn't figured out how to do that.

We found Don in the bread aisle talking to a group of elderly men. His eyes lit up.

"What brings you to Hawaii?"

"Checking in," I said. "Making sure you're doing good."

"I've never been better." There was the warmest smile on his face.

"Want to get a drink?" Gian said.

"It's ten in the morning."

"Hair of the dog? I need a Bloody Mary."

"In a while. These are new widowers. I'm teaching them how to shop for themselves."

"This is my store back home," Gian said. "Can I recommend a few things?"

Don gestured toward the men.

"Hello, gentlemen. I'm Don's friend, Gian. If you'll let me, I have easy meals to share."

"Much appreciated, son," a man in a white bucket hat said.

"That's very kind," the youngest looking in the group replied.

Another man went on a five-minute diatribe about the wonders of mustard.

Gian brought us over to the packaged meat aisle.

"Pork tenderloin is an easy meal." He held one up. "The best is the Teriyaki. No need to cook it all at once. Divide it in half or thirds and freeze the rest. Throw in some canned vegetables and a box of rice; you have yourself a meal."

"One note," Don said. "If you defrost meat, don't refreeze it later. You'll get real sick defrosting it a second time."

"Yeah," I said, remembering getting my whole family sick doing just that.

The men all picked out a loin for themselves. Don sat back, taking notes for them.

"While we're here, let me show you a trick your wives probably did to keep you healthy." Gian walked over to the poultry section and held up a package. "Tacos are one of the easiest meals. Ground turkey is a great substitute."

"Grace used to do that for me," a man said.

"With the seasonings, I bet you couldn't tell it wasn't beef," Gian said.

"Reef?" a man asked.

"Beef. Beef," another said. "For tacos."

"Why is he holding up chicken?"

"It's turkey. Healthier," the first man said.

It took everything I had not to laugh.

"The best part is you'll have easy leftovers for days," Gian said, speaking louder.

It warmed my heart how patient he was. When it was time, he would make a great father.

After two more meal suggestions, Gian handed the group back to Don.

"Do you have any tips?" he asked me.

"What I can offer are hugs."

The man in the bucket hat started crying. I embraced him.

"I'm sorry," he sobbed.

I stroked his back. "It's all right. I understand what you're going through. Hold on as long as you need."

The last of the men was the only one who didn't cry, but he whispered thank you in my ear.

"I think this is a good place to stop for the day," Don said. "Let's do this same time next week, but we'll meet at Costco. Follow me. I'll pay for your groceries."

That produced an uproar in the men. No one was about to let anyone pay for their food. A frail man acted along, but the way he had carefully checked the prices said otherwise. I slipped a hundred from my wallet and pretended to pick it off the floor.

"Excuse me, you dropped this." I winked.

He smiled at me, confused, and then smiled wider.

"You're an angel."

I slid the bill into his shirt pocket. "So are you."

"Would you care to join me for breakfast?" Don asked Gian and me. "There's a place by the harbor that's the best."

"Give us a half hour. We'll find you," I said, dragging Gian out of the store.

"I need your cock," I growled in his ear.

"Old guys do that to you?" he joked.

"No," I laughed. "I can feel you flopping around in your shorts. It's the best."

It grew erect. He reached in and positioned it up and out of the way. His cock was so hard it protruded above his waistband. The wind blew against him, outlining the head through his shirt.

"Let's go to Don's house. Wait, no, let's go to that beach we like. Buy a towel. I'll meet you in the dunes."

138

I materialized above the beach and walked along the ridge until I found a secluded area with a view of the surf below. It was lovely sitting alone with the sun caressing my body.

Gian materialized next to me. He handed over a beach towel and a bottle of water.

"Thanks." I downed half the bottle.

He spread the towel out and started unbuckling his belt. I grabbed his hand to stop him. I liked getting it out. That was half the fun.

I rubbed his cock through his shorts. My other hand slid up his leg to caress his balls. I wanted to rip his shorts open but took my time.

I unbuckled his belt and unzipped. His cock was outlined through his underwear. I placed my lips against the soft fabric, rubbing and nibbling. He gripped the back of my head, pushing me closer. That made me want it more. I lowered his underwear, freeing his perfect cock. It dazzled in the sunlight. His succulent scent drew me in. I grabbed hold and slid him down my throat. That, in my opinion, is the best way to greet a cock. The impossibility of the act shows he's a part of me. He fits. He's mine.

"It feels good," he moaned.

His words stoked my fire. I worked him with my hand and mouth, stroking long and hard. I felt, from his perspective, my tongue sliding the length of his shaft. I narrowed my focus to flicks and licks. It was glorious.

"You're the best."

I smiled wide, screwing up my rhythm, and slipped him from my mouth to stroke. That was even better. No wonder guys masturbate so much.

Before the slickness dried, I took him back into my mouth. I traced the outline of his head, and my tongue found the hole. There was barely any feeling from his side. The pleasure came from my end and the curiosity of it all.

I teased him at the end, backing my hand off when he was getting close, resetting him for a few more minutes.

"Let me come, baby."

I stroked him hard with my mouth over his head. His breathing grew heavy, and his hips heaved as he came. The electricity in his brain activated mine, letting me tag along. This was a strong one. I enjoyed every second as he released into my mouth. The taste was delectable.

I let his cum drizzle to my palm and ran my tongue through before wiping it off in the sand. A small dollop emerged from his cock. I licked it off while smiling at him. Another eased its way out. Each one tasting better than the last.

I left his cock out and cuddled up, kissing him deeply. I loved this man so much.

Gian remained hard. He unbuttoned my shorts with a mischievous smile.

"My period," I said, shocked.

He shrugged. I was frozen in silence as he lowered his face to me, snatching the tampon string in his teeth and flipping it aside. Trepidation turned to lust as he maneuvered his cock to my hips and entered me. I'm glad he had backed his face away. I couldn't have handled him eating me out.

Shallow thrusts worked wonders on my cramps. He sank deeper, hitting my magical spot. Pleasure engulfed my body, ebbing through me like a soft caress of my soul.

We didn't have a lot of time. I moaned louder, hoping to speed things up. It wasn't working. I asked for a rain check on the orgasm. Faking one with the Touch wasn't an option.

Gian let me relax while he headed out for tampons. How could I have left the villa without extra?

It was pleasant in the sun with the afterglow, but we had promised we'd be there in a half hour.

Don was in the same restaurant where we first saw him. He insisted we order the Loco Moco. It was a wonderful mixture of rice and egg, topped with a hamburger patty, covered in a dark beef and mushroom gravy. We'd be walking the meal off later.

There was a sadness in the air. I wasn't sure where it came from. It wasn't my own.

"Did I tell you I went surfing yesterday?" Don said.

I couldn't picture him surfing. "What? Shut up."

"I used to be good."

"How did you do?" Gian asked.

"Not well," he said, laughing. "But I was able to, and that was enough."

"I hate to cut this short," Gian said. He leaned over and took my hand. "We need to visit Rowanda. Something's making her sad."

"I was sensing that too."

"We'll get this meal." Gian laid a hundred on the table.

"That's nice of you," Don said. "Mahalo."

"What does that mean?" I asked.

Don backed his head away. "Wow, you haven't spent much time here. It's Hawaiian for gratitude. Mostly, thank you."

"Mahalo for showing us how good people can be," Gian said.

"Where would the respect be in living my last days selfishly?" Don asked.

I couldn't help crying. "I have to go."

Gian caught up with me in the parking lot.

"How can we kill this guy?" I said. "I can't. I won't."

Gian held me tenderly. "I don't think we have a choice."

A hug with the Touch is a magical feeling. It was a tornado of love cleansing my tears.

We walked to our landing spot and vanished. Rowanda was in her apartment alone.

"Sup. Come on in," she said, answering the door.

I took her hand. "Are you OK? We felt your sadness."

"That's weird. I'm just packing for New Orleans. There's no time to come back here. I'll miss the Caribbean, that's all."

"But you're going home," I said with a smile.

"I am. They're giving me immunity for my testimony. Momma's gonna be so excited."

Nera spoke in my ear. I repeated her warning. "Don't surprise your mom. Call her to get a doctor to check her heart."

"What? Momma's ill?" She searched around and found her phone.

"Tell her you saw it in a vision."

I tipped a finger goodbye and followed Gian to his condo to change clothes for Alaska.

"Can you log into the account we made for Rowanda?" he asked, moving away from his computer. "I want to make sure she won't get arrested."

I entered the password.

He read through all the documents the CEO sent. We didn't head to Alaska until he was satisfied.

Janet had two days left. We needed to spend more time with her. We found her in a baby store checkout, purchasing a pram.

"Let me help you with that." Gian took the cart.

I zipped up her coat before going outside.

She held her stomach. "I've talked to him. He's a good boy. He's not evil."

"Oh, Janet." I should have said more, but what was the point? Could passing with ignorance be what she needed?

"Are you at peace with yourself?" Gian asked.

"No," she cried. "How could I be at peace with myself?"

"When you go, they'll think you died from complications from your fall," he said. "Eddie will be charged with murder."

"How can peace come from spite?" she asked.

142

Neither of us knew the answer.

"Would you like help putting it together?" I asked.

"That would be nice."

"Why don't you head home," I told Gian. "Janet needs some girl time."

"Say no more." Gian kissed me and walked away. He was a little too quick with his exit. I didn't care for that.

I climbed into the passenger side of her truck. The parking lot was plowed. It was unsettling to see all the snow on the roads. I hoped she was a decent driver.

"You have a handsome boyfriend," Janet said. "Like super handsome."

"I'm lucky. I didn't mean lucky. I don't want to do this, Janet. Know that. We have no choice."

"You're not telling me everything. Why do you have to do this? Who's behind all this?"

"I can't. I just… I can't tell you. Everything will be explained when you cross over."

Nera spoke in my head. *Tell her Jesus is waiting for her.*

*Is he?* I thought. There was no response.

"What?" Janet said.

I put my hand to my heart. "I've been told that Jesus is waiting for you."

Janet skidded to the side of the road. She leaned out the door like she was going to throw up but pulled herself together. "You know when you're crushing hard, and your love suddenly appears, making you sick in your stomach? Jesus."

How she looked at me when she said Jesus made me laugh.

"I have to get to confession."

"There's time tomorrow."

"When does it happen?"

"You sure you want to know?"

"Yes."

"12:05 a.m. Thursday."

"Tomorrow is my last day?"

"Yeah," I said, wishing it wasn't.

Janet sobbed quietly. "Will you and Gian be there?"

"We have to be. We're the conduit."

The conversation grew silent. I gave her as much time as she needed.

She pulled into a driveway lined with pine trees. We came to a stop in a carport by the garage.

"This my parent's house."

"It's nice."

"They're mad that I quit school."

"Treat them kindly. Don't leave them with regrets."

She found a tissue in her pocket, wiped her eyes, and blew her nose. I didn't know what to do to comfort her.

We lugged the box up to her room. I liked that she wasn't apprehensive about the instructions. Janet took charge of the assembly.

She was holding a piece up to another, confused.

"I think that's for the left side," I said.

"Shit, you're right. Oh, oh." She covered her mouth.

"They're only words," I said. "It's OK to swear."

"Will it hurt? Dying."

"Not at all. It's so fast you won't feel anything."

"That's good." She tightened a screw with an Allen wrench. "So, what do you do when you're not killing people?"

"I'm in a transitional stage. Who knows what's next? Our old life is over."

"What did you use to do?"

"You ever watch Buffy the Vampire Slayer?"

"Yeah."

"I was Buffy, except I left the killing to my family."

"Right," she laughed.

"It's true, but with another kind of monster. My boyfriend was one of them. I guess it was more a Romeo and Juliet scenario."

"You're kidding me?"

144

"I wish I wasn't. Many people died because of me."

"Linsey, there's no way it could be your fault."

"It doesn't make it better."

I could feel Gian. He had remained in town but was now deep in the mountains. Why the hell was he out there alone?

"Will you excuse me for a moment," I said and disappeared.

Gian was invisible when I arrived. He materialized with me. "Hey, sunshine."

I was up to my waist in snow. "What are you doing out here alone?"

"Hunting for gold. No need to dig it up." He showed me his new GPS reader. "I can record the exact coordinates and guess the depth."

"Shouldn't you be practicing for your tournament?"

"I will."

"Don't wear yourself out. You could get hurt."

"I won't, Ma."

Being called Ma bugged me, but I let it go. "I have to get to Janet. Be safe."

Back in her room, I sat where I had been before and materialized. Janet was staring at me wide-eyed.

"That is so cool."

I took a seated bow.

She brushed snow off my legs. "Tell me about the monsters?"

*No* was all Nera said.

"I'm being told I can't."

"Who is telling you this?"

"That I really can't tell you. I want to hear about you. What were you going to college for?"

"You're very frustrating. I was studying to be a veterinarian. A horse vet."

"You look like a horse girl. What will you call your clinic?"

145

She perked up. "I wanted Arctic Equine Veterinary Clinic, but the name's taken."

"You can always buy them out."

"I think I will," she said, playing along.

"So, have you talked to your friends lately?"

Tears welled, but she pulled them back. "No."

"What are you waiting for?"

"They won't talk to me."

"Invite them to dinner tomorrow night."

"I can't."

*I'll get them to go,* Nera told me.

"They'll come," I said.

"You sure?"

I nodded.

She grabbed her phone and started a group text. I took her arm before she hit send.

"Wait an hour."

"OK," she said excitedly. "If this happens, I'll be so happy."

Janet tightened the last screw in the pram.

"Take her for a spin," I said.

She pushed it around the room with perfect posture like English royalty. We fell over laughing.

"When can you even use something like this?" I asked.

"It's not always snowy here. The summers are spectacular."

Her phone rang. "It's my best friend." She held the phone to her chest.

"Answer. Go on."

"Hey Tracy, what's up?" As she listened, her smile crept wide. "That sounds fun. I'll be there."

"Well?"

"My friends invited me to dinner tomorrow night at the Crow's Nest. Thank you."

"That wasn't me. It's the good in you bringing everyone together."

"Yeah, right." She hugged me. "I think I'll take my family out tonight. Want to join us?"

"I probably shouldn't."

"It's all right. I have a big day tomorrow to plan anyway."

"You sure you're OK? I can stay for a bit. I need to go rescue Gian, though."

"I'm actually good. Am I at peace with myself?"

"I believe you are. Come here."

She felt comfortable in my arms. Love emanated from her body.

Hanging onto her, I saw her mom losing a ring. It was as clear as if I was there. Nera was working her magic. "I know where your mom's wedding ring is," I said.

"How did you know about that?"

"I saw it when we hugged. Follow me."

We grabbed a shovel and a weeding trowel from the shed.

"I'll go invisible. Show me your mom's garden."

I followed Janet and noticed the faint glow of the diamond. I materialized and started digging out the snow. She joined in.

"Just until we see the surface," I said. "We don't want to damage it."

Once I saw dirt, I turned invisible again and narrowed our digging area. I sank my shovel in the soil and turned invisible. The blade was lower than the ring. Using my weight, I broke through the frozen dirt. I checked one last time.

"Have a look. It's right in the shovel."

She broke apart the dirt and jumped. There in the pile was a silver band. She picked it up. I was invisible but still at her side. The faint glow of the diamond moved to her heart.

I left to find Gian. He was leaning against a tree for support, looking over with a worried look.

"I overdid it. Got greedy. I found so many."

I hoisted him up, propping him on my shoulder. "Let's go to your place. We can have dinner with your parents."

"I'd like that." He was groggy. I had to get there fast.

I steered us through the portal. Gian collapsed, with me breaking his fall.

"I'm going to lay here for a bit," he said.

"I'll get you a blanket."

"No, just hold me."

It was nice having him need me. We napped for a while, using his coat as a pillow.

"Do you have a Bible?" I asked when he awoke.

"I don't think so."

I pulled one up on my phone. "We should learn a prayer to send Janet off."

"Of course. You're the sweetest. How did your day go?"

"It went well. I think she's ready. I'm not."

"Me neither," he said. "I'm sorry I've put her on you. I can't handle it. You're stronger than me."

I appreciated the compliment, but it felt like a copout.

Gian's phone rang. "Hi, Mom. You're on speaker. Linsey's here."

"Hello, Linsey."

"Hi, Leonora."

"So, Gian, you're in town and don't even tell us?"

He rolled his eyes, "It's not like that. We were going to see if you wanted to have dinner tonight."

"We're eating at Enzo and Pippa's at six. We can surprise them."

"Is it just you guys? We're beat."

"Sure."

"Mom?"

"I said sure."

"Love you too." He hung up.

I was excited. I adored Enzo and Pippa.

We napped in Gian's bed for a couple more hours, then headed to his great-grandparents. They lived in a rambler outside Seattle. I saw Pippa peering through the side window. Our eyes locked and she shouted. "Enzo, it's Gian and Linsey!"

"Well, let them in," he yelled.

Gian opened the door and Pippa came rushing out for hugs. I loved the iridescent green fitted coat she wore. It had a crazy wide collar that flowed halfway down the front. A green and blue scarf was on her head, tied into a turban. The topper was her bright red lipstick. I wish I could be as brave as her with fashion.

"What are you doing in town? I thought you were on a mission."

"We are. It lets us travel around a bit," Gian said.

"Come in. Come in."

There was a wall of windows opposite the entryway. The place was like a large C, with the opening facing the woods. A stone courtyard sat in the middle of the two wings. A table with four settings was outside. His parents kept their word. Gian hadn't thought they would. I had mentally prepared for an onslaught of family.

Their kitchen and living room was off to our right. Enzo was in a crazy green checkered suit. It went well with his wild beard and curled mustache. I knew from Gian that he wore socks matching the color scheme.

"Love the socks," I said as if I could see them.

Enzo lifted a pant leg, showing his pair. They were an exact match of the lighter green. Pippa walked behind him. Their outfits complimented each other.

Leonora and Carlino were dressed casually—well, casually for their family. I'm glad Gian had me change into a dress.

"It's good to see you, Dad," He gave Carlino a one-armed hug.

Enzo had a big grin. "What a treat. Set two more plates."

He didn't ask if we wanted wine. He just poured the glasses. "Drink up."

"I hope you're staying safe," Pippa said.

I put my hand where my birth control had been. Gian shook his head at how wrong I took the statement.

"It's not a dangerous mission," Gian said. "That's not to say it's easy."

"This is the hardest thing I've ever done," I said.

"You're tough," Pippa said. "You'll be fine. What I want is to see your ring."

I held it up for her.

"Oh, it's glorious. Look at this beautiful ring, Enzo."

"Welcome to the family," he said.

Leonora held my hand to admire the ring. "It's good to have a daughter. I've waited so long for one of the boys to settle down. Grow up a little."

"Don't listen to her," Enzo said to Gian. "With the Dark Times over, there's no need to grow up. Enjoy life and everything it has to offer."

Pippa and Leonora glanced at each other. Usually, I would have asked myself why women are the only ones who have to grow up, but after my talk with Gian, the thought comforted me.

"What's for dinner?" Gian asked. "It smells divine."

"Baked ziti," Pippa said.

"You're in for a treat," Gian said to me.

"Will there be enough?" I asked.

They all laughed.

"So, what is this mission you can't talk about?" Enzo said.

"Grandpa," Carlino said.

"It's OK," Gian said. "I'd want to know about it, too. But we really can't talk about it. People will die if we do."

"No more death," Enzo said.

I wish that could be true. It made me think of Janet. I excused myself and had a good cry in the bathroom.

When I came back to the kitchen, everyone but Pippa was outside. I headed for the door to join the others.

"Linsey, stay," Pippa said in Italian. "I sent them away so we can talk. I missed my girl."

She reached into the fridge and retrieved a pitcher of limoncello. "Let's start our meal with dessert?"

Her pour was to the top of the tiny glasses. We clinked together and I took a sip. This was a strong batch.

Pippa coughed with a laugh. "I may have used a little too much Everclear."

Leonora walked in from the outside. "I missed you, Linsey." She gave me a motherly hug. Pippa poured her a limoncello.

"To my new daughter." Leonora drained her glass with barely a reaction. It was kind of badass. Limoncello is a sipping drink.

"I'll drink to that," Pippa said.

---

We looked in on Janet four times the next day but only appeared to her twice. She had a full list of activities planned. We rode with her that evening to the restaurant, with Gian sitting in the middle. Janet was nervously chatty.

"I've never been to the Crow's Nest. It sounds super fancy," she said. "You should get a table. You're dressed for it."

Nera had told us to dress up a bit. I pulled up the restaurant's web page. "The view from the dining room is gorgeous. Look at the mountains, hon."

"Call 'em," he said.

I didn't think I would get a reservation, but I humored him. "Serious, you have a table for two?"

"We just had a cancellation," the man at the restaurant said. "If you can make it by six, it's yours."

151

I looked at the clock on the dash. That was in fifteen minutes. "Can we make it by six?" I asked Janet.

"That's when my reservation is."

"Six is perfect," I told the man.

"What name can I put you down for?"

"Lombardo."

"We'll see you in a few."

I hung up. "We're eating well this week," I said.

"Too good." Gian patted his belly.

"There's the Crow's Nest." Janet pointed to the right-hand tower in a complex of black and brown buildings. "The restaurant's at the top."

Gian leaned into the window to get a better look. "Super modern."

"It's not all Hicksville," she said.

"I wouldn't call Alaska that at all," I said. "I think you have to be tough to live here."

"You get used to the cold. It becomes a part of you."

"Or you've grown numb," Gian said.

Janet laughed. "Probably." Her expression tightened.

"What's the matter," I asked.

"I'm nervous. I can't drink because of the baby. I don't remember how to be myself."

"You'll be fine," I said.

Our table was two over from Janet's. She didn't need our support. Seven of her friends showed up. They were fun, loving, and attentive. I hope it was them knowing and not a spell.

Janet handled herself well, only breaking down once. She covered it up, saying the tears were happy tears. I followed her to the bathroom to help calm her down. Gian said her friends spoke wonderfully about her when she was gone.

The dinner was long, but the girls wanted it longer. Janet forced herself to leave and be with her family.

Back at the house, Gian and I waited in her room, listening at the door to their conversations. I bawled as silently as I could.

"You're going to scare her." He wiped away my tears. "Pull it together."

His resolve impressed me, knowing how difficult this was for him. He gave me strength.

At midnight, Janet excused herself. The last words the family said to each other were, "I love you." It was how it should be.

We disappeared as footsteps approached. I peeked my head through the wall. It was only her. She started crying when she saw us. I caught her as she fell to the floor.

"I'm so scared," she said.

"You're doing great," I said. "Would you like me to recite a prayer?"

Janet nodded.

I'd been memorizing all day. I hoped I didn't screw this up. I wasn't using notes.

"Lord Jesus, holy and compassionate:
forgive Janet's sins.
By dying, you unlock the gates of life
for those like Janet who believe in you:
do not let our sister be parted from you,
but by your glorious power, give her light,
joy and peace in heaven where you live and reign
forever and ever.
Amen."

She was smiling.

"I'm excited for where you're going," Gian said.

"You'll be magnificent," I added, choking back my tears.

Janet's body relaxed and she leaned her head back, eyes closed.

153

I placed my hands on her head. Gian completed the connection. When the countdown reached zero, she sank in our arms. Janet was gone. I started bawling.

Gian stood up and knocked a glass off the shelf in anger, shattering it. I heard her parents stir downstairs. We vanished. Janet's aura was gone. The fading glow of her child was all that remained. It was a horrific sight.

I followed Gian to Sicily. He let out an animalistic howl and fell onto our bed. I screamed and pounded on the mattress.

"I can't do this," I said.

Gian's body was shaking. He wrapped me in his arms and held me tightly, sobbing.

How could we complete our task? We were fond of all of them. Even Robert was growing on us.

Gian pulled himself together enough to make espresso. His mind was so off it took him three times to do it right. I moved to the balcony so I wouldn't laugh.

I was on a stool at our breakfast table. The morning sun usually brightened my mood, but even that was failing. Gian set the coffee down and joined me. His foot rested against my leg. It bugged me, but I left it there in case I was giving him comfort.

"Hello?" Nera said, knocking on the doorframe.

We both acknowledged her presence with a nod, barely uttering a word.

She sat on the stool between us. "I'm proud of you. That wasn't easy. You performed your duties with compassion. Janet passed in peace."

"What happens if they're not at peace?" Gian asked.

"That's not something we'll find out. You did well. I want you to take the day off. Troy's time isn't for ten days." She handed over a sheet of paper. "I've booked a room in Venice."

I perked up and looked at Gian with a smile. He had a pained expression.

154

"Quit with the guilt," Nera said. "Her life saved thousands."

"I liked her," he said.

"I told you not to get attached. Hold out your hands. Both of you. Palms up."

A large garment box appeared for each of us.

"These are for your trip," she said.

"Thank you." I peeked inside.

"Bianca calls the design Deconstructed Proper."

I held the dress out in front of me. The bottom was almost conservative, but two wide straps crossed the back, coming over the top straight down the front. Gian was going to love how revealing this would be.

"It's gorgeous," I said, unsure if I'd have the confidence to wear it. But they wouldn't have given it to me if I didn't.

They'd made Gian a new pinstriped suit that looked gangster.

"Sweet threads," he said.

"Be on time for your dinner reservation. It's the best seat in Italy. Don't be sad," she said. "You'll be fine. And if not, drink the night away. You have two hours until check-in." With that, she vanished.

---

We materialized on the bottom floor of the building we were staying in. Our aim was getting better. The stone hallway was more of a dungeon than a hotel entrance. Off to our left was a side room leading to an arched canal opening. If I were the owner, I'd put a coffee table there, but a dirty boat was pulled onto the stones. Off to our right was a courtyard overgrown with weeds. The surroundings offered little hope for our room.

A motherly woman checked us in from a quaint home office. She sent us on our way to the top floor. A shared space was off our room. We were told this is where they serve breakfast. I doubted we'd be up in time.

The room was magnificent despite my doubts. It was hundreds of years old. I loved the red fainting couch in front of the bed. We didn't have a balcony, but each of the three windows faced our canal. I was looking through one when Gian popped his head out the other and waved.

I moved to the bathroom to change. Inside the box was tape to secure my chest. I sucked up my insecurities and slipped the dress over my head. With the straps positioned as well as possible, I taped myself in place. There was a moment of hesitation before I turned to face the full-length mirror. Gian was going to love the dress. It was side boob galore.

When I was training, I always looked manish in clothes. My muscle mass had decreased significantly. The dress made me look so feminine. I turned to get different angles. They all pleased me. Bianca did well. Still, there was a lot of skin.

*Confidence,* I told myself and headed back into the room.

Gian was in his suit, looking fabulous. "Holy fuck!" His mouth gaped. "Let's show the city, my girl."

"It's not too much?"

"Honey, you're too much." He kissed me and took my hand, leading us from the room.

The streets of Venice are a maze. We ended up in a quiet courtyard.

He gestured to a restaurant with outdoor seating.

"Let's get a drink."

The maître d' spoke to Gian in Italian. I had to answer for him. The man switched to English.

"You choose the poison," I said to Gian.

"Rum and Coke," he said without thought.

"Rome and Coke?" The man asked.

"Rum," Gian said.

"It's rhoom," I said. "Like you're revving a motorcycle."

"Ah, rum and Coca-Cola," the man said.

I held up two fingers. He looked at me funny.

"Due."

I wondered what my gesture meant. I'm such a nerd. I'd learned the language, not the passion.

Our drinks arrived with three cubes each. One of the few things I don't like about Europe is how stingy they are with ice. It had become a joke between us.

Gian lifted his glass. "To Janet."

"Janet."

The drink didn't go down well. We sat in silence, watching the people stroll by.

"Did we do right?" I asked.

"All I know is I'm going to drink until it feels like we did."

"I know what we're missing," I said. "Close your eyes." I did the same. "In your mind, forgive yourself. If it doesn't work, keep forgiving until it does."

It took me three times until I was at peace. I opened my eyes and gazed over at Gian. He had a relaxed droop in his eyes.

"I felt it."

I was about to say Grandpa taught me, but he would ask why I needed to forgive myself.

When dinner hour arrived, we had a slight buzz going. Nera wasn't kidding about our table. The waiter brought us to an open-air seat facing the canal. Where the wall should have been, there was a floor-to-ceiling opening like a huge door was missing. A stone footbridge was to our left, and another was in front of us from a connecting canal. People on the closest bridge would stop to take our picture as if we were famous. Gian had fun pretending to be annoyed at being recognized.

We enjoyed a slow meal. The bridge's underside lit up whenever a boat approached, and then it appeared pushing a wave from the bow. With two canals intersecting, there was plenty to watch.

It was eleven when we finished our dinner. We would have ended sooner, but this jackass kept asking when we were going to free up the table. If he wanted it so badly, he should have made a reservation. Gian topped his meal off with grappa. I chose limoncello.

Venice is a stunning city. Everywhere in the streets would make for a perfect picture. We stopped in three bars on the way to St. Mark's Square, each time having them point the way. It was one in the morning when we arrived. A small orchestra of eight was playing next to a restaurant. We chose an outer seat. There were plenty open.

I was lost in the atmosphere. A hundred people tops were in the whole square. A street vendor was demonstrating a wind-up bird. Off in the distance was the echo of a loud clatter followed by laughter. Through it all, the band played a haunting piece. Once they finished, an ensemble across the way played the next song. The small crowd watching our group walked to the other. There was one other minor symphony in the area. After each performance, they would rotate in competition.

The experience was magical, but I had Gian get the bill after one drink. I was getting too sloppy for the public.

"Seattle made a copy of that bell tower." I pointed up at it. "I never thought I'd get to see the original."

"I know the one you're talking about. It's at the train station." He pulled out his camera. "Stand in front of it."

"Are we supposed to take pictures?"

"Get up there."

He waited until I evened my chest to take it.

Back at our table, the waiter set the bill down and thanked us.

Gian glanced at the total. "Jesus Christ!"

I looked around nervously. Italians are intensely religious.

He slid the bill over, and I said it louder. Our drinks were forty-two euros each for a rum and coke. I'm glad we only had one.

"I guess we're paying for the band." He set a hundred on the table.

"Just the seat," I said.

I followed Gian to St. Mark's Basilica. We strolled along the open-air archway, admiring the architecture. He stopped at an enormous wooden door. There was a heavy rope hanging next to it. He pulled with his body. From the size of the rope, I expected loud bells, but it was a funny, muffled "Bling, Bling" sound.

A nun appeared at the window next to us, startling me. "The church is closed. Quit ringing da bell."

My heart sank when Gian yanked the rope again.

Bling. Bling.

A Priest appeared at the window. His face was kind, emanating love. "Eh, quit ringing da bell," he scolded.

Gian looked at him with a smile and pulled the rope.

Bling. Bling.

The man pleaded softly with his gaze. "I'll calla de police."

Gian rang the bell again, and I fell to the floor laughing, with a hand on my chest to hold things in place.

The man had the phone to his ear. "It's a ringing."

Gian helped me up from the ground and we took off, apologizing as we left.

That's the last memory I have from the evening. I guess my muse drove my drunken ass around for a night. Not a bad city for it.

We had a late checkout, but even that was rough. My stomach was a mess, and my pussy destroyed. I hoped it was me with him, but it amused me thinking of Teriko getting fucked. It didn't bother me too much. Gian was as happy as can be.

"You were an animal last night. That was the best sex I've ever had."

"Venice," I said. Now I really hoped it was me.

"I can't believe you let me pee in your mouth." He rubbed his cock against me. "That was so dirty."

*Teriko?* I thought accusingly.

"What are you chuckling at," Gian said.

"Nothing. Just embarrassed."

"Don't be. I loved it."

On the ground floor, Gian left momentarily to bring our bags home. He returned to explore the city.

Venice in the daylight was horrible. There were at least ten thousand people in St. Mark's Square. Shopping on the side streets was fun, but we headed to our quiet square for peace and a late lunch.

A woman approaching caught my eye. It was Nera. She waved.

"Can you take this hangover away?" I pleaded.

"We can't fix what is self-inflicted. You know that. Looks like you had fun."

"Venice," Gian said. "It was one of the best nights of my life. The days, however. What's up with all the people?"

"Cruise ships," was all she needed to say. "When you're up to it, I want you to check in on Troy. Find out what he's running from."

He had nine days. I didn't want to grow close to him.

"I hate to say this here, but I almost had to kill Janet's baby."

"Damn it," Gian said.

"That was you. Breaking the glass brought the parents to the room. CPR almost kept him alive. Be more mindful. It would have destroyed me having to kill a baby."

What did she think it did to us? I rose and hugged her but didn't get much back.

Nera snatched an olive from our tray. "You'll have to wait until Troy's done racing for the day. He's on the Baja. I left clothes in your villa. Ciao."

I looked at Gian. "There's so much going on in my head."

160

"I doubt that," he said dryly and started laughing.

His callousness pissed me off. I was waiting for him to stop so we could talk.

"Hey, whoa," he said. "I was joking."

"That's not cool."

"You know I love you, right?"

"Yeah."

"If there's an opportunity to say something funny, we should be able to."

"At my expense?"

"Not at your expense, with you. I was laughing with you. Don't you and your brother rip each other?"

"That's different."

"Only because we're even closer. I didn't get to laugh a lot while cursed. I want every one I can have. I'll never say anything that makes you look bad in front of people."

"Promise?"

"I promise." He leaned over and kissed me. "Just let me laugh."

His phone rang. It was Dr. Killourie. He put it on speaker. "Hi, Lorie."

"Don't hi Lorie me."

"What?"

"Robert's a raging asshole. I'm not helping that man. How could you recommend him?"

"He said he would try."

"Well, he didn't. Tell him to lose my number," she said and hung up.

"We're going to fail," I said.

"We'll give him a good last day. Did Nera say Troy was racing on the Baja?"

"Yeah. How cool is that?"

"I really like the guy."

"Don't get attached."

Gian sank his head. "I know."

161

We headed to our villa for a good night's sleep. As soon as Gian was out, I drifted away. There's too much going on in his body when he's awake. Lying quietly, I can feel it all.

---

The clothes Nera left looked like desert finds. I put on the tan cargo pants and the heavy boots. I liked the shirt. It was an olive, short-sleeved, breathable cotton. Gian matched, except his shirt was a faded white. Add a brown leather jacket, and he'd look like an Italian Indiana Jones.

"All you need is a whip," I said.

"And a hat." He found one in the bedroom, but it didn't match his look. I threw it on the couch.

"Ready?"

He answered by turning invisible. I followed his trail, but we couldn't materialize right away. There were too many people around Troy. We had to walk a few blocks to the backside of the small Mexican village and made our way along the edge of town to stay out of sight.

"We're nomads," I said.

"Honey, we have a villa and a condo."

"Alto," a man said from behind. We kept walking until I heard the cocking of a gun.

I turned around. A man in his forties had an old Colt aimed at us. He was serious.

"What now?" Gian said.

The man gestured with the gun for us to come to him.

"What do we do?" Gian asked.

"Whatever he says."

His finger on the trigger was worrisome. Getting the gun away would be risky. Should we turn invisible, making the witches have to kill him? I didn't want to draw attention.

"Dinero." The man rubbed his thumb and finger together.

I pulled out my wallet and counted out a few hundred. The man was agitated. He wanted the whole billfold.

"Forget that," I said, putting the money away.

He drew the gun to my head. As he raised it, I popped his wrist higher and jammed the gun out of his hands. He was looking at it confused when Gian nailed him in the balls. I slammed his chin onto my knee and dropped two bills near his head.

"Let's get out of here." I tossed the emptied gun into a thatch of cactus.

We ran into the desert laughing and made a wide arc to Troy's camp.

"Back there, I had a racist thought," Gian said. "I hope it's not coming back."

"What he did has nothing to do with race. Remember when Robert called you a wop? That wasn't so fun to hear."

"In his defense, we are here to kill him. Calling me a wet wipe was funny, though. Anyway, fuck that guy back there."

I laughed.

"You were badass," he said. "The gun was out of his hand so fast."

"We didn't come this far to get killed by a petty thief."

"You shouldn't have given him money."

"Someone has to pay for his broken jaw."

The men sitting by a motorhome directed us to a Baja racer with a light underneath. Two legs stuck out.

"Troy, it's Gian and Linsey."

"Hang on a second. I'm almost done."

We checked out the car while he worked. It was a closed-top two-seater in dark blue. I loved the color. An identical orange racer was parked next to it.

Troy rolled out and shook our hands. "Aren't these awesome?"

"They truly are." I found a rag to wipe the oil from my hands.

"The suspension alone is worth more than any car I've owned."

"Are you racing?" Gian asked.

"Practicing. I missed the Baja 250. Next up is the 500, but I won't be around."

"How are you here?" Gian asked.

"I have mad skills in hydraulics. An offer to pay for a helicopter spotter at the 500 sealed the deal."

"That's not cheating?" I asked.

"Not at all. It's an advantage of the rich. But you still need a good driver. Which again, the richer teams have."

"You're the coolest guy I've ever met." Gian had a total man crush.

"Don't get too attached," Troy said.

Gian and I looked at each other.

"So, what brings you to Mexico?" Troy asked.

"We were told to talk with you," I said. "Find out what you're running from?"

"Running? I'm not running. Just enjoying my last days."

"You don't seem scared," Gian said.

"I don't get scared. When it's my time, I want to go jumping from a plane. We can make it look like an accident. Can you imagine dying that way? What a rush. Will you do that for me?"

"You want us to jump out of a fucking plane?" I said. "No." My heart was pounding just thinking about it.

"Come on. It'll be wild."

"I'm in," Gian said.

"Wait," I said. "We can't stay invisible in a plane. We'll fly right out like what happened in the helicopter."

"I'll rent one. I'm a pilot."

"Of course you are," Gian said.

"It'll just be us," Troy said.

The idea of it all freaked me out. "I'll agree to this if you agree to talk openly. Right now."

"It's a deal," Troy said. My heart sank. I didn't think that would work.

"We'll need cervezas," he said.

We grabbed two beers each and carried folded chairs into the desert.

"You have a gun?" I asked.

Troy lifted his shirt.

"Good. We almost got robbed walking over here."

"You want to stay away from town in these parts."

"Already noted," Gian said.

We crossed a dirt road.

"This is the Baja race track." He climbed up a small embankment and sat overlooking the road. "So, what do you want to know?"

"If you were running, what would it be from?" Gian asked.

"My parents? But I'm not running. We're estranged. It's mutual. They're not good people."

"Have you tried talking to them?" Gian asked.

"Many times. They pretty much suck."

"Have you forgiven them?" I asked. "It helps clear the soul."

"Multiple times. They don't give a shit."

"Forgiveness isn't for them. It's for you," I said. "It frees your mind."

"Believe me. I don't waste time thinking about those fucks."

"Do you have any siblings?" Gian asked.

"I have a brother. This is going to kill him. I'm afraid to talk."

I thought about Max. Losing him would be devastating. "That's what you're running from," I said. "Fly him out."

"What am I supposed to say?"

"Nothing. Just give him love. Give him some time with you. Otherwise, he'll be left with regret."

"Jeff's been trying to get me to Vegas to go on a couple rides. The fool thinks he can scare me."

"Go," I said. "Do Vegas. Do it right."

"Yeah?"

I leaned back and was amazed at how clear the Milky Way was. I'd never seen it so bright.

"It'll be good for you," Gian said. "No one can get into trouble like brothers in Vegas."

"I'll do it. Maybe get a suite. Now I need something from you. What day and time do I die? Mountain Daylight Time."

I pulled myself away from stargazing to check the time zone app on my phone. "One week from tomorrow. At 2:47 p.m."

"Eight days! How long have I been out here? Can you transport me home?"

*No*, Nera said. I shook my head.

"I'll get a ride to the airport in the morning. I have to finish the suspension. Thanks for stopping by," he said and took off toward camp.

I barely touched my beer. My stomach was still churning from Venice.

"You forgot your chairs," I said to Troy and disappeared.

Gian followed me to his condo. I was changing when he arrived.

"Where are we headed?" he asked.

"I thought we'd say hi to Rowanda. See how she's doing. We can't go to New Orleans looking like archeologists."

We'd moved more of my clothes to his place. Gian dressed in black pants and a blood-red button-up shirt. I held up a T-shirt Max found for me at a thrift store. It was white with a skeleton in a top hat. New Orleans was stenciled across the top.

166

"That one's perfect," he said. "Plus, it's super cute."

I changed into a white bra and slipped the T-shirt over my head. One look at my chest stretching out the tee and he was hard.

"Later." I gave his cock a playful tweak. I didn't want to miss Rowanda.

# Chapter 8

We found Rowanda relaxing on the fenced patio of a neighborhood bar. She was eating a plate of crawfish. The spices from the chef's massive cooking pot sent my eyes watering.

I was familiar with New Orleans from the book *A Confederacy of Dunces*. I could picture the protagonist, Ignatius, getting kicked out of a place like this.

Rowanda noticed us. "Hey, where y'at?" Her accent had returned full force.

"Right here," Gian said.

"Have a seat. You have to try these. Best crawfish in Nawlins."

Gian snatched one off the plate. It was whole, head and all.

"Come on." She held out the plate for me.

"How do you eat it?" he asked.

"You pinch the tail and suck the head."

"OK?" I laughed.

She picked one up. "Break the tail off."

We followed her lead.

"With the head, you squeeze, bite and suck all at once."

Whatever I was chewing had a brilliant combination of spices and flavoring. Then came the heat.

"Holy shit, that's good," Gian said. "Hot. Fucking hot."

He downed half of Rowanda's beer. I finished the rest. It didn't help.

"For the tail, you remove the first ring. Then squeeze the tip." She pulled out a sizable chunk of meat with her teeth.

I was scared of the heat but finished mine. The delicacy was worth the pain. I needed more. "Grab some beers. I'll get a plate."

"Yeah, you right," Rowanda said.

The crawfish were addicting. I couldn't stop eating them.

"I'm going to pay for this in the morning," I said.

"Ain't nobody worry about tomorrow but me," Rowanda said.

"Sorry." I could hear Grandpa telling me to quit saying sorry, but this time, I was.

Gian returned with a pitcher of beer to put out the fire. "So, how's your boss?" he asked.

"That bitch is going down. Hang on a sec. I have to wash up. You've got to see her photo."

She returned, wiping her hands on her pants. "They never have enough paper towels on crawfish night." She pulled out her phone. "Lookie here."

The picture was Margaret being escorted from her office in handcuffs. Her face was steeped in rage.

"My officemate took that. To get her to look, she yelled, *Fuck you, Margaret*. Look at that bitch face."

She brought the picture out wider. It was from the newspaper. "Front page. Thank you very much. Seeing Momma was all I needed. You were right about her heart."

"Will she be OK?" I asked.

"I hope so. Just needs to diet and walk. I'm helping with that." She stared into my eyes. "Is there anything I can do to stop this? She needs me."

"I wish." I was struggling with guilt. How could we, her executioners, sit with her all chummy?

"It's strange. I'm so happy and scared all at once. You say I'm supposed to find peace with myself. How am I supposed to do that with this dark clock ticking?"

"Good always balances out the bad," I said. "Maybe you need to do a little balancing."

"You're off to a good start," he said. "You've already made life at your old work better."

"Infinitely," she said.

"Keep it going. Spread the joy," he said.

"I'm not a giver. It wouldn't be real."

"Joy is in the eye of the beholder. Doesn't matter if it's real or not."

Nera placed a thought in my head. "Being good can be simple. You know that homeless man you pass on the way to the market. Learn his name. Say hi when you pass him. Acknowledge his existence. It's the little things that lift people."

"Buy him lunch," Gian said. "Your crime was monetary. The balance may be giving it back."

"I did give it back."

"No, honey, we did," I said. "You didn't even offer to buy our crawfish."

"It's hard," Rowanda said. "No one's ever helped me. Everything I've ever done, I did myself. Momma says I have the devil in me. But you're right. Tonight's on me. What'll you have?"

"We've never been here," he said. "Can we do Bourbon Street?"

"It's only three blocks away," she said. "We're about to pass a good time."

Rowanda's expressions were cracking me up. After washing our hands, Gian and I followed her to the door in the fence.

I whispered to her, "Maybe thank the chef?"

"Ey, Antoine, best batch ever." She handed him a five.

His eyes lit up. "Thanks, miss."

Bourbon Street was packed with a boisterous crowd of drunkards. I was expecting cars, but it was pedestrian only. The old buildings radiated the Louisiana vibe.

"It's packed. Isn't it a Tuesday?" I said.

"You should see it on Fridays," she said. "Let's start with Jazz."

She walked us a few blocks to the Jazz Playhouse. The band was in the middle of a Louis Armstrong tune. Their trumpeter was brilliant. You have to be if you're playing Louie's music.

My father would have been upset with my choice of drink. I sullied my whiskey with Seven Up to cool the fire in my belly.

Rowanda took out a credit card to pay. I grabbed her wrist.

She put it away and paid cash. "I'm not a good person."

"Enough," I said.

"I know what I can do. I'll be right back." She stepped outside.

She had a smile on her face upon returning. "You have the room connecting to mine. Don't worry. I'll pay cash."

"Let's rip this place a new one," Gian said. "Another round."

I wasn't so gung ho.

We made our way through four more bars. I was surprised at how I had rebounded.

The crowd in the street had grown. A heavy disco beat from down the block drew me in. The outdoor dance floor was calling.

"Wanna dance?" I asked.

"You asking someone from New Orleans if they want to dance? It's a way a life."

"Let's go," I said, leading our group through the gate.

I had never been to a dance club with Gian. The only thing close was the end-of-the-curse celebrations. It was freeing not to have the focus on us.

Rowanda was a fun dancer and so creative. Best of all, she was aware of what we were doing and matched our moves or enhanced them.

"See how you're linked with us in your dance," I said. "Would a selfish person do that?"

"If they wanted to fool around," she said.

"That's not a good idea," I said, shooting her down.

"Come on." She reached down and wrapped her hand around Gian's cock. He grew hard.

"Ain't you lucky," she said to me.

My emotions were torn between decking her and thoughts of his cock.

Gian removed her hand.

Rowanda's face soured. "Can we at least be fucking when you kill me?" She straightened his collar. "Take me out feelin' loved."

She was crossing a line.

"You're drunk," he said.

"And you're avoiding my wish."

"We're not genies," I said.

"That's too bad 'cause I want to rub your lamp."

She turned to a group walking in. "Hey, college boy," she said, grabbing a tall blond and bringing him close. "Wanna fuck?"

He looked her up and down. "Why not? I'll meet you back here," he said to his friends.

"How did that work?" I said to Gian.

"How could it not?"

"Follow me," Rowanda said to us. "I'll show you your room."

"I'm not paying for this, am I?" the boy said.

"What the fuck? I'm not a whore. Do us a favor and stop talking."

"Whatever."

Rowanda led us back the way we came. We turned at the same road as the crawfish bar. She stopped at a dark metal wall and unlocked a hidden door to her room. It had an old-school elegance to it. I wasn't expecting the charm. But then I noticed all the dildos lined up by size on the headboard.

"Why aren't you staying with your mom?" I asked.

"I love the woman, but she drives me crazy."

"It's been like two days," Gian said.

"I know," Rowanda said and laughed.

"I'll do her too," the guy said, "but the dude has to leave."

"Don't flatter yourself," I said.

We searched around for our key but couldn't find it. Gian tried the connecting door and it opened. The key was on our coffee table.

Rowanda pulled the boy close. "Saddle up, cowboy. We're doing it in the ass tonight."

He had a massive grin on his face.

"Have fun," I said and locked the deadbolt behind us.

Our room was a suite with a purple velvet couch in the sitting area. The color made me think of Prince and his muse. I hoped Sty Ling was doing better. Gian took a peek outside.

"This place kicks ass. There's a pool in the courtyard." He began undressing and was soon naked. "Let's go swimming."

"No way."

"Come on. No one's out there."

I grabbed one of the robes from the bathroom. "At least put this on."

He held his arms up like a child, and I slipped them inside the robe.

"It's not going to be any fun without you."

"Fine."

I drunkenly undressed and he helped me with my robe. We ran outside giggling. He ditched his robe and nonchalantly dropped into the pool.

After surfacing, he stared, waiting for me. I tried being as cool as him, but public nudity is far outside my comfort. I ended up speed-walking to the pool and tripped into it.

He brought me into his arms. "Such grace."

I laughed with him. He was right. Laughing with each other was freeing.

"I love you," I said.

"Hop on."

I held onto his back and he swam us to a dark corner. The Touch was odd in the water as we were both floating. It felt more out of body than usual.

I wrapped my leg against his and rubbed his ankle. This simple act had his juices flowing. We let go of the edge and slipped underwater. He traced my thighs, running his hands up and down my body. I reached for a nipple and was delighted at its connection to his cock. The slightest touch produced a tremor below.

I surfaced, continuing to play with his nipples. He reached down and stroked mine as lightly as I was. The slowness lit up all my senses.

Gian backed me up against the pool wall and held us up with a firm grip on the edge. He slipped inside me, going from tepid water to slick warmth. Unfortunately, with each thrust, I lost more lubricant to the pool. It was a slow go, which increased our want.

"What the hell are you doing," a woman shrieked. Our backs tightened at the same time.

The boy she was lifting was frantically pulling up his sweatpants to hide his shame.

"Where the fuck did boner boy come from?" Gian said.

"How dare you," the woman screamed at us.

I shrank down.

"We didn't know he was there," Gian said. "I swear."

175

Lights were coming on in a few of the rooms. I ducked under the water and wanted to vanish. I could hear Gian laughing nervously from up above. I surfaced away from him.

We waited in the shadows for the place to calm down. Eventually, the lights went off, but I was sure there was peeping.

A woman in a hotel uniform came out. We were so busted.

She found my bathrobe and opened it wide by the ladder. "Quickly, girl."

I slipped out as gracefully as my drunk ass allowed.

"Hang on a second." I raced to the room. Gian was exiting the pool naked when I returned.

I slipped a sizeable tip into the woman's hand.

"Thanks, darling," she said. "I'd recommend staying in your room. Momma looked pissed."

"We didn't even know that little shit was there."

"It's no worry."

I couldn't get to the room fast enough. Gian plopped on the sofa with his arms wide, motioning me over. He was unfazed by the experience. His confidence fed my lust. I sat on his cock and rode him, thrusting forcefully. He held my waist, keeping me almost weightless. We smelled of chlorine, but his alluring scent soon prevailed.

Without warning, he flipped me onto my back. The thrill brought a shocked laugh from me. With one leg on the floor for stability, he plowed into me. I screamed out in ecstasy. He laughed and put a hushed finger to my lips. I bit it playfully.

He snatched my neck, holding me tightly at bay. The move was frighteningly fast and terrifying.

"What was that?" he said with pained guilt.

My heart was racing. Was there a little monster left inside? No wonder he didn't like it too rough.

"It's OK," I said and kissed his forehead.

"It's not OK."

176

I thrust my hip toward him to get him moving. He slid my leg down and fucked me missionary. It took a while for him to calm down. Eventually, his focus was back on me.

I slid him out and rolled onto my knees. He lowered and started tonguing my ass. I gasped in shock as he circled my hole. I was cleansed from the pool, but it was still miles out of my comfort zone. He was enjoying himself, so I relaxed. The slick skin felt soft against his tongue. My thoughts drifted to Joan as he rimmed me. She was going to laugh when she heard I was thinking about her during this.

Gian rose to his feet and slid his cock along my crack. I reached between my legs and positioned it on my cooch. He laughed and slid inside.

A clump of my hair in each of his hands momentarily became reins. I moaned and bucked wildly. We went at it so hard that we fell off the couch.

He picked me up and bent me over the sofa. His hands were firmly over mine, holding me in place. I was a prisoner of his lust. The power in his grip resonated. His thrust flowed rhythmically through his body.

My vision narrowed as the world blackened. I leaned my head back as pulses raced through me, exploding outward. I lost consciousness and woke up on the floor. He stirred next to me.

"I wish that wouldn't happen," he said.

"The Touch can be touchy." It was so stupid he fake laughed.

"Let's get in bed," he said, taking my hand.

Once there, I tried to keep things going with a handy.

"I'm too drunk to come."

I liked the challenge and took him in my mouth. It wasn't working, so I stroked the slickness wildly.

"Holy crap," he said.

I stroked harder, relentlessly. I slicked him back up and worked him some more. He clawed at the bed, the sheet crumpling in his grip.

His orgasm was a fireworks show shooting all over his belly. I raised my hand high and smacked the pool on his stomach. His juices splashed everywhere. I had the worst case of the giggles, which had Gian going.

He cleaned up with a towel the best he could, and we snuggled off to sleep.

I woke up sweating profusely and came within seconds of missing the toilet. The spices from the night before were racing through me like lava. Gian knocked lightly. Aside from a slight hangover, his stomach was fine. How is that possible?

"Can you go for a walk?" I pleaded.

"Head back to the villa. I'll meet you when you're feeling better."

"I'm not leaving you alone with that woman. You go."

"I just thought you'd be more comfortable at home. I'm not going to fuck Rowanda. Why would you even think that?"

"You may have to." I had softened to the idea of her going out that way. Who was I to deny her wish?

"I'm not fucking her to death."

"You may have to," I said firmer. "It's what she wants. Oh, God." I was trying my hardest to hold things in.

"I'll see you back home." I felt him slip out the door to the street. His midsection was convulsing. He was laughing at me.

I cried from embarrassment and pain, but he had me laughing. At least I could suffer alone.

Hours later, I was motionless in the hotel bed, waiting for my body to stop betraying me. An incoming text vibrated. It was a picture of Gian and a bronze statue of an odd-looking man in a hunter's cap.

It's Ignatius from A
Confederacy of Dunces.

He had his arm around my favorite literary character of all time.

That is the coolest.

It's three blocks away. Meet
me here. We can have
breakfast. I found the best
café.

I wish. I'm going to head to
Sicily. I'm dying.

Poor baby. Do you mind if I
eat first?

Not at all. See you in a bit.

I knocked on the connecting door to Rowanda's. There was no answer. I unlocked the deadbolt and placed the key on her table. Her room had a foul stench. I turned invisible and aimed for the villa's bathroom, throwing up on arrival.

Gian showed up a few hours later with a to-go order of biscuits and gravy.

"I hope you can eat these. They're so good."

I followed him to the balcony, where he set a table for me.

"I think I can. I'm feeling a little better. The crawfish."

"I wish we'd been there sooner. Rowanda said Antoine added more spices to the pot once the first batch was done. She called our batch atomic."

"When did she tell you this?"

"Jesus, I wasn't fucking her."

"I know that. I was just asking."

"I met her at Mother's."

"Her mother's?"

"No, the restaurant. Mother's is supposed to be the best breakfast in town. Seeing her there confirmed it."

I took a bite. "This is delicious."

"I know, right."

"How do they make the gravy so flavorful?"

"No idea. Yours is still the best."

"You're sweet, but I know when I'm beaten."

Even as good as it was, I could only eat half. I pushed the rest away, satisfied.

I spaced out on our view. I loved the hillside across the way but wished we could see the Mediterranean.

He smirked. "Did you see all of Rowanda's dildos?"

"Why does she need so many?"

"No idea," he laughed.

It really bothered me how jealous I had been of Rowanda. I thought about his past loves. Having sex with different people is what kept him alive. Still, I didn't want him cheating on me. I had to get ahead of this. "Gian, if you need to, I'll allow you to sleep with one person a year."

"Where is this coming from? You don't need to do that."

"Your sex life went from multiple women to one. You had multiple women to live. I'm OK with this as long as you let me know before. I don't need to be there. I just need to know it's happening."

He smiled, pulling back a grin. "Let's hold onto this idea. I want you to know I don't need it right now. And no, you're not OK with this."

No, I wasn't. I was glad he turned me down. What the hell was I thinking?

"So, who should we visit today?" he asked.

"Not Robert," I said. "I don't have the stomach for him. Let's say hi to Don. Maybe catch him at sunset. I want to see the green flash."

"I like that idea. Mind if I take a nap?"

"You're looking at my day."

He kissed me and headed to the bedroom. I went inside to find a new book.

---

Kauai is twelve hours behind. We set the alarm to wake us in time for the sunset. It came too soon.

"Don's heading to our favorite beach," I said. "What's the name of it?"

Gian pulled up a map. "Palihale. Look at how big it is. This is where we go." He pointed to an area by the park.

"It's the coolest beach I've seen."

"We haven't been to the ones in Sicily."

"I know. What's up with that?" I asked.

"We've been kind of busy."

"You can never be too busy for the beach. Let's make a day of it sometime?"

"It's a date," he said and kissed me.

"The sunset is in forty minutes. Get dressed. I want to grab snacks."

I wish I thought of food earlier. I would have made an antipasto dish. We had to settle for a deli in Hawaii. I used Aunt Pia's picnic basket. I felt bad for not returning it. We may as well use it.

Don looked over casually as we approached.

"Are you high?" I asked.

"Not at all. Just content. Pull up a seat." He had two extra chairs. "I had a feeling you'd show up."

"We brought food," I said.

"Thanks. If I stopped, I would have missed God's show."

The sun was low on the horizon, sending a golden trail across the water. We had just made it. I set the picnic up and handed him and Gian a plate. My boyfriend's

181

contribution was beer. I stuck with water. I wasn't drinking for a while.

Gian's face glowed from the sun. He looked like an adorable beach bum with his messy hair and two-day stubble.

"This may not be a good one," Don said. "The sky is unusually cloudless."

"Do you think we'll see the green flash?" I asked.

He smiled. "I do."

"Then it will be a good one."

We didn't talk a lot. There was no mention of charity. Or the two weeks he had left. We sat enjoying our meal, basking in the gloriousness that was Palihale.

"It's weird," I said. "We were in Monday, and now we're back to Sunday."

"You're time travelers," Don said.

Gian took my hand as the last of the sun sank behind the sea. The bright orange sliver dipped below the horizon, producing a neon green flash. It struck me deeply, almost spiritually—more than I expected.

"Now you'll never go wrong in your love," Don said.

I had a wide grin. Gian kissed my silly face.

"So when is your wedding?" Don asked.

Gian and I looked at each other. We hadn't discussed the wedding.

"We haven't even begun to plan," I said.

"It's selfish to think of ourselves during this time."

Don shrugged. "Life goes on."

"Life can wait," I said. "Right now, we're here for you." I took Don's hand.

He brought the back of mine to his lips and gave me a soft kiss. "Mahalo."

The wind was picking up. I gathered our food before the sand started pelting us.

"Would you mind driving back with me? It's a long way. I'll buy shave ice. The best isn't far."

"That sounds nice," Gian said.

The five miles of dirt road leading to the main highway was fun. Don was a crazy man speeding along, only slowing for the giant dirt speed bumps.

He said it was usually sunny on this side of the island, which is why the humidity was better. The tradeoff was an arid climate.

We'd made it to Waimea but were disappointed to find Jo Jo's closed. They'd left at six. I thought Don had said shaved ice wrong, forgetting the d at the end, but the sign said shave ice.

"I guess they wanted to see the sunset, too."

"We'll have to come back," Gian said.

It was a couple-hour drive back to his place. There's one main road on the island, so traffic gets heavy. We picked up a supreme pizza by his place. I'd never experienced everyone in a group choosing the same type. We were synced.

"I bet the argument about pineapple on pizza is nonexistent in Hawaii," Gian said.

Don shook his head in frustration. "When did society get to the point where we shun people for the food they like?"

"That's a good question," I said.

There was a beat-up truck in his driveway.

I wasn't in the mood for confrontation. "Now what?"

"You stay here," Gian said to Don.

"Do you have a gun?" I asked him.

"Why would we need a gun?" he asked.

I disappeared and moved to the front of the house, returning soon after with Gian.

"It's maintenance," I said.

Don was chill. He grabbed the pizza box casually. "Come on."

The man in the back apologized profusely. "Sorry to disturb you. A sprinkler busted. It was sending off alarms. I'm almost done."

"No worries," Don said, handing him a beer. "Take a slice on your way out."

"Mahalo."

It was almost ten, and the humidity was still brutal. We ate inside, basking in the coolness of the air conditioner.

"So, how goes the giving?" I asked.

"It's been amazing. But I'm almost out of money. I'm trying to unload my house but it's not selling. I can't even cancel this place early. I'm stuck."

"Maybe not," Gian said.

I followed him to our bedroom, wondering what he was up to.

"What would you think of giving Don some of our gold?"

I didn't have to think about it. "Yes. Do it."

Gian laughed. "That was quick."

"Give him the big one."

"I don't think Hawaii is known for gold. We'll have to stick to smaller pieces. Besides, that one's our future."

I meant the baseball-sized one, not the giant nugget, but didn't correct him.

He looked up gold in Hawaii. "Yeah, it's only been found in a few streams. I'll be back." I felt him heading to his condo.

"Would you like another beer?" I asked Don.

"Sure, can I get you anything?"

"I'm off liquor for a while. New Orleans ruined me."

He laughed. "I bet. How was it?"

"Have you been to Vegas?"

"Sure. There's no casinos on the Islands."

"New Orleans is like Vegas but real, if that makes sense."

I felt Gian heading to our stash in Alaska and smiled.

"What?" Don asked.

"Nothing. Just wait. I'm having a gummy if there are any left."

"Can I have a little?" Don asked.

"You're free to them anytime."

"I didn't want to bogart your stash."

I was surprised by his hip lingo.

"I wasn't always so stuffy."

"I don't think you're stuffy at all." I headed to my room for a couple edibles.

I found a knife in the kitchen and quartered the gummy. Don took half. A year ago, I never would have thought I'd be getting high on my own. I blamed it on the stress.

"Gian's back."

He walked in with a leather satchel like you'd have for college. I halved another gummy and offered him a piece. He smiled and had me pop it in his mouth.

"We should get more," I said, "of this kind. I like it."

"Take a picture. We'll pick it up the next time we're in Seattle." He patted his bag. "Should I wait until our high kicks in?"

"Show him," I said.

He unbuckled the clasps. "We want you to have this, Don. It's not stolen. We gathered it in the Alaskan wilderness."

"You remember how we found that gold ring?"

"Get a load of this," Gian said, emptying the gold onto the chopping block in the kitchen. The pile was significant. And these were just the small pieces.

"Holy moly!" Don said. "Is this real?"

"Pick one up."

He cried, rolling a nugget in his hand. "I can do so much with this."

"Why does he have to go?" I bawled.

"Nera's here," Gian said.

She was waiting in our room with tears in her eyes.

"What's up?" I whispered.

185

"You guys are so sweet. I needed to hug you."

She brought us in, hanging on tightly.

"Do you want a drink?" I asked. "Don makes a mean piña colada."

"I can't be seen. Stay good." With that, she vanished.

Don had a bathroom scale out. He was weighing himself holding the sack.

"Nine point two pounds. How much is this worth? A million?"

"Surprisingly not," Gian said. "You're looking at maybe a hundred eighty."

"Thousand?"

"Yeah. Less with the processing fee."

"I can make that work," Don said.

"We can get more if you want."

"No, this is fine. It's plenty. Let's bring chairs to my beach. This calls for a celebration." He found a bottle of Prosecco in the fridge.

"Oh, Christ," I said. "Twist my arm."

---

The only place to sell raw gold in Hawaii was Honolulu. For the price of his last-minute ticket, Don could have chartered a private plane.

Gian and I brought the gold with us. TSA would have had a field day with that bounty.

We sat in a coffee shop waiting for Don. I was playing on my phone. "You were right about Janet's rapist. His charges are manslaughter now. Bail revoked." I hadn't thought of Janet all day. The guilt smothered my senses.

Gian read through the article. When he handed the phone back, it was on her obituary. That was too real. Too final. I closed the page.

Don waved from the door. He approached the counter and ordered drip coffee. I expected nothing less.

When he joined us, I slid the bag over. Don set it on his lap, holding it protectively with one hand like a baby.

"Thanks for doing all this. It means the world."

"No mahalo?" I said.

"Of course. Mahalo. I'm nervous. What if they ask where it came from?"

"Laugh and say, wouldn't you like to know," Gian said.

"What if they rob me?"

"A place like that won't," I said. "They should have a security officer or two on site. You'll be fine. We'll walk you there."

Don breathed in deeply. "OK, let's go before I lose my nerve."

He was shaking when we reached the block.

"Don't let the gold out of your site," Gian said.

We let him slip ahead and watched from a distance. As we passed the entrance, we saw him talking to security. We grabbed a cab to Waikiki Beach.

Gian was ready to leave after walking a block. We'd been spoiled with Kauai.

"Too many people here. Let's explore Sicily," he said.

We headed home, but it was still nighttime. The sun wouldn't be rising for another hour.

"Can we go here?" I asked, pointing to Cafalù in my travel guide. It was a beach town northwest of ours. I wanted to see the old houses lining the waterfront.

"Of course."

There were plenty of places to materialize. I couldn't see anyone awake.

Gian was delayed in joining me. "Sorry, I didn't know you meant now."

"It's all good. You're going to love this."

I led him to the end of a stone pier. The ancient buildings along the waterfront were lit by moonlight. The sight was more beautiful than expected — almost spiritual.

"This place is gorgeous," Gian said.

I leaned my head on his shoulder and took in the view. I had a selfish thought, wishing the Don had given us a villa here. Our town was so isolated.

"Let's walk on the beach," Gian said, leading me to the sand at the base of the pier. It wasn't as soft as in Hawaii, but that didn't make it any less special.

"I hate to cut this short. Do you mind if I practice my game? We can come back during the day." Talking about the tournament sent his heart racing.

"I don't mind at all. Can I be there for you?"

"If I make it far enough."

"You will."

We headed into the city to find a place to disappear.

"I'm kind of freaking out," Gian said back at our place. "I couldn't join any tournaments with the curse."

"You'll be fine."

"I sure hope so. It's a €10,000 entrance fee."

Now my nerves were racing. "You'll be fine," I said again, more to myself.

"You know I can feel your heart."

"I just don't think we should use the witch's money like that."

"It's mine. I've been taking out fifteen hundred a day from the ATM.

I had wondered why he kept going to the same spot. That made me feel better. I kissed him on the cheek. "Will it bother you if I go work out? Maybe fight a little?"

"Not at all. I bought a cable to bring the laptop into the bathroom. It was the brown package that came with Friday's mail."

"It's on top of the microwave."

"Thanks," he said and kissed me. "The metal's blocking the wifi."

We needed to fix that. I liked having my phone in the bathroom.

188

I dialed Joan. "Hey, girlfriend. I need to get back into working out. Want to join me?"

"Sure, I'd like that."

"Meet me in the garage."

I gave her ten minutes, then stepped through to their guest room. A clear signal from a video camera flowed from the wall. The rest of the house was clear. I materialized in the stairway.

I found the camera built into the new frame on my favorite painting. I ripped the electronics from the back and crumpled it in my hand. The rage I felt was overwhelming.

I texted Gian. "Isolate yourself in the bathroom. I need to fight."

I changed into my sparring clothes and headed to the garage.

Both Max and Joan were in there.

"Hey, sis," Max said.

"Don't hey sis me. What the fuck?" I said, throwing the camera at his feet.

"How did you find that?"

"Wrong answer! Why are you spying on us?"

"I wanted to see how you're getting here."

"Do you want to die? The witches will have to kill you if you see that. Gear up." I threw him a set of gloves.

"Hey, come on."

I reached for my own. "Fuck you."

My anger was out of control. I walked to a corner of the cage and closed my eyes. My coach, TJ, would have told me, don't let your rage overtake you. Use it. I wasn't sure that would be possible.

"You ready," Max said and touched my shoulder.

I elbowed him in the chin, striking his headgear. It dazed him. I came in strong with four hits to his head.

"Linsey? I wasn't ready."

I heard Joan laughing off to the side.

I stepped back and allowed him to get his stance back.

He dodged my hit and tackled me around the waist. I was spun around and held tight from behind.

"Calm down."

"I'm the king of calm," I said.

He let me go and we rose to our feet.

"I shouldn't have spied on you." He dropped his arms to his side. "Hit me."

I swung hard to the side of his head. He took it but was rattled.

"Hit me!"

I swung harder.

"Hit me!" he screamed.

I rushed, picked him up, and slammed him onto his back. I was on top of him, fist raised.

"Don't," Joan screamed.

I slammed my fist onto the mat, close to his head. I struck a couple more times and lost control of my tears.

"This isn't a game," I said through a warbled cry. "They have us killing people. Good people."

"Why do you still get to kill people?" Max said.

"Fuck you!" I couldn't stop my tears. I decked him hard in the chin.

Joan offered a hand and helped me to my feet. She hung onto me.

"You should go," she said to Max.

He slunk from the garage. At the door, he looked back. "I didn't mean anything. I guess I'm jealous."

"I had to kill a pregnant woman. When she died, I watched as the energy faded from her baby. There's nothing fun about what we're doing."

"Can I help? How do we get you out of this?"

"Just be there for me. It's not a lot to ask. We only have fifteen more days."

"I'm always here," he said and left.

"Hey," I called out.

He popped his head back in.

"I got to use Dad's trick for getting a gun away from someone. It worked."

"That's awesome."

"The guy was a bit of an idiot. It may have helped."

"No, that was all you. You practiced and practiced. It's your drive that kept us alive."

"The role of a Huntress weighed heavy."

"You do it well."

"Did it," I corrected.

He smiled and closed the door behind him.

"So you're not going after the Dread?"

"Joan, you can't ask questions."

"I'm sorry."

"And no, we're not going after them. They're not our enemy. Gian's family are some of the nicest people I've met. Besides, the curse is gone. They're not Dread anymore."

"I didn't mean anything by that. Grab a jump rope," she said. "When's the last time you worked out?"

"I do pushups and sit-ups every day. Other than that, I haven't exercised since leaving for Europe."

"Let's not go too heavy then."

"Thanks. I want to stay toned. I'm liking my figure."

Joan looked down at her muscles. "I like this." She kissed her bicep.

I laughed. Thankfully, she joined in.

"Did Max tell you we started a business?"

"No, what? Flipping houses?"

"PI work. Your Dad and Grandpa are helping. We want to flip houses but don't have the capital."

"Gian and I can help with money when all this is done."

"Serious?"

"Sure, it would be no problem."

"That's good. PI work sucks. It's mostly weirdos looking for something weirder. I don't even want to talk about our last client. Such a freak. It's not like on TV."

"You've got to tell me."

"You don't want to know. Trust me."

I swung the jump rope over my head and hopped in time. I forgot how much work this simple exercise was.

Max joined us for a run through the park. When I returned to Sicily, Gian was still in the bathroom. Opera was blasting in the room, and he was singing along. I sat on the floor listening. The music seeped into my soul. I needed to take him to an Italian Opera.

He didn't sing with the next song. I startled him when I opened the door. My man was in the tub relaxing on cushions from the front room couch.

"Hey, sunshine." He rose to kiss me.

"Sorry about being short on my text. My brother had a video camera in my bedroom to catch me materializing."

"What the fuck?"

"He's jealous. I was so freakin pissed. Max kind of let me beat the crap out of him."

"What the hell is he jealous of? The shit we're doing is horrible."

I couldn't tell him he missed killing. "Brothers."

"Yeah."

"Hey, would you mind if I invite people to your tournament?"

"Hang on a second. I need to bet. Never mind. I fold. What if I don't make it through?"

"Then we have a good time at the beach."

"Who do you want to invite?"

"Your aunt and uncle. Maybe the witches we slept with. It would be fun to see them again."

"It sure would," Gian said a little too eagerly.

"Have you eaten?" I asked, ignoring his comment.

"Just a snack."

"Keep playing. I'll make that spicy sausage dish you like with the fusilli noodles."

"Let's skip the pepper flakes. The sausage is hot enough."

192

I was still traumatized from the atomic crawfish. Not only was I skipping the pepper flakes, I had the butcher mix in regular sausage with the spicy.

Gian followed me to the kitchen and sat at the counter to watch me cook. "Dante's in this game."

I walked in front of the computer and found his brother in the upper right corner. I waved. He gave me a quick flick of his wrist and returned to his cards. He was focused.

"Are you up a hundred and eighty thousand?" I asked excitedly.

"It's not real money," Gian said.

"Still."

"Dante's up a half a million."

"Quit gabbing," Dante said.

Gian unmuted. "Sorry."

I noticed two of the tabs in his browser were porn. Did he put up the metal sheeting so I couldn't feel him masturbating? There wasn't much I could say. I'd much rather he did that than sleep with other women. What made me happy was the program he used to write music was also open.

# Chapter 9

Exercising with Joan left me exhausted. I fell into a deep slumber and was out all night. When I awoke, Gian was cuddled up with me.

"Hey, sweetheart," he said.

I stretched my arms wide. "Morning."

"Don't get too comfortable. Nera wants us to visit Robert."

"Well, shit."

"I know."

"When?"

"Soon. Do you need a shower?"

"Just a quickie. To wake me up."

"Speaking of quickies, can you jerk me off? I had the dirtiest dream."

"Of course."

He flipped onto his back and threw the sheets off him. There was lube in his dresser for when I overcame my fear of anal. I might as well use it for something. It was cold, dripping onto his cock. I soon warmed it up. The slickness allowed me to find a smooth rhythm. I was too eager. It took only a couple of minutes before he came in a flood. Must have been a hell of a dream. I hoped it was about me.

The corners of his lips curled mischievously. "How about putting it in your coffee."

Boys are so nasty. "Really?"

He nodded with a wicked smile.

"For you," I said, talking myself into it.

I returned from the kitchen with a cup and spoon. He flinched when the cold metal touched his stomach. Gathering his goodness was odd yet fun.

"Cappuccino," I said, handing him the cup and heading to the bathroom.

My coffee was on the bathroom counter when I stepped out of the shower. The only difference in taste was a slight metallic twinge. Knowing he was in it brightened my morning.

I applied the bare minimum of makeup, enough to bring life to my eyes. The weather report for Dunster was sunny and fifty-eight with a slight breeze. I wore the dress I chose for our visit with Sir Donald. Thoughts of that afternoon left me daydreaming.

"Oh, yeah," Gian said when I rounded the corner. He was making scrambled eggs and bacon. The aroma reminded me of Sundays with Grandpa.

"I'll change after we eat," he said.

"Your sweater's fine."

"It was until you walked in."

"You make a good cup of coffee," I said.

He giggled. "That's so dirty."

"It's not bad. Try some."

I was kidding, but he took a sip. He had a curious look on his face. "I can't taste it, but I can tell it's there."

I shook my head.

"What's mine is yours... Is mine? I forget the expression."

"Just cook the breakfast."

We found Robert in his backyard. I wasn't expecting such an exquisite garden. Close to the cottage was a stone patio with a metal table and two chairs. A wide path led to a gate at the edge of the woods. Weeping trees on both sides formed an enchanting tunnel with their bunches of yellow flowers. The plants and bushes looked randomly placed, but they had a purpose. The pattern in the giant purple bulbs gave it away. Robert was on his knees weeding. He had an unfamiliar calm about him. There was even a smile.

"Robert?" I asked.

He laughed. "Working with me hands has a calming effect. It's how I've kept my job."

I'd been wondering about that. He seemed unemployable. Why he was still working was beyond me.

"Your yard is gorgeous," I said.

He stood up and looked around proudly.

"What are these trees?" I asked.

"Laburnum. Golden rain. In a few weeks, they live up to the name. I guess I won't have to clean up this year."

"So, Dr. Killourie called," Gian said.

Why was he bringing that up now? There goes the peace.

Robert laughed.

"You said you would try."

"I did. She was getting in me head."

"She's a psychologist. That's her job. She would have helped you. I've seen her. She's the best. Linsey even went to her."

"I can't recommend her more."

"I'll give it another shot," he said.

"There's no way. I don't know what you said to her."

"I was brutal," he said, laughing. "She's a daft cow. I'm fine."

"You're not fine. There's something seriously wrong with you," Gian said.

Quit prodding the bull.

"They say I'm not batting with a full wicket."

The phrase made me giggle. Gian's demeanor changed from annoyance to laughter.

"I didn't mean to insult her," Robert said. "She was all right."

Gian gestured with both hands at him. "That, right there. Why can't you be like that?"

"It was forced. The insults came naturally."

"When I was a shy teenager, my grandfather taught me to fake confidence until I wasn't faking anymore," I said. "Maybe you could fake compliments."

Robert went back to tilling his garden. "I can't stop me mouth. I can tell what I say is wrong as it's coming out. But I can't stop it."

"Then just apologize after."

"People don't stick around long enough."

"How are we supposed to ensure you're at peace when you go?" Gian said.

"It's not today, is it?"

"No, you have a few weeks."

"Good. There's something I need help with. It may bring me peace. Can ye get my friend Jake to talk with me? My lawyer needs his National Insurance Number. I'm giving my cottage to him."

"That right there could get you to the promised land," Gian said.

"Wasn't trying," Robert said. "Jake's a good man. He doesn't deserve me, but he could sure use the house."

"What's his address?"

Robert entered it into Gian's phone. "He'll probably be at Three Lions watching the match."

"Why don't you take a shower? We'll see if Jake will talk with you."

"I'll throw on a clean shirt," he said.

"You're a little ripe," I said.

"Fine, I'll meet you in town." He looked up earnestly. "When it's time, can you have tea with me and send me off in my garden?"

"Of course," I said.

Once we were out of earshot, I whispered to Gian, "How is the craziest guy's wish the sanest?"

"Don't try to figure out that man."

Charlie looked up as we walked into his bar. "No! No more. Robert came back. Not again!"

"Damn it," I said. "He said he wouldn't."

"He says a lot of things."

"He's dying," Gian said.

"Shut up. I'm not barmy."

Gian laughed. "Barmy?"

I liked the dying statement in Gian's plea for sympathy. I added to it. "It's a brain tumor. He has weeks to live."

Charlie huffed loudly, then grunted. "Fine. He can come in. But only if you're with him. Keep that wanker under control."

"Will do. Is there a Jake Willington here?"

"He's the bloke in the sweater."

I looked around. Everyone was in a sweater.

"Corner table. Next to the Juke."

I set a ten-pound note on the bar. "Whatever he's having."

Charlie poured a tall stout.

Jake was a rough-looking man with unkempt hair. I figured the length was more because he didn't like going to the barber than for fashion.

He barely looked at us. "I've seen you with Robert. Leave me alone."

I set the pint in front of him. "He's dying, Jake."

"Good."

"Robert wants to leave you his house," Gian said.

"Bollocks."

"He does."

"Why?"

"He said you used to be mates. He'll be gone within the month. Probably sooner."

*Show him the MRI in your photos,* Nera said. *There's a tumor on the top left side.*

What was she talking about? I opened my photos to humor her. The last photo was a scan. How did she get that on there so fast?

I showed Jake. "He has a tumor in his brain."

199

He handed the phone back. "Is that why he's such an arse?"

"That's from his fall," I said. "This is something different. Maybe God's putting him out of his misery."

"I think he's putting the town out of our misery."

I laughed.

"Fine. Go get the git."

I looked up "git" outside the bar. It meant idiot. I showed Gian and he laughed.

We waited for Robert at an outdoor table.

Charlie brought us two pints of Guinness. It was usually night when we were here. The town was as adorable in the daylight. It was like being in a pleasant chapter of a Dicken's fable.

Robert joined us. "You'll have to bring him out. I can't go in there anymore."

"Charlie says you're fine if you're with us," Gian said.

"Just with us. Don't come in here alone anymore."

Gian stopped him at the door. "We told him you have a brain tumor."

I was worried he wouldn't go along with the ruse. Robert backed away.

"How do you know about that?"

It felt like my stomach dropped to my feet. "Wait, you do have cancer?" Why the hell hadn't Nera told us? It would have lessened the guilt. Or had she told us? My guess of a brain tumor was a little specific. I was so confused.

"Me headaches sent me to the doctor," Robert said. "I guess I was doomed no matter what."

I pulled up the MRI and zoomed in on the patient's name. It was his actual MRI. *Come on, Nera.*

"You ready? Jake agreed to talk with you."

"Bloody hell. Really?"

"You be nice," I said.

He nodded. "I will."

200

Jake waved to Robert and we walked over. Gian and I snagged the table next to them.

Robert sat down and tried to speak but couldn't. He started crying. "I am so sorry, Jake."

Jake's angry façade withered. He put his arm around his old friend and Robert cried harder.

I went up to the bar to talk with Charlie. "Would it be OK if we left them to it? I think he's in good hands."

"Yeah. That's fine. I didn't think Jake would talk with him. He's as stubborn as they come."

I walked back to Robert. "We're heading out. You're cool to stay."

He turned to Charlie, who nodded.

I patted Robert on the shoulder. "Take care."

Outside, I asked if Gian had a picture of the scotch he took from Sir Donald.

"Shit. Yeah. I forgot about that."

We headed to Scotland for a replacement. It took a few hours to find the correct year. A shop in Aberdeen had it. The bottle was shockingly expensive. We had to head back to Sicily for more money.

Gian's heart was racing. I thought it was from the purchase, but he was looking at the time.

"We can head back after we return the bottle," I said.

"Thanks. There's a qualifying round tonight. I'm getting a little antsy."

"What? Why didn't you tell me?"

"I thought I had. Must be nerves."

"Should I get us a room by the casino in case people want to join us?"

"We won't need one. It's a straight shot from our place."

Nothing was a straight shot from our place. Either direction was winding mountain roads.

A safe place to vanish was behind the whisky shop. "Let's show up by the guard house," I said. "I want to walk the road to the castle."

"We can't materialize."

"It will still be nice."

"Lead me through," he said. "I want to hold your hand."

We arrived on the bridge. I could see the energy of two men inside the guard house. I wanted to say hi to Gregory so badly.

The canopy of beech trees lining the entrance had energy like they were alive. Their auras swayed into the wind with a mist.

What was emanating from the castle was menacing, dark blue, and cold. Gian led me through the main door and down a set of steps.

We materialized in an impressive stone wine cellar. Full shelves lined the walls, and a tasting table was in the center. He placed the bottle in an empty slot.

"How are there no ghosts here?" I asked

"Right? I did see one in the forest just off the road. Looked like a soldier."

I missed that. I was kind of glad.

"Before we head home, let's have a look at your land."

"We can see it from the hills of Lochiel," I said and headed there.

Gian materialized in front of me. The ground under him gave way and he tumbled off the cliff. I reached out for him, helpless. He fell so far.

The ground shook as he landed behind me. His heart was racing.

"You scared me," I said.

He held a hand up as he caught his breath. "Fuck that was intense. What a big ass cliff."

I wrapped my arms around him. He turned me so I was facing the valley. The view was magnificent. Below was the stable house where we had stayed. He pointed out the remaining tower of the old castle. Achnacarry Estate stood proudly at the edge of the Arkig River. I wanted to wander the grounds.

"We have to come back."

"We're welcome any time," he said.

I was lost in the view.

"Do you think you could dance for me?"

"Is there time?"

"There's always time for dancing." He found two sticks and placed them in a cross in the dirt.

I wanted to grab my dancing shoes, but the boots I was wearing would do. I started a short Highland song on my phone and had him hold it.

It was magical dancing on the cliff above the land of the Cameron Clan. I leaped and bound with grace and confidence.

Gian clapped as I bowed. "I love watching you dance."

"You're very sweet. Let's get you ready." I disappeared and headed back to our villa.

Gian dressed in a tight bowling shirt. His dark glasses completely obscured his eyes, blocking out the last remnants of emotion. He was practicing his stone face.

"Where's the tournament at?" I asked. "In case your aunt and uncle can make it tomorrow?"

"It's close. You take our road south to the ocean, and it's off to the right. In the RG Naxos."

Close is a relative term. That was still an hour's drive. Plus, there's that massive section missing from the road.

"I should get going."

"You don't want anything to eat?"

"I'll grab a bite after I sign in. There's a couple-hour gap until qualifying begins."

"Wait, your hat."

"I'm good without it."

"I thought it was lucky."

"Nah, I only wear it sometimes."

The villa was quiet without Gian. It was nice having it to myself. I used the alone time to tidy up and do laundry.

Content with my housework, I flopped onto the couch, worn out. A strange feeling arose from Gian. He was walking along a beach, shuffling his feet in the sand. I looked at the clock. They must have postponed the start.

I dialed Angela with nervous energy. We hadn't spoken since we'd slept with her and the three other witches. I got a little wet thinking about it.

"Linsey? Is that you?"

"It is. How are you doing?" I said in Italian.

She stuck with English. "It's so good to hear from you. Mom said to give you space, that you're on an important mission."

"What? We would have made time for you. I was wondering why you hadn't called. I thought maybe things were weird after that night."

"Not at all. We had fun."

"Speaking of fun, do you and Alfonso want to join us tomorrow evening? Maybe bring Chiara and Orlando."

"We're not friends with them anymore. But Alfonso and I would love to come. What did you have in mind?"

"Gian's in a poker tournament at the RG Naxos. I thought it would be exciting to watch. We could hang out at our villa afterward."

"At the RG Naxos Hotel?"

"Hotel? It's not a casino?"

"No. We don't have casinos. What do you mean a poker tournament? Is this underground? They're illegal in Sicily."

My chest tightened in panic. This could be why Gian was walking with such a defeated gait. I didn't think he was hurt. I would have known.

"I have to go. We'll do something soon. I promise."

I thrust my feet into the first pair of shoes I found and headed to Gian's location. He was alone on a rock jetty at the end of a sandy beach. I stepped behind an abandoned restaurant and materialized.

Gian was slumped over, sitting upon an ancient lava flow. He could feel me walking up but remained still. I sat down with my arm around him. He rested his head on my shoulder.

"It was a scam," he said, his voice choking up. "The room was locked when it was game time."

"Oh honey, I'm so sorry. Troy is heading to Vegas. I'm sure we'll get pulled there. Maybe you can find a tournament."

He lifted his head and removed his glasses. "The entrance fee is gone."

I didn't know what to say. I thought humor would be the best. "Should have worn your lucky hat." I couldn't fake a laugh, but my smirk had him going. It soon turned into tears. "It's not your fault. You were blinded by passion."

"I have to hand it to them. It was a good heist. There were at least five hundred players. That's a huge haul. Millions."

"Did you call the police?"

"The concierge told me I could get in trouble if I went to them. Besides, the police are probably in on it. I don't see how it could have been done without them."

"Will we be all right? Financially?"

"Yeah. We should have enough to get us through until we sell the gold."

"Well then, let's let this be a lesson."

He looked up at me in disbelief.

"That was my dad talking. Fuck those people."

I pulled out my phone. There were a bunch of restaurants around the corner.

"Come on," I said, standing up. "Let's walk this off."

"I feel like an idiot."

I rubbed my hand along his shoulder. "You feel all right to me."

He didn't laugh at my brother's joke. I took his hand and we headed out in silence.

Around the bend was a private neighborhood with fancy beach villas. The luxurious sights momentarily took Gian's mind off his troubles. He would crack a smile every so often.

We reached the boardwalk leading to the beachfront restaurants.

"Are you hungry?" I asked.

"Let's get a drink first."

I was starving, but he brought us toward the beach. I saw what was attracting him. A waiter was serving a couple in lounge chairs. I was surprised there were chairs still out. The sun was setting. Gian rented two loungers off to the side.

A young waiter around eighteen approached.

"Buonasera," I said. "Is there a local drink you recommend? Something happy."

"A Garibaldi. Campari-Orange."

I looked at Gian. He nodded.

"Due Garibaldis per fevore."

"I could have said that," Gian said.

A man my dad's age walked over and introduced himself. "Sorry to bother you. Did I see you at the tournament?" he said with air quotes.

"Yeah," Gian said.

"What are we supposed to do?" the man whispered. "I'm freaking out. Are they bringing cops in? Can we get in trouble for this?"

"I doubt anyone will go to the police. I think we're fucked. We shouldn't even be seen together."

"You're right." He looked back at a woman leaning on a railing. "My wife's going to kill me." The man sulked away.

"You have anything funny to say about that?" Gian asked me.

"Hey, come on."

"Sorry. I'm pissed."

"After this drink, we'll get some food in you. I'll find a good restaurant. What are you in the mood for?"

"Italian."

I don't know why I found that so funny.

The waiter returned with peach-colored drinks in festive glasses. Gian took a sip and coughed.

"They're so bitter."

So are you, I thought and took a drink. Garibaldis are horrible. Bitter was an understatement. They couldn't have been made correctly.

"I'll order something else," I said.

"No. This matches my mood."

I smirked but pulled it back.

The waiter stopped by and asked how our drinks were.

Gian responded, "Molto bene." It wasn't even close to the correct response but was perfect for this drink.

The waiter said, "OK. OK," sarcastically.

I started laughing.

"What?" Gian said.

"Nothing."

Dinner didn't help. When we arrived home, Gian was still in a pissy mood. I was going to suggest heading to Hawaii, but I didn't want to bring negativity to Don.

A call came from the street. I pressed the button on the wall intercom.

"There's a package for you," I yelled to Gian.

"Can you get it?"

"They said you need to sign for it."

Gian shuffled to the stairs and returned with a small box. He threw it on the kitchen counter and sulked to the balcony.

I picked it up and followed him out. "Open it."

"I can't take any more bad news. Have at it."

I turned on the party lights and sat in the lounger next to him. Another package with a note was inside.

*Gian, it would be best if you hadn't been at the hotel. Here's double your money back. Be more careful.*

There wasn't a return address on the package. I couldn't suppress my smile.

"What?"

I handed him the note. After he read it, I tossed the package onto his lap. A thick stack of used hundreds was inside.

"I still feel like an idiot. Don't," he said as I reached for his arm.

I laughed at the stupid joke he didn't let me make.

"I'm going to find the guy who talked to me."

"Why?"

"To right a wrong." He handed over half the money and disappeared.

I was overcome with guilt. My thought at seeing the money was to keep it all.

Gian was back within minutes.

"That was fast."

"I think the witches helped. I found him a little too easy. Boy was he happy."

"If the witches wanted to help, they could have warned you it was a scam."

"I know, right?"

"Do you think Don Trentino was behind this?" I asked.

"There's a good chance. I'm starting to think he's not a good guy." His delivery was so dry. For the first time that evening, he truly laughed.

"So, what do you feel like doing?" I asked.

"Don't take this the wrong way. I need some alone time."

"You've been alone your whole life. Let me help you through this."

"Please."

I was hurt that he didn't want my help. "Don't beat yourself up too hard," I said and vanished.

I headed to Connecticut to check out a women's shelter I found for Kristen. The place was as secure as their website stated. Two doors had to be opened by a guard. She would be safe there. Hopefully, there was room.

I waited in the lobby for the manager. She was off running an errand. It was a full hour before she showed up. You can do a lot of thinking in an hour. I still couldn't figure out why I had been so greedy with the stolen money. It really bothered me.

"Here's Sandy now," the guard said. She was an older woman with a giving face. Even for her, they opened one door at a time.

I rose to meet her. "Hi Sandy, I'm Linsey."

"Hello. I hope you weren't waiting long. Please come with me." A loving hand was placed on my waist. Her motherly vibe put me at ease.

"Thank you for meeting with me," I said.

She closed the door to her office. "This first step is the hardest. You're courageous and brave."

I wanted to tell her those are the same thing. "I'm actually here for a classmate from my old high school. She's in a physically abusive relationship."

"Is your friend willing to be saved? Not everyone is."

"No idea. She threw me out. But if she does, I want to make sure she's safe here. Your security looks great but is the program?"

"I know how to put your mind at ease. Would you excuse me for a minute?"

She met a young, short-haired redhead in the hall. The woman's arms were crossed, not for comfort but as if she needed to hold herself. They both looked my way.

"I guess so," the woman said.

"This is Amy. She's a resident. Ask her anything."

I sensed how uncomfortable she was. Hopefully, I could get my answer in one question. "Is this place good to you?"

A genuine smile grew on her face. "They're the best. They saved my life."

"That's all I needed to hear."

Amy sighed, relieved, and excused herself before I could thank her.

"Well, that was easy," Sandy said. "Here's my contact info. Your friend can call anytime."

The business card was for Balloon City. I was confused.

"She can't have a card for a woman's shelter on her."

"Smart. I'll do all I can to get her here."

"You're a good friend."

"We're not friends. She was my high school bully."

"That makes you an even better person."

I didn't feel like it. I was doing this more for me than Kirsten. I figured helping her would give me closure. I couldn't beat her up anymore. Life had done that already.

Sandy walked me out. Leaving was as big a process. Safety was their first concern.

"Please thank Amy for me."

"I will. It was a pleasure meeting you."

After finding a place to vanish, I jumped to Hartford.

Kristen wasn't at home. I found her at the third strip club I tried. Walking through the place, I grew sad for the girls. Sad that this was her life.

I was about to leave when Kristen walked out topless. The expression on her face reminded me of her bullying. My anger was hard to suppress. She saw me and moved her arms protectively over her chest.

"What are you doing here?"

"I want to talk."

"Look, I'm sorry I picked on you. I was a bitch. Is that what you want to hear?"

"I'm not here for that. You need to leave your husband. He'll end up killing you."

"And go where? I'm trapped."

"I found a woman's shelter in Greenwich. They have a room for you."

"Why are you doing this?"

I looked at the floor. "That day I stopped by. I wanted to hurt you."

"Jesus."

"I know. Hearing your husband hit you gave me a glimpse of your life."

"You don't know the half of it."

"I know your father abused you."

She crumbled in my arms. I brought us to a couch.

"How do you know?"

"That's not important. It's not too late for you to have a good life."

"Yes, it is. I'm nobody. I'm trash."

"That's your husband speaking. He's trash. That's your father speaking. He's trash."

"I don't have the strength for this."

"I'll be your strength. All you have to do is get up. Let's go. I can get your stuff."

She sat still. I held her under her armpits and lifted. "We're leaving," I said sternly.

A short man with a greasy haircut and a crooked nose stepped in our way. "Where the fuck you goin?" He had an air about him as if he were the manager or the owner.

I got in his face. "She's sick. I have to get her home."

"She don't look sick."

"Back the fuck up." I pushed him aside. "Take a swing. I dare you." A bouncer in the corner was trying unsuccessfully to hide his smirk.

The man walked away with a huff. "You're off the schedule!"

"Let's get out of here," Kristen said.

211

My persistence had won. I followed her to a dingy dressing room. She was shaking too hard to change. I helped her with her hoodie and into her pants.

"I can't do this."

"Yes, you can. Let's get that makeup off. I want to see the girl I remember." There were wipes on the table. I gingerly cleansed her face. She kept her eyes closed. I thought I detected a hint of a smile but it faded quickly.

Except for the new shiner, she looked so much better fresh-faced. I hid the bruising under concealer and applied minimal makeup, bringing innocence to her look.

I handed her a mirror and forced a compliment.

"You have a natural beauty."

She shied her eyes away. "My looks have always been a betrayal."

"Fuck that. It's shitty men who betrayed you." I took her hand. "Let's go."

I paid the train ticket in cash and waited with her on the platform. She was trembling against my shoulder. This should have brought sympathy, but thoughts of her tormenting me flooded in. There was no way I was going to be able to sit with her for a whole train ride. I concentrated on disabling tracking on her phone and handed it back.

"It'll be all right. When you get off the train, find the hospital. Then head a block East on William Street."

"You're not coming with me?"

"I have to get your stuff."

There was panic in her eyes. "I'll go with you."

"No. You have to go. Now. The shelter will be the second building on the right, past the church. Ask for Sandy. I'll come shortly with your stuff. If you get lost, call this number." I handed her Sandy's card. "The address is on there."

"I don't know if I'm strong enough."

"You are. This is your train." I helped her up. "I want you to be brave."

"Why are you doing this?"

"To right a wrong." It was a simple answer but the truth.

"How can I repay you?"

"When you're healthy, you can get in the ring with me."

She laughed, thinking it was a joke.

I boarded the train invisibly to ensure she stayed on through the next stop before heading to her place. I hoped her boyfriend was there so I could beat on him some more. The place was empty.

Under their bed was a suitcase and a large backpack. I only took items for her new life, makeup and regular clothes. I added a sexy nighty that looked expensive. I'm glad I checked the medicine cabinet. She had prescriptions.

I vanished, holding the bags. There was a glowing circuit in the suitcase. I set the other packs down. It was the only one with an oddity.

I materialized again. That fucker had a tracker inside the lining. I headed north to a truck stop in Springfield and placed it in the glove box of a semi, but I had a vision of her husband hurting the owner. I found a high shelf in the restroom to hide it.

I was back at her place, invisible, and about to leave when I spotted gold under the mattress. I materialized. An envelope with jewelry was taped under the bed. I checked the room one last time and left.

I wanted to meet Kristen at the train station, but the timing would be suspicious. I hailed a cab in Greenwich and had the driver wait down the road from the shelter.

Sandy didn't like that I let Kristen ride the train alone. There would be a room for her if she came. I hung up, doubting myself. I should have toughed it out and stayed with my bully.

I was so proud when I saw her approaching. I told the driver to pull forward. He was leaving when she walked up.

"How did you get here so fast?" she asked.

"Traffic was a breeze. I should have had you ride with me, but I didn't want you to go home. To have time to change your mind. Here's your stuff."

"How can I do this?"

"You made it this far. If it will help, your asshole husband had a tracker on your luggage." I showed her the picture.

"What the hell? Do you think there's more?"

"No, you're good. I checked everything. Come on, let's get you inside."

The door buzzed. I held it open for her.

"Are you not coming in?"

"I can't. The first step must be done on your own. You'll be fine."

She came back out and hugged me.

"I believe in you."

"Thank you." She took a deep breath and walked inside.

My hands grew sweaty and my stomach tightened. I was having a panic attack. I'm glad it didn't happen minutes earlier. Something awful was happening to Troy. I was getting a read of astonishing terror. He doesn't get scared. I raced around the corner and headed his way.

There were too many people on the roof he was on to materialize quickly. Troy was in the front row of a car full of people. It was tipping off the edge of the building. At the last second, it stopped. He was on a ride—some kind of teeter-totter. Off in the distance, a bright blue ball of energy shot into the sky. I found a far corner to materialize. We were on top of the Stratosphere. The Vegas strip was off in the distance.

Troy was white as he unbuckled himself. He pushed past what I assumed was his brother. The hair on the side of his head had grown in a bit. He didn't look like he had a mohawk anymore. They were both in suits with no ties, looking handsome and so Vegas.

"I got you." His brother raised his arms triumphantly. "X-Scream!"

Troy bent over to catch his breath. "That scared the shit out of me. It's so simple. Why is it so terrifying?"

"Wait until you ride Big Shot." He looked up at the people screaming from a drop-fall ride.

"Tomorrow. I don't think my heart can handle it. Let's get drunk. Hi Linsey." He did a double-take.

"Who was that?" his brother asked.

"Hang on a second." He walked back to me. "I need more time with my brother."

"Of course. We can hang back all you want."

He handed me a folded-up piece of paper. There were coordinates on it and a time 2:30 p.m.

"Meet me there Saturday. I'll pick you up in a plane."

I caved in on myself, thinking about the horror of skydiving. "You're really going to make me jump out of it?"

"Quit your worrying. You'll love it."

"Won't picking us up draw attention?"

"Nah. It's between the hills. If we do it quickly, air traffic shouldn't notice."

"What are you doing until then?"

"Living like my days are numbered."

"Don't die early."

"I'll try." He gave me a manly chuck on my shoulder.

Another full car was teetering over the edge. The ride looked terrifying. Troy wouldn't even look at it. He left to catch up with his brother.

It didn't feel right being in Vegas without Gian. I headed to New Orleans. Rowanda was in a courthouse office. Was she offering her testimony? I stopped in Minnesota and headed to Hawaii, knowing Don was home.

I scared him coming out of the bedroom.

"You're going to give me a heart attack." He looked in the room. "Where's your man?"

"At home."

"Well, give him my thanks."

I forgot about the gold. "How much did you get?"

"$127,540 after fees and taxes. Thank you both so much."

"I love that you paid taxes."

"That wasn't on me. They're taken out there."

"You would have done it anyway. You're a good man. The best I've met."

"That's sweet of you. I didn't think they were going to take the gold. They asked so many questions. Even did a background check. My clean record sealed the deal."

I followed him to the kitchen. "Where did you say you found it?"

"In a stream below the volcano. There are thousands of them. Good luck there." He laughed.

"The next time we're in Alaska, we'll grab a few nuggets to sprinkle around for people to find."

"Can I do that?"

"Sure."

"Would you like to join me for a celebratory cocktail?"

"You know what I'd like? Can we go snorkeling?"

"Absolutely. I'll meet you on the patio."

We snorkeled for a solid hour, wearing me out. There were three turtles in the bay. I didn't want to leave.

My nap turned into a full sleep. When I woke, I felt Don on the other side of the island. I went to the kitchen for coffee and sat on his lanai to wake up. The solitude was nice but I needed Gian.

# Chapter 10

I had one last stop on the way to our villa, St Mark's Basilica. There were too many people inside to materialize. It took over an hour to get in. When people say, "Ah, Venice," they have to be talking about at night when the hordes of tourists leave the city.

I walked through the church and was giving up on finding the man I was looking for. As I was leaving, I saw him gathering papers at the pulpit. My younger self wouldn't have the courage to approach him. I was proud of how I walked right over.

"Pardon me, Father. I've come to apologize for the other night."

He gazed at me with a warm smile. "Whatever for?" There was a hint of recognition in his eyes and he laughed. "Quit a ringing the bell."

I felt my cheeks flush. "I am so sorry for waking you."

"Why? It made for a funny sermon. You gave me a story. What better gift can you give?"

"Thank you?" I wasn't sure why I was thanking him.

"No, I mean it. What better gift can you give?"

I stood stunned. What could I offer him?

"Ha, I fooled you. Now we are even."

"Only after I get a hug."

His eyes lit up. He offered a warm embrace.

"You're a wonderful man," I said.

"More souls are saved with kindness."

That sat heavily with me. I walked through the backstreets deep in thought, ending up in a local neighborhood. The people were a bit standoffish. Was it because I was a tourist, or could they tell I had been a huntress? I didn't stick around to find out.

Gian was in our town but not in the villa. I had a feeling he was at his aunt and uncle's. I headed back to our place.

He materialized shortly after. "You should have come over."

"I didn't want to disturb you."

"You could never disturb me." He kissed me on the cheek. "No visit for Robert?"

"I will never be alone with that man."

"Yeah, that's wise. I have to get back. They think I'm in the john. Come join us."

"I'll be right there."

Aunt Pia's beauty intimidates me. I spent time on my makeup and picked a cute top to wear.

Their place was a quick stroll from ours. Gian answered the door before I knocked.

"Look at you, sexy girl."

I blushed.

"Come in. We're out on the patio." He leaned in and whispered, "Don't mention the tournament."

Aunt Pia saw me approaching. Her dress was simple, but her face elevated the look. I found her stunning. "What a treat." She kissed me on both cheeks.

Uncle Emilio stood up and greeted me. I still wasn't over how much he looked like Gian's dad. "It's always a pleasure."

"Another glass," Aunt Pia said to her husband.

Uncle Emilio returned and offered a generous pour.

"You'll like this one. It's smooth, gentle on the palate."

I took a sip. The flavor was deep yet subtle. There was nothing acidic about it. I could drink it all night long. "This is wonderful," I said.

"It's a Sicilian Rosso."

"I much approve," I said. "So, have you found your next house? You were saying you wanted a place with a view."

"We've put that on hold until you finish your mission. There is safety in this villa."

"I didn't give them any details," Gian said.

"We're going to set things right. Hopefully, everything will be wrapped up in two weeks."

Gian sank into his chair at the weight of it all.

"You are strong. You will get through this," Uncle Emilio said.

"Let me see your ring," Pia said.

I felt guilty. I hadn't seen them since the morning of our picnic. Shit! The picnic basket.

"It was my mom's." I held the ring out prominently.

"It's glorious. Will you be taking the family name? That was rude of me. You're a modern woman. That's a choice only you can make."

"It wasn't rude at all. I am proudly taking the Lombardo name."

"Linsey Lombardo. It flows nicely," Uncle Emilio said.

"I quite agree," I said.

"Linsey Cameron Lombardo," Gian said, to include my family. "LCL. That would be a good girl's name, Elsey Elle."

"Are you pregnant," Aunt Pia said. She almost knocked her glass over in excitement.

"No. I don't think so. Am I?"

Gian shook his head.

Pia looked confused at why I was asking Gian. "You would make beautiful children." Coming from her, I ate the compliment up. "But, you're young. There is plenty of time. It might be best to wait until you are done with the witches. You need wine to get you through this."

"Sound advice," I said, taking a sip.

"I don't know this use of the word sound," Pia said.

"It means sensible. I apologize."

"No need," she said. "We are taking the English classes. I was only curious."

219

"Il mio Italiano sta progredendo," Gian said.

"Perfetto," Pia said.

"We would be honored if you joined us for dinner," Emilio said. "There's a lasagna in the oven. Pia makes the best."

"That's the wonderful aroma. I would love to stay for dinner."

"This calls for more vino," Emilio said. "Come help me pick the bottles, Linsey."

"I would love to."

Inside his wine cellar, he spoke in Italian. "Are you keeping my nephew safe? I can't lose Gian. He's my favorite. Even with the curse, there was goodness."

"You have nothing to worry about," I lied. His family asking had me plenty worried. "Do you have any more of that Chianti?" I asked.

"I bought four bottles for the next time you were over."

"What are you having?" I said.

He laughed.

After dinner, we invited them to our place for a nightcap. I went ahead to our bedroom and shut the bathroom door. The new metal sheeting would raise questions. They had seen the room before.

Aunt Pia went to open it, but I stopped her. "It's a mess. Boys," I said, looking at Gian.

"It's not just you anymore," she scolded. "Be good to Linsey."

"I'll clean it tomorrow. Would you care for a drink out on the terrace?"

"I wouldn't even mind one in the street," Emilio joked.

"How about a Moscato," Gian asked.

"Certo." Emilio gestured a kiss with his fingers.

We had said goodbye to his aunt and uncle when Nera appeared on the stairs. "Get to Robert. He's about to shoot himself. He can't die yet."

"Fuck," I said. "Can you take us there? We've had a bit of wine."

"Of course." She took my hand, and I held onto Gian.

Nera stayed invisible when we arrived in Robert's cottage. He had a shotgun barrel in his mouth. Seeing us appear, he jumped, giving me a start.

"Hold on, Robert. You're not ready. You have to make peace with yourself. I thought you wanted to go out in your garden?"

"Don't do it this way," Gian said.

Robert removed the gun from his mouth but kept it pointed at his face. "What do I have to live for? This tumor will kill me anyway."

He pulled the trigger. Water shot from the barrel, soaking his face.

We were stunned into silence. Robert let out a long, piercing scream and crumpled over. I grabbed the shotgun with shaking hands and pulled the slide back. There were two shells loaded and no water. I removed them and handed the gun to Gian. Nera was gone.

"You have a few weeks." I sat in front of him and stroked his hair tenderly. "Live your life."

He was avoiding eye contact. "Jake's ignoring my calls. No one in town likes me. And my doctor's after me to start radiation." He scoffed. "Not doing that."

"Get Jake away from everyone," Gian said. "Have him come over to help with something here."

"He's not coming over for nothin'."

"You're giving your house to him. Tell him you're cleaning up and need help moving things."

"That might work," he said with little enthusiasm.

"It will work if you treat him right," I said.

"Be on your best behavior," Gian said. "Ease up on the whisky so you can stay in control."

"You guys talk to me like I'm five."

221

"We're just trying to help," Gian said. "About your doctor. Tell him you'll start in three weeks."

"That'll learn him," Robert said with a laugh.

I wanted him to be around people. It felt like what he needed. "Let's go to the pub."

"If you can get me in, I guess so," Robert said.

Charlie wasn't pleased to see us. Gian had Robert wait at the door with him. I slipped Charlie a hundred.

"Make it three," he said. "That's how much I lose when he's here."

I tried to get Robert to follow me to a corner table, but he walked straight to the bar. Gian raced after him. I joined them for support.

Robert laid a debit card on the counter. "Drinks are on me tonight."

"What will you have," Charlie asked Gian and me.

"For the house," Robert said.

"Are you sure?" Charlie said.

"As much as they want. Do you mind if I say something?"

"Only if you're good."

"I promise."

Charlie gripped his arm tightly. "I mean it. If you dump on my customers, I will never allow you in here again."

"I won't," Robert said.

Charlie put two fingers in his mouth and whistled. "Oy! Listen up. Robert is buying your drinks tonight. He has something to say. Don't worry, he's promised to behave."

Robert sat still for quite a while, looking at the floor. I wasn't sure he would get the words out, but they eventually came.

"Pour the house a round of scotch, will you, Charlie? I have little time left. There's a tumor in me head. Tonight, I tried to kill myself. Stuck a shotgun barrel in my mouth. My friends here stopped me. They're good people. But I haven't

222

been. I don't mean to be an asshole. There's something wrong in here." He knocked on his head. "I can't stop the words. I don't mean them. I'm sorry for any harm I've caused. William, I didn't mean what I said about your wife. She's a good woman. Tory, I won't repeat what I said, but know I didn't mean it. I'm actually jealous of your son. Russ, oh Russ." He started crying. "I can't go on. Know that I am sorry."

Gian stepped up. "Drink up, everyone. How about we make this a living celebration? Who has a story?"

"I have one," Jake said from the doorway. I hadn't noticed him coming in. He walked up and put his arm around Robert. "As kids, my friend and I were in town late one night. As a joke, I tried the door to old man Leonard's chocolate shop and was shocked when it opened. Robert made me close it and walk away. We could have had our fill. He said no. That's how good of a person he was. I'm so sorry for abandoning you, my friend."

Robert was crying and smiling, his face contorting in a humorous and charming way. He couldn't talk and brought his friend in close for a hug.

An older woman stood up. "Years ago, stormwater ran into my house. My husband was off on business. I was frantically digging a trench along the side. Robert was maybe fifteen at the time. He gathered his friends, and in the pouring rain, they dug the rest of the ditch for me. He even had his father over to ensure we sealed the hole in the foundation properly. Thank you, Robert," she said, raising her glass.

I was crying. I whispered in Gian's ear, "This is the sweetest gesture I've ever seen. You did well."

A frumpy yet slender woman Robert's age stood up. "I can't believe I'm saying this. In our twenties, Robert and I were. How do I say this nicely? Friends with benefits."

Robert chuckled to himself.

"He ruined me for other partners. No one could compare. So creative and passionate."

The crowd gave him cat whistles.

"I still am," he whispered to me. I pushed him away.

A gentleman stood up. "A few years back, Robert called me a land whale. I didn't take too kindly to his observation." The room laughed. "I've lost over fifty kilos. Doc said I saved my life. Thank you, Robert."

"I'm sorry, Terry," Robert said.

"It's all good, mate."

Many of the patrons had a story about young Robert. I've never been so touched. How cruel that an accident could rob him of his goodness.

I woke up next to Gian in a strange bed. It wasn't until I was in the hall that I recognized Robert's place. Pieces of the evening were coming back. We'd ripped it up. Having started with wine, I thought cognac would be the best progression. I was wrong. It was all I could do to keep things down. I stumbled into the kitchen for a glass of water and saw Robert outside weeding his garden. There was still coffee in the pot. I poured myself a cup and joined him.

"That's not tea, is it?" He was panicked.

"No. It's not time."

"Good. I was afraid to make any with you here. Hey, love. I appreciate ya taking me to the pub. I enjoyed the hell out of that. You two can drink."

I slumped into a chair. "I can feel it."

He pulled a pill bottle from his pocket. "Percocet? It'll take that hangover away."

I held my hand out mindlessly. Two fell in my palm. I saved one for Gian. I'm not a fan of pills, but damn if it didn't make me feel better.

Gian stumbled out a while later and sat beside me in the dirt. "I have to get home," he said, not looking up.

"Sure, honey." I checked my pockets and had everything I came with. "It's been a pleasure, Robert. Will you be all right?"

"I think so. Just had myself a moment."

"Hang in there, buddy," Gian said, taking my hand.

I wasn't sure there were cameras out back. I led him to the front room and headed to our villa.

Gian curled up in a blanket on one of our loungers. I walked onto the balcony, skipping to a beat in my head.

"How are you not hung over," he asked.

I held up a pill. "Robert gave us a couple Percocets."

"Yes, please." He opened his mouth and I dropped the pill inside.

I sat next to him with the sun caressing my face. "I hope this is a down day. I need one."

"Ditto," he moaned. "Did you feel Troy's tracker last night? I couldn't figure out what was up until I saw he was at Six Flags. His being on a roller coaster was trippy."

"I thought it was the spins." I looked at my shoes. "I don't want to jump out of a plane. It's freaking me out."

"We have to."

"Why?"

"You're the one that's been pushing the importance of granting last wishes. Wouldn't you want yours granted?"

"I guess so."

"There's no way we can get hurt."

"I could have a heart attack from fear."

"You'll be fine."

"I'll be fine when it's over," I said. "I've been thinking about Robert's tumor. Do you think it's his tracker? Remember when I punched him in the head? Maybe I dislodged it."

"Huh?" He paused too long before adding, "It wasn't you."

Nera stayed silent throughout the day. Not only did we have a free one, but we also had time the following afternoon to prospect in Alaska. Marking the gold's locations on the GPS made for quick work. By the time we left, we had thirty new locations and twelve nuggets that were in easy reach. I was on a quest to get as much as we could so I could provide seed money for my family. Gian hadn't minded that I made the promise without him.

We spent that night at Gian's condo so we wouldn't oversleep. As good as his mattress was, I hardly slept. The thought of jumping out of a plane freaked me out so bad I had Gian run to the store for an enema kit so I wouldn't shit myself in the air. It worked wonders. Health-wise, I felt fantastic.

Gian handed me sunblock. "You better put this on. We're meeting him in the flats. Make sure to get under your nose. I heard the sunlight reflects off the salt." He applied a little to show me how.

"I don't know if I can do this," I said. "I didn't get a wink of sleep."

"Yeah, you kept me up. It'll be OK. This is just a new adventure. What a way to go. I'm going to miss this guy."

"He's pretty badass."

"You ready?"

I looked at the clock on the stove. "We have an hour."

"Salt Lake is an hour ahead."

My heart dropped. Thinking about time put the countdown in my head. There wasn't much left at all.

"It'll be all right," he said and vanished.

The visual of the salt flats was unlike anything I had experienced. They stretched on endlessly. It was like being on another planet.

I could sense Troy's plane getting closer. "Let's try to open a portal while he's landing. The less he's on the ground, the less suspicious Traffic Control will be."

"Yeah, didn't Troy say we'd be hidden in a valley? What the fuck? This is a clear shot back to the city. Here he comes."

I spotted his plane approaching. I swallowed, hoping to dampen my fear. All it did was bring vomit close to my throat.

Troy did a flyby and waved, then came back around to land. Judging by his descent, we jumped to a closer spot.

His wheels had barely touched the ground when we appeared inside the plane.

"Go, go, go," Gian said.

Troy looked back, wide-eyed, and floored it. We made our way up front. Gian gave me the passenger seat. It was a sweet gesture. Troy handed us both headsets.

"Nice plane," Gian said.

"I needed cruise control. Don't worry. The owner's a dick. How much time do we have?"

"Sixteen minutes," I said.

Troy pulled the wheel back. We climbed steeply. "I'll try and reach 13,000 feet. That will give us a solid minute of jump time."

We were already at twelve minutes. Time was moving too fast. My heart was beating so strongly I thought it would explode. Gian leaned forward and put his hand on my leg. It helped.

"Once we reach our altitude, I'll put the plane in a circle. It will keep that up until the fuel's gone. I've been dropping most of it, so that won't be long."

"What about airline traffic?" Gian asked.

"Commercial airlines are coming in from the East. We're cool."

"How you holding up?" I asked. I needed talking. I needed a distraction.

"If you want the truth, I don't want to die."

"I don't want you to either," I said.

"But are you ready?" Gian asked. "Are you good with yourself?"

"As good as I can be. You guys were right about meeting up with my brother. We bonded."

"You'll see him again," Gian said. "This is one of many planes. Who knows, your next existence could even be better."

"This one has been fun," Troy said.

I called out four minutes. My hands shook uncontrollably.

"Eleven thousand it is." Troy set the cruise control and walked hunched over to the back. I was confused why he was reaching for a parachute.

"Why are you using a chute?" I asked.

"Jeff can't think I killed myself. It'll open when I get close to the ground. How much time's left?"

"Two minutes." I was in a bad nightmare.

"We're jumping into a turn. Dive down so the tail doesn't hit you. Everyone goes at once. Tell me when we're at forty seconds."

He walked over to the door and opened it. His confidence somehow fed into my fear. The wind whipping into the plane sent my whole body shaking. I took place behind Gian, but he put me in the middle.

"Forty," I screamed.

Troy didn't hesitate to jump. Gian followed, pushing me out the door.

I woke up having fainted and was falling. The three of us were positioned in a triangle, with them holding my hands. I tried to speak, but the air flowing past moved too swiftly. The ground was so far away it wasn't real. I was flying. The thrill of the moment was overwhelming, a manifestation of a dream.

I shouted from the rush. Gian's smile receded. It was time.

I mouthed goodbye to Troy. A tear leaked upward from his eye and shot skyward. That started the waterworks in Gian and me.

I let go of Gian's hand and maneuvered to Troy's chest. Gian was on his back. We spun wildly. Troy had a crazed grin on his face. He was loving this. Our hands landed on his head and Troy went lifeless. All that was left was the shell of his body. It was that noticeable. He was gone.

I held onto Gian, floating away. Troy's body was crumpled inward, falling below us.

I wanted to open a portal, but Gian held up a finger to wait. The ground was getting close. Troy's chute opened automatically.

Now, Gian mouthed. I vanished and jumped to our villa, rolling upon arrival. The energy in the wall absorbed my motion as if it were rubber. I bounced backward and materialized next to him.

As the adrenaline receded, I was soon shaking. Gian held onto me and cried.

"I wasn't ready," he said. "I didn't want Troy to go."

"I can't do this anymore," I said.

Nera appeared. "I'm proud of both of you. I know how hard this is. Hugs all around."

I could barely stand. It took two attempts. As good as her hug was, another trip would have been a better distraction. I guess that was a one-time deal. She was gone.

"How about we go to your place and get high as shit?"

"Who are you?" Gian asked.

"Not that nerd you first met."

He looked me in the eyes. "You were smart, not a nerd."

"Just make the sorrow go away," I pleaded and jumped to his condo.

It was early afternoon in Seattle. The sun was shining, a rarity for spring. I poured myself an OrangeGian and waited for him to return from the pot shop. It was selfish not thinking of Gian. I made a drink for him.

He appeared, walking out of thin air. "They were out of our brand." He tossed over an odd box with six sides. "It's still CBG. Only do half. Promise me you won't take more."

"I promise."

It took a while to figure out how to open the lid. The gummies were square, making them easier to divide. I expected him to take the remaining piece, but he did a whole one.

"What the hell?" I said.

"My tolerance is higher. We'll be about even."

"Thanks, I guess." I handed him his cocktail.

"Let's walk around," he said. "It's a beautiful day."

"I'm not in the mood for people."

"How about people watching? We can go to the park. Come on. It'll be a nice distraction." He retrieved a couple of to-go cups from the cupboard.

"Fine, but keep people away. I'm not up for social hour."

I found a soft velour blanket in his closet. "Do you mind if we take this?"

"That's the one I would have picked," he said, smiling.

"Hold up. I'll make a pitcher of drinks," I said.

"I knew there was a reason I wanted to marry you. Sorry, that sounded horrible."

"I know what you meant."

Not only did he carry the blanket and pitcher, but he also held my hand the whole way to the park. He picked one further from his. We chose a spot near the fountain with a buffer from the other people. A teenage boy was throwing a frisbee for his dog. They both were locked in the moment, oblivious to their surroundings. Maybe when life returns to normal, we could have a dog.

"Is this Capitol Hill?" I asked.

He nodded.

"I love this part of town. The people watching is off the charts."

A lesbian with a noticeable mustache walked by. I wanted to compliment her boldness but wasn't sure that would be taken too kindly.

"This is a cool park," I said.

"You fit right in."

Was he saying I was cool, or I had a mustache?

"I have to pee." I headed to the bathrooms we passed at the bottom of the sloped hill.

Gian caught up to me with all our stuff. The pot was hitting me on the way. I couldn't get rid of my silly grin. The high struck hard in the stall. My hands were clammy and I was shaking.

"I'm here for you, Linsey," Gian said into the room. He had felt me freaking out.

I looked out from under the stall. No one was in the room. I washed my hands and fled.

"I'm way too high," I whispered to Gian.

"It'll pass. You know how it comes in strong but mellows. Let's sit for a minute."

He picked a spot next to a skate park at the edge of the baseball diamond. The ramps were homemade, like teens had taken over a tennis court. It was so Seattle to leave it that way.

"I should have brought my board."

"Go borrow one. Watching you will take my mind away."

"You sure?"

I think I said yes, but I probably nodded. My high wasn't getting any easier. I would stick to a quarter from now on. I was glad he talked me out of a whole one. The soft velour of the blanket was helping. I was rubbing it for comfort.

Gian easily borrowed a board. I panicked, thinking he was going to hurt himself being so high. Yelling out to save him would be foolish. I peeked through my fingers. He ground along a rail, landing with ease. A block of wood lay in his path. He kicked the tail up at the last minute and landed on the other side. Every movement was fluid as if the board was part of him. It was a trip feeling all the ways his body was balancing. The learned skills were automatic like second nature.

He took a tumble off a ramp but rolled on the landing into a standing position, barely hurting himself. After a couple more tricks, he gave the board back. On the way out, he slipped the kid something.

"Did you give that boy drugs?"

"What?" he laughed. "No. It was a ten. He's plenty high."

"That's not cool."

"There's the nerd."

I gasped, then giggled uncontrollably.

"I think I laughed my high down."

"Want to head home?"

"Yes, I do."

My body felt fantastic. I couldn't believe what I was thinking. Would I have the courage? Then again, I did jump out of a plane without a chute.

"What are you grinning at?" he asked.

"I'm going to let you fuck me."

"In the butt?" he said wide-eyed.

"In. The. Butt."

We both laughed at how I said that. But here I was, nervous again.

"I felt you tense up. You'll be fine. It only hurts for a little while."

I wasn't sure it would even fit. I sat on a bench to pour myself another glass of courage.

Back home, Gian eagerly spread the velour blanket on his bed. There was no time for backing out. He returned from the bathroom with a damp washcloth and set it on his nightstand.

"You sure you're cool with this?"

"It's now or never," I said.

He pulled his smirk back. "Lay on your chest and relax your body." He pulled a bottle of lube from his nightstand and set it on top. "You're so tense. Let me rub those knots out."

I melted into the soft blanket with my fear receding. He found a knot under my shoulder blade and focused diligently until it was gone. Soon, there was none.

His hand was on my ass, and a slick finger entered. My eyes grew wide in shock. I let out a gasp.

"I thought you would have felt it coming."

Me too. I didn't respond for fear of talking myself out of the act.

He removed the finger and poured lube onto my backside. His finger was back inside but holding still. There was a stinging pain that I tried to ignore. He slowly moved in and out. I wanted him to stop, but he had let me fuck him. No way I was backing out. It wasn't so bad anymore. Then a second finger was inserted. I clenched tightly, locking his fingers in place.

"Are you OK?"

"Yeah," I lied.

He spread his fingers, stretching me, but he knew when to stop and restart. The pain wasn't going away as he had promised. It was a relief when he pulled out. The washcloth was there to wipe his hands. I saw him reaching for the lube again. It was go time, and I wasn't ready for launch.

Cold lube dripped onto me, causing my back to arch. "I'll be real slow," he whispered.

I lifted my hips, but he pressed me back down flat. His approach was gingerly at first, then more forceful. I was relieved when he couldn't get it in.

"You have to relax," he said.

As soon as I did, the head slipped inside with a pop. I gasped. The pain was immense, but the pleasure from his end was astronomical. I was wonderfully tight. It was painful and so good.

"It's OK. It's OK. Hold still," he said. "You're doing great."

He held me by my waist and pushed farther.

I wanted to yell, get out! "It hurts," I said. "It feels so good."

"I know." He held still.

When the pain subsided, he pushed in deeper and held still again, adding more lube.

That helped. Pleasure stifled the pain when he pulled back and inserted again.

"I think I can do this."

He pushed almost all the way in. I tried hard to concentrate on what he was feeling.

"You're so tight."

"I know," I said.

He went in for a few strokes and stopped.

"Keep going."

He kept a slow roll of his body. Eventually, the pain became bearable. I was about to say you can go faster, but he knew. His thrusts became deep strokes.

"I need to look at you," I said.

He rolled me on my side and propped up my outer leg. I stared into his eyes as he fucked me. His satisfaction reverberated across his face, which became animated with each thrust. Gritting of his teeth. A clenched smile morphing to a grin. All of it handsome. All of it drawing me in.

I had reached a point where the pain was almost gone. The light sting was still there, but the dueling pleasure drowned it out.

"As hard as you want," I said.

"I can't go too hard. I could hurt you."

"Harder!" I demanded.

Dormant nerve endings were awakening. I reveled in the pleasure. He was the king as he pounded away, and the king was getting close.

"Do it inside me," I demanded.

He slowed his rhythm into long, deep strokes. A tightness in his back stretched his skull. I was overwhelmed by the physical sensation of his orgasm. It was so intense that I was sure I would pass out, but the earlier pain was enough to keep us conscious. Gian rolled me back onto my stomach and collapsed on top of me to catch his breath. It was nice having him out of me.

I excused myself to clean up. When I returned, the blanket and the lube were gone, and he was smiling proudly.

"You conquered two fears today," he said.

"It's been a crazy one." My mind drifted to Troy. Gian must have seen it on my face.

"None of that." He forced me onto my back and dove on my pussy, eating it with a fury. I tried to forgive myself for Troy's death but couldn't concentrate.

Gian lifted his glistening face. "My high is making me smile. I hope that isn't striking you weird."

I thrust his head back down. "No talking." He was almost fucking me with his tongue. Sticking it in me, then across my clit, back and forth until he focused solely on it. He flicked swiftly as if his tongue was vibrating. I leaned back and grabbed a couple of slats on his headboard.

He backed off frustratingly. I begged for my release. When it grew close again, he backed off. I gripped him by his hair to raise his head.

"Make me come," I said in a comically deep voice. I didn't mean to say it that way, and we both laughed.

He managed to pull himself together and was back to business. The manic flicking was back. My clit danced with his tongue. The inner tightness spread to my legs and up across my torso. I screamed out as my release shot through the universe. Gian's face remained buried in me, riding it out. I fell back on the bed like pudding.

He rolled over onto his back, panting heavily. "I thought I was going to get a cramp in my tongue. It was good, wasn't it?"

"Like nothing on this earth."

I stared up at his skateboard light, catching my breath. It was an artifact of our old life. Now a symbol of hope.

"You want to go sit in Don's hot tub?" Gian asked. "We'll have the place to ourselves. He's in that town with the shaved ice."

I didn't correct him for saying it wrong. Shave ice sounds weird to me. "I could use some on my ass."

That sent us into giggles.

Don was still in Waimea when we arrived. My high was wearing off, letting bits of the day slip in. I took a quarter gummy to chase the bad thoughts away. The clock showed one thirty. We'd gone back in time to before Troy died. If only it were true, I could tell him how much knowing him had affected me. I closed my eyes and forgave myself.

We had to wait for the hot tub to heat up. That didn't take long at all. I disrobed and entered naked, sinking into the warm water, and let myself drift toward Gian. He caught me in his lap, holding me close.

Clouds rolled in, bringing a dull gray. The rain was delightful on my face. As fast as it left, the sun was back. A teenage couple appeared below the edge of the lawn. It was rare to see people this far down the beach.

"Sorry," the boy said upon seeing us. The girl moved behind him shyly.

"No one owns the beaches," Gian said.

The boy gave us the two-finger solute the English use to tell people to fuck off.

Gian and I looked at each other and laughed.

"Are you trying to do this," Gian said, showing him the hang loose sign.

"Yeah," the kid said.

"Aloha," Gian said. "Hold up a sec. I have something for you."

He covered himself as he stood up, and headed to the house to retrieve a gummy, returning in a swimsuit. I didn't think he should be giving kids drugs. They must have been older than I thought.

I couldn't hear what he said to the couple.

"No shit," the boy said, smiling. He gladly took the edible.

"Nice house," he yelled back as they walked away.

236

"It is a nice house," I said, looking around. "You think we could afford this?"

"We'd have to do a lot more prospecting." Gian ditched the shorts and joined me.

"We could rent it out when we're not here."

"We'd still have to do a lot more prospecting."

"I'm game," I said. "I'll be too traumatized to work for a while."

"We could do spring here, summers in Seattle, and winters in Sicily."

"Sounds perfect. We don't need this exact place. I like Hawaii."

"I do, too. The vibe fits," he said. "Don's heading back. Should we take off?"

"No, we need to check in. Is what you said about the beaches true?"

"That no one owns them?"

I nodded.

"No matter how rich you are in Hawaii, the beach belongs to everyone. Don talked about it at breakfast."

"My mind must have been elsewhere."

"It's a good rule. No one should own a beach."

Don arrived well under two hours. We'd been swimming in the pool and jumped back in the tub when we felt him enter the house. He rummaged in the kitchen, then walked onto the patio naked. Don screamed when he saw us. He almost lost his drink.

"Seriously, you're going to be the end of me," he said, grabbing his heart with one hand and covering himself with the drink. "I'll get my suit."

"Don't worry about it," I said. "We're all naked."

"You sure? I'm not the greatest view."

"Get in."

"There's a gummy in our room if you want some?" Gian said.

"That sounds nice. I had the best day. Would you like a piña colada?"

237

"Yes, please," I said. "We had a shitty one."

Don looked into my eyes. "It was someone's time, wasn't it?"

"Second of five," Gian said. "I'll take one also."

Don walked away deep in thought. That was a lot to take in. He returned in shorts with our drinks in plastic cups.

"You'll make us uncomfortable," I said. "Off with them."

He laughed and stepped out of his suit. I neither looked at him nor away.

I took too long of a drink and was struck with a brain freeze. It was too good to stop. Gian suffered with me. "Why is this so yummy?"

"I used coconut ice cream."

"It's fucking good," Gian said.

"Sorry about your day," Don said.

"Thanks," I said. "I don't want to talk about it. What did you do that was so wonderful?"

"You're both swearing a lot more than usual. You sure it won't do you good to let it out?"

"Very. I need positivity."

"That's all my day was. I started in a soup kitchen. With each meal, I slipped a twenty into the napkin. It was fun watching people find the money. What warmed my heart most was when someone was kind enough to point the bills out to others. From there, I went to a high school on the other side of the island and paid off all the student lunch debt. I bought meals for twenty of the poorest kids for the rest of the year. The best part is the principal called this single mother to see if I could help her. Tracy's living in her car with three kids. I'm meeting with her tomorrow to get a roof over their head."

"You're the sweetest man I've ever met."

"You should've seen me last month."

"We did," Gian said. "Oh man, I forgot my wallet again."

"Gian!" I said.

Don laughed. "That man is no more. I don't have to meet with Tracy until five tomorrow. Maybe I'll take the work crew out for lunch. That'll shock the hell out of them."

"They kind of seemed like jerks," I said.

"No, that was me. They're a good team. I'm going to do it."

"They won't recognize you," I said.

"Truly," Gian said.

"I've lived more in these last few days than I have in years. Plus, it's fun hanging out with you guys," Don said. "I never had cool friends."

"Me neither," I said.

"You grossly underestimate your worth," Don said.

My classmate Chase had told me the same thing when we first met for coffee. How many times did I have to hear it before I believed people? I should call him. We hadn't talked in ages.

"You're pretty. You're cool. You're pretty cool," Gian said. He sat up straight. "We have to get to New Orleans."

Rowanda's mother had passed. "I thought she was getting better."

"Don, it's been a pleasure," Gian said. "Can I ask you something? Are you a religious man?"

"Not really. Would it help?"

He shook his head. "I was just wondering where the good faith was coming from. You're more spiritual than anyone I've met. You'll get right in."

"All I want is to be with my wife. I don't care where as long as it's with her."

"You will," I said.

We headed to our bedroom to find appropriate clothes for the journey. Rowanda was at her mother's house. Who was being wheeled out to a hearse at the moment. We materialized when Rowanda shut the front door. She was leaning with her forehead against it and turned around.

239

"Why did you have to take her?" she screamed.

I shook my head. "We didn't do this."

"She's all I had." Her back was against the door. She slid to the floor.

I kneeled and held onto her. "Time is precious. You spent it with her. You made her happy."

"I should have stayed here. Oh, Momma, why'd you have to go? I gotta get out of here." She flung the door open and ran down the block.

"Let her go," I said. "We'll meet up with her."

Nera appeared. "I'll help clean up." She tilted her head to the bedroom.

"Oh God," I said.

Her mom died while taking a nap. Not a bad way to go. I was happy to see a mattress protector. We threw that and the sheets away. Rowanda didn't need to deal with the mess. I found clean bedding. Nera headed out when we were done. She never explained why she didn't have Rowanda move back in with her mom.

We found Rowanda hanging onto an iron fence, crying. The house in front of us was a gorgeous Victorian.

"This was Mom's favorite place. See the corn shaped into the fence?"

The corn wasn't just shaped into the fence; it was the fence. There were rows of deep green metal stalks with ears painted a dull yellow.

"That's so cool," I said, touching an ear.

"I wanted to stay here tonight. Looks like they're selling the place."

"Why don't we go for a walk," I said and took her hand.

"Is this the street Brad Pitt lives on?" Gian asked. "I've seen these buildings in a picture."

"That's a few blocks over," she said. "I can take you there. You have any more ganja?"

"Is it that noticeable?" I asked.

"Only on you."

Gian reached into his pocket for an edible. "Start with half."

She shoved the whole gummy in her mouth.

"Whoa, come on, spit out half. That's some strong shit," he said. "You can keep the other half." He handed her the plastic wrapper from the ground.

"Fine," she said and spat it into her palm. It was a mangled mess. There was no way to get that back in the wrapper.

"Just do the whole thing," Gian said.

She ate it back up and washed in a dog's water dish. I shuddered at the thought of germs.

A horse-drawn carriage rolled past with a young couple in the back. "This street is gorgeous," I said. "So much different than Bourbon Street."

"Royal has class," she said. "History. So, I have a question. When am I going?"

"This Friday evening," Gian said.

"What time?"

"Eleven thirty-two," I said.

"Jesus, you have it down to the minute."

"To the second," Gian said.

"I'm gonna throw a party at Momma's house."

I was about to object, but Nera told me it was all right. "Go out big."

"Don't think you're getting out of your part, honey," she told Gian. "I'll be up in my room at eleven."

"Fine," he said.

I let out a huff.

Rowanda crossed Royal, proceeding in the same direction, then crossed back to the side we had been on.

"What's wrong?" I asked.

"LaLourie Mansion." She motioned with a nod to the building she had avoided. "It's haunted."

The building had a dark vibe. I'd like to see it when invisible.

"This is Brad's street." She led us down a block and a half. "He's not here anymore. They're selling it."

"I bet this was a fun place to live. Seems like a town that would leave him alone."

The house was unassuming. Even shorter than the ones on each side. The second-floor balcony stretched the width of the house. I adored the place. It was a perfect home.

"Too bad it's Saturday," she said. "There's a great restaurant down the road. No way they have a table free."

"Who knows? Try," I said.

She called to humor me. "Really?" She covered the mic. "Can you hang around for an hour? It's Creole-Italian."

I would have said no if she'd made a Creole-Italian sexual innuendo. It was still bugging me that they were going to fuck. I made a mental note to purchase condoms.

"That's fine," Gian said.

"Eight works, thanks, darling." She gave her name. "Is there a band tonight? Perfect."

"There's a jazz band in the bar. We can hang out while we wait for our table. It'll be nice and loud, so we don't have to think."

"We also lost someone today," Gian said.

"Did you lose someone or kill them?"

"We don't want any of you to die," I said. "It was hard."

"Did they suffer?"

"Not at all," Gian said. "One second he was there, and the next, he wasn't. Your body's just a shell."

"Good, I hate pain. I guess I'll see Momma soon enough."

His shell comment struck home. It was so noticeable when Troy left his body, probably because he was full of life.

The packed bar in Adolfo's was tiny. A waitress came down the stairs with menus. "Hiney party of two."

A couple stepped away from the standing table in front of us. We snagged it.

"Hiney party," Gian giggled.

The jazz trio started with a loud piece. A man with a standing bass barely fit on the tiny stage. The trumpeter and the saxophonist faced outward to give him room.

Rowanda was right. It was too loud to think. I enjoyed the hell out of not talking. Her sadness seemed to fade as the edible kicked in. She had a pleasant smile, listening to the band.

The dining room upstairs was kitschy, with red-and-white checkered tablecloths. The walls were a deep red, covered in framed pictures. We lucked out with a table tucked away in a nook.

Looking through the menu, my eyes went straight to one of my favorite dishes. More importantly, it wasn't something they would make spicy. I closed the menu.

"That was fast," Rowanda said. "What are you having."

"Spaghetti Vongole."

She nodded in agreement. "Nice choice."

# Chapter 11

The next day, we jumped to Robert's living room. He was in his bedroom getting lucky. The energy from their sex created a fuchsia glow permeating from the center of their bodies. We moved to his garden to materialize. I was happy to see no cameras. Both of us were grinning.

"Do you think that's his old fuck buddy?" Gian asked.

"I hope so. She seemed sweet," I said. "Since we're here, can we explore the castle on the hill?"

"Sure, lead the way."

I vanished and found a pathway in the woods by the upper parking lot. Gian appeared behind me. Dunster Castle was impressive as it came into view.

"That's about as castle as castle can be," I said.

There was a small queue to get inside. I noticed the man in front of us holding a ticket.

I tapped him on the shoulder. "Excuse me. Where did you get the tickets?"

"Hey, Americans. USA," he chanted.

His wife rolled her eyes. "Follow the signs to the Great Gatehouse. The ticket booth is past that on the left. I'm surprised you missed it."

"The scenery was a little distracting."

"It sure is." She locked eyes with Gian.

"Hey," the man said.

I could see why they called it the Great Gatehouse. It was so massive that the path wound through it. I would have been happy just touring that building. It looked hundreds of years old.

"We're closing in forty-five minutes," the woman at the ticket counter said. "You may want to come back tomorrow."

"We'll be fast." I handed over a couple of twenties.

She had me sign the guestbook.

"I hope you used fake names," Gian said as we walked away.

"Damn, I should have. I only put our first names."

We were back in line at the castle. One of the poles for the thick queue ropes held a plaque with an overview of the castle's history. Gian was absorbed in the story.

"The Battle of Hastings was here. I've heard of that one."

"I have, too. Weird."

He gasped. "We need to get out of here."

Gian wouldn't slow down. "Wait." I held his arm firmly to stop him. "What's the matter?"

"It was the Normans who conquered this town. Right around the same time they were exterminating my people in Sicily."

"Weren't the Normans the ones who allowed the Moors to stay once they were defeated?"

"I guess. It's still too big of a coincidence. I don't like it."

A man with slicked-back hair and a gray three-piece suit was approaching. He had a crooked English nose. I loved the odd characteristics of my kin. His pace slowed and he stared at us with trepidation.

"Pardon the interruption," he said in a posh accent. "Are you Gian Lombardo and Linsey Cameron?"

Gian raised an eyebrow at me.

"It is you, isn't it?"

I nodded.

"A friend thought he saw people last week who matched your description. Where are my manners? I'm Stephen, the House Manager."

He offered his hand.

"I hope you don't mind. I had my ticket takers look out for you. When I was sixteen, I went on a business trip to

Milan with my father." He looked around before whispering, "Dad was murdered in our hotel by a Dread."

I felt Gian's shoulders sink a little. He didn't need this guilt. Why was this guy talking to us? It bothered me.

"The monster toyed with me through the crack in the closet doors. Security shot him before he got to me. I'll never forget the thirst in his eyes for my death."

"I am so sorry," Gian said.

Stephen could barely look at him. "Don't be. You broke the curse. No one will ever have to go through what I did."

Hearing that made me feel a little better. "You'll be happy to know that Gian never killed anyone."

Stephen forced himself to look at him. His knees buckled and I caught him. "You look so much like that Dread. I... I... need a moment. If you meet me back here at four, I'll give you a private tour without all the people."

"You sure you can do this?" I asked.

"Pretty sure."

"Can you give us a ghost tour?" Gian asked.

I shot him a look. The man just told us about losing his father.

"Can I ever. You're looking at one of the most haunted castles in England. Head down the road to the left. It will take you to the old mill. By the time you return, all the tourists will be gone."

I found the mill at the bottom of the hill on our map. We were going to jump, but the path kept getting prettier. The old mill did not disappoint. I liked the spinning water wheels working in tandem. I'd never seen two.

I was distracted by a sign pointing to Lover's Bridge. Off in the distance was a stone bridge spanning the river with two arches for water to flow through. It was adorable.

"Come on," Gian said, taking my hand.

A seat was built into the brick wall in the middle of the bridge. We relaxed and enjoyed the view of the sprawling field past the stream.

247

"I wonder why they call it Lover's Bridge?" he asked.

"Couldn't possibly be the loveseat we're on," I said. He'd asked for that.

Back at the gatehouse, a guard stepped into the path, blocking our way. His face was slumped from exhaustion like he'd had a challenging day with the public. "Castle's closed. You'll have to come back tomorrow."

"Stephen is meeting us at four," I said.

He kicked his heels, standing taller. "But of course. Please proceed."

We were ten minutes late. I hoped the House Manager was still there.

Stephen stepped from a side door and held it open for us. He had removed his blazer and rolled up his sleeves. The relaxed vest look made him seem less stuffy until he talked.

"A handful of guests are still inside. We'll tour the Crypt while they clear out."

We entered a hall resembling an English manor. Most of the stone was covered in plaster. At the far end was a sweeping staircase. The ornate woodwork was gorgeous. We had spent so much time in Italy. It was nice being immersed in English history.

"This is the Inner Hall. It's said to be haunted by National Trust volunteer Mrs. Hooper."

"Oh, Mrs. Hooper," Gian said, playing along.

Stephen ignored him, but he'd made me laugh. "She's been spotted at the piano over yonder or ascending the staircase. Some have even heard her speak to them."

A chill crept up my back. I reached protectively for Gian's hand.

We followed Stephen down the stairs to the Crypt. It was spooky and looked every bit like I was expecting, with dirty stone walls and archways. But I wasn't sure why it was called a crypt. There weren't any graves that I could see.

"Do you happen to know when the Normans were defeated?" Gian asked.

"In Dunster?"

"Yes."

"They never were. There were a few uprisings against them, but none succeeded. The King of England made William the Conqueror's grandson the Earl of Somerset, and the bloodline slowly adjusted to our way of life. We had to bring them kicking and fighting, but they adapted. It's funny that you brought up the Normans. They're the reason I moved here. I wanted to learn as much as possible about the Dread without being too close. No offense, but I wanted to kill them."

"I would have too if I were in your shoes," Gian said.

"You don't need to feel uncomfortable in here. This castle was built years after the Normans invaded. The only building remaining from that era is the Gatehouse and the remnants of a few original towers."

"Thanks. It freaked me out when I read about them in line. I was trying to get Linsey to leave when you showed up."

"Don't hate the Normans too much. They're part of your lineage. The reason for your European features."

Gian had to sit down. I joined him. What a mind trip it must have been to know that the people who helped defeat his people seeded their heritage. But then again, he's engaged to a woman whose family would have exterminated them if given the chance.

"Back to the ghosts," Stephen said. "This room is the only one I've experienced anything in. I was working late one evening when a hand pressed against my shoulder. There was the indent of fingers in the fabric but nothing else."

A hand grasped my shoulder and I shrieked. If that wasn't embarrassing enough, it echoed across the stone walls. The hand was Gian's. I felt it approaching and it still scared me. He was soon on the floor, rolling with laughter. My heart was racing too fast to find the humor.

An associate called over the radio, letting Stephen know we had the place to ourselves. I was glad we were leaving the crypt.

The castle tour made me uneasy, but I felt no ghosts. I was surprised. If anyone could feel them, it should be us. I bet if we went invisible, they would be everywhere.

Upstairs in the King Charles bedroom, Stephen stopped in his tracks.

"Where did all these belongings come from? That's not right."

There were clothes on a chair and personal items on the writing table as if someone was staying in the room. A half-empty cup was on the side of the bed. He picked it up and swung his arm toward us. We both recoiled.

He held the cup upside down, laughing. It was a prop with the "liquid" staying in place.

"Best tour ever," Gian said.

"It gets better. There's a secret passageway to the left of the bed."

As we approached the wall, part of it was indented a few feet, opening to a slender hallway.

"Tourists aren't allowed in here, but you're guests. If you want to take it, I'll meet you on the other side."

"Will we fit?" Gian asked.

"If you go sideways."

"You first," I said.

Gian sidled right along.

"Don't get too far ahead," I said.

My tits were tight against the wall. I was afraid I'd get stuck. Claustrophobia was setting in fast.

The passage wound around and ended in a small library where Stephen was waiting.

"That was awesome," Gian said. "Secret passage!" He waited for me to give him a double high five. "Don't leave me hanging."

I looked at Stephen. "Have you ever high-fived?"

"No." He walked toward Gian. "But I've low-fived." Their hands connected with a smack. Seeing a proper gentleman do that was amusing.

I went to high-five Gian, but the moment was over.

"I was afraid you were going to turn the lights out to scare us," I said.

"I wouldn't do that to you," Stephen said.

He brought us to the Leather Room, which he said was the most haunted in the castle. I was creeped out but didn't sense any ghosts. The Morning Room and Victorian kitchen sent chills, but that was all. There were no doors slamming, footsteps, or dropping temperatures.

While Stephen locked up, we waited out front. He had his blazer back on when he joined us.

"It's too bad we didn't see any ghosts," he said. "But maybe we'll see one in the Gatehouse. If you'll follow me."

He led us down the hill and into the side of the stone structure.

"My dog won't go up these stairs. He sits at the bottom and growls."

"Where does it lead to?" I asked.

"The dungeon pit." He pulled a flashlight from his coat and led us up the stairway.

Standing above the dungeon was creepy. Something was pressing on my body from all sides. I'm sure it was ghosts. A lot of bad happened in that room.

In the corner, I heard the rattle of an old set of keys. I held Gian tightly. We walked closer. There was only silence. Then the rattle rose again, clearer. My heart was beating out of my chest.

"Damn it!" Stephen picked up the phone playing the sound. "My coworkers are always trying to scare each other."

I had my hand to my heart and was trying to catch my breath. "That was so scary."

"It was the best," Gian said.

Stephen brought us to the main house. "Did you walk or drive?"

"Walked," I said.

"Follow the road until you see a wide path on the right. That will lead you to West Street. It was a pleasure meeting both of you. I can't thank you enough for ending the curse. It's comforting to know there'll be no more murders."

"Can you tell your friend we need to keep a low profile?" I said.

"Don't worry. It's only him. I met Lawrence in an online support group. He lost his brother to a Dread. I apologize. Let's not end this on a negative. How about a pint?"

"Normally, we would love to," Gian said. "But we're meeting a friend."

"Crazy Robert," Stephen said. "It's a small town."

"I'm hoping he's just Robert today," I said. "Can I get a hug?"

He gave me a stiff English hug. Gian went in for one.

"I can't," Stephen said.

"Totally understand."

"That was rude of me." He offered Gian a distant hug but soon held firmer. I could see his shoulder shaking. He was crying. Gian rubbed his back.

"I appreciate you meeting with me. It offered a wee bit of closure."

"I'm glad we could help," I said. "I want you to do something if Gian will play along. Look into his eyes as the eyes of your father's murderer and forgive him."

"I can't." He shied away.

"Do it for your sanity," Gian said.

He stared into Gian's eyes and started crying.

"You don't have to do this," I said.

"I do," he said. "I forgive you."

Stephen would have quite the story for his support group.

Gian offered me the crook of his arm and we headed down the road. We were silent for quite a distance. I hoped I hadn't upset him.

It wasn't too far from Robert's. We decided to walk the rest of the way.

"Sorry about the high-five," I said.

"No worries. It was silly."

"Since when is silly bad?"

I had never pressed the bell at Robert's cottage. It took a while for him to greet us. He was in sweatpants, a sweater, and thick wool house socks. A genuine smile made him look almost normal.

"There are my mates." He came in strong and hugged us both, one-armed.

"You're sure in good spirits," I said.

"I got laid," he said proudly.

"Robert?" I said, trying to look shocked.

"Was it the woman at the bar?" Gian asked. "The one from your twenties?"

"Aye, it was indeed. Sally's more of a wildcat than before. I'm sure glad her man is dead."

"Do not tell her that," I said.

"She knows I don't mean what I say."

"Still, she doesn't want to hear it," I said. "Are you up for a pint?"

"I would, but I'm in the middle of a sketch. I have to get it out of my head. Thanks for the invite and for bringing Sally back into me life."

"That's all on you," Gian said. "We just nudged the night along."

"Well, I appreciate it."

"I'm happy for you," I said and vanished to head to our villa.

Gian had a grin on his face when he arrived. "That went weirdly well. Do you think he's changed?"

I shrugged, not wanting to speak my doubts.

"I'm rooting for him."

"Do you mind if I invite Angela and Alfonso over for dinner tomorrow?"

The mere mention of them stiffened his cock. "Not at all. That would be fun."

I ignored his arousal. I was inviting them for friendship.

---

Our guests were arriving any minute. Gian was stressing about the meal. His first batch of homemade pasta didn't turn out like he wanted. I thought it looked fine. He was hanging the second batch on the pasta dryer. The main dish was carbonara. My contribution was a salad with gorgonzola, crushed candied pecans, halved raspberries, and raspberry vinaigrette. It was more of a dessert than a salad.

The intercom chimed. We rushed down the stairs to greet our friends. On the landing, we laughed at our excitement. Gian opened the door, still laughing.

"You're blonde?" I said. With the color, Angela resembled her mom. I wondered if someday she would become the high priestess. "How did you grow it so fast?"

"I was always blonde. I made you see black."

"That's so weirdly awesome," I said, hugging her.

Alfonso handed Gian a crate of his homemade orange Italian soda.

"Thanks, man," Gian said.

"Honey, you need to wash your hands," Angela said.

"The fuck? I did wash 'em." He curled his fingers into his palm to check his nails.

"Nothing wrong with working hands," I said. His rugged handsomeness was alluring. He didn't have a typical Italian look. His face was hardened and cool like a rock star. Thoughts of our witch orgy produced a tingling below.

"Come on in. We'll show you around." Gian led us upstairs.

Angela held her hand to her heart upon seeing the front room. "I love this place. It's so you."

Gian retrieved a plate of four quarter-pieces of gummies from the fridge. "Marijuana," he said, offering it as an hors d'oeuvre.

Angela took one. "Yes, please."

I waited to make sure everyone was doing it before I ate mine.

On the tour of our bedroom, Angela noticed the metal plating in the bathroom.

"I don't understand. Is the curse still on?"

"No, that was left over from the previous owner," Gian said, selling it poorly.

We were heading to the patio when I felt a pinch on his arm. I turned around.

"Dude," Angela said.

"We have to track each other," Gian said.

"Wait a minute? Both of you have it? Oh, we are having fun tonight."

Well, there was the icebreaker. I felt Gian grow semi-erect.

Alfonso was on the balcony gazing out toward the valley, calm and collected. "Love your view."

Angela moved in behind and held onto her man.

"I'll make us a pitcher of OrangeGian," I said.

Gian's breadsticks were baking in the oven. I had my salad individually bowled in the fridge. All I needed to add was the dressing. The prosciutto in the carbonara gave our kitchen a hearty aroma, making me hungry.

I thought I'd added enough vodka to the pitcher, but Gian poured more. He filled four glasses with ice. We didn't follow the three-cube rule in our place.

Our guests had come back inside.

"I forgot to ask. Is anyone a vegetarian?" I said.

"Meat. Meat," Angela said, pointing at her and Alfonso.

"I'm ready to serve." Gian looked proudly at the large bowl of carbonara.

It was a pleasant enough evening to eat outside. I had worried about the wind, but it died down. We seated our guests and brought out the food.

Alfonso waited until everyone was served before taking a bite. "Gian, you've outdone yourself."

"My grandma taught me."

"She taught you well," Angela said.

I took a bite and sank inward. It was the best carbonara I've ever had.

"Linsey made the salad."

"It's marvelous," Angela said. "The whole meal is."

It was growing dark. I turned on the strings of party lights over the balcony. I love the vibe they bring.

"Do you mind me asking why you're no longer friends with Chiara and Orlando?" I said.

Angela's eye twitched. "That bitch," she muttered. "I woke up early the morning that the curse partially came back. I saw Chiara walking back from the lake. I know it was her. Thankfully she screwed up like everything else she does."

"I don't think it was her," I said. "Talk to Nera."

"I have. And to Mom. They won't tell me anything."

I wondered if the muses drove Chiara to try and reinstate the curse. Maybe it was her.

"What?" Angela said. "You have doubts."

"She may have been controlled. I can't talk about it. I'm so sorry."

"Don't be sorry," Angela said. "Mom says your task is difficult. How are you holding up?"

I looked over at Gian for support. I didn't want to talk about it.

"It's brutal," he said. "We're killing people. And it's horrible."

Angela took my hand.

"We'll get through it," I said.

"I want you to know we're here if you ever need a friend."

"I appreciate that," I said. "Friendships were a rarity in my past role."

Alfonso had a glazed look of bewilderment. "I'm getting kind of buzzed."

"It's the pot," I said.

He was confused.

"The marijuana. We call it pot back home for some reason."

"I forgot we took that." He sat back in his chair. "I can feel it coming on. It's nice."

The heavy meal mellowed the group. After clearing the table, we relaxed on lounge chairs, listening to music. It was pleasant having friends over.

A shooting star streaked across the sky.

"Do you believe in aliens?" Angela asked.

I was so confused. Surely they knew about the muses. Next, she was going to say she still believes in Pan. I went to ask her but couldn't.

*Were you seriously going to tell witches that one of their Gods is made up?* Nera said. *Come on, Linsey.*

*She can read minds,* I told her.

*Not today. We put a blocking spell on her.*

I barely heard what Alfonso was saying about aliens. Gian's response that it would be a waste of space was familiar as if it were from a movie.

*Looks like I need to leave,* Nera said. *See ya.*

Angela was staring into my eyes.

"What?" I said, but I knew what was what.

"You guys want to fool around?"

"Gian's hard cock is your answer," I said.

Angela walked over to his lounger and ran a hand across his jeans. I joined her and undid his pants. His big cock flipped up onto his stomach. She bent down and licked the shaft as I attacked his head. Alfonso worked his pants off and sauntered over.

"Mi scusi." He moved us off Gian. "Lift your leg," he told him. Alfonso positioned himself facing Gian with their legs intertwined and their cocks together for us. It was a porny thing to do, but really turned me on. Angela and I sucked and rubbed their cocks, sometimes holding them together as one. I was psyched that this was happening again. Yay, witch orgy.

Gian had trimmed his bush neatly with his balls shaved smooth. I let my fingers wander and found his hole bare. That sent dirty thoughts brewing.

I felt Alfonso kissing Gian and gasped. Alfonso had been adamantly against anything like that at the witch's celebration. The boys made out passionately. Alfonso was an incredible kisser.

"Let's go inside," I said. "Meet me in the front room."

I joined them with a comforter for the floor, a bottle of lube, a wet washcloth, and condoms. Gian smiled.

"This isn't for me," I said.

I loved seeing his eyes grow wide with concern.

The aroma of cooked prosciutto was heavy in the air, creating a heavenly mix with the musky scent of cock.

I didn't think Alfonso would be too fond of the request I was about to make. What could it hurt asking? "I know this could be *way* out of your comfort zone, Alfonso, but can you... fuck Gian? It would feel so good to me."

"What? No. Kissing him was grade school fun. I'm not gay."

"Neither am I," Gian said. "She just likes it."

Alfonso sat silently.

"You're only gay if you have fantasies," I said. "You can go down on me while you do it. Please."

"Fine. This isn't gay," he repeated more to himself.

Angela disrobed and lay on her back, tempting Gian. We were soon all naked, with Gian entering her. I closed my eyes and reveled at the warmth of it all.

"You'll have to prep," Alfonso told me in Italian. "I'm not fingering a dude."

"I'd rather have her do it anyway," Gian said.

I lubed my finger and massaged the outside of Gian's hole. His cock throbbed when I slipped inside. I didn't want him to come too fast, so I concentrated on the stretch.

I grabbed the washcloth and wiped the lube from my hands.

Alfonso was only semi-erect. I sucked on him through the condom until he was hard.

"You first," he said.

I straddled Gian, facing Alfonso. It took a bit of contortion to present myself. Resting my legs on Alfonso's shoulders helped. He lowered his face onto my pussy. Gian moaned deeply as Alfonso's tongue lapped across my lips. I felt Alfonso's cock pressing against Gian's ass. He pushed too hard entering. Our backs stiffened. But maybe the pain would keep us from passing out. Alfonso let out a surprised gasp. He was slow and steady in his thrusts.

The pain soon turned to pleasure. I demanded he speed up. Angela's pussy felt like bliss, Gian's prostate was singing out, and Alfonso was a master at cunnilingus. I was drifting and smacked Gian as hard as I could on the side of his ass.

I closed my eyes. Stars appeared from the darkness. Each thrust or lick was a booster, propelling me further into the abyss. The stars warped inward as if my clit was commanding their presence.

Was I getting close? My God. I brought Alfonso tighter against me. He didn't skip a beat and stayed with what was working, a firm upward stroking across my clit.

"I can't hold it." Gian pulled out and shot onto Angela's stomach. Some of it must have landed in her mouth. Her yummy sound of appreciation made me smile.

The stars imploded into my body and pressed outward, reaching as far as my fingertips. I screamed out as the release overtook me. Alfonso held my weight as I crumbled. Gian backed deeply onto Alfonso's cock. A sharp pain kept us in the present. Alfonso pulled out abruptly.

"The fuck, dude?"

"I didn't mean anything," Gian said. "Pain is the only thing keeping us from passing out during sex. It's a messed up side effect of the Touch."

"That must get interesting," Angela said.

"It's a delicate balance," Gian said. "I don't want to be a monster again. I've felt it deep inside like a temper."

"Maybe it is just temper," Angela said.

That would be wonderful. Tempers can be managed. I rolled onto the floor to catch my breath. Alfonso returned from the bathroom and slipped inside Angela.

"You want him to do you?" she said.

"No offense, Gian, but that's a hard no."

"You said hard," Gian said.

Hearing dirty stoned boy innuendo during sex struck me funny. I was already laughing at how stereotypically Italian "that's a hard no" sounded.

Alfonso scooped up some of Gian's cum with a couple of fingers and fed it to Angela. She licked her lips and moaned.

"More," she repeatedly demanded until her stomach was clean.

"Come here," she said, calling me over.

I straddled her on wobbly legs. She grabbed my ass, bringing my pussy to her face. It was amazing, but the position wasn't working.

"Hang on." I moved to a spot on the couch.

"Get on your knees," I demanded of Angela. She rested my legs on her back.

Afonso entered her from behind as she licked and fingered me. I felt a mouth on Gian and looked up. Alfonso was sucking him off. And not lightly. But he never broke his stride with Angela. She started in again, driving me toward the brink.

Alfonso soon lost interest in Gian. "Any way you ladies could stack up like you did at our celebration?"

"Of course." I motioned for Angela to sit on me.

Alfonso dove in, attacking each of us in turn. His hunger was insatiable as he moved from pussy to pussy.

"Let me come," Angela begged.

"Can I do it?" Gian asked.

We separated. Alfonso focused on me, and Gian pleasured Angela. He was using Alfonso's move he'd learned at the witch orgy. With each flick of the tongue, she moaned louder. She screamed out as she came.

Angela recovered quickly and teamed up with Alfonso.

"Move over a second," she told him.

She stuck a finger inside me, and he brought his face back. It felt like she was using a vibrator, hitting me deeply. It must have been magic. I let out a moan and my hips curled upward. She had my nerves standing at attention like they were absorbing energy from the room. Alfonso coaxed me along from the front. It was almost too much to handle.

A warm sensation in the center of my body grew like my muscles were a rubber band stretching. I grabbed at the couch, trying to hang on. I didn't know if I could stand the tension any longer. I thought I would explode when it snapped. For a brief moment, I felt everything and nothing. It was like I was back skydiving and falling thousands of feet. The orgasm spread in waves across my body, increasing in intensity like an earthquake of unbearable pleasure. My muscles shuddered as it released.

I was left sweaty and flushed. My legs continued to tremble as I coiled into a ball of relaxed mush. The steamy aroma of sex was heavy in the air. I breathed in, absorbing our lust.

Angela held onto me in the afterglow. I felt safe in her arms.

"God damn," Gian said.

God damn, indeed.

The boys were so giving. So adventuresome. I swallowed my fear and picked Angela up, spinning her around to face me. She pressed her hips forward, landing on my face. As much as I tried, I couldn't get into it. The same as the first time, I was mechanical in my technique.

"Relax," Angela said.

"I'll help you." Gian began licking me.

I mirrored his actions, catching up to his moves and syncing each time. His latest was a tongue-swirling circular motion around the base of her clit.

"Don't stop," Angela moaned. She quivered, and her body shook at the power of my passion. Having Gian on me scrambled my thoughts. It made me not worry about what I was doing. It set me free. I dove in and made her come again more fiercely, only stopping momentarily as Gian brought me to orgasm. I was floating to another world, like my soul had left my body. It sent shivers down my spine and left me drained and happy.

Alfonso held onto Gian from behind and jerked him with long, manly strokes while humping the crack of his ass. He slowed almost to a stop. I felt his cum raining on Gian's back. Alfonso had the guiltiest look on his face when he let go.

Angela slid off the couch. I joined her, and we all cuddled on the blanket, catching our breath.

"Looks like I'll have something new to talk about at therapy," Alfonso said.

"It was the pot," I said.

Gian was insatiably horny the next day. No matter how many times I made him come, he wanted more. The fifth time, he got off himself.

He took a deep breath and stared at the ceiling.

"Last night was so dirty."

I snuggled up to him, placing my head on his chest.

"It was fun."

"There's a threesome," he said. "What do you call it with four people? There has to be a better word than foursome?"

"Fourplay?"

That made him giggle.

"I need a nap," he said, spooning up against me. We woke up hours later. Gian made sausage and eggs while I straightened up the villa.

"I was thinking of cleaning Rowanda's backyard for her party," he said.

"It's a mess. I don't think her mom's been out there in years."

"Do you see Rowanda doing it?"

I did not. "I'm in. What the hell?"

She wasn't home when we arrived. I headed to Seattle for my lock-picking kit to break into the shed. While there, I grabbed a stack of yard waste bags. I thought we should start on the front since it was easier, but Gian insisted the back would make for a better surprise.

Six hours of work and all we had to show for it was weedless flower gardens. The grass was so long you couldn't tell we had done anything. We brought the yard waste to a swamp so she wouldn't know we'd been there.

I needed a soak and jumped to Hawaii. Don wasn't home, but he was heading our way. I left a note on the counter so we wouldn't scare him this time. We showered outside and slipped into the tub in bathing suits.

I was asleep relaxing on Gian when Don woke us both up by popping the top off a beer.

"Hi, Don," I said. "Do you have any more? That sounds so good."

"Have mine."

There's nothing better than a cold beer after a hard day's work. He went to retrieve two more. I joined him at the edge of the pool.

"I helped the woman living in the car. I have Tracy in an apartment with a year paid, so she has time to get on her feet. The joy on her kids' faces when they saw their bedroom." He smiled wide with his head tipped slightly back.

"What put her in the situation?" I asked.

"Medical bills from her husband's cancer treatment. Their insurance was crap, and the hospital didn't let her know about the charity program. She could have been out of debt years ago. After a visit from my lawyer, the hospital said she'll be taken care of in a few days."

"I don't understand why they didn't help her before?"

"Must have slipped through the cracks. But it's over, and she's happy."

I leaned my head onto his shoulder. He put his arm around mine. Of the five, Don was the one I liked the most. It was going to be hard letting him go.

Gian stepped into the pool and swam up to us. "Can we take you out to dinner?" he asked.

"I would like that," Don said. "We can go to Hanalei. You'll love this town. It's old-school Hawaii."

The town he brought us to was more for tourists than locals, but the visitors from the other side of the island had left by this hour. The shops were in old plantation-style buildings. Don took us to a bar that was his new favorite. He promised they made excellent food. He did not lie.

New Orleans is four hours ahead of Hawaii. We had to leave at six to be there at ten in the morning. My body ached from the previous day's work. We trimmed bushes until Rowanda woke up.

"Are you cleaning up for my party?" she asked from the back door. "Aren't you sweet."

I waved. "Morning, Rowanda."

Gian wiped the sweat from his brow.

"I'll make some breakfast," she said.

With her up, we could be louder. Once we weed-whacked the yard, mowing went quickly. We had cleared a good amount of space for guests.

"Why don't we take down that old playset," Rowanda said.

"Perfect," Gian said.

It was an eyesore, but we had been afraid to say anything in case it had memories attached.

"I'll ask Antoine if he can set up his kitchen back here. I was putting him in the house."

"Is he the one who cooked the crawfish?" I asked.

"He sure is."

"Now it's a party," I said.

Once we had the playset apart and in the back of her mom's truck, I moved inside to help tidy up. We had the place deep cleaned in a few hours.

My body was aching, but Rowanda wanted to eat dinner with us. Her friends had canceled on her.

We showered at Gian's. It took every ounce of energy not to climb into bed. I didn't want two groups canceling on her. That would be rough.

"This is crazy," I said, seeing all the people on Bourbon Street.

"Yeah, I like it earlier in the week," Rowanda said.

This was Wednesday. The weekends must be insane.

She turned onto a side street to a place called Arnaud's. The inside was charming with a touch of class. I'm glad we dressed up.

"I've already ordered the sampler," Rowanda said after we were seated. "They need a couple days' notice for the request. Tonight's on me."

"That's sweet of you," I said.

"Can't take it with you," she said.

"You seem to be in a better place," Gian said. "Happy almost."

"I've been through every emotion since you told me my fate. I guess I've accepted it. Life's hard. Maybe this is a blessing. At least I'll have friends to see me on my way."

"How many are coming?" he asked.

"A few hundred. It'll be a rager. I hope you can make it."

"I hope so, too," I said.

"You have to come," she said. "I insist."

We were on our third course. "Arnaud's famous turtle soup," the waiter said. "Enjoy."

I looked at my dish with reservation. How could I eat a turtle? They're so majestic.

Gian didn't have the same problem. He dug right in. "This is delicious."

I carefully selected the broth.

"Get some meat. Trust me."

"Fine." I expected to gag it down, but damn was it good.

"Told you." He laughed.

"Sorry," I said to the bowl and dug in.

Gian gasped. "Oh no, the turtles." I'm sure he was thinking of Hawaii.

The meal was six courses. I didn't think I could fit in the dessert, but the chocolate-themed baked Alaska was too delicious.

"They'll have to roll us out of here," I said.

"Do you mind if we head home after this?" Gian said. "We've been cleaning your place for two days."

"I was wondering how you worked so fast. Of course. I appreciate the help. You've made the party."

"No, you've made the party," I said.

---

Rowanda wanted her last full day to herself. I respected her wishes and headed to Connecticut to check on Kristen. The guard at the women's shelter wouldn't let me past the first gate. I wasn't listed as an approved guest. Why did she not include me?

"I just want to check if she's all right," I said.

"She's not here. That's all I can tell you."

I walked away dejected. I hoped she hadn't gone back to her husband.

"Oh, duh." I walked back up to the door.

"I gave you the wrong name. She knows me as Janice."

"Oh. You're cool. She left a letter for you." The guard slid it through the gate.

"Thank you."

It took a while for me to read it. I hoped she gained faith in herself.

Janice,

Thank you for being there for me. I feel like shit for the way I treated you in school. I hope you forgive me. I'm giving this program a chance. Not for you but for me. You made me believe in myself, even if only for a moment.

*My therapist has me off drugs and is tearing down the walls to find me. It may take a while but I'm in it for the long haul. I'm hoping she can find the person I was supposed to be.*

*Kristen*

*P.S. How sweet of you for finding Grandma's jewelry.*

I held the letter to my chest, relieved but guilty for doubting she would make it. My good mood increased as the day wore on. I could finally let my bully go.

---

We could hear Rowanda's party from three blocks away. I doubted any neighbors would complain about live jazz.

The place was hopping. It took us a while to find her. She was in the backyard talking to Antoine. His crawfish pot had a prominent spot in the corner.

Rowanda saw us and rushed over. "Welcome. Welcome. I wasn't sure if you could be seen. Glad you made it."

"We wouldn't miss it," I said.

"Speaking of missing things," Gian said. "We didn't miss the first batch of crawfish, did we?"

"I saved a plate. The spices." She smacked her lips. "Ooh wee."

My stomach rumbled thinking about it. "I don't know if I can do it."

"You'll be fine," she said. "The first batch isn't as hot. Let me get you a drink first." She headed off to the kitchen.

A drunk guy had pleaded with the band to let him sing. He was going on about Salt Peanuts.

Rowanda returned and handed us two red party cups. Behind her, a guy was trying to get our attention. Judging by his conservative attire, he was probably from her old work. He pointed to his cup and held onto his neck like he was dying. Had she put something in our drink? She was looking away. I stopped Gian from drinking his and dumped a little out of my cup. He did the same, confused. Rowanda looked pleased, thinking we had drunk some.

What the hell had she put in there? I thought we were friends.

"I'll be back. Enjoy. My home is your home," she said and walked away.

Her workmate headed over. "I'm glad you figured out what I was saying. Holy shit. What do you think she put in your drink? It was so much."

"That bitch," Gian said.

"Come on, we don't know what it was." I looked over at the man. "Don't say anything. She's in enough trouble."

"OK, but damn."

"Do you know what the drink was so we can make a clean one?" Gian said.

"Whiskey Seven, I believe."

"Thank you. You're a good man."

We headed into the house to get new cups and made drinks without Rowanda seeing us.

"Why are you being so cool?" Gian said. "She tried to kill us."

"I think it was just spiked to knock us out, so we miss the moment."

"You have more faith than I do. Let's check out the upstairs to see where we can get her alone tonight."

"You're not still fucking her, are you?"

"No. She ruined that. Ruined for her, I mean."

I couldn't wipe the smile from my face.

The first door led to a spooky attic space. The other one was a bedroom. We laughed when we saw all the dildos on the headboard.

"What is up with all the dildos?" Gian said.

"Who knows?" I said, shaking my head.

I shut the door behind us and Nera appeared.

"What the hell, Nera? Why didn't you warn us?"

"Do you think I would let her do that? And it wasn't just spiked. She added rat poison. A shit ton."

"That bitch" I said.

"Don't worry. I swapped it out earlier today with nutmeg. I was curious if she would go through with it. The girl has moxie. I'll get her up here at eleven, so you have time to talk. She has some unfinished business."

I gave her a stern look.

"Not that. You're doing well. It'll be over soon." She vanished.

"What are we supposed to do?" I said. "Act like nothing happened?"

"She wants us sick. Let's give her sick."

I followed him downstairs. We found the guy who warned us. Gian whispered in his ear. The man nodded in agreement.

As soon as he saw Rowanda, Gian crumpled in and steadied himself on the man. I held my stomach with a pained face. My acting skills weren't as refined.

"Are you OK?" the man asked.

"No. Can you help us out of here?"

"Yeah, let me call you a cab."

He walked us to the front yard, where we waited. I thought he was playing along, but he had called us a cab.

"To the Ignatius statue," Gian told the driver. It was sweet of him to remember I hadn't seen it.

Rowanda came running out.

I lowered the window. "We're sick. Can't even transport."

Gian rolled his head as if using the last of his effort.

"You probably don't want this then." She was holding the plate of crawfish she saved for us. "They're to die for."

I took the dish. "Maybe for later."

"Have fun," Gian said.

The cab pulled into the street. I slid down in my seat to peek out the back. Rowanda was skipping to the house. At least she would enjoy the party.

"She didn't bring us water," Gian said.

The driver held two bottles up. He also had napkins.

Without the intense heat, the flavors were even more prevalent. Antoine's crawfish *were* to die for. But she was still a cunt for saying that.

After seeing the statue of Ignatius, we walked to the paddle boat. I checked the schedule, but there wasn't enough time for a ride. We ended up exploring the riverfront. Eleven was approaching fast.

"I wish we could go somewhere after this," I said. "I want to hit Paris, but the timing with Don is too close."

"No way. I looked into taking you to Paris after this."

"We can still go for a few hours. I'd love to walk along the river looking through those green booths."

"I love that out of everything Paris offers, that's what you want to see."

I didn't admit it was from a chapter I read in a romance novel.

Being Friday evening, finding a secluded area to vanish took a while. I thought we were late, but we made it five minutes early. In walked Rowanda ahead of Nera.

Rowanda's eyes widened and she turned to leave, but Nera blocked the closed door. She screamed, but nothing came out. "I don't want to die. Let me out of here?"

"Honey, no one does," Nera said.

"Well, I guess we need to get to fucking," Rowanda said.

"Yeah, no," Gian said. "You blew that when you tried to kill us."

"Come on. It was an honest mistake." She went to reach for his junk.

He grabbed her wrist. "I said no."

"I want you to call your sister," Nera said.

"Wait, you told me you were an only child," I said.

"She's not my sister."

"Honey," Nera said. "She didn't steal Terrance. He was using you to get to her. He's the one you should be mad at. They've divorced. Did you know he almost beat her to death?"

"No." Her voice crackled.

"That could have been you. Call her. There's time. Give me your phone."

Nera didn't even hit the keys and it started ringing. She vanished when Rowanda put it to her ear, but she remained in the room.

"Gina, it's Wanda. I'm so sorry."

I couldn't tell if Gina was angry or happy. She sure had a lot to say.

"It's OK. It's OK. Why don't you come over tomorrow? I'm at Momma's house. She died this week. I know. I know. I'm a bitch for not calling."

They had a good cry. I was watching the time. It was getting close. I motioned for her to hang up.

"Baby, I have to go. I'll talk to you tomorrow. I love you."

She put the phone to her heart. "Thank you. That meant the world. How much time do we have?"

"Two minutes," I said.

"Can I at least get a hug?"

"Of course," Gian said.

She approached with her arms wide, then pushed us over and ran from the room.

Nera materialized. "Don't bother following her. You can do it while invisible."

272

Now she tells us. We vanished and found Rowanda in front of the band. A crowd of auras danced around her. She was going out big. Maybe it would be easier not having to look at her. I was angry and didn't want to enjoy it.

Seconds remained. We placed our hands on both sides of her head. A bright flash shot outward from the center of her brain, and then all her energy imploded. She dropped to the ground with the auras of her guests flowing inward to help. A ball of energy rose from her body. It was the brightest blue I've ever seen, almost blinding. The light hovered momentarily, then shot into the sky. That's what the blue streaks I had been seeing were, people dying.

I chased Gian to Paris. We found an alley a few blocks from the Seine to materialize in. The area smelled of piss and garbage. On the main street, the delicious odors of pastries wafted from the open door of a bakery. I wished we'd materialized there.

"Dying at your own party," Gian said. "What a rookie mistake."

I didn't want to think about her, but I couldn't rid my thoughts of what I believed was the soul leaving her body. It gave me a whole new appreciation for death.

He took my hand and we walked to the green shops. I was disappointed to see them closed. It wasn't even seven in the morning. We could always come back.

Gian hailed a passing cab.

"Can you take us to the Eiffel Tower?"

"You're not even making an effort," the man said.

"Our flight just got in," I said.

"You need to say your formalities. Bonjour, would you drive us to the Eiffel Tower, s'il vous plaît?"

"Bonjour," Gian said, "would you drive us to the Eiffel Tower, s'il vous plate?"

"It would be my pleasure," he said, pulling into traffic. "And its s'il vous plaît not plate."

Gian repeated the phrase correctly.

Our driver took us past the Louvre and up the Champs-Élysées. We circled the Arc de Triomphe a few times. There was no order to the four lanes of traffic. Cars wove in and out randomly. It was the most terrifying drive of my life. Finally, he exited down a side road and stopped in front of a large building.

"The best introduction to Paris is ahead on the right, between the two buildings."

"Thank you so much," I said.

He shook his head. "Merci beaucoup. It's not that difficult."

"I am so sorry. Merci beaucoup."

Gian slipped him two hundred euros.

"Merci," the man said, surprised, and handed us a receipt.

After he drove away, I realized he hadn't given us a receipt but rather a list of ten French phrases and their phonetic pronunciation. Our driver was helping France one ignorant tourist at a time.

Gian held the list up as we walked. We were concentrating so hard we didn't notice the view in the distance until we got much closer. Centered between the two buildings, past the stone square, was the Eiffel Tower in all its glory. The sight took my breath away. Gian walked us to the edge and swept me dramatically into his arms, kissing me passionately.

# Chapter 12

Don's last day was approaching and I wasn't handling it well. Someone as good as him ought to stay. The world needed him. I needed him.

We spent the night at his place. When I woke, I sensed him on the other side of the island.

While waiting for the coffee to brew, I found a note on the kitchen counter. I brought it and our cups to the bedroom.

"Don wants us to meet him for shave ice at one." I held up the note.

Gian rubbed the sleep out of his eyes. "What time is it?"

"Noon."

"I slept like hell last night," he said.

"Me too."

"I'm going for a dip."

He didn't bother showering first. I found that disrespectful and had a quick rinse before joining him.

"Should we get something to eat first?" I asked.

"I think starting the day with dessert is a sweet start for a sweet man. Oh, honey, I didn't mean to make you cry."

"I can't help it. I don't want to do this."

"It's best not to dwell on it."

"Says the man who was up all night because of Don."

The employees at Jo Jo's took island time to a whole new level, but their attention to detail was worth it. Gian and I were sharing a Berry Berry. I expected the syrup to be excessively sweet, but it was perfection. The homemade vanilla ice cream at the bottom was a wonderful surprise.

Don drove us down a side road to a secluded stretch of beach. He was ready with a towel for Gian and me.

275

"We haven't talked about this," I said. "What do you want to do tomorrow?" It was such a tough question I couldn't phrase it correctly. I hoped he understood.

"I just want to relax at home," he said.

"Your home or the beach house."

"The beach house is my home now. Let's not talk about this. Just be here for me." He took a spoonful of his shave ice and stared at the sea.

"Of course." I forced a smile. It's unbearable mourning a man who's sitting next to you.

"Did I tell you I took the work crew out for steaks?"

"No. You were talking about doing that."

"It was fun. I hope that made up for my cheapness."

"I'm sure they were glad to spend time with you," Gian said.

"It made me realize how much I hated working. I don't think people were made for it. The snake in the Adam and Eve story is their boss, and the apple was the knowledge that they have to work their whole lives. A blissful existence in paradise is best. Even if it is brief."

I was trembling from trying to conceal my tears. Gian poked me with his elbow. I tried pulling the tears back, but it made them worse. I handed the bowl to Gian and ran down the beach.

Don showed up at my side. "There's no need to be sad for me. I'll be with my wife soon. Let's make the best of this."

"You are so good," I said, bawling.

Don smirked.

"What?"

"Let's get out of here," he said after looking at the time.

On the way home, he stopped at an airstrip to watch the helicopters. "You'll never look at life the same after this."

"I never will," I said.

276

"No, this," he said, pointing at the field. "Come with me."

"Serious?" Gian said.

My fear of flying got the worst of me. Being in the cargo helicopter had seemed like a good idea. The ones parked in front of us were tiny and frightening.

Gian must have felt the tightening in my chest. "You going to be all right?"

"Are you afraid of flying?" Don asked.

"A little."

"You don't have to do this. Gian and I can go."

"No, I want to."

"I know what will help."

Don found a pill bottle in the glove box. "Xanax will take the worry away."

"Two might be better?"

"These are strong. One is plenty."

Gian held out his hand for drugs even though he had no signs of fear in his body.

We had a twenty-minute wait before our pilot, Hudson, introduced himself. It was just enough time to adequately freak myself out. Hudson was a bright-faced kid around our age. This didn't instill confidence, but he said he'd been flying with the company for several years.

His helicopter seated four people, including himself. The worst part was the lack of doors. The Xanax hardly helped. Gian sitting in the back with me brought the most comfort. He even double-checked that I was buckled in tightly.

Helicopters don't fly smoothly like planes. That first minute of weird, almost weightlessness nearly did me in, but it grew fun once I was used to the flight. It was the height that scared me the most. Having the doors off didn't help.

Hudson gave me options at certain parts of the journey: the easy way or the more adventurous one. I always chose the latter for Don. The one near the tail end of

Waimea Canyon was a bad decision. The helicopter dipped drastically from an intense headwind as we crested the top. I was sure we were done for, but Hudson's smile put me at ease. If he wasn't scared, why should I be?

We asked for two slight detours: one over our favorite beach and the other a flyby of the house Don was renting. From the air, his place was huge.

The last leg of our journey was flat and windless, which I enjoyed the most. When we landed, I was brimming with life. There's nothing like facing fear. Even so, I needed a drink.

"That was the best," I said to Don.

"I knew you'd enjoy it. You did well. We barely heard you screaming at the beginning."

I laughed.

We were starving but waited until we were closer to home to treat Don to a meal. I didn't want his last hours stuck in traffic.

Don recommended a place by the beach house. The wait for a table on the covered patio was worth it. He eased into his seat with a relaxed smile.

I thought he was joking about ordering lobster, but realizing this was his last full day struck me hard. We ordered the same. If he could celebrate, so could we.

"This is where I learned to put coconut ice cream in my piña coladas. You'll love these."

He wasn't kidding. They were divine.

I held up my second one for a toast. "To Don Fernau, the greatest man one could know."

"I'll drink to that," Gian said.

"Mahalo. For dinner," Don said. "I've given so much away I'm down to eighty bucks."

"We have you covered. Whatever you need," Gian said.

"All I can think of is mixer. I imagine there will be drinking tonight." Even his needs were selfless.

Back at the beach house, we were in for the long haul. Don brought a thick envelope into the kitchen.

"This is my will. I made a copy for you."

"You didn't add us to it?" Gian said.

"Of course not. Well, I tried to make you the executor, but I physically couldn't. Sorry, I wasn't thinking."

"Yeah, that wouldn't be good," I said.

"There's a list of charities I've made in case anything gets contested. I don't trust lawyers."

"What about your family?" I asked.

"I trust them even less."

I was wondering why he never talked about family.

"You up for a game of dice?" Don asked. "My friend in college used to play Ten Thousand with me. I think it would be fun."

"I think so, too," Gian said.

We had a mellow evening with Don—just how he wanted. And like he predicted, we did drink a bit.

My bladder woke me up early. I was in the kitchen filling my water glass when I spotted Don. He was sitting with his legs hanging over the edge of the yard. I grabbed my phone and snapped a picture. He looked so peaceful.

I walked out to join him. The humidity seemed worse. I was expecting the opposite this early. Don had rings under his eyes and a glass of champagne in his hand. An empty bottle was upside down in the sand.

"Did you not sleep?" I asked, taking a seat next to him.

"It would be a waste of time," he said. "You missed the turtles. Six of them came up to the beach with me. It was the most spiritual experience I've ever had."

"Did you get a picture?"

"Some moments are sacred," Don said. "I want you to do something for me."

"Anything."

"Try and lose your fear of flying. Travel is a gift. You're a banana. Don't be afraid to lose your peel. That's when you become great."

"Did you get into our edibles?"

"A little," he said, laughing. "But seriously, lose that fear."

"I'll do it for you."

"Do it for you. When you get on the plane, is the crew afraid? When there's rough weather, are they running around screaming? Think of turbulence as a ride on a coaster."

"But I don't like roller coasters."

"You haven't discovered that you love them."

"I will do my best," I said. "Do you have any other advice?"

"Stay away from what they call politics today. It's anger theater. Most of us believe a lot of the same things. We're being artificially divided, mostly by outside forces. Just stay clear of it. But still, vote in every election."

"My father taught me the importance of voting." I don't know why I said that. We were never able to vote. I would register for Don.

"Your dad sounds like a good man."

"He's getting there."

We talked until Gian woke up. I could have sat there all day soaking up Don's wisdom.

Gian and I cleared our bedroom, moving all our belongings to Seattle. We wiped every surface and had Don grab the handles to add his prints. I wasn't sure why we were going to all the trouble. His passing would look natural.

We had as relaxing a day as we could at his beach house. Don's time came too soon. There were fifteen minutes left. We hadn't told him when it was happening. He was in a lounger under the covered patio, napping. We decided it was best not to wake him.

I had the strongest feeling that there was someone in the yard. It would screw up everything. I disappeared and walked onto the patio. As I moved closer to Don, a ghost took form. She was kneeling with her hand on his. It was his wife. I was sure. I backed up and she faded. That's why we couldn't see a lot of ghosts. They're only visible when close. She leaned over and kissed his hand.

I materialized inside by Gian.

"What are you smiling about?"

"Go invisible and walk to Don."

He disappeared for a few minutes, then materialized with tears streaming down his face.

"Where do you think we go when we die?" I asked.

"I have no idea. But I like that this isn't final. If I go first, I'll wait for you."

"That's the most romantic thing I've ever heard."

When it was time, we crept up on Don. Gian brought his hands to his head. I reluctantly followed. Don's eyes opened, and he gasped with a smile. He was with his wife.

I slumped down on a lounger facing him and held his hand while I bawled. Don had a peaceful look on his face. He died adorably.

"Go free, my friend," Gian said.

I cried for a solid hour. I needed to be someplace loud and distracting. I pulled up Eli Strut's website and saw he was playing Madison Square Garden. I checked the time in New York. He was an hour into his set. That was fine.

I took Gian's hand. "Come with me."

"Where are we going?"

"Away."

After changing at his place, we headed to New York. We arrived on stage next to Eli. His aura was brighter than anyone I had seen while invisible. Fuchsia energy emanated from almost every crotch in the audience. It was absorbing into him in streams, feeding him. His aura pulsed fuchsia from their love. He did a bunch of excited forward kicks and ran through us. The glow from our orbs increased in intensity, turning the air around us fuchsia. Eli toppled over and stared in our direction as if he could see us. His aura was now a dying brown.

"Get out of there," Nera screamed in our heads. "You're killing him."

Oh shit. Not Eli. I went to open a portal. Nothing happened. Gian raced off the end of the stage. I followed. Eli was getting to his feet when I looked back. We didn't stop running until we were clear of the stadium. I led us to an alley but couldn't materialize. We weren't able to for another three blocks.

"I thought we were stuck," Gian said, catching his breath. "What was that?"

"I think Eli's energy from the crowd shorted out the potenza."

"Eli Strut?"

I nodded.

"We were totally on stage with him."

Yeah, and we may have totally killed him.

As we walked uptown along Fifth Avenue, people turned toward us, drawn in by our presence. We walked faster, but the people followed us as if we were famous. I understood the hassle stars feel. The New York Library was up ahead. How weird that we ended up at the place we met. I led us inside and found an open study room.

Nera appeared. She held our wrists, looking closely. "They seem unharmed. Try opening a portal."

"Wait, is Eli OK?"

"Yeah, he's fine."

I breathed a sigh of relief. "That would have killed me."

"Try opening a portal," Nera said.

I turned invisible and thought of being in our villa. The slit barely opened an inch. I reappeared. So did Gian.

"I could see it, but it wouldn't open," he said.

"I'll get you home," Nera said.

"They went this way," a voice in the hall said.

We formed a chain and headed to Sicily.

"I wasn't sure that would work," Nera said, relieved. "Stay here for a while. Something's screwed up."

She was uncomfortably close and wrapped her arm around my waist. Her hand was traveling south. She shook her head and backed off.

"I have to get out of here. The attraction is too strong."

She vanished, and Gian and I dove for each other's lips. My lust was insatiable to the point I couldn't think clearly. We dropped to the living room floor and worked on each other's clothes. My brother wouldn't be happy with what I did to his favorite shirt, but I couldn't stop myself. It was as if I was possessed by a sex demon.

Gian's chest was perfection. I attacked his nipple so ferociously I was gnawing at it. He forced me off and ripped the rest of my shirt apart. The bra wasn't so easy. I tried to undo it, but he tore the front, springing my tits free. He grabbed the sides, pressing them together, sucking both nipples at the same time.

I broke the zipper on his shorts opening them too fast and yanked them down. His cock was bursting as he wrestled my shorts off. I'd never felt him so hard. He dove onto my pussy, and I twisted around until his cock was in my mouth.

My lust was primal. I stroked and sucked with wild abandon. Not even the overpowering sensation of being eaten out could stop me. He was deep in my throat when I felt him getting close. That was fast. I slid up his cock until just the head was in my mouth. Eating his cum was all I could think of. I stroked a few times and felt him unload. His body shook with a rumble at the end. He spun around and started kissing me, fighting for his load. It was the dirtiest thing I've ever experienced.

He backed away a few inches from my face. "I don't know what's happening."

I shoved his glistening face back to my crotch. His shaft had a little cum left in it. I squeezed to get it out until I was hurting him.

Gian licked hard against my clit. He slammed a couple fingers inside, fucking me with his digits. Two could play at that. I licked a finger and shoved it in his ass. He lifted his head in ecstasy. I gripped his cock in my other hand and spindled him, stroking vigorously and thumbing the underside of his head on the upstroke. I plunged my mouth upon him, being a little aggressive on the head, nibbling on it. He grasped a chunk of my hair, pulling back.

The onslaught of sensations was shocking. I'd never had an orgasm come on so fast. Feeling his prostate lighting up may have helped. The release was like a freight train ripping through me with sparks shooting from the wheels.

There was no time to stop. He was back on my pussy, pressing his face tightly as if trying to get inside. I could feel how soaked his face was. He spread me open with his fingers, bringing my energy away from my clit and redirecting it, expanding the waves outward into my stomach and down my quivering legs. I grasped for the floor and held on as another orgasm erupted. My trembling reverberated across his face.

He picked me up and slammed my back against the wall. I wrapped my legs around his waist as he pushed himself inside. He pounded into me to the point where my back was banging into the wall. I didn't care about the pain, but he stopped and carried us over to the couch, knocking our vase over on the way. I landed in a seated position. He barely missed a beat and was back to fucking me as soon as I was down. I wanted more. I wanted it harder. The couch shifted toward the wall with each thrust. After it banged firmly in place, his power was relentless. I couldn't hold back and screamed out as he punished me below. I wrapped my hands around the back of his neck and pulled myself closer. My hips rocked in sync with his rhythm.

Another orgasm was brewing. They had become rapid fire. I held on so tightly I was almost choking him. Waves of ecstasy flooded every part of my body. I was powerless as the relief brought me to tears.

The energy driving us waned as if it was leaking out. As quickly as the lust came, it was gone. In its place was warmth, peace, and relaxation. Gian laughed and fell on me, exhausted, his chest heaving.

"Where did that come from?" I said. "Wow!"

We shared a confusing silence.

The unrelenting sex had blocked thoughts of Don. His death came crashing home. The world lost the best man I have ever known. I cried until it hurt.

It was dark when I awoke. Gian was curled up behind me. I turned invisible and tried to open a portal to the bedroom. I was happy when it worked. I jumped to the front room and materialized. He was awake and turned to me.

"I just stepped through a portal."

"Oh, good. I thought we broke them. Although it would have been worth it."

"Totally," I said.

"We should check in on Robert. He doesn't have much time left."

I looked at the clock on the nightstand. "It's four in the morning."

We headed to the bedroom. I was the little spoon, wrapping myself in his arms. In two more days, our mission would be over. Hopefully Robert's death would be easier to handle.

As tired as I was, I couldn't sleep. There was a nagging urge to visit the gate to the Underworld. I woke Gian.

"Can you come with me? There's something I need to check."

"Sure," he said, groggily.

I had us dress in our winter gear. Gian thought we were going prospecting.

"Follow me," I said.

We materialized, hidden under a tree. The gate was covered in a deep layer of snow at the bottom of a raised crater. We walked to the top and gazed out at Crater Lake. Pictures don't do it justice. It was gorgeous. The lake offered majestic reflections of the surrounding snow-covered cliffs.

"Hey, this is the gate to the Underworld," Gian said.

"Over there," I said, jumping recklessly out in the open to a flat field in the distance. Gian followed. I walked into the center, but once there, my drive vanished.

"What's wrong?"

"I don't know what brought me here. What the hell is going on? Let's head home."

"Wait," Nera screamed. "Don't move."

"What?" I said, looking over. She was naked in the snow.

"There are witches all over you. Walk slowly this way. Don't go invisible."

I looked around but couldn't see anything. It was creepy knowing they were on us. We walked over to Nera.

"Slower."

Her face relaxed when we were at her side.

"Let me make sure there are none still on you." She vanished and reappeared. "You're good. They are so angry. Let's get out of here. Don't look back. They'll lure you in."

We met up in our villa. I retrieved a robe and slippers for her.

"Thank you. That was so cold. Why were you on Wizard Island?" she asked.

"Something drew me there," I said.

"Did you recognize who it was?"

I shook my head. "It seemed like it was my idea." I was concerned about how easily I had been controlled.

"What was that place?" Gian asked.

"It's a jail for malevolent witches. A pen. It would have been devastating if they escaped. I should have warned you but didn't think you knew where the portal was. I have to go. I need to find out who did this. Whoever it was knew I was in the Underworld."

"I'm sorry this happened," I said.

"It's not your fault," she said and vanished. The bathrobe fell to the floor.

"Two days left and I almost ruined the world."

I wrapped my arms around Gian from behind, squeezing harder until I knew I was back in control of myself.

He was looking up something on Maps and showed me the phone. "It's actually called Wizard Island. How weird is that?"

We headed to Dunster in the late afternoon. Robert's tracker brought us to a restaurant in town. We materialized around the corner. A man passed us, and he and Gian turned and looked at each other but kept walking.

"That's the man Robert would have killed," he said.

"Are you sure? How do you know?"

"No idea, but it's not sitting right."

Nera rushed toward us. "You have to get out of here."

Gian shook off her hold. "That guy's not a scientist. He's military. Something's wrong."

"I would know," she said. "I would see it. Trust me. Trust the muses. Have lunch with Robert. Stay away from that man. Go." She gestured for us to leave.

"How did you know he wasn't a scientist?" I asked.

"How did I know it was him? There's something messed up here."

I grabbed his arm. "Let's get some food in you. Nera will look into this." Although I wasn't so sure she would. She seemed so sure. I guess that happens when you can see the future.

Robert was eating with his lady friend. We were only going to say hi, but Sally insisted we stay.

"They have the best fish and chips in town," Robert said.

She was speaking my language. I couldn't wait to have English fish and chips.

I noticed Sally's hand on his knee. "So, what's going on here? You two an item?"

Robert blushed. He actually blushed.

"He's a keeper," Sally said. She had a shy way about her like she worked in the back of a library. But that could have been from her frumpy dress.

The waiter stopped by for our order. Robert barked at the man, "Fish and chips."

Sally laid her hand on his shoulder. "Honey, let the ladies order first."

"So sorry. Yes, please, what would you like?" His demeanor had changed entirely. Sally was a miracle worker.

Gian added a pint and a whisky chaser to his order. He was freaking me out. I ordered the same.

Robert winked at me. "That a girl."

Sally excused herself and headed for the restroom.

"She's after me money," Robert said. "But I don't mind. She can have some. It's a good way to go out. The cottage and enough to cover taxes are still going to Jake."

"You're a man of your word," Gian said. "I respect that."

"I think she honestly likes you," I said. "I'm going to check on her."

I found Sally washing up in the loo.

"Hi," I said. "Can we talk?"

"Sure. What's up?" She backed up a few feet nervously. I didn't mean to intimidate her.

"It's Robert. I have a feeling he doesn't have much time left. Can you give him a good couple of days?"

"I've had this feeling all week," she said. "It hit home when he quit working. I treat every day like it's his last."

"Good. I'm so glad you found each other."

"You made that happen," she said.

Gian did, I wanted to say. "No matter what he does, don't give up on him. He'll take care of you."

"I don't want his money. I love Robert. Flaws and all."

For the first time, I felt we would succeed. Robert was going to die in peace.

Our drinks were on the table when we returned. The meal arrived soon after. It was conversation stopping good. I'd go as far as to say it was the best fish and chips I'd ever had.

"Tell Linsey what you call your bucket list," Sally said.

"It's me fuckit list," Robert said, laughing. "We don't have time for some of the big items, but we're making progress."

---

The following morning, I jumped to Hawaii to mail a letter to Kauai's local newspaper, The Garden Island. I sent it from Oahu to give Don enough time to be found. He wouldn't have appreciated us going to the media, but his story had to be told. He was our hero, but keeping him to ourselves would be selfish. Most importantly, the publicity would help save a few of his charities. The tale of him finding gold and giving all the money away would make him a local legend.

I returned to Sicily and dressed for England. Gian and I were avoiding eye contact. Robert's day had arrived. Neither of us was ready. He was so happy lately. Well, happy for Robert.

"I don't want to do this," Gian said.

"I don't either." I took his hand, letting him lead the way.

Robert was asleep in Sally's arms. I wasn't sure how to get him away from her.

*I've knocked her out,* Nera said in my head.

"Robert." I rubbed his shoulder. "Wake up."

He looked up at me with glazed eyes. "Hello, love."

"Let's go have that tea."

His shoulders sank in. "No," he whined.

"It's time."

"But life has become so much better."

"I know, my friend. You're brave. You can do this. Don't run. It will happen wherever you are."

I stepped out of the room and waited in his kitchen with Gian. Robert emerged barefoot in an English pair of striped pajamas. He found his slippers warming by the stove and slipped them on.

"Sally wouldn't wake up. I really shook her."

"She's OK," Gian said. "We had to knock her out. She can't be with you for this."

"I need her more than ever."

I took him in my arms. He was gentle with his embrace. "Why don't you make the tea? We have time to enjoy it."

He rooted through the back of his pantry and pulled out a box. "I bought this special for the occasion, but I want me standard."

"Go with what you love," Gian said.

His use of the word go sat heavy with me. I wasn't sure I would find the strength to do this.

290

Robert's hands shook as he prepped the tea. Time was moving fast, but I didn't want to rush him. He made a tray for us and we headed outside.

"Can we sit in me garden? Right on the ground."

"I would like that," I said.

He sat with his legs crossed at the base of one of the flowering trees. We both joined him. The garden was calming.

"Sugar?" he asked.

*It's only sugar*, Nera said.

"Yes, please," I said. Gian nodded.

I added a teaspoon and stirred. The scent of the tea leaves came to life as I took a sip. "Robert, this is delicious."

He tipped the cup to his lips and his shoulders relaxed. "I'm not ready. Is there any way we can extend this a few days?"

"We can't. It's like a timer. Relax. We're here for you. It won't hurt at all."

Robert started crying. "I don't want to die."

I scooched over next to him. He leaned his head and sobbed on my shoulder. Gian moved to his other side.

"We're going to remove the pain from your tumor so your last moments will be in peace," Gian said. "Hold still."

He smiled at us. "Thank you."

I kissed him on the forehead. "I love you, Robert."

We brought our hands to his head and his body slumped over. He passed with a slight smile of peace that gave me hope.

I didn't think his death would affect me so drastically, but I started bawling. Gian helped me to my feet and held me.

"We need to get inside before someone sees us."

I gathered the tray and cups but left Robert's by his side. Gian found a branch to wipe our presence away. Back in the kitchen, I washed our dishes and put them in the cupboard.

I slipped the teabags into their wrappers and took them to Sicily. Nera was waiting for us in the front room.

Her smile was a warm greeting. "All five were at peace with themselves. You did it."

The phrase struck me funny. Max says *You did it* when his cat does a trick.

Gian's look was pained. "Something isn't right. Take us to Penderdash." The look of terror in his eyes was scaring me.

"What?" Nera said.

"I need to see Penderdash. Now!"

She cocked her head, confused.

"For fuck's sake, Nera," he said.

"Let me contact him. You'll see everything is fine." She lay flat on the floor and closed her eyes.

"What the hell is going on?" I asked Gian.

"I think that English guy was supposed to die. Only bits are coming to me."

I was lightheaded and steadied myself against the doorframe. Penderdash wouldn't lie to us. The five had to die. They had to. If we killed innocent people, it would destroy me.

Without using her arms, Nera's upper body rose to a sitting position and her eyes opened. "He'll see us."

"Wait, hang on," I said. "I have a gift for Sty Ling."

I retrieved a purple sweatsuit from our closet. "This is from Prince's bedroom. I hope it's all right?"

"That's sweet, but you can only bring what you wear. How will you fit into such a tiny outfit?"

I folded the arms in on themselves and did the same with the pants to wear on my arms. "Will that work?"

"Maybe. Lose the ring. I'll bring pants for you." She vanished.

"I was wondering why you stopped in Minneapolis last week," Gian said. "I would have gone to Paisley Park with you."

"There were cameras everywhere. We'll have to tour that one in the daylight."

"Still."

I thought it best not to tell him I saw Prince's ghost.

It wasn't easy getting his clothes onto my arms. The doubled-upped pajama bottoms fit, but the sleeves in the top were too small. I had to go through the bottom of the shirt with my hands out the neck hole. Gian cinched the loose fabric with the arms.

Nera returned with a stack of silk clothing. Hers was yards of fabric that she had me wrap onto her. "I couldn't show up next to Prince's outfit wearing cotton."

"Let's get moving," Gian said impatiently.

After dressing, Nera took our hands, and we headed on the journey to the Underworld.

Penderdash met us at the cleansing room. We disrobed before emerging. "What is the meaning of this? Why have you called for me?"

"The man we saved from Robert still needs to die," Gian said. "What is going on?"

"I don't appreciate this tone," Penderdash said. "The visions were clear."

"You had the visions?" Gian asked.

"Not me," Penderdash said.

"Let me guess. It was Judas's muse who had them?"

Penderdash laughed. "No, but that's funny." He turned to the alien behind him. "Bring me Jornata."

We walked with Penderdash out of the rock tunnel to the grassy meadow. The warm air was nice on my nakedness.

"Is that purple fabric for Sty Ling?" he asked me.

I had folded the outfit in a neat pile. "This isn't just fabric. Prince wore this. I'm hoping it will cheer her up." The cleansing chamber had ruined the best part. I could no longer smell him on the clothes.

He looked into my eyes with a warm smile. "I do not consider this stealing. She will treasure this gift. Her grief

293

has been crippling." He set it on the grass. Gian and Nera added their clothes to the pile.

The muse returned with who I assumed was Jornata. His smile dropped when he saw us.

"Gian said there's something wrong," Penderdash said. "That the last man saved was supposed to die."

Jornata sang his answer back.

"In English," Penderdash scolded. "We have guests."

"Everything went as the vision foresaw."

Penderdash tilted his head like a curious puppy. He reached for Jornata, but the muse backed away.

"What have you done?"

"Nothing. Everything is as it should be."

"Come here," Penderdash said forcefully.

Jornata didn't move.

"Come here!" Penderdash shouted. His tone tore through my core. I doubt he had raised his voice in years. He put his hands on the alien's forehead and closed his eyes. Penderdash gasped.

"I'm tired of being trapped here," Jornata said.

"And what? You were going to let the humans destroy themselves."

I reached for Gian. He seemed to be a million miles away. Panic overtook my senses. We had been played.

"Do you think the Collective would allow us to move to the surface? They would come for us next. You've put us all in grave danger."

Penderdash whistled. A giant of a beast came lumbering over the hill. It looked more dinosaur than animal. The monster galloped closer and roared, showing a triple row of sharp teeth. Jornata screamed and shielded his face as the mouth crashed down. He was picked up in one bite. The crunching as it chewed was horrifying.

Penderdash was shaking.

"Why didn't I see this?" Nera said.

"Tell me we didn't kill innocent people," I demanded.

"No, no. You can't change fate. It was their time."

"Even Don?" Gian asked.

"Even Don. Jornata used the distraction of your mission to trick us. I can't ask more from you, as I promised." He whispered in Nera's ear.

She looked over at us, horrified. "Would you see it in your heart to eliminate the two men about to destroy our world? I'll help."

"What do they do?" I asked.

"They start a nuclear apocalypse," Gian said.

Penderdash nodded.

"Fuck, of course," I said.

"Time is of the essence. Get them to the Admiral," he said to Nera.

"I love you, Penderdash," I said.

He smiled. "I love you too. We were impressed with both of you. Your task was difficult, yet your hearts remained pure." His body rose until he was eye level with Nera. "There's no time to explain." He placed his hands on her forehead.

She jerked her head back, wide-eyed. "We are not killing the leaders of these nations."

"No. No. That would be too high profile. Eliminating the Admirals will break the manipulation."

"We need to go now," she said to us.

Nera raced us back to Sicily. We only had minutes to recover from the trip. My head was killing me.

"I thought they were nonviolent," I said. "That beast."

"Focus on the task," Nera said. "Don't worry about clothes. We're not going to materialize. This first one is tricky. We're heading to a nuclear submarine north of Scotland."

She lined us up, and we jumped to a small room surrounded by glowing circuits. We had to walk forward to stay in place. A man at the console held a tiny device in his hands. The glow of its circuits moved in a cross pattern as he blessed himself. Nera rushed toward him and sank a tracker in his head. It glowed brightly, then faded. The man's arms dropped to his side, but he remained seated. I was surprised at how calm I was. I wasn't sure where the strength was coming from. Gian and I placed our hands on his head. There was no countdown. Would this even work? The tracker flashed and he slid to the floor. The blinding light of his soul emerged, drifting backward as if not knowing where to go.

Nera snagged the device, and we were whisked off to a war room in China. A man was pulling his arm back from a wall of circuits. Nera touched the area and sparks flew. I hoped we made it in time.

She placed a tracker in the man's head and we disposed of him. His soul shot into the air like Rowanda's had. As spectacular as it was seeing life leave a body, saving the world was anticlimactic.

I headed back to Sicily and materialized. My headache had turned into a debilitating migraine.

"Let me help you with that." Nera removed the pain, and I collapsed.

Gian didn't want her to remove his pain.

"It will kill you," she said and removed it for him.

"You did well, my friends." She was looking at the USB drives in her hand. "How can something this small cause so much carnage?"

"I don't understand what could have happened," I said. "Jornata is dead. Why didn't the plan end with him?"

"The manipulation was already in place. So was Jornata's alibi. He planned to launch a nuclear weapon at Russia and another to the US. These two missiles would have caused an extinction-level reaction. Few would survive. You saved humanity, my friends."

The magnitude of what we had accomplished washed over me like a tidal wave. My body shook as the adrenaline receded. "What about the man we ran into that was supposed to die."

"That was the General in the submarine," Gian said. "He was in Dunster to say goodbye to his family."

Nera's eyes rolled back and she swayed slightly on her feet. Her gaze returned to normal. "Penderdash has a parting gift for you, Linsey." She took my hands. "Your mother is coming."

I couldn't comprehend what she was saying. The biggest wish I've had in life was to see my mother again, but the realization it could be happening was fighting with reality.

"I don't know how this was arranged. Those who pass can visit but can't be seen by family or loved ones. He's breaking so many rules. She only has seconds. Go invisible. Go."

The tears vanished as I did. Standing in front of me was my mom's spirit. She was beautiful. Radiant. I went to hug her and passed through. She smiled with a tilt of her head. I placed my hands in hers as best I could.

"I love you," she mouthed.

"I love you, Mom. I love you so much." I hoped my words reached her.

She placed a hand over her heart and said, "Proud." Her gaze was deep as her spirit rolled into a ball of energy that shot to the sky. I fell to my knees and watched until I couldn't see her light anymore.

It wasn't easy to catch my breath after materializing. The tears came flooding in. I hadn't cried like that in years. I think every tear I'd suppressed for her came pouring out. Gian held onto me from behind, stroking my hair lightly.

Reasoning pulled me from the grief. How did Penderdash arrange that? Were humans aliens? The way Mom left was the same as when people died. Was that their soul or just how we traveled? What struck the deepest was the glowing blue light looked the same regardless of the person's skin. I stared at the shell that is my body and back at Gian, confused. "Are we aliens?"

"Are we?"

"There are no aliens," Nera said. "Just different species in the universe."

Gian helped me to my feet. I grabbed my wrist in agony and watched as the potenza worked its way out of my flesh. It dropped to the floor and melted, fading from bright blue to a dull gray. I stumbled backward. Gian's fell out and rolled under the counter. A puff of smoke drifted away.

The connection from inside him began to fade. We reached out to each other in desperation. The Touch was receding.

# Chapter 13

We waited until early summer to head to Alaska. I'm glad we did. The price of an ounce of gold had risen almost a hundred dollars. Our flight from Seattle to Anchorage was ridiculously bumpy. I was doing my best to cage my fears. Don's advice to watch the flight attendants wasn't working. They abruptly stopped the drink service and strapped themselves in. How was that helping? It didn't seem to bother Gian, which somehow made my anxiety worse. The flying itself is what Gian hated.

"Why couldn't we keep the potenza?" he said. "This is bullshit."

"Be humble. We can fly back in first."

"We could take a Lear Jet if we wanted."

"Not if we want to keep the money."

Gian's grumpiness carried well into Anchorage. His knowing I had a gun purchase arranged wasn't helping, but the amount of gold we were after required protection.

The sun warmed my face as I stepped from Granny's Guns. It had been cloudy when I went inside. Lush trees were abundant downtown. The peaks of the surrounding mountains sat whitecapped, like a crown upon the city. Anchorage was just as gorgeous in the summer, even in this part of town.

Gian pulled me close, but recoiled. Feeling the holster must have triggered him.

"It's OK, Gian. You're right here with me. We're in Anchorage." I was using the same technique Aunt Pia used on her husband during his PTSD episode.

He looked up at me. "What? I was thinking about the first day you came back in my life. At the hotel after you took off your holster." He placed my hand on his hard cock.

I wanted to smack him but his smile caressed my soul. We walked down the street hand in hand.

"I have our truck," he said.

Every vehicle was a truck.

He pointed to a beat-up red Toyota with a sturdy brush guard. "That one."

The color worried me. It would stand out in the wilderness.

I reached the passenger side and smacked the roof with my palm. "Old red looks solid."

He slid into the driver's seat, meeting me inside. "I can't believe you've never hiked before."

"My family didn't like leaving the house unsecured." I looked at him, flush with guilt.

He let it go. "I love hiking. Being in the forest was the only time I was free."

"You'll have a new sense of freedom on this one," I said.

"There's so much gold."

"Your window's open," I said.

He slunk in his seat and checked that no one heard.

"Hence the gun."

He laughed. "Just be careful."

"Safety was the first thing I learned."

Our last stop was to pick up the gear we ordered. The metal detector almost didn't arrive in time. It showed up with only two days to spare. Metal detectors aren't very reliable with gold, but this one was supposed to work the best. With the locations marked on the GPS, any hit should be our gold.

We booked a room and headed out at dawn. It was a two-hour drive to our first site but less than a mile hike. With our digging gear, it seemed like four. This was the shortest of the eight hikes.

The river was down from what I remembered. "We should have marked where that big nugget was in the middle."

"Totally. That's at our next stop. Maybe the detector will find it."

"It was buried deep."

"Plus, how do we dig in water?"

Gian found a flat spot high above the river for our campsite. He picked the location for the morning shade. After pitching the tent, we rinsed off at the shore. He sat on a boulder with the water filter, filling a bottle, looking manly and rugged.

"Try this," he said, handing over the water.

I took a large swig. It was mountain fresh and ice cold.

He responded to my smile. "That's hiking."

"This is hiking," I said, gesturing with an open arm toward the scenery. Mountains towered over our valley.

"That's the best part. It's like owning the finest property in the world." He turned on the GPS. "You ready to get rich?"

"I'm so ready."

He led us through the brush and stopped in a meadow to read the notes on the screen. "This one's about four feet deep. Might as well get the deepest one first."

Gian swept the metal detector but couldn't find anything. He adjusted the sensitivity and kept coming to the same spot. His headphones fell off he was laughing so hard.

"You have to hear the sound it makes when it's locked into something deep."

I put the headgear on and swept the area. The locator sounded like an excited country boy yelling whoo. I wished we had two headphones. It was hilarious.

Digging the hole wasn't so funny. We weren't even halfway after an hour.

"Do we have enough food for a few days?" I asked.

"I was thinking the same thing. If not, we can catch some trout."

"This isn't easy."

"You can't get rich without putting in the effort." He swept the detector until he was near the side of the hole. "The first mark was off. This is the gold."

He carved out the side with the shovel and dug down a bit. Then swept again. "There she is."

I took over digging. The ground wasn't bad this deep. We switched off back and forth—one on the shovel and the other with the detector.

"You're right on top of it," he said.

"I want you to have the honor."

I leaned back, stretching my spine. In my peripheral, I swore I saw the movement of a jacket. Looking closer, it was a clump of leaves. My heart was pounding. I didn't like how close we were to the road.

Gian slid the shovel under where I was marking. I sat down with the detector. There was a metallic clunk. He adjusted his pitch and lifted from underneath. The sun glistened off the gold. Gian picked it up and rolled the nugget around in his palm.

"Don't shout out," I whispered. "Be cool."

He looked around. "Eight, nine ounces? What do you think?"

I caught his toss. The gold was heavy, but I had no idea by how much. "We should have brought a scale."

"Could be $10,000 here."

"Nice. Onward." I turned on the GPS and scrolled to the next entry.

He checked which one I chose. "Let's hit the furthest and work our way back."

"Smart."

"I'm not still here because of my looks."

"Maybe not, but I am."

"You're getting good at your snark."

"Thanks," I said.

With eleven nuggets in our satchel, we called it a day. My body was wrecked. Digging is hard work. We were filthy and bathed in the stream. The water was freezing, but you wouldn't know if you looked at Gian. That boy doesn't know the word shrinkage.

We had one small towel. He was a gentleman, letting me dry off first. I changed into new underwear and warm clothes. Being clean didn't take away the aching in my muscles.

"I don't have the energy to fish," he said.

"Yeah, this is so hard." I pretended to cast. "Ow!" My shoulder screamed out in pain.

He laughed and held up two freeze-dried meals.

"Beef stroganoff or lasagna."

I pointed to the stroganoff.

"I was hoping you picked that. These are easy. I'll get it ready. But first, I have something you'll like."

He retrieved our air mattresses from the tent. After letting out a little air, he folded one in thirds and tightened the side straps. It became a low chair. That was why he'd put the weird covers on them.

"Best hiking invention ever."

Gian wasn't kidding. Sitting with a backrest was a game changer.

After dumping boiling water into the pouch, our meal was ready in a few minutes. He divided the stroganoff between two plates. The dish was better than I expected. There was actual flavor and texture.

"Are they all this good?"

"No." He laughed. "They're horrible. But the scrambled eggs and bacon are all right. Biscuits and gravy is good, too."

"How about the lasagna?"

He shrugged. "The cheese is a little off. I brought you a treat." He pulled a plastic hiking bladder from his pack. "It's not twenty-five years old, but it's the one you like."

"You're my hero. Is there any Percocet in that magical pack?"

"I wish. Settle for ibuprofen?"

I held a hand out. "Two, please."

After the sun dipped behind the mountains, the air grew brisk. I shivered and had to walk off a cramp. Gian retrieved a flannel top for me from the tent.

"You have bottoms if you need 'em."

"I'm good for now."

Watching me put on the flannel turned him on. I didn't need the Touch to see that. He was rubbing his bulge slowly.

I stood up trying to hide my agony, and walked him to the tent. The last thing I remember was being on top, making out. I must have fallen asleep.

A loud clomping outside woke me up. Something huge was near. I found the gun and unzipped the tent flap as quietly as possible. About twenty feet away was a giant bear trying to get to our food. The beast locked eyes with me. I was frozen in terror. In the dark, I couldn't tell if it was brown or black. I didn't know how to react. I showed him my gun as if he would know what it was. He let out a tremendous roar.

"What the fuck is that?" Gian said.

I aimed at the hill behind the bear and fired. Gian screamed. The bear jumped back, terrified. I couldn't see him in the underbrush, but the shrubbery was flattening in his wake.

"Did you scare a bear away?" he asked.

The adrenaline was receding, and I was freaking out.

Gian held me from behind. "Your heart's going to fly out of your chest."

"Let's move the food. That bear was huge."

"Fire another off. So he's good and scared." He poked his head out of the tent. "Hit that stick on the ground."

"Cover your ears."

The bullet struck the ground a few inches in front of the stick. I was surprised I got that close.

304

"Nice shot."

We moved the food to a tree across the way, tying it higher. My heart was still racing. I wasn't going to be able to get back to sleep.

"Can we dig up the rest and get the hell out of here?" Gian asked. "We've already hit the deep ones."

"Sure. I don't want to be around when he comes back." I eyed his bulge. "You need a quick handy?"

He slid his pants right down. My arm was sore within minutes. It gave me the giggles. I switched to my left hand, but that pain was worse. Digging would be miserable. Gian took over and finished. We both fell on our backs, exhausted.

After cleaning up, he worked a T-shirt on with a groan. "Let's get it over with."

There were seventeen more nuggets in our area. All but three were shallow. We had them dug in under four hours. The sunrise was glorious. It crested the mountaintop as we hiked out.

I liked morning hiking. Sure, we had pain, but the cold kept it at bay. Seeing the truck still there was a pleasant relief.

Getting the gold processed was a three-hour ordeal. We took the advice Gian gave to Don and never let it out of our sight. In the end, we were handed a check for $212,056. Neither of us had the patience to upgrade our room. We took a quick shower and slept into the evening. In the morning, Gian arranged for a sports masseuse to come up.

We chartered a helicopter for the rest of the digs. This would save time and energy. Plus, we read that firing a gun is a dinner bell for bears. They've learned from hunters. We're lucky I hadn't drawn more.

Our pilot was more seasoned than the one we had in Hawaii. Austin was a super chill dude in his fifties. He had been a pilot in the Iraq War. The sun brightened his face as he helped me into the helicopter. His eyes were a stunning blue, but his infectious smile drew me in the most.

305

He had me up front with him. "You ever been in a helicopter?" he asked over the mic in the headsets.

I found the talk button on the side. "Yeah, we're cool."

"Let's do it," Austin said and took off.

That initial weightlessness and unsteadiness still freaked me out, but I wasn't as scared.

"I didn't need any Xanax this time," I said.

Austin chuckled to himself, his smile never waning.

What would have taken half a day was a mere twenty-minute flight.

"We'll need about four hours," Gian said. "Can you pick us up at six?"

"Call when you're ready." He handed over a satellite phone. "I'll be fishing on the other side of that mountain range."

Gian spent longer than he should have trying to find the large nugget in the middle of the river. Even with hip waders, I wasn't happy with him out there. The current was strong.

I pulled him away to find the gold we marked. Only one of the sites was deep. We had all of them dug in a few hours. The nuggets at this site were huge. We had around nine pounds. At this rate, we'd never have to work again. It felt like a dream.

Our shower was a small waterfall. I shrieked as I stepped under. Gian's balls retreated, almost going inside him. He caught me looking and grew erect. I kneeled and worshipped him while immersed in the frigid falls. I had to stop. It was too cold.

"After lunch," I said.

We lathered up. The soap we picked was harder to wash off than the first. I wished we hadn't left it at our last camp. Having to stay under the falls for so long was torture. We ran for the sun, shivering. I brought him into my arms for warmth, with his cock pressing against me.

"Let's eat quickly," he said.

306

That morning, I found a fancy deli while Gian arranged our transportation. Everything stayed fresh in the cooler. I was starving but took my time making the sandwiches.

With a helicopter, we could bring actual chairs and a small table. Gian took them to the river bank and relaxed his legs on a flat boulder.

I set a plate on his lap. "Thanks. I'm famished." He took a bite of his sandwich and looked over wide-eyed.

I tried mine. The bread was moist, the lettuce crisp, and the roast beef perfection.

"It may be because I'm hungry, but this is the best sandwich I've ever had."

I stopped myself from saying it was the bread. Why is it so hard to accept a compliment? "Thank you."

The pasta salad was phenomenal, almost as good as the sandwich.

Gian didn't leave a scrap on his plate. He held up his hands to surrender. "I'm leaving lunch to you while we're here. There's no way I could top this."

"You can top something else, baby." That came out so corny, but he smiled.

"Whenever you're ready."

"Let's get the cooler up high first."

I set my holster in the grass away from our blanket. He brought it closer.

We wrestled our clothes off. The minerals in the glacier water left Gian's skin silky smooth. His abs were the best as I ran my fingers across the contours. "Fuck, you're a sexy man."

"You're the sexy one. There's not a day that I don't appreciate being with you. It's not just your looks."

What a sweetheart. How could I be so lucky?

Gian kissed me from above as I lowered to my back. He entered, not having the energy for foreplay. I didn't mind. Having him inside me was the closest I could get to the Touch.

His thrusts were slow and methodical from his core. That quickly changed to a steady swing of his hips. I didn't think he could keep his normal moves up. Just watching had hurt my back. Soft kisses accented his lust. The open-air nature of it all left me captivated in his being.

An eagle rested on a branch high above. He leaped into the air with a bounce and soared away from us. I needed to fly, and positioned myself on top.

My muscles were soon screaming. I powered on until he came, then faked an orgasm and collapsed onto my back next to him.

We cuddled in the afterglow as a float plane crossed overhead. I heard it reverse course and covered up. Gian leaned back, giving the plane an eyeful. They didn't return.

"I think we have time for at least one more location," I said.

"Do you have the energy?"

"I'll find it. The more we dig, the quicker we're done."

I changed back into my dirty clothes, wondering why we had showered.

Austin brought us to our third spot, but we had to cut the dig short due to the approaching evening. We forgot headlamps. He called ahead to have the refinery stay open. The staff was abuzz when we returned. Everyone wanted to know our secret.

The owner, Gerry, was out of state. He wasn't comfortable letting us go out again alone and hired a security guard for our next trip. Gus was military through and through, including his buzz cut. He and Austin were night and day. Gus had us touch down in multiple spots to throw people off our track.

"Make two more stops after this," he told Austin.

Gus stood vigilant as we dug each new hole. However, he studied us as if looking for our secret. I would have, too.

It was an exhausting ten hours before we wrapped up our final location. Gian hoisted the pack of gold onto his shoulder. I caught his subtle smile as he shifted the weight.

"That's it for digging," Gian said.

"I hope you don't mind me asking," Gus said. "How did you know where it was? You walked right to it each time."

I looked at Gian, not knowing what to say.

"We marked it all ahead," he said.

"But, how did you find it then?"

"That is what we're not telling," I said.

"Can I get the model of your metal detector?"

"You can have it," Gian said, handing it over.

"Freeze," a voice in front of us demanded.

Mother fucker. I was more angry than scared.

Gus unholstered his gun. Two men fifty yards apart popped up from the underbrush.

"You're gonna lose," Gus yelled.

I liked this guy. My gun was out, aimed at the man on my side.

"We have a sniper in the hills behind you."

"He's bluffing," Gian whispered.

"Drop your gun and walk over," the man on the left demanded.

"No," Gus said defiantly.

"Send the man with the gold."

"Go fuck yourself," Gian said. Looks like he was as mad as I was. This was our gold.

The two guys glanced at each other dumbfounded.

"We'll come over," the first guy said. We were dealing with idiots.

"Lock in," Gus said. "Feel the moment."

*Nera, please help me knock his gun out of his hand.*

She didn't answer. I hadn't heard her since the potenza was removed.

The man furthest away stumbled and nearly lost his footing.

309

Gus and I fired. My man's gun flew from his hand as if we were in a movie. "Holy fuck!" Thank you, Nera.

"Dude," Gian said staring at me wide-eyed.

Gus's man was down. We took off running toward our guy. Gian dove on him. I slid around and put the man in a choke. He stopped resisting once I applied strength to his throat. I could have killed him but stopped.

There were large zip ties and a roll of duct tape on the man's belt. What were they going to do to us? Gian secured his hands behind his back. I bound his legs.

"John. John!" the man yelled.

Gian taped his mouth shut.

I headed over to see if Gus needed help. A pool of blood was widening under his target's head. John was dead.

"You kill the other guy?" Gus asked.

"I shot the gun from his hand."

"Shut up." He laughed.

"Lucky shot," I said.

"Linsey, don't ruin the story. Own it. Would have been better to kill him, though. I'll call it in."

I'm glad I didn't kill him. There would be no more death from me. We walked over to Gian.

"How did you know he was lying about the sniper?" Gus asked.

"He blinked too much."

Life Flight and three police helicopters arrived in short order. Police love a good shooting.

Gerry, showed up in his private helicopter. He had an incredible bushy mustache, which went well with his cowboy hat. His gait was confident, almost cocky.

The lead detective, Ryan Neason, was very New York. It could have been his suit, or all the Law & Order I watched.

We couldn't reach Austin. Detective Neason suspected he was involved in the robbery. I couldn't imagine.

Austin called an hour into the investigation, apologizing. He said he fell asleep in the sun with his phone accidentally on mute. The police weren't buying his story. They had him fly back to be escorted to town.

"I can take them," Gerry said about Gian and me. "I'm damn glad they're alive."

Neason held his hand up. "Sorry, Gerry. They're coming with me."

"I'm riding with them," Gus said.

"That's not happening either." He pointed at two officers. "You and you." Then he picked up our sack of gold with a grunt. "And I'm afraid this is evidence."

"That's fine," Gian said. "As long as you weigh it first and we get it back."

"Everything will be done accordingly." It was a non-answer that didn't sit well.

"Can we make one last stop?" I asked. "We have another bag hidden. Plus a huge nugget that's at least a ten-pounder."

Gian looked over at me.

"I'd like a police escort," I said.

"Let me check with the sergeant."

"Thank you."

We were given approval for the last haul. Even though there was a detective and two officers with us, I would have felt safer if they'd let me keep my gun.

Our hiding place was higher in the mountains where there was still snow on the ground. We trudged through it with the entourage. It was difficult getting past the bushes. We always just jumped there. Gian slid his back along the cliff and reached into the crevice for the satchel.

"Fuck! The big one is gone."

My dreams popped like balloons. Served us right for drawing so much attention. "We'll still have enough for a good start," I said, more to myself than him.

"I don't want just a start," Gian said, pouting.

"What are you complaining about?" Neason said, looking in the bag. "There's half a million in there alone. That's not evidence. It's yours."

"This nugget was huge."

"We got greedy," I said. "Life didn't let us keep it." And by life, I meant the muses.

A small boulder rolled from the cliff above and slammed into the ground a few feet away. Yeah, yeah, we get it. "Come on, let's go," I said.

At the police station, they found a tracker in our pack. The only people who could have placed it there were from Gerry's company. This cleared Austin.

On the way to the hotel, Gian calculated our bounty. Even without the large nugget, we would have close to two million once the evidence cleared. Not a bad haul, but not enough to fully help my family. It was enough to purchase a house to flip. Maybe I could get a business degree to help run things. Gian and I could take design classes. That's work we could do from anywhere.

Two officers searched our room before heading out. One was left behind for our safety. As soon as he moved to the hall, Nera appeared.

"I know," I said, "we got greedy."

"We saved the world," Gian said. "Doesn't that count for something?"

"It does, but you were drawing too much attention."

"A little more wouldn't hurt," he said.

"That is exactly what I told Penderdash when I pleaded to give it back."

"You tried," I said. "We appreciate the effort. Sorry we drew so much attention."

"Don't be. You'll draw a little more when you return for your nugget."

Tears built in my eyes. This was happening.

Nera nodded with a smile. "Penderdash used a passed out hiker to bury it below your hiding place. It's under the rock that fell. I was trying to tell you."

"How come you can't talk in my head anymore?" I asked.

"That left with the potenza."

"Can you hear my thoughts?"

"Not at all."

"So it was me that shot the gun out of the man's hand?"

"It was all you," Nera said. "You visualized your target and connected."

I almost said it was dumb luck but remembered Gus's advice.

"How come Angela and Chiara can read thoughts?" I asked.

"The witches today have so much power. Especially Angela. She's the strongest in our coven. Stronger than Bianca. She'll be High Priestess one day.

I was surprised she talked so freely, but they did allow us to remember everything. I thought for sure our minds would be wiped.

We hired Austin to help retrieve the large nugget. It was our way of saying we trust him and to apologize financially for his troubles. I let Detective Neason know we were heading back to the hiding spot. He demanded that we have the two officers accompany us. I didn't have a problem with that. Gus was busy.

I gathered our team once we landed. They still hadn't returned my weapon. I felt naked without it. "Can you go guns out?" I asked the cops. "I don't trust anyone anymore."

"I don't blame you," the blond officer, Ryan, said, unholstering his pistol.

Gian led the group. I followed from behind. My heart sank when I saw the bushes cut in front of our hiding spot. The stone protecting the crevice was now a pile of rubble.

"You fucking cops do this?" I asked.

"Whoa, come on," Randal, the seasoned officer, said. "We wouldn't do that."

"Is it gone?" Ryan asked.

"No," Gian and I said in unison.

The boulder that almost hit us was in the same spot. He moved it aside and swept the area with the metal detector. We had borrowed it from Gus.

"How did they not find it?" he said. "It's right at the surface."

I knew how. The muses gave us one last gift.

Gian drew the shape of the nugget in the dirt. He passed the detector over it one last time to make sure he had it right.

"There's no way it's that big," Austin said.

"It's massive," I said.

Gian was digging around the shape when his shovel clinked loudly.

"God, damn it," he said. "Oh, it's just a rock."

He moved his shovel out a few inches. It took an hour of digging to get to the nugget. He was meticulous so he wouldn't damage the gold. Once a trench surrounded it, a hard knock to the side freed the remaining dirt in a mini slide. The nugget glistened in the sunshine. Everyone gasped.

"What the fuck," Austin said. "Can I hold it?"

"When we're safely in the chopper," I said.

Gian wrapped the nugget in canvas like a child and we rushed to our ride. It was a thrilling takeoff. We were safe.

Back on the ground, we handed Austin a cashier's check for $14,000. It was the largest gift we could give without him being taxed.

"I hope that makes up for your troubles," I said.

"It makes up for everything." His warm smile was beaming.

A police escort drove us from the airport to the refinery. The nugget weighed in at almost thirteen pounds.

Gerry wanted us to keep it in his safe. A bank vault felt safer.

We never caved for an interview, but the media had our picture from security footage. The news vans hadn't found our new location. We were in the same complex where Janet ate with her friends. This was our sixth hotel since the shooting. I felt the media was paying the hotel staff for our locations.

"The auction's about to start." Gian set his laptop on the coffee table. There was our nugget sitting in all its glory. It looked smaller on our screen.

Bidding started at one million. Once it reached two, we couldn't stop laughing. I was glad we weren't there live. Our laughter would have ruined everything. The news coverage had worked in our favor. A couple of bidders were determined to get the nugget. An eccentric peanut farmer took the win.

We were shocked at the final total. Gian ran the numbers, working in taxes and the auction fees. He slid the phone over. I stared at the $6,532,450 in disbelief.

I turned to Gian, dumbfounded. "Holy fuck."

"Holy fuck indeed." He slumped in his chair.

Gian is so good with numbers that he was only off by two dollars. Seeing the amount in our bank account was a trip. The first call was to a lawyer for help setting up the Don Fund. Ten percent of everything would go to our charity. Don wouldn't have it any other way.

It was another week before we were cleared to leave Alaska. I was happy to get out of our room. Being holed up for so long isn't healthy.

A chartered jet snuck us into Washington. The cost was less than expected. We stopped in to see our families before leaving for Hawaii.

"So what are you going to do with all that money?" Dad asked.

"We're taking our time to figure that out," I said.

"Wise move," Grandpa said.

Maxwell wasn't hiding his jealousy.

I handed over a check. "This is to get the family business off the ground. You'll be able to flip a couple houses at a time."

"Holy fuck!" he said.

Dad took it from him. He looked like he was about to cry upon seeing the million-dollar amount. But it might have been from who the check was made out, Cameron Lombardo Construction.

"You don't have to go with the name, but it's available," Gian said. "Cameron Construction was taken."

"The name's perfect," Dad said.

"Gian and I will be silent partners. We need a break."

"We'll only take a profit if we work on a house."

"I've been saving Sir Donald's scotch," Grandpa said. "I can't think of a better celebration than this."

Maxwell brought me out to the deck. "You didn't have to do this. I appreciate it."

"Family first," I said.

"Yeah, but you're starting a new family. This was really generous."

"You would have done the same thing."

"I'd like to think I'm that good."

"Shut up," I said, hitting him on the shoulder. "This is probably a good time to tell you I ruined your favorite shirt."

"I think we can call it even."

His dry humor made me laugh.

"What are we celebrating," Joan said from the living room. "Oh my God!" she screamed.

Max and I both laughed.

"You have a good girl there."

"I love her with all my heart."

We rented a condo in Kauai for a month to hide out. Sadly, Don's place was off the rental market. We were a week into our stay. I was out on the lanai reading a book in the shade. Gian was playing on his phone.

We had been fighting. Twice that week, he hid what he was doing on his laptop. It really upset me.

He passed his phone to me. There was a listing for Don's place. I saw the price and almost choked. "We can't afford that."

"No, but we can tour it. Pay our respects."

"Why is it so expensive?"

"There're two guest houses on the property."

He called the listing agent to arrange a tour. "Today is fine. Fantastic."

He brought up our bank account and took a screenshot. "She needs proof we have money."

"Blur out the account number."

It was an hour's drive to Anini Beach. Pulling into the driveway was like coming home. I felt Don's positive energy as I stepped through the front door. I hoped his spirit wasn't trapped. But I could think of worse places to be.

"Do you feel him?" Gian asked.

"That's the vibe he left here."

"No, it's him. We need to buy this place."

"There's no way. Even with two million down, the loan payments would bankrupt us."

"Not if you put all three houses in the rental pool," the listing agent, Jennifer, said. "Let other people pay it off."

"Could we carve out time for us to stay here?" I asked. "Or maybe live in one of the guest houses."

"How long you stay each year depends on how fast you want to pay it off."

"We can keep my place in Seattle, and we'll always have Sicily," Gian said.

Jennifer led us to the main bedroom. The beams in the high ceiling created a diamond shape with the point directing my eye to the bay. I wanted to wake up to that view.

I looked at Gian. "Let's do it before I lose my nerve."

Jennifer couldn't stop the smile spreading across her face. She was getting the listing and selling fee. We made a new friend that day.

Waiting a month for the loan to close was torture, but we passed the time planning our wedding. It would be at Don's house. There was no discussion. It just was.

The day the house was ours had arrived. We pulled into the drive to get the key.

"I need a picture," Jennifer said. We stood at the door astonished.

"Please don't post that," Gian said.

"It's only for you."

Three months later, I was in our bedroom with the blinds drawn for privacy.

"It's almost time," Joan said. "You look gorgeous."

A knock came from the door. "You ready, Peaches? There's a nice break in the weather."

"Give us five minutes, Dad."

I poured glasses of Moscato and handed one to Joan, my maid of honor. The other three went to my bridesmaids, Bianca, Nera, and Angela. We had grown close from the Bachelorette party. Mine was in New Orleans, having won the city from Gian. He had his in Vegas.

I lifted my glass. "Thank you for making the long trek. I appreciate the love. And thank you for this wonderful dress," That last remark was directed at Bianca. "It's the most beautiful wedding dress I've ever seen."

She looked at me with a confident smile. "Only the best for you. Let's make sure you're perfect." She adjusted the strapless back.

Gian was first attracted to me because he thought I looked like a princess. Now, I felt like one. The cut was elegant yet light for the climate. Bianca nailed the fit. The fabric molded to my figure. My hair was thankfully perfect.

I was worried that the old dirty blond would come in strong but it has been a slow change. I love how sun kissed it looks.

"You deserve everything," Joan said. "Someday, hopefully, we'll be sisters."

"We already are," I said. "And no one deserves anything. We're on this planet to be good."

Nera pulled me into the corner and whispered, "When I arrived this morning, I saw Don and his wife on the lanai."

"Is Mom here?"

"I don't know. But I doubt she would miss this."

I closed my eyes, hoping to feel her presence. I'd like to believe I did.

I let Dad in. He was clean shaven. A day into the humidity, off went his beard. One look at me and he teared up.

"I told myself I wouldn't cry." The crinkle in his eye was adorable.

"It's OK," I said, hugging him.

"I'll see you out there," Joan said, leaving with the girls.

"I'm nervous, Dad."

"You'll be fine."

This struck me funny. I had felt him tremble when we embraced. Dad wasn't a fan of crowds.

"You ready," I said.

"I'm so proud of you," he said.

It took everything not to cry. The walk around the corner was surreal. The first person I saw was Gian standing before the seated rows of guests. His beauty dominated the handsome tan suit. I was glad he ditched the tie. The look went better with our tropical theme.

The Hawaiian version of Somewhere Over the Rainbow began playing. Gian turned his head in my direction. His eyes sparked to life upon seeing me.

Our family history could not be more divided, yet as the crowd shifted in their seats to look, both sides were together, mixed as one. I spotted Gian's aunt and uncle. They said they couldn't make it. What a pleasant surprise. Behind them was a familiar face. It was Sir Donald. I almost didn't recognize him in his Hawaiian shirt. The moppy white hair and crazy eyebrows gave him away. He held up his glass of scotch to say hello. His presence blew me away.

Chase had made it with his new boyfriend. They looked happy. I leaned over and kissed my friend on the cheek.

"You're gorgeous," he said.

We reached the front and Dad walked me to Gian.

"I consider you a son," he said. "I love you, peaches." On the way to his seat he shook Gian's father's hand.

Gian took me in his arms.

"You were always the one. I love you so much," he said.

I couldn't hold back my tears. He squeezed my hands in comfort.

"I love you, baby."

Our preacher, Hoku, was a biker, which was an odd juxtaposition to his role. He was a large Hawaiian with a beautiful personality—a gentle giant. He was the perfect choice. I adored him.

"We are here this day to share with Gian and Linsey a most important moment in their lives," Hoku said. He looked at both of us. "Before we begin, I want you to turn and face your friends and family. Without their love and support, your lives would be incomplete."

That moment hit me deeply. The day wasn't only about us. I scanned the loving faces staring back. All these people flew in for us.

A song began playing. From Gian's first haunting line, "Love at first sight is a right to be earned," I was sobbing.

"Is this what you were hiding from me?"

He nodded with a smile.

"I am so sorry."

"It's all right, baby."

At the end of the song, the line "time to say goodbye" was turned into "there's no more goodbyes." Applause broke out. I could hear people asking if that was Gian singing.

Hoku had us face each other, holding hands. Off in the distance was our life-size bronze statue of Don sitting with his legs dangling over the yard's edge, forever facing the sea. It was so lifelike I expected him to turn and wink. I looked at the lanai and smiled, hoping he and his wife were watching.

"Gian and Linsey stand before us today to declare their promises openly and happily. Gian."

How were we already at our vows? I had missed the reverend's whole speech.

Gian held the printed vows at his side. He'd memorized them. "I bring myself to you, Linsey. I promise to be a faithful mate and to unfailingly share and support your hopes, dreams, and goals. I vow to be there for you always. When you fall, I will catch you. When you cry, I will comfort you. When you laugh, I will share your joy. Everything I am and everything I have is yours, from this moment forth and for eternity."

I couldn't stop the tears. This is why wedding makeup sessions cost more. It has to take a beating.

My mind was blank. Even though my vows were the same, I had to read them. It was Gian's turn to cry.

"Would the best man please present the rings."

Gian's brother, Dante, handed over each ring. Hoku spoke as we were putting them on each other.

"These rings symbolize the vows taken, a circle of wholeness, the perfect form. They mark the beginning of a long journey together filled with wonder, surprise, tears, laughter, celebrations, grief, and joy. May these rings glow in reflection of the warmth and life which flow through the wearers today."

His mention of glowing reminded me of gold and why we were in this fantastic house. We were truly blessed.

Hoku made a slow turn to the crowd. "Gian, will you take Linsey to be your wedded wife? Will you love, honor, and cherish her in sickness and health, be true and loyal to her, as long as you both shall live?"

"I will."

"Linsey, will you take Gian to be your wedded husband? Will you love, honor, and cherish him in sickness and health, be true and loyal to him, as long as you both shall live?"

"I will."

"By the power vested in me by the state of Hawaii, I pronounce you husband and wife. You may now seal this blessed union with a kiss."

Gian gave me a perfect kiss. It was light, yet passionate, but not too much for the families. I exaggerated being weak-kneed, but not by much.

"Friends and family, I give you Gian and Linsey."

I've never felt love more than from the faces smiling upon us. After the applause faded, my brother handed each of us a glass of the good champagne.

"You're so jizz," he said.

His dumb saying made me laugh. The humor was a perfect stress reliever.

"I fucking love you," Gian said to him.

"Thanks, brother." It was the first time Max had called him that. I was touched. "I'm going to go find Joan."

"Love you," I said.

Dad came up to congratulate us. "Linsey, I'm so happy for you. Son," he said, shaking Gian's hand. "Welcome to the family."

"Introduce your father to our special guest?" Gian said.

"He doesn't know?"

"I had him sneak in."

"You're just full of surprises. Dad, I want you to meet someone." I walked him over to Sir Donald.

He rose from his seat. That was no small feat. His body obviously ached. "Linsey, Gian, that was a wonderful ceremony. Nice and short."

I could imagine the pomp and circumstance he had to endure. "It's such an honor that you're here. Dad, I'd like you to meet Sir Donald, the Chief of the Cameron Clan."

"The honor is all mine," Sir Donald said.

Dad looked at me, then back at Donald. He was speechless. "I am humbled."

Sir Donald chuckled. "We're family. No need to be humble. If anyone should be, it is me. The love of your daughter and this fine man saved humanity."

He had no idea how much.

"Thank you for the bottle of scotch," Dad said. "We treasured every drop."

My heart sank. He would know we stole it.

"You saved it," Sir Donald said to Gian and me. I relaxed. He was talking about the first bottle he gave us. "There's more in the house. I hope ye don't mind. I opened one of them. There's a case."

His generosity floored me, but I felt being overly thankful would be insulting. "Your presence was gift enough. I would be honored to share a toast."

"The open bottle is in yer pantry," Sir Donald said.

"The rest is in the garage," Gian said.

We brought Max and Grandpa with us. They had no idea who they were walking in with. Things were about to get very Scottish for my family.

The day was a blur. Everything went perfectly. Gian was a gentleman with his offering of cake. Our dance was heaven. Aunt Pia had secretly recorded their performance of Time to Say Goodbye. We were both expecting the original. It was magical dancing to their singing. Once we were done, the DJ kept people on the floor. What I liked most was the love from our friends and family. It hit me to my core.

By one in the morning, most of the older relatives had returned to their hotels or rooms. I was beat myself and searched for Gian. Weddings are exhausting when they're your own. Nera pulled me aside.

"Come with me," she said, leading me to the guest bathroom.

I checked myself out in the mirror. Did my makeup need fixing? It could have been the humidity, but I was glowing.

"Your night will be wrapping up soon. Let's get you ready for your man."

"Oh, Nera. You are so sweet."

"It's been a pleasure."

She rinsed a washcloth off in the sink and gingerly cleansed the exposed parts of my body. My deodorant appeared in her hand. I rolled it on. She flicked it into thin air. My dental floss, toothbrush, and paste appeared next.

"Take your time. I'll be outside with the girls."

"Thank you, Nera."

"You're welcome."

Gian loves the taste of sweat on me. I washed up, careful not to get too close. I ditched my panties in a drawer. Should I lose the bra, too? I removed it and made sure it wasn't too noticeable with my top back on.

Outside, I ran into the girls. Gian sauntered up and kissed my cheek. "I think it's time to say good night, Mrs. Lombardo."

"Go," Nera said. "We'll see you in the morning."

I followed Gian to the door. He turned and faced the remaining guests. "Good night, everyone. It's been a pleasure. Stay as long as you want. All night. Don't worry about the noise."

"I love you all," I called out.

He picked me up, carrying me over the threshold. I felt weightless in his love. Inside, he planted a kiss while I was still in his arms.

"Minty," he said.

We walked hand in hand to our bedroom. I panicked. The girls and I had destroyed the place.

He opened the door and stepped back. Candles lit up the room. Tropical flowers were scattered on the bed and floor.

"It's beautiful, Gian."

"You're beautiful. I love you so much it hurts."

"You're the sweetest man I've ever met. How could I be so lucky."

"It's not luck. It's destiny. You and I were made for each other."

"It was destiny."

He kicked off his sandals and walked behind me, setting the pace as he slowly unzipped my back. I removed his shirt before he helped me out of my dress.

He was surprised I wasn't wearing my bra and panties. "God, damn."

The appreciation fueled my lust. I removed his jacket and shirt, then undid his pants, sliding them and his underwear to the floor. His cock pressed hard against his stomach, eager to please me.

He walked me over to the bed and spooned up behind me. I wasn't expecting that at all. His embrace was tight, as if he never wanted to let go. I had my arms crossed, holding his, pressing against him. His scent, mixed with the flowers, was heavenly.

"I knew from that first moment at the train station that I would spend the rest of my life with you."

I melted with the romance of it all. He used the opportunity to roll me onto my back and embraced me in a kiss. I could feel his heart pounding against mine.

"I love you so much."

I want you inside me."

Gian moved with confidence as he entered me. He lifted his head so he could stare into my eyes.

"I love every ounce of your being."

He thrust with love behind each motion. His kiss was delicate yet passionate. The squeezes of his embrace, the rolling of his body, all sent me to heaven. Overcome with emotion, I let my tears flow. His smile grew as my vision blurred. We were married. He was husband. It was such a trip. The sex was blowing my mind. It was so fucking good.

"You're blowing my mind," he said, thrusting deeper. "You're so fucking good."

"What the hell?" I said.

"What?" He laughed.

"I was just thinking that."

"Body and mind, baby. Body and mind."

He pulled out of me and sat cross-legged. I straddled him with my legs wrapped around his back. We held each other up in our embrace. Him thrusting rhythmically, my body working with him in unison. We'd never been in this position. Our bodies merged as one.

His cock pressed deep, to that spot he knew too well from the Touch. He picked up the pace, working to make me come. He wouldn't last much longer. I positioned my hips forward so my clit slid along his shaft with each thrust.

I was concentrating too hard on my release. I let go, closing my eyes, and my body responded with a tightening deep inside.

"It's coming, baby."

"I can't hold off."

He moaned deeply, and his body shook slightly as his head fell back, mouth open in ecstasy.

I know how sensitive he gets after he comes, but he powered through, biting his lip, thrusting harder, faster.

My breathing increased and I dropped my head to his chest. Flowers bounced on the sheet, dancing to the beat of our lovemaking. The petals rose as my eyes lifted skyward. I wasn't sure if I was seeing things or if the witches were doing this. The flowers reached the rafters and pulsed in unison with my breath. I closed my eyes and let the orgasm wash over me. The petals rained upon our bodies. When I opened my eyes, they were on the bed exactly where they had been.

Gian relaxed onto his back, stretching his legs, still inside me. I fell on top of him with my head resting on his chest. His breathing lifted my body up and down.

He didn't mention the floating petals, only that he loved me. We soon drifted off into a deep slumber.

---

The witches gifted us a honeymoon in Tahiti, one week on a private island and another in the end unit of a row of dock houses. It had been ten days since the wedding. We were leaving in the morning.

Nera materialized in our bedroom with a suspicious grin on her face.

"What are you up to?"

"Penderdash has a gift for saving the world. Come here." She reached for our heads.

We backed off.

She gasped at the audacity. "I'm not here to kill you. Come here."

She gently held the back of our heads and brought us to her forehead.

"It will take a while for the Touch to return fully."

"No way." I held Gian's wrist and felt him, all of him. His heart was beating wildly.

"I fucking love you, Nera," Gian said.

"I love you too," she said and kissed his cheek. I felt her lips connect.

Our private Island was beyond anything I imagined. A chef and the staff were housed on an adjacent island. They treated us like royalty. There were three cottages, a main house, a kitchen hut, and a covered bar area for dining and entertaining.

The staff had gone home for the evening. Before leaving, they'd set up loungers in the lagoon. A pitcher of Tahitian Vanilla Punch sat between us and another in the fridge. I was topless for Gian.

"This week went so fast," he said.

"It was like being in a dream."

"I don't want to wake up. This was the best week of my life." He rotated his hips and I felt his cock shift in his shorts. The Touch was entirely back, and I loved it.

I slipped out of my bikini bottoms and straddled him. He kissed me passionately, tasting of punch. I reached down and, with his help, worked his shorts off. It was wonderful feeling his side of slipping into me. I took him deep and rocked my hips in long, slow undulations, watching his face the whole time.

"You're missing the sunset," he said.

"I can see it in your eyes."

He sat up and brought my mouth to his. The kiss was warm and gentle but soon flowed with passion. We were locked in the moment. I rode him with shorter movements so as not to break us apart. I loved kissing him — my husband.

The loungers on the deck of our second honeymoon location were sublime. Our house was the end unit on the dock, looking out at three islands. I'm glad the witches had included the place. After a week on the island, we were ready for company. The night before, we had dinner with newlyweds from Canada.

Gian approached from behind and I felt him handing over my drink. I met his hand without looking.

"Rum and pineapple juice."

I giggled to myself. That was the drink Joy had made me before we had that crazy threesome.

Nera walked around the corner.

"Hi, Nera," I said. "What are you doing here?"

"Stopping you from drinking that." She took the cocktail from me.

"What are you talking about?"

Tears streamed down Gian's cheeks. "Is she pregnant?"

Nera nodded. "It's only a day old, but I can see the faint glow of his energy."

"His. We're having a boy?"

I stood up in shock and hugged Gian.

He placed a hand on my belly. "How did you know?"

"I was in the Underworld yesterday when Teriko let it slip. I'd already had a vision of your labor. Please let me be there for the delivery."

We looked at Gian. The smirks on our faces turned to laughter at the thought of him experiencing childbirth. He didn't find it as humorous.

"Of course you're our midwife," I said.

"Actually, Bianca will be your midwife. I'll assist her."

What an honor that the High Priestess would assume the duty. It made sense not to put the Priestess of Death in the role.

# Chapter 14

My due date was a week away. Staying in Italy for the birth may have been a mistake. The closest hospital was an hour away. But it was too late to head home. Even if we'd stayed in Hawaii, the conditions were the same. Washington was out. During the birth, our families would see that Gian has the Touch. My only consolation was that Bianca would make sure I was safe.

I wanted the baby out of me. I was sick of the aches. Sick of the pain. And beyond sick of Gian complaining. He was a bigger baby than I was. How could I blame him, though? He felt everything that I did. At least we were past morning sickness. It was now a dull queasiness I could work through. Laying down was the worst. Everything hurt. There wasn't a position that gave me relief. My stomach was too large and heavy. I was miserable.

The baby kicked with a stretch that I felt in my ribs. I put my hand on my belly and smiled.

"I'll see you soon."

If I ignored my bladder any longer, I'd pee myself. I removed the pillow from between my legs and shuffled to the side of the bed without waking Gian. I teetered over the edge with a grunt, catching the weight on my knees, and headed to the bathroom, hunched over like an old man.

As I wiped, I could almost touch my boy. He was so low. Bianca said it was nothing to worry about.

Gian knocked on the bathroom door a few hours later. I was on my knees scrubbing the area around the toilet. I have no idea where this obsession with cleaning came from. There was no stopping me until the room was sterilized.

"What are you doing? You should be in bed. I'll do that."

I held up a hand. "I have to do it." I was possessed. I wondered if this is what people with OCD went through.

"I don't know where you're getting the energy. But thanks for letting me sleep in. How about I make breakfast? What are you in the mood for?"

I had a guilty smile. "There is something I've been craving. It's kind of weird."

"Lay it on me. I could use a drive."

"All right. I want a large slice of plain cheesecake smothered in Big Mac's secret sauce. Like tons of it oozing over the sides."

He laughed. "I'm on it."

I caught him shaking his head as he turned the corner.

Gian was dressed when he stuck his back head in. "There's a McDonald's in Milazzo. I have the grocery list. Can you think of anything else?"

I couldn't. "I'll text you if something comes to mind."

"Want me to fix you breakfast before I go?"

"No, I'll have the leftover pizza."

"I love you, baby," he said. "You're beautiful."

"You talkin' to me or the baby?" That came out rather snotty.

"You. I love you, sunshine. And the baby."

I should have felt bad, but I was months beyond regrets.

Gian returned hours later. I was resting on the sofa, ready to start cleaning the living room. His back was to me in the kitchen, but I could feel him assembling the cheesecake. It didn't sound good anymore.

He turned around, one hand under the plate and the other palm up, gesturing toward it like a prize on a game show. His goofy smile was fitting.

"I... I don't want it." I didn't offer an apology.

My rudeness didn't faze him. I think he was happy to have been away from my aches and pains. He shrugged and sank the fork in for a bite.

"Please don't," I pleaded. "I'll puke."

He set the plate out of sight and opened the package he'd brought in. "How about cereal? Your brother sent Cap'n Crunch with Crunch Berries."

I can't believe Max listened. All they had in Sicily was the original version. "Use the big bowl."

That evening, contractions woke me up. It wasn't as painful as I had read. The roof of my mouth hurt worse from the cereal.

I shook Gian awake. Bianca appeared at the end of the bed. Her blond hair was a ratted mess. I checked the clock. It was four in the morning. Gian looked at both of us confused.

"He's coming," I said.

Gian's face lit up.

Bianca shook her head, no. "This is false labor. You'll know when the baby is coming and laugh, thinking *this* is pain."

I didn't care for the sound of that. Another contraction began, but shifting my waist made it go away.

"How did you do that?" Gian said. "Not that I'm complaining."

I shrugged.

"Your body is prepping for the birth," Bianca said. "Getting your uterus ready." Her usual stern face softened almost to a smile. "I'm so excited for both of you."

That Saturday, we watched a Sicilian movie on the front room couch. Gian's Italian had progressed far enough that he turned the subtitles off. I was proud of his effort.

My body tensed up — every part of it. A contraction started. *OK, this is something. Definitely worse than before.* Gian glanced at me, excited but nervous. The second contraction came so fast. This was it. The baby was coming.

333

Bianca and Nera ran out of thin air. "This is it!" Bianca said. "Your boy's on the way."

"He's coming so fast," Nera said. "You're so lucky. Bianca's first labor took twenty hours."

"Twenty-two," she corrected.

Gian had the timer going on his phone. Two minutes later, the tightening in my body warned of another contraction. A dull pain grew in my back. My stomach became rock hard as if it was trying to push the baby through. I screamed out as the pain overwhelmed me. Gian joined my screaming. I had no control over the contractions. The witches were doing this. Gian was rolling on the floor, bent over, holding his stomach. Bianca and Nera couldn't help laughing at him.

"Shut up!" I screamed. "Everybody shut up!"

The contraction lasted only ten seconds, but it was an eternity. Then it was gone as if nothing had happened, and I was fine. Gian was crying. The witches were, too, but from laughter.

"No more helping," I told them. "Quit pushing for me."

"That's not us," Bianca said. "Your body is taking over. It wants the baby out. That's nature."

"OK, but everyone needs to stop talking during the contractions. No laughing. Everyone just shut up!"

"Sure. Sure," Nera said.

Bianca gestured toward Gian. "You have to admit this is funny."

"It's not funny." Tears streamed down his face. "I don't think I can handle this."

"Oh, you will," I said sternly.

Bianca took my hand. "Your scream is wrong. I want it more guttural. Don't scream from your throat. Yell from your gut. Roar. Give it a try."

My yell was more of a moan. It sounded horrible but felt right, especially from below.

Gian was inflating the birthing tub. "You sound like a duck." That struck the witches funny.

"You sound like a duck," I said. "Oh shit! Here comes another one."

*It's only ten seconds*, I kept telling myself, but holy fuck. The pain was unimaginable. Everything below my chest was on fire, like I was being ripped open from the inside. I yelled as Gian screamed.

"I can't do it," he said when the contraction ceased. "Give her drugs. Make the pain go away."

"Shut up," I said. "The baby is not coming out of you. Man the fuck up."

He left the room. "I'm just getting the hose," he said, popping his head around the corner.

Gian meticulously worked to reach the proper pool temperature of ninety-nine degrees. I lost my patience.

"If it's close, let me in," I pleaded.

"Sure, I'll work around you." He moved the hose to the opposite end of the hand-holds. Bianca and Nera helped me into a standing position.

The weight of my belly lightened as I slipped into the warm water. There was little time to enjoy it. The next contraction was so intense I was twisting, trying to escape the agony. My body was no longer mine. Gian had fallen to the stone floor out of sight. Nera placed the hose back in the pool.

I wasn't doing the birthing breathing. It didn't seem to help. All I could focus on was shutting everyone out. I needed them to vanish. I thrust my hips upwards, but Bianca pushed my stomach down so my lower half was under the water. I don't know if Nera read my mind and mistook my intentions, but she vanished.

The contraction ended, and I fell back against the side of the pool, exhausted. I shifted my body until I was comfortable.

"If you keep moving, it will help the baby along," Bianca said.

"Great," I said sarcastically and shifted my hips around.

Nera reappeared. "The people in your building are knocked out."

Bianca glanced over at Gian accusingly.

"Yeah, yeah," he said. "You all win. Childbirth is way worse than getting kicked in the balls."

We all laughed. How men could think it was even a contest was beyond me.

Gian stayed upright during the next contraction. He was loving and attentive.

"Don't look at me!" I yelled. He froze, not sure what to do. There was no pleasing me.

Three hours into the labor, the baby was right there, but nothing was happening. Bianca sat on the floor to rest. Something caught her eye. She had me lift my hips.

"Oh, he's still in the sack. Do you want me to break your water?"

"What will that do?"

"The sack is taking up room. He'll be easier to push out."

"Hell, yes. Break it. Get this fucking thing out of me."

An instrument resembling an ancient knitting needle appeared in her hand. She waved her hand across it, and the tool grew sparkling clean. She had her hand inside me when a contraction approached.

"The next push, he's coming out. Get down here to catch him," Bianca said to Gian.

She guided the needle safely home. As she pulled her hand out, the baby followed. He was ripping me open. I screamed bloody murder. The baby came out in one horrifically painful push. His exit rattled my bones like bumps in a neglected road. Gian passed out from the torture, sliding down the side of the pool until he wasn't visible.

This is the last bit, I thought. It's almost done. And then it was. The baby was out. The pain was gone. My headache was gone. My heartburn, gone. It was amazing.

Bianca held the baby submerged. I sat up easier than I had in months and stared at him. My little boy lay on his back, calmly in the water. Gian joined me at my side. It was such a surreal moment. I expected the water to be gross, but it was a pinkish hue.

"They usually come out slower," Bianca said. "You should have had to push again to get past his shoulders."

"He's stretching like he did in the womb," I said.

I don't know if he could see us, but he opened his eyes.

"Look at his little tinkle bean," I said.

"I think it's big for his age," Gian said, not trying to be funny, but it came out that way.

Bianca lifted our baby into the air and he took his first breath. He was covered in white blotches like he'd been rolled in oatmeal.

"This is normal," Bianca said. "It's a natural coating that helps prevent... What is the word? They're like grapes. Prunes. Pruning. Let it come off naturally. It's good for the skin."

Gian grabbed a towel. "Let's get you out of the tub."

"Not yet," Bianca said. "There's still work."

After taking our boy's vitals, they handed him to me, umbilical still attached. He was the most beautiful thing I'd ever created. I was in love.

Gian was bawling. "Hello, Lino."

Our son opened his eyes and stared at him. He recognized Gian's voice.

Bianca handed a sharp set of shears to Gian. "It's time to cut the cord."

"Will it hurt," he asked.

"Not at all, to her or the baby."

She used a string to cinch the cord, then placed another set of knots a few inches higher.

"Cut right in the middle," she instructed.

Gian was confident yet gentle. The baby rested in my arms, free of its tether. I've never been more at bliss than at that moment. I was so in love with our baby. It didn't bother me when the contractions for the placenta started. They were nothing after the hell I just went through. I let my body do the work. Bianca assisted by pushing my stomach down.

Once the placenta was out, Nera put it in a bowl and checked it carefully.

"It's all here," she said.

Bianca placed a soft hand on my shoulder. "You were fantastic. It's all over."

"Are you sure he didn't rip me open?"

"There would be more blood. To be safe, let's have a look."

I lifted my hips, loving how much lighter I was.

Bianca smiled and I knew everything was well.

"You're all good. You can climb out now."

We moved to the couch with the baby, cuddling in a fuzzy blanket. Lino found a nipple and began suckling.

"Is that normal?" Gian asked. "She's cramping with each suckle." I wondered the same, but I was so caught up in the moment that I couldn't speak.

"That's her uterus contracting back," Bianca said. "It will happen for a few days. Perfectly normal."

Gian caught my eye. "When he was coming out, I could see him drop from your stomach. It was the weirdest."

Nera held up the placenta bowl. "We'll keep this safe. In case you need the cells."

"Thank you," I said. "For everything."

"Why don't you go in the bedroom? We'll clean up."

"Thank you," Gian said.

He helped me into bed and placed Lino in my arms. I held the covers open and he crawled in next to me.

"I'm so proud of you," he said, kissing me lightly. "I love you more than ever. I love our family."

# Epilogue

Lino was now three and a half. He was the most beautiful boy I'd ever seen — the spitting image of his father.

Max and Joan were visiting us in Hawaii. The news that morning was talk of a pandemic. We hoped it was nothing. Their daughter's third birthday was in a month. We would be in Washington to celebrate. I thought Elsie would have Joan's red hair, but the Cameron blond dominated. She did have her mom's devilish smile.

Gian placed a second tray of piña coladas on a table next to our loungers and handed them out.

"This is the life," Max said, taking a long drink.

Little Elsie was a ball of energy. At least they'd managed to get her shrieking under control. It was ear-piercing. The kids ran around the yard, Elsie chasing our naked boy.

"Look, Mommy," she yelled. "I'm hunting him. I'm hunting him."

The adults looked at each other. I mouthed, "What the fuck?"

# Acknowledgments

A massive thank you to my cousin, friend, and writing partner, Camille English.

Thank you to the early readers: Vicki, Kim, Mom, Tami, Stephanie, Shelley, Robin, Niccole, Nancy, Melissa, Lori, Lisa, Deb, DeAnna, Cynthia, Colleen, Connie, and Debbie. Your feedback is much appreciated, especially Vicki's. She is always the first to read my work.

A huge shout out to the experts for their knowledge and patience:

Dunster Castle and Gardens: Charlie Hornsby, Business Services Coordinator.

Massage: Sara Freeborn

Natural Birthing: Laura Holman

Firearms: Wade, Josh, and Spike at Wade's Eastside Guns.

Self-Defense: Joe Porras

Mixed Martial Arts: Claire "Grizzly" Guthrie.

Psychology: Stephanie Self-Bence, LICSW.

Stregheria:

While researching Sicilian witchcraft, I was drawn so strongly to Marguerite Rigoglioso Ph.D., it was as if she had called to me. A paper she wrote, Stregoneria: The Old Religion in Italy from Historical to Modern Times, helped create a fictional version of the religion and the streghe. The article has disappeared, making me wonder if it was ever there.

According to Marguerite, the term strega is used disparagingly to describe someone who practices malevolent magic in Sicily. Unfortunately, the witches' preferred term of maga has been politically adopted in the United States. For this story, strega and the plural streghe are used positively to describe the witches.

I respect the secrecy enshrouding the stregonerian traditions. Portions of the rituals and history were changed to protect their covens or fit the storyline.

Marguerite's teachings can be found at:
www.SevenSistersMysterySchool.com

Photo by Bradley Taylor. Sicily 2023

Markus Taylor writes under the pen name Jackie Notter. He lives at Alki Beach, Seattle. During the book's development, the cruelty of cancer took his love, Marc Broderick. If something in this book made you laugh, it is likely Marc's witty remark. His encouragement remains strong.

Both books in this series are IPPY Award winners:
2022 Independent Publisher Book Award for The Mirror's Touch
2025 Independent Publisher Book Award for Five Must Die

347